THE BODY NEXT DOOR

THE BODY NEXT DOOR

MAIA CHANCE

MIRA

MIRA™

ISBN-13: 978-0-7783-1041-9

The Body Next Door

Mira
22 Adelaide St. West, 41st Floor
Toronto, Ontario M5H 4E3, Canada
MIRABooks.com

Printed in U.S.A.

For Zach

PART ONE

NOW

HANNAH

I'm not completely okay with being one of those spoiled, pretty women you see in new luxury SUVs on their way to power barre, or to get microneedled, or running into Nordstrom to return some cashmere before picking up their children at prep school and going home to their hot, rich husbands.

That's not me. Those women don't smell like lost love the way I do. They don't smell of death. But I have studied those women so carefully, and I imitate their ways so well, that I outdo them all.

So when my friend from the Seattle Tennis Club, Jorie Henries, calls with the news from Orcas Island, I freeze like an animal in a flashlight beam. My hiding place has been sniffed out, I think. This time, I'm caught.

It's quarter to two, more than an hour before Oliver and Sibley's school pickup, but I have been summoned by the head of school, Mr. Preller, to talk. He said it was time-sensitive but didn't elaborate. The meeting must be about the school's fundraising auction: I've sat on the committee for five years and counting. Or maybe the school is going to come at me, shark-like, for more of Allan's money. They aren't shy.

Jorie pings my mobile phone just as I'm making my exit onto Capitol Hill. I ignore it until I'm safely off I-5. Rush hour in Seattle starts at one thirty these days, and it doesn't let up until after seven. Getting across town to the Huxley School and back is basically my job.

I pick up the phone, redial the call, and switch to Speaker. I gas my Range Rover into a left turn.

Jorie's bright voice says, "Hannah! How are you?"

"Great. Heading over to the school. I'm guessing I'm about to get roped into even more auction stuff."

Jorie laughs. "That's why I always just say *no* to the school. I would never have *any* me time if I let the school have their way with me. God, as it is, the girls' lacrosse schedule is running me *ragged*. Listen, I'm calling because I just found out about the news on Orcas, and I wanted to see if everything's all right. With your island house, I mean. And with you."

At the word *Orcas*, my throat clicks shut. I keep my eyes on the wet asphalt rolling out of sight under the Rover's hood. "I'm not sure I know what you're—"

"Oh, that's right, you *hate* current events, don't you?" Jorie laughs again. This time I hear a lilt of condescension. Jorie has an MBA from Stanford and considers herself to have the intellectual upper hand over me, who can only boast of a high-school diploma and subsequent (brief) flight-attendant career. Not that Jorie has ever used her business degree for anything besides making sure she didn't get screwed in her prenup. "They dug up a dead body yesterday on Orcas Island," she says. "Someone is excavating for a new house. A woman's body—"

Allan, I think.

My fingers slip and fumble the phone. Just as I catch it, my vision fills up with the red glow of brake lights. I slam my own brakes, jolting hard against my seat belt. I have stopped with maybe a couple of inches between my front fender and a Prius.

My heart beats quick and small. It's a rabbit's heart. The heart of a victim.

I carefully drive forward.

Jorie is still talking. "—near Deer Harbor. Isn't that where your island house is? I would just *hate* it if something like that happened near one of our homes." A pause. "Hannah? Are you there?"

"Yes. Hi. I hadn't heard about that, Jorie. Thanks so much for telling me— Oh! Sorry, I have another call. Is there—"

"No, no. See you Monday at the club." Jorie's voice is replaced with dead air.

There is no incoming call, only someone honking their horn wrathfully behind me. I pull through the intersection and then, half-blind, turn onto the first side street.

Dead leaves are gunking up the gutters, and cars pack both curbs. The houses are large, well-kept, and close together. Does wealth always look so desolate? Maybe it's just because it's November. I double-park and, without switching off my engine, open the web browser on my phone. Ghostly plumes of exhaust coil around my car.

Allan, I think again.

I have a choice here, I tell myself. No one is forcing me to search for anything. I can turn away and refuse to look. I can lock this news in the box in my mind with all the other junk I can't deal with, and I can carry on. I'm good at that.

But instead I type the search terms into my phone.

I'm jittery. I misspell every word. Despite that, the news item from the *Seattle Times* is easy to find: Human Remains Unearthed on Orcas Island.

> Construction workers on Orcas Island, Washington, made a gruesome discovery yesterday when they excavated the remains of an adolescent female on a secluded waterfront

lot. A spokesperson for the San Juan County Sheriff's Office reports that the remains were found in a shallow grave, and there is evidence of blunt force trauma to the female's skull. Foul play is suspected. Based on preliminary observations, the female appears to have been deceased between five and ten years.

Rural Orcas Island, with only around 6,000 year-round residents, made national news in the summer of 2015 as the home of the Kinfolk Community, a group of self-professed "radical homesteaders" led by Chris Garnock, who was known to his followers as Uncle. The community, which was flagged by watchdog organization Cult Watch, disbanded after a standoff with the Bureau of Alcohol, Tobacco, Firearms and Explosives that left an ATF agent, Garnock, and fourteen-year-old Kinfolk Community boy Quill Stroufe dead. The remains discovered yesterday were unearthed on land neighboring what was once the Kinfolk Community's parcel.

The deceased female was wearing a braided leather bracelet with a small pottery disc attached, printed with the emblem of the Kinfolk Community: a seedling with two leaves. Cult expert Dr. Anthony Chin of the Department of Psychology at the University of Washington notes that the emblem signifies the "new springtime" that Garnock and his followers believed they would experience following an environmental apocalypse. A spokesperson for the San Juan County Sheriff's Office says that, while not conclusive, the evidence strongly points to the possibility of the female having been a member of or visitor to the Kinfolk Community but adds that no persons linked to the community were ever reported missing.

The remains have been transported to the Snohomish County Medical Examiner's Office for autopsy. Officials ask that anyone with information about the female's identity contact the San Juan County Sheriff's Office.

I read the article twice. Then I squeeze my eyes shut.

I would like to cry, except I've forgotten how.

Fifteen minutes later, I park in the fire lane in front of the Huxley School. Lawns sprawl around the stately old redbrick main building. Modern structures—the new library, the slick sports complex—stand off to the side, their windows glowing in the dull autumn afternoon. The school's air of smug, liberal-minded money always makes me feel trashy.

I get out of the car. I'm not worried about being towed from the fire lane. My husband's considerable annual donation to the scholarship fund has its perks.

I have pulled it together. Pulling it together, keeping it together, that's in my skill set. With my quietly luxurious outfit—belted vicuña coat, jeans, Italian suede booties, chocolate-brown Birkin bag—I know I look like any pampered Huxley mom. Except that I'm younger and even more pampered than most.

It's just a vacation home, I recite to myself as I wait to be buzzed into the school. *Just a vacation home. And dead bodies are gross; anyone would be upset.*

I make my way through the school's empty hallways to the administrative offices.

"Mrs. McCullough," the receptionist says. "Welcome. Mr. Preller is waiting for you." She gestures to Preller's office door.

I think I see a flicker of anxiety on her face before she turns back to her computer screen.

"I'll get straight to the point, Mrs. McCullough," Preller says once I have taken a seat and declined refreshment. "It's about Oliver."

"Oliver," I repeat. This isn't about the auction? Not about the scholarship fund?

"Surely that doesn't come as a complete surprise. Your son's behavior has been a problem since he began here…" Preller's voice tapers off, as though he's waiting for me to interject.

I remain silent, my spine rigid.

Preller says, "In some ways, Oliver has made progress—I understand he's been in behavioral-cognitive therapy, and his impulse control seems to be improving. However, we've had several complaints from parents just this term, and I'm afraid that at this juncture we simply cannot fail to take some sort of action. I called you and your husband here today—it's unfortunate he couldn't come—to tell you that we have decided it would be best to…to suspend Oliver."

"I'm sorry. I don't think I quite understand." I use the tone Jorie calls my flight attendant's chirp.

In the back of my brain, a nasty little voice whispers, See? *See?* I told you we're not safe.

"This morning he exhibited extraordinarily aggressive behavior toward one of our fourth-years," Preller says.

"Aggressive?"

"At first, Oliver limited himself to berating the other student after their basketball accidentally hit him in the sport court—"

"Was Oliver hurt?"

"He *terrified* the other student. He screamed—he called the other student a freak and a monster—"

"He said that?"

"I'm afraid so. When the other student made a swipe at Oliver—"

"So the other child hit him first."

"—Oliver tackled him to the ground and *bit* him. Bit his cheek. Not hard enough to break the skin, but contusions and swelling are present. The child has been taken to the doctor, because human bites carry a heavy risk of infection. The parents have threatened to sue the school."

"Oliver is only twelve years old. Kids do weird things."

"He should know better. He *does* know better."

"How long is the suspension?"

"In January he may return to school, and we will reassess his behavior. You must realize that Oliver is being given extraordinary consideration here. Almost any other student would have been expelled—*expelled*, not suspended—years ago."

"So, what? I'm supposed to be grateful to you? Grateful that now I have to hire some kind of private tutor just so he won't fall behind, after my husband and I—"

"Your husband is one of our more generous donors, and for that we are grateful."

Your husband is generous. Not *you*. It's the same kind of microslight as Jorie laughing at my lack of interest in current events. But Jorie is at least a social peer. Preller is just a glorified minion.

"Your daughter is doing well, both academically and socially, here at Huxley, so I do hope—"

"Thank you, Mr. Preller." I'm on my feet, gripping my handbag. "My husband and I will be in touch about whether or not we'll be keeping our children at Huxley." I give him an ostentatiously fake flight attendant's smile. *Pretzels? Something to drink?* I say, "Have a *great* afternoon."

All I can see are bones.

Big bones clumped with dirt and something gluey and fibrous. Delicate little bird bones flittering away in the wind. The bones are entangled with the name that keeps whispering in my mind: *Allan*.

"Daddy says everyone has their price," my eight-year-old daughter, Sibley, says on the car ride home from school. "All you have to do is figure out what it is."

"What?" I say, glancing at her in the rearview mirror. She sits straight and alert on her booster seat, her dark blond curls wisping around owlish glasses. "Daddy said that to you?"

"It's for his work," she says. "For being good at it."

"Oh, okay," I say, relaxing. "That makes sense."

Sibley is a funny kid. Imaginative, precocious with art and

language, but a little behind her peers in terms of emotional development. She is happiest playing alone for hours with her Calico Critters. Moving the tiny toy animals around in their plastic treehouse, making them have conversations with each other.

Oliver rides in the seat beside me. I haven't mentioned the suspension to him yet, but I think he knows. His fair head is bent over his phone. He's playing a game. Frown—swipe—frown—swipe—

I do not dare speak to him. I can't reveal how desperately I need him to interact, or he'll shut down even more. But this isn't about my needs. It's about his.

Once a month, I meet with Oliver's therapist, Patti, one-on-one. She, who knows more of the truth than anyone else, suggested I see a separate therapist for myself. I declined. No way am I going to rip off those old scabs.

And now, Oliver's suspension. How am I going to broach the subject with Allan? He'll start pushing again to send Oliver to that boarding school in Montana, the one for screwed-up rich kids. Oliver won't make it in a savage place like that.

"Is Daddy coming home today?" Sibley asks, as though she can read my thoughts. Sibley is an empath, her preschool teacher told me years ago, sadly, almost as though she were saying *Sibley is defective.*

"Yes, Daddy's coming home," I say.

I imagine that I hear a gentle tapping sound, the one that seeps from the locked-up part of my brain sometimes. It is soft, but so persistent.

We arrive fifteen minutes later at our large brick Tudor Revival home in Briarcliff, a moneyed neighborhood north of downtown. Perched high on a slope and framed by twisty madrone trees, there's usually a view of Puget Sound, Bainbridge Island, and the Olympic Mountains, but not today. Too misty, too dark even at 3:45 in the afternoon.

The house was built in 1927. It has English-style mullion windows, a turret, creeping ivy, and a picturesque garage built to look like horse stables. A century ago, Seattle's new rich wanted to cover up their grubby backgrounds by pretending they were British landed gentry. I know Allan bought this house for the same reason.

I park in the driveway. The garage doors are open, and I can see Allan's black Tesla Model S inside, next to his Porsche.

"Daddy!" Sibley cries, unbuckling and flinging open her door. "I see him!" She dashes to the garage, hair flying, and knocks on the window of Allan's Tesla, bouncing up and down. "Daddy, Daddy! Get off the phone!"

For the first time that afternoon, I'm alone with Oliver. I decide I won't mention his suspension yet, but I want him to know I'm on his side. That, no matter what, I'll always be on his side.

"Oliver, sweetheart." I reach over to touch his still-round cheek. "Little—"

He pushes my hand away. "Stop it."

My hand falls to my lap, limp and defeated. "Sorry. You're right. You're not a little kid anymore. But..." I turn to look at him, his profile so like my own, especially the slightly undersize nose with the faintest upward slope to the round tip. My mother had that same nose. So did my sister.

Oliver gets out of the car. Leaving his door open, he lopes toward the house.

I gather up my handbag, then get out, and circle around to gather the kids' backpacks and close their doors.

In the garage, Allan has gotten out of his own car. He is crouching to talk eye to eye with Sibley, his phone in his fist. He is red-faced and in running clothes. A triangle of sweat darkens his T-shirt. He has just come back from a run. He is fifty-one years old and more than a little apprehensive about his own mortality, so there's nothing weird about him squeezing in a run after a long flight.

What *is* weird is that he would sit inside his car—his precious custom Tesla with its soft leather seats—in sweaty clothes.

He was on the phone. He was trying to keep the call private, using the Tesla as a sort of high-privacy zone.

He sees me approaching. He smiles.

ALLAN

I see my wife walking toward me and I think, There's nothing to connect me to that corpse. Nothing but the unfortunate coincidence of my owning real estate next door.

Sometimes when I'm traveling, I look down on the patchwork of land from the air or forests blurring outside a car window, and I imagine the rotting bodies they must hide. Most will never be discovered. Of those that are found, still fewer will give up their stories.

Have you ever perused a human-remains database? It's quite the eye-opener. Entry after entry describe decaying jeans, soil-clotted wounds, bones licked clean by rodents. They describe fields behind Walmarts. Ditches beside train tracks. Rotting trailers. Burned-out cars. Non-people in non-places, because whatever once made those remains people—social connections, a pulse, a soul if you insist—is gone. They have become things.

Do I sound loathsome? Vicious? Do you suspect me already? Listen. I'm a collector. I *love* things. I love how you can make things say what you want them to say. How you can place even the humblest specimen in a velvet-lined case and shine the spotlight just right, and suddenly it glows, the most beautiful thing you've ever seen.

One man's trash, I think, and I kiss my wife. I was aiming for her lips, but somehow I end up kissing her cold cheek instead. She smells like makeup.

"Hey, beautiful," I say. That sounds normal, I think. I'm still breathing hard from my run and from the stress of that phone call, but I sound like a normal husband. A nice guy.

Hannah smiles. Even though it's growing dark, Chanel sunglasses hide her eyes. The curl of her lips looks genuine enough. "How was your trip, sweetie?"

"Exhausting." I adjust my grip on the phone. It's slippery with sweat. I wonder if, from behind her sunglasses, Hannah is looking at it. "I'm glad to be home."

"Looks like you got in a run." Now she's looking at my sweaty T-shirt or, perhaps, the highly developed muscles to which it clings. I'm not a tall man, and I never was handsome, but I buy the best food, the best personal trainers, the best skincare, the best-fitting clothes. Not that I'm vain. My dad wasn't completely wrong when he called me an *ugly little shit*. I guess you could say I've discovered how to optimize what I have. Hair thinning? Shave it all off and make it look like a choice. Only five seven? Weight training makes you look masculine and powerful. Face like a pit bull? Well, I'm told I have nice eyes.

As Sibley chatters about velociraptors, we go into the house through the kitchen door.

I press my hand to the small of Hannah's back, feeling the curve of her bottom through her coat. It almost seems like she stiffens under my touch. I don't remove my hand, though. I mean, she's my *wife*.

Inside, Sibley disappears deeper into the house. The latest au pair is in the kitchen unpacking bags of groceries. She's a mousy little twenty-one-year-old from France. She's been with us since the summer, the previous au pair having been dismissed by Hannah for reasons I never asked about.

"Hi, Mr. and Mrs. McCullough," the au pair says. She's looking at me, not Hannah. Her eyes are big and hopeful. She's still not pretty. "As soon as I put these away, I will fix the children their snack."

"Thanks, Tilde," Hannah says.

That's right. *Tilde.* I can't keep track of these girls.

To me, Hannah says, "Something happened today at school. Oliver—"

I stop her with a lifted hand. "I know. I just spoke with Preller on the phone."

"That's who you were talking to? Preller?"

"Yeah." I glance at Tilde, then back to Hannah. "I need a shower." I move close enough to smell Hannah's skin under the makeup. I touch my lips to hers, breathing her innate scent, the one that always makes lust roll over and wake up. My mouth lingers until she responds as she always does. Arching her neck. Sighing a little. Her eyes are open, though, and trained sidelong in Tilde's direction.

But I've got her, I think as I kiss her harder. I've got her now.

Tilde is turning away, opening the refrigerator.

I push my hand inside Hannah's coat and run it down the warmth of her waist, her hip—

She pulls away. "Babe," she whispers, half laughing, half reproving. Hannah's reprimands are never harsher than this. They're so sweet and sultry, they're practically invitations.

Tilde is still rummaging in the refrigerator. Her ears, which stick out, have turned red.

"It's not my fault," I murmur. "You're so goddamn beautiful."

I discovered Hannah like a shipwreck's treasure on a beach. I alone saw her for what she could become. I fixed her. Polished her. I *made* her. And after all that, after all these years, she still cries out for someone else in her sleep?

Hannah turns her back on me. She pulls things out of a grocery bag. A package of celery hearts. A carton of milk. "Go and take your shower, you sweaty beast," she says, glancing over her shoulder at me. Her voice sounds flirtatious, but her eyes are as cold as pebbles.

CAROLINE

Trey works out at the CrossFit place in Eastsound on Mondays, Wednesdays, Thursdays, and Saturdays at two o'clock. I have never actually seen him working out. The gym doesn't have windows. Even the glass door is covered up with plastic film. But it is worth the wait just to see him get out of his car and enter the building.

I staked out the CrossFit place for a few weeks—this was in July—until I figured out his exact schedule. I am self-employed so my hours are flexible enough to do that kind of thing. I would park at the far end of the parking lot, which, since it was summer, was always crowded with vacationers' cars. I would wear my canvas bucket hat and sit with the ice cubes in my coffee melting and my heart beating so slowly. Like some creature only half-alive, waiting for hibernation to end.

As I was piecing together Trey's CrossFit schedule, I learned that after his workouts he usually drives the few blocks in his old green Jeep Cherokee to the Island Market. He will go into the supermarket for five or ten minutes and come out with a bag of groceries.

Such a bachelor, I always think as I watch from the edge of the parking lot. Instead of stocking a week's worth of food, he goes shopping every time he needs a square meal. He probably loads up on junk from the hot deli counter, too. He needs a woman to take care of him.

He needs me.

Trey—Treyson Paul Higgins, born Sacramento, California, on March 3, 1995—thinks we first met when he was introduced to me as the new youth minister at Orcas Bible Church in September. True, that was our first official meeting, and it was memorable in its own way. I was wearing my chambray dress from the TJ Maxx on the mainland. My hair was in its usual neat French braid. During fellowship after service, Pastor Mike came over to where I stood at the coffee urn. I was holding my cup, pulling on the lever, but nothing was coming out of the spout. The coffee was gone, and I was imagining exactly what I would like to say to the greedy pigs who had drained the urn dry when Pastor Mike said, "Caroline, there's someone I would like you to meet."

The man Pastor Mike introduced to me had been going for daily runs down my shady dirt road every morning since mid-June. Peering between the curtains of my kitchen window, I had watched the tanned strappy muscles of his thighs, the rhythmic pumping of his arms, his sweat-soaked shirt. Later, in the August heat wave that pushed the temperatures into the nineties, I saw him running without any shirt at all.

He is younger than I am. I realize that. He is only a few years older than my own son. Yet all summer I could not resist watching for him every morning, for his fit smooth body, his mop of honey-colored hair flowing back. First he ran away, but he always ran back.

Now I am waiting in the Island Market parking lot. I sit there with the bottles of Pine-Sol and Scrubbing Bubbles, the dirty floor mop, and the too-full vacuum cleaner stinking up my back seat. I hold my work-reddened fingers clasped in my lap. I am a stone.

And here is his Jeep, enough minutes behind schedule for me to wonder if he lingered at CrossFit to flirt with some little whore in short shorts. When I glimpse his face, I think, There he is. There is my beloved.

When he disappears through the store's automatic glass doors, a voice in my head says *Go*. The voice is so firm, I do not think to question it. I go.

Inside the Island Market, I pull out a shopping cart and roll it to the right. One of the wheels squeaks and spins. Everything smells like fried chicken and damp cardboard, and the fluorescent lighting seems to shudder. A pop song whines in the background. None of that matters, though, because I see him, Trey, standing at the deli counter with his back to me, looking at his phone while the employee behind the counter weighs something.

I can't breathe. I certainly can't approach him.

I turn my cart abruptly to the left and up the first aisle. I roll along past shelves of bread in plastic bags. The cart's bad wheel chitters.

This is a terrible mistake. It isn't time to run into Trey. Not yet. He needs to get to know me better through church before we—

How am I supposed to get to know him through church, another voice asks, *when he's always surrounded by that gaggle of teenage sluts from the youth group?*

That percussive word—*sluts*—sends blood rushing to my head. The women in my unmarried women's fellowship group have counseled me to cast out that voice with prayer. They have told me with calm authority that the voice is not mine but Satan's. This knowledge is reassuring because it explains why I cannot stop the voice. Satan's will is like steel. I am just a woman, so my own will, the fellowship group says, is soft and sweet and pliable. Like cookie dough, I imagine.

I reach the end of the bread aisle. I mean to go left to the dairy section, but I find myself going right into produce. It is as though God has guided my cart.

Well, I think, I'll take one last, nourishing look at Trey over at the deli counter, and then I'll buy something and leave.

But Trey is no longer at the deli counter. He is just steps away, hovering over the bright pile of oranges. He looks up and sees me.

My heart seems to stop.

His face is at first a blank, but then it lights with recognition, and he smiles. *Smiles.* At me. He has such white teeth. One dimple in a smooth tan cheek. "Hey," he says. "You're—you go to Orcas Bible, right?"

I am mute.

He looks back to the oranges. He picks one up, squeezes it gently, puts it down. "It's… Caroline, right?"

He remembers my name. I smile. My face is stiff, disused from all of my waiting, but now, here, at last, in this hallowed space fragrant with bittersweet citrus, is the moment for which I have been waiting. "Yes," I say. "Caroline Cooper." My voice sounds wispy. Feminine. "And you're Trey. The new youth minister."

"That's right." He selects another orange, feels it, and places it in the bag with the others.

Say something else before it's too late, the voice commands in my head. *Say something about being neighbors.*

I do not stop to wonder whether this is my own mind's command or an intrusion. I say, "I think we're neighbors, too."

"Really? Duncan Road?"

"I'm in the little red cabin, the last house before Camp Praise property."

"Yeah, okay. I drive—or run—past your house, like, every day."

I tuck a strand of hair behind my ear. "So you must—do you work at Camp Praise? Isn't it empty at this time of year?" As though I don't know. As though I have not searched for and devoured scraps of information about this man. From the internet. From people at church. Following him in my car. Hoarding copies of the church bulletin that happen to have his picture in them. Once in September, after the campers were all gone and I knew Trey was safely at CrossFit, I even drove down the road to the camp with the intention of stealing a bag of his garbage. Unfortunately, the bin had been empty. I have not worked up the courage to try that again.

"I originally came out to be a counselor at the beginning of the summer," he says, "but I really like it here, and they needed a new winter caretaker for the camp, so I was like, sign me up."

"And then the youth minister position opened up at Orcas Bible."

"Yeah." He smiles again, a flash of boyishness. "It really felt like God wanted me here. Like there's some reason I needed to stay." He places the bag of oranges in his basket. He is going to leave, he is turning, opening his mouth to say goodbye, but then he stops and turns back to me. "Hey, since we're neighbors, maybe we should—want to come over for Bible study sometime?"

"Do I…" My words die. First, a real conversation with Trey, and now, an invitation? To his home? It is too much bounty.

"I always learn so much more studying with someone else, you know? Especially someone more…" His eyes flick down and up my heavy body in its navy blue raincoat, slack beige dress, and sensible shoes. "Someone who has life wisdom. My Friday evenings are good, if—"

"Sure," I say. "Yes! I'd love to." I sound too eager, like one of those teenage sluts.

"Seven o'clock Friday?"

"Sure. Seven o'clock Friday."

"Awesome," he says, and then he walks away.

I go through the store in a daze. I might laugh, or weep. I am lit up, electric with joy.

Bible study with Trey. I do not deserve it. Him. And yet God in His wisdom has chosen for this to happen. He designed all of this, so it is right and good.

Blindly, I dump a few cans of soup, a box of store-brand saltines, and a few nonfat yogurts into my cart.

There are no lines at the Island Market checkout. Not at this time of year. The store's one cashier is scanning and bagging the cartload of groceries of the woman in front of me. I have seen both of them around the island, many times. Most of the year-round residents look familiar, but outside of my church community and the clients I clean house for, I do not personally know many people.

"True," the cashier is saying to the customer in an excited whisper, running a can of Folgers across her scanner. *Blip.* "I know, 'cause my boyfriend's brother is one of the guys who was out there. I mean, he wasn't the one operating the digger, but he was standing *right there*, and he *saw* it."

"Oh my gosh," the customer said. "Is it—was it—"

"He said it was, like, only about a foot under?"

"Well, there's no topsoil to speak of—"

"Exactly, especially down on that part of the—"

The two women notice that I am listening in on their conversation, and they fall silent.

The cashier turns to me. "Did you hear?"

I pull my tongue from the roof of my mouth, making a sound like a kiss. "Hear—" I clear my throat. "Hear what?"

The customer says, "It's been all over the news, I'm sure she's—"

"I don't follow the news," I say. "What happened?"

"Guys digging for a house foundation down past Deer Harbor found a dead body."

A hissing starts up in my ears. "Of a—of—"

"Of a girl—a teenager."

The customer gives me a sympathetic look. "You okay?"

"Oh. Yes." I hold tight to the shopping cart.

Trey, Trey, Trey! my brain stutters. If, if, if—if Trey finds out, then he—then he—

"The skeleton is probably a hundred years old," the cashier says.

"That's not what *I*—"

The cashier gives the customer a cutting look and turns back to me. "You clean houses, right? I think I've seen you working at Janet Kerrigan's Airbnb?"

"Yes."

Now the customer's smile is, almost imperceptibly, condescending. She probably has a real job as a schoolteacher or a bank teller. A husband and a house with central heating. But I have not seen her at Orcas Bible Church, which means she is bound for Hell, and that is some consolation.

I purchase my groceries, go out to my car, start the engine. Fear is like a frozen pond inside of me.

THEN

GREENE

It was mostly dark out when Mom drove the old Toyota hatchback over a little bridge and onto the ferry.

"Okay, okay, jeez," she muttered as a ferry worker waved her closer and closer to the bumper of the car in front of them.

The ferry worker flipped his palm up: *stop*.

Mom switched off the engine and sighed. She sighed a lot. "Want to go up and have something to eat? Kit told me there's supposed to be a cafeteria or something. Are you hungry? It's after dinnertime."

"Okay," Greene said.

"Let's go, then." Mom grabbed her jacket from the passenger seat. Greene already had on his turquoise windbreaker with the *Tennis Champion* patch on the arm, a hand-me-down from Mom's friend's son back in Idaho. The jacket was humiliatingly out of fashion, like something you'd see on a really old rerun of *Sesame Street*. Greene slid his hand into the pocket—his Matchbox cars were in there. Beauty and Fred. He wrapped his fingers around their comforting solid shapes.

Greene and Mom squeezed between tight-packed vehicles on

the car deck and started upstairs. The entire boat vibrated with the huge grinding engine buried deep inside.

Greene took hold of the metal stair railing—

—calloused rough ones and sticky candy ones and grabbing squeezing they go up—

—and jerked his hand away as though the railing were hot. Now he heard, he felt, only the boat's engine again.

Upstairs, he followed Mom past brown seats and big dark windows. They found a bright cafeteria that smelled of coffee and chili and exhaust. Greene wanted Doritos and one of those fruit yogurts and an intriguing packet of sugar- and cinnamon-coated doughnuts, but no way would Mom okay those, so he chose a stale-looking bagel with a little squeeze-pack of cream cheese instead. Mom got a cup of tea.

They were in line for the cashier, Mom nudging their tray along the metal track, when…

There was the man.

He was medium height, with muscled slim legs in worn jeans. He wore a chunky brown sweater coat. Dark gold shaggy hair covered his ears. His neck, his head, his jawbone were so clear-cut, like a head on a coin.

Mom whisked in a little air through her nose when she saw him. Greene cringed inwardly at the sound because he knew what it meant: she was hooked again. Hooked like the little brook trout Greene caught last year when he went fishing with Harrison, Mom's boyfriend before the last boyfriend, who Greene was not supposed to even know *was* a boyfriend because he already had a family. Greene had been horrified at what he'd done, watching the gemlike little fish flipping and palpitating with the hook in its cheek. Pain had bloomed in Greene's own cheek as he fought back tears. Harrison said, "Your first catch, buddy! We'll fry her up with a little butter—you'll love it," and unhooked the little thing and, holding it by its tail, slapped it on a rock, and it was dead.

The man with the shaggy gold hair flicked his eyes. Eyes that were black, too black for human eyes, black and shiny like the eyes of a garter snake, and he flicked them right at Mom.

Mom sighed a different kind of sigh.

The man turned his back. He picked up a paper cup.

Now it was Mom's turn to pay, and she dropped the change on the floor, laughed, and apologized to the cashier as Greene knelt to gather it up.

Mom carried the tray to a table next to a window. She sat with her back to the cashier, and Greene sat across from her. He tried not to look at the man, whose eyes were hot black dots.

Greene tore open the cream cheese packet, but it was too cold to spread on the bagel and the plastic knife was too bendy, so he started to eat the bagel plain and dry.

Outside, black humps of islands—were they islands?—passed by, with a few lonely lights twinkling. The churn of the engine and the noise of all the things at the cafeteria table—*Shush, I'm—I want to want to dip-dip!—he tied it, tied it tight*—filled up Greene's head. Straight down from the window, way, way down, he saw white froth winging out from the ferry boat's side.

The man had paid the cashier and now he was sitting down at the table next to theirs. He had a newspaper, which he unfolded across the tabletop. Mom was fiddling with her cup, turning it around and around. Even though she wasn't looking at the man and the man wasn't looking at her, Greene felt them listening to each other.

His stomach started to hurt.

He took Beauty out of his pocket. Beauty was a red Porsche with silver fenders and dark windows. He set her on the tabletop, next to the bagel. He reached into his pocket again and pulled out Fred. Fred was a green pickup truck.

Beauty and Fred were Matchbox cars, so they didn't have faces like some toy vehicles. But when Greene looked at them, it felt like he knew them personally. It was impossible to explain this to anyone. Once he'd tried with Mom, and she said he'd always had such a wonderful imagination.

Mom flipped her wheat-colored hair over her shoulder and turned toward the man. She hesitated, softly cleared her throat, then said, "Looks like the weather should be nice this week."

There was a second or two when it seemed as if the man hadn't heard. Mom was about to say something else when he turned his head. "Rain and clouds," he said. "That's *nice*?"

"It is if you love the rain. And I do—love it, I mean. We're moving out to Orcas from Idaho, so any rain is welcome."

"That so?" The man's eyes went back to his newspaper.

Eagerly, Mom said, "I've—we've—never been, but everyone says it's the most magical place in the world."

"It's pretty magical, all right," the man said. He sounded like he was making fun of something. "What part of the island are you moving to?"

"Oh, well, we're not—not quite sure yet." A nervous breathy laugh. "We're going to stay with a friend of mine for a while, to get things straightened out—"

"Do you have a job on the island? There aren't many jobs."

"No." Another laugh. "Our move was kind of sudden."

The man had seemed bored, but now he turned to face Mom. "So, what?" he said. "Clearing out from a bad situation back in Idaho? Maybe a rotten husband? Is he going to come for the kid?"

Greene squeezed Beauty in his hand so tight—*no, no, no!*—he could have melted her. He let up, thinking but not saying *Sorry*.

"His dad is long gone. It's not about— It was just time to make a fresh start." Mom smiled. "I'm Caroline, by the way. Caroline Cooper."

"Nice to meet you, Caroline." The man looked Mom over, the same way Mom herself looked over grapefruits at Safeway. Greene could picture him squeezing Mom's face in that same skeptical, searching way. "People call me Uncle."

"Uncle what?"

"Just Uncle."

"Do you have lots of nieces and nephews?"

"Not by blood, but yeah, I do."

"Adopted?"

"Informally, I guess. I'm not big on bureaucracy."

"Well, pleased to meet you, Uncle. Oh! And this is Greene."

"Like the color?"

"Like Graham. His dad liked the writer Graham Greene." Mom stressed the word *liked*.

"Isn't he too old to play with toy cars? How old is he? Ten?"

"He just turned eight."

"He ought to be working. My littlest nieces and nephews, they're out on the farm working every day. You're never too young to learn how to take care of yourself."

"Working?" Mom was half laughing.

What Greene wanted was to get away from Uncle. Just get up and go. But you couldn't do that on a boat. So he made up his mind to focus on Fred and Beauty, on the line of Beauty's roof sliding down to her rear bumper; he pictured her zooming along a highway. He didn't dare drive her on the tabletop, though, because the man would definitely make fun of him.

Mom talked with the man—Uncle—for a while. At some point, Uncle joined them at their table, sitting next to Mom.

Greene stopped listening, but he couldn't stop noticing. How Mom leaned toward Uncle. How Uncle's smiles seemed like they were hiding a mean secret.

"I'm going to grab more tea," Mom said, getting to her feet. "You want anything?"

"Get me another coffee," Uncle said. "Black."

"Sure. Back in a sec, Greene. Hey, I thought you were really hungry. Why aren't you eating your bagel?"

"I'm not hungry anymore," Greene whispered.

As Greene watched Mom walk away, he thought, Don't go. Don't leave me with this weirdo.

Mom kept on going.

Uncle turned his eyes on Greene. They were so black, so shiny, and his skin had a golden sheen that made it look like plastic.

Greene stared down at the tabletop, at Fred the pickup sitting there on a crumpled napkin.

"You *are* too old for toys, you know," Uncle said.

Greene thought, Hurry up, Mom. He could see her filling a cup at the coffee dispenser.

"Hey, is that a killer whale out there?" Uncle said.

"Really?" Greene pressed his forehead against the window and looked out at the black water. "Where?"

"Aw, my mistake. Trick of the light, I guess."

Greene rubbed the cold condensation off his forehead. "Where's Fred?" he said.

"Who's Fred?"

"My truck!"

"You mean that dumb little toy?"

"Yeah."

"Maybe it fell on the floor."

Greene dipped his head under the table. Nothing down there but an old Cheetos bag.

He sat up. "You took him," he whispered to Uncle without meeting his eye.

"Whoa, whoa, whoa. Face it, buddy. You lost your toy. What do you need that shit for, anyway? It's from a sweatshop in China. Kids your age in a factory with no mommy or daddy, making junk for fourteen hours a day for spoiled materialistic American kids? That's sick. Maybe you need to figure out how to go without. American kids are just little trash-makers, and they grow up to be big trash-makers."

Greene pictured his belongings, all of which fit into a wicker laundry basket stuffed in the Toyota. *Was* he just a trash-maker?

Here came Mom, carrying two steaming cups.

Uncle leaned toward Greene and said softly, "There's going to come a time when *all* this shit will be meaningless. Adapt or die, buddy."

Mom was sitting down, setting Uncle's coffee in front of him, beaming. "Look at the two of you having a nice boys' chat." Her smile slipped off. "Greene! What's the matter?"

"I—"

"He lost his toy truck," Uncle said.

"You lost Ted?" Mom said to Greene.

"Fred," Greene said. "How could I lose him? He was on the table, and now he's gone. He's not on the floor. There's nowhere he can be."

"How about in one of your pockets?" Mom asked.

Greene patted his windbreaker pockets and his jeans pockets, just to humor Mom. But he knew exactly what had happened to Fred.

Mom said, "Are you sure you didn't leave Fred down in the—"

"He was sitting right here!"

"Greene, don't yell."

"I don't remember seeing a toy truck," Uncle said.

Mom said to Greene, "Listen. I'll get you a new truck, how about that?"

"But I want Fred!"

"Kids," Mom said to Uncle. "They think their toys can, I don't know, *talk*. Greene's not usually like this, by the way. He's had a really big day, that's all. Look at him. Dark circles under his eyes."

"He looks all right to me."

Uncle and Mom fell into grown-ups' conversation again. Mom told him how she was a graduate student in botany at the university in Moscow, how she was planning on going back but she needed some time to get her head on straight. She asked Uncle a lot of questions about himself and mostly he talked about his farm on the island, how he grew plums and kale, how they had chickens and goats and it was all surrounded by trees with trunks so thick even he, Uncle, couldn't reach his arms around them.

"Gosh, it sounds like paradise," Mom said, propping her chin in her hand.

"It's a lot of work, but it's all worth it to be self-sufficient. Nothing feels better. I don't owe anybody anything, and I'd survive even if the entire country got nuked."

Greene sat quiet and wondered how he could get Fred back from Uncle. But Greene was just a kid, and Uncle was a grown man who had everything. He even had Mom now.

Mom had told Greene, earlier in the car, that Kit's house was near the beach, that you walked along a trail through the woods and there it was, all pebbly and with water like green Jell-O. Mom had said they could look for clamshells and cool rocks and pieces of driftwood there all day long—they'd bring peanut butter sandwiches and a bag of potato chips. She'd said they could go to the beach even if it rained. She promised.

So all Greene had to do was wait. Ignore Uncle until he passed out of their lives.

They went for a walk on the ferry deck, even though it was dark and raindrops blasted around the corners like needles in the wind. Greene walked behind Mom and Uncle, shaking with cold, worrying about Fred.

Then back inside to the warm cafeteria again, and as they were sitting down at the same table they'd sat at before, Uncle picked something up off the floor. "Well, how about that," he said. "It's your lost toy." He pushed his fist across the table, holding it in front of Greene a second too long before opening his fingers. And there was Fred.

"Uncle!" Mom was laughing. "How—"

"It was on the floor."

"Well, thank you—Greene, say thank-you."

Greene mumbled thanks. He picked up Fred. Fred felt like how it would feel to have an angry wasp in your hand, only without any motion or any biting. Just the *sense* of that vivid anger, the sense of someone raging *no, no, no, no, no!* without making a sound. Not a regular sound, anyway, that anyone else could hear.

"You're a lifesaver," Mom said to Uncle. "He and that truck have been inseparable for at least a year, and with all the changes..." Her eyes were shiny. The black stuff she always drew around her eyes was starting to smear.

Uncle was just watching.

Watching.

"Sorry," Mom said, wiping under her eyes with a finger. "I drove four hundred miles today and, well, it's also...it's just that it's so nice to see Greene have a positive interaction with a man. His dad took off when he was just a baby and...oh, never mind. What is it about you that's making me spill my guts like this?"

"I'm a great listener," Uncle said. "Everyone tells me that."

When the voice on the loudspeaker announced that they were arriving at Orcas Island and needed to return to their vehicles, Mom said to Uncle, "Wow. Well, it was so nice to meet you, Uncle, and I hope—I hope I'll see you around the island?"

"Sure." Uncle was standing up. He seemed bored again. Almost like he *hated* Mom now. "Good luck with everything—was it... Kathy?"

"Caroline."

"Oh, right. See you round, Caroline."

Mom looked shrunken as she watched Uncle walk out of the cafeteria. Greene was glad to see Uncle go, but he felt shrunken, too.

The loudspeaker voice said something else about passengers returning to their vehicles.

"Mom?" Greene said. "I think we're supposed to go to our—"

"I know. I *know.*"

Back in the Toyota, Fred sat in Greene's palm and told him in a rush how Uncle took him off the table and what it was like in Uncle's pocket. Fred had feelings about it. Thing feelings, which were different than human feelings. It was a story, but not a story in the way a human would tell it. Greene was used to hearing such stories and knew exactly how to listen to them. Listen in the special way that was more like feeling.

"Wow, what a great guy," Mom said, holding the steering wheel tight even though they were still waiting for the ferry to dock. She was looking in the rearview mirror, then peering at the cars ahead of them. "Wasn't he nice? Uncle?"

Greene wanted to shout that Uncle wasn't nice at all, that he was mean—no, worse than mean, he was a freak. A monster. Couldn't Mom see his eyes were too black? That there was something the matter with the way he held his shoulders and the way his skin looked like plastic? But Greene didn't say anything.

They drove off the ferry in the slow line of cars, windshield wipers squawking and rain slanting through their headlight beams.

"Kit told me to park in front of the store by the ferry dock," Mom said. "She said to turn right and we can't miss it."

They turned right and parked at the curb. The store was closed. No other cars were waiting.

Mom had said that Kit lived off the grid, which meant she didn't have electricity or running water or even an address, since her house was built on the edge of her parents' land and wasn't really supposed to be there. She'd told Mom that she would meet them and lead them to her cabin because it was impossible to find, especially in the dark.

They waited. Mom fidgeted with her hair. Greene needed to go to the bathroom but decided to hold it.

Also, Kit didn't have a telephone.

After a time, maybe twenty minutes, during which Greene concentrated on holding his pee, a pickup truck pulled up beside them. Mom rolled down her window. Rain sprayed in.

The truck's driver-side window inched jerkily down. But it wasn't Kit. It was Uncle. "Your friend's a no-show?" he called through the hissing rain.

"It's starting to look that way," Mom called back.

"How long are you going to wait?"

Greene felt the suck of Uncle's black-dot eyes.

"I don't know," Mom said.

"Sleep at my farm tonight," Uncle said. "There's plenty of room." He cranked up his window before Mom could answer.

They followed Uncle's red taillights into the night.

NOW

HANNAH

After Allan leaves for his shower, I stay to help Tilde put away the rest of the groceries. Not because I enjoy Tilde's company, but because our housekeeper is on vacation until after Thanksgiving. Also, I want to give Allan a head start upstairs.

I eliminated all candidates with even a hint of prettiness when I was screening the new options from the au pair agency. I'm not stupid: even the youngest wife doesn't stay young forever. All the same, Tilde has developed a hard, hot crush on the man of the house. I know this because she lets her needy adoration for Allan show all over her face. It makes me queasy with shame for her. Doesn't she know she's doing it wrong? You can't let men see the truth. You have to bury it deep.

I give Tilde instructions for starting dinner, and then I go up the main staircase. I love these stairs with their heavy carved banister. I love the whole rambling house with its polished wood and high ceilings, the sumptuous custom furniture and the artwork Allan has collected over the years.

Sometimes when I'm alone in the house, I'll walk slowly from room to room, surveying my kingdom, so different from the dumpy houses I grew up in. I'll check to make sure the housekeeper has vacuumed up every speck of dust. I'll look with satisfaction inside the refrigerator and the pantry at all the neatly stored food. I'll run my manicured fingers with their shimmering diamond rings over the fine, expensive things and think, I belong here.

I'm not sure I completely believe it.

I crack the door of the primary suite and hear the shushing sound of the shower. I go to the walk-in closet. Allan's running clothes are balled-up on the floor next to his running shoes. His phone is on a chair.

I grab the phone, swipe it to life, and punch in the passcode, which years ago I deduced through discreet spying.

I open up the recent calls.

At 3:23, Allan made a call to a number with a 360 area code that lasted for 22 minutes and 17 seconds.

Allan, I think. Allan, what did you do?

Because it's not Head of School Preller's number. It's not even Preller's area code. Allan lied about this call.

I check up on Allan's emails and texts routinely, even though I have never caught him in an affair. But I will. I'm getting older by the second. There's nothing I can do to stop the decay of my tissues. For a certain type of man, a decaying woman is unforgivable. It reminds them of how they're dying, too.

One day, Allan will divorce me, just like he divorced his first two wives. Just like them, I will be ravaged by the prenup I signed nine years ago.

How did you two meet? people always ask, with smiles that say *Tell us your love story*, but with a flintiness in their eyes that adds *you little gold digger.* And isn't it just classic, the story of the middle-aged businessman and the pretty young flight attendant in the first-class cabin? It's familiar, with flavors of Cinderella and soft porn. It's a bitter story, too, because probably there's a cast-off middle-aged wife in the plot, maybe even cast-off children. Still, everyone wants to hear it.

Men picture me, a version of me so young I'm like the tenderest cut in the butcher's case, and think *Well, of course Allan fell in love with her.* Women's responses are more complicated. Some picture themselves in my shoes. They sympathize with jumping at the opportunity to land the trophy-wife gig. Other women are condescending, assuming with my looks and lack of a college degree I must be an idiot. Still others—women who were themselves thrown away for younger women, or whose mother or friend or sister suffered that fate—can barely contain their hostility.

He swept me off my feet, I tell anyone who asks. *He was my rock. He was there for me when I needed him.*

That last part is the truth. I always add it so there's enough truth mixed in with the lies to put them off the scent.

We met on the red-eye from LaGuardia to Sea-Tac, I say. *Everyone was asleep in the cabin except for Allan, who stayed awake working on his laptop. We got to talking. We just clicked.*

I can conjure in an instant Allan's face the day we met. The texture of the graying stubble on his suntanned cheeks, the gleam of intelligence in his eyes. He was wearing a blue Mariners cap. Expensive-looking jeans. A black, techy-looking The North Face jacket. He was neither handsome nor tall, but he exuded an energetic self-assurance that more than made up for it.

His eyes met mine, and I watched them change from tired and distant to bright and alert. He didn't smile. He lifted a hand like a king and beckoned me. And I, his willing slave, went.

Maybe it's weird to revisit that moment so much. But I find myself returning in my mind to that day, that moment, again and again, as though I'm still trying to figure it out. What happened, exactly? Which step was the wrong step?

This phone number, though, this is something different than an affair. Probably. Because I happen to know that a number with a 360 area code followed by 376 is an Orcas Island number.

It has to be about the horrible thing those construction workers found. That—those buried—

"Hannah?" Allan says behind me. "Is—is that my phone?"

I try to set the phone down on the chair, but my hands are shaking, so it clunks to the floor. I stoop to pick it up and then Allan is beside me—bare-chested, damp towel clutched at his waist—snatching it up himself.

I step back. Allan is frowning at the phone's screen. It's in lock mode again. Maybe he won't realize I got in.

"Do you…know my passcode?" He sounds almost childishly hurt.

"Of course I don't know your passcode. I heard it ringing and thought I'd bring it to you in the—"

"Really?" Now he sounds skeptical. He unlocks the phone. The screen still displays the list of recent calls. "I don't see any calls in the last few minutes. Why are you… How do you know my passcode?"

"I'm your *wife*."

"You heard the news. About the island house. You thought—"

"What about Oliver?" I say quickly, because suddenly I'm terrified to go there. To the grave. To the dead girl. To what I thought when I saw that island phone number. "Aren't we going to talk about *him*?"

"You're changing the subject."

"We need to talk about it."

"Fine. You want to know what to do about Oliver? I'll tell you. He belongs in a special school, like I've been saying for years. You know what? I'm calling Larches Academy right now. I assume a place like that accepts new students year-round." Allan is stabbing and swiping on his phone. Searching for the school's number, I guess.

"*No.* You are not taking him away from me."

"He needs more help than we can give him."

"He's seeing Patti."

"She's a quack."

"He needs to be with his family. With people who love him."

"You call that *love*, Hannah?" Allan looks up from his phone. "Letting him get away with this shit? Letting him push the line and push the line until we have a monster on our hands?"

"Don't call him that."

"Preller said that kid's family is threatening to sue. *Sue*, Hannah. And what if he hurts Sibley? How will you feel if you let that happen?"

"I— He wouldn't..."

The walls of the closet are closing in. The racks of beautiful clothes, the dim, expensive lighting, the odors of laundry detergent and leather and my husband's shower gel—it's all suffocating me. I'm hyperaware that I'm about to rip a hole in our perfect marriage. I have never made any demands on Allan, never asked him uncomfortable questions. I can't remember the last time I even told him *no*.

I have tried so hard to be the perfect wife—honey-sweet and yielding, beautiful, fit, fashionable, and smiling—for the sake of the kids. And Allan has been a good husband, a decent father, and an exceptionally generous provider. He's in love with me, I know, or he's in love with the version I let him see. I was never in love with him, but I've grown fond of him, in a way.

But if he knows something about that dead girl, if he's hiding what he knows from me? Even *I* can't pretend that's okay.

I have to say something, and there will be no going back.

I take a breath, so deep it hurts. I let it out. "Why did you call an Orcas Island number? You were in your sweaty running clothes in your car. You were hiding that call, Allan. What did you do?"

There's a long pause. Allan watches me closely, his eyes darting over my features, trying to read my thoughts. But I'm still safely hidden. He will never see me. He never has.

Finally he says, "Where is this coming from, Hannah?"

"I just want to know."

"What's gotten into you? This isn't like you at all."

"Just answer my question." I stumble over the words. It's like speaking a foreign tongue, confronting him like this. "Who did you call on Orcas Island?"

Now Allan's expression is guarded. Almost mean. He's never looked at me like this before.

"I'm warning you, Hannah," he says. "Don't you breathe a word of anything—*anything*—to anyone. Your entire life is built on it. You *wanted* it."

It, I think. Our original sin.

I whisper back, "Your entire life is built on it, too."

Allan draws back. His eyes narrow. "Is that...is that a threat?"

"Are you serious? How could I— In what world would that even—"

"Because if you're threatening me, Hannah, you need to remember that I always, *always* win—"

"I didn't—"

"So keep that in mind before you even *think* about—"

"Allan. Please." My heart is tiny and pattering again, the victimy rabbit's heart.

Finally, his eyes soften. He steps close, wraps his arms around me, nuzzles his mouth against my cheekbone. I force myself not to recoil. "Everything I do, Hannah, I do for *you*," he says softly. "What would become of Sibley, of Oliver, if you went to prison?"

Run, I think. Hide.

Tomorrow, after Allan leaves for work, I'll take the kids and run. But to whom? I have no one. All of my friends are married to Allan's friends. All of my relatives are either estranged or dead.

Allan says, "You should be grateful, Hannah. Look at your life. Look at what you *have*." He gestures around the closet as though the clothes and shoes and handbags are the sum total of our life together.

In a way, they are. There are the exquisite Loro Piana jackets to wear to playdates and soccer games. Moncler ski suits for our winter trips to Park City and Aspen. Cute little French tennis dresses for my lessons at the club, bikinis and coverups and sundresses for vacations in Hawaii and the Virgin Islands, the perfect Dior trench coat I bought in Paris, the sexy dresses for date nights with Allan, more conservative dresses for mingling with Allan's business associates. This closet is a catalog of my life as a rich mom. A life that, as of this afternoon, no longer feels secure.

Allan says, "You want to throw all this away for—for what?"

"I *am* grateful," I say softly. "I am."

"What would have happened to you if you hadn't met me?"

"I don't think about that."

"Well, maybe you should, because you would have been so screwed, and you know it. Okay. What's going to happen is I'm going to enroll Oliver at Larches and fly him out there as soon as possible, and you're going to stop thinking whatever crazy stuff you're thinking. We have a great life, babe. Don't screw it up."

He kisses me on the mouth, and I submit as I have trained myself to do. But I'm not thinking about him; I'm thinking that even though I may have no one to run to, there is some*place*. There is the island house.

It would be crazy to go there right now. That house, that island...they make me feel trapped. Sometimes it feels like Allan brings me out there just to punish me.

Besides, human remains have been dug up near the house—and they are *remains*, I tell myself. Not a person. Not even really a body anymore.

But what other option do I have? It's either let Allan pack Oliver off to Montana, let Allan make threats and call the shots and tell lies. Or run and hide. And the island house could make a great hiding place. Allan knows I hate it there. It will be the last place he'll think to look for me.

I should probably be paying more attention to how the island is quietly, steadily pulling me back.

JOSH

The Sibelius *Violin Concerto* has three movements—the first majestic, the second sobbing and slow, the last a virtuosic feat—all of them bogged down with existential despair. I never feel that despair. But according to the music critics, I make *other* people feel it. Or I usually do.

Things are not happening as they usually do this afternoon.

I'm standing downstage at the Béla Bartók National Concert Hall in Budapest, the center of attention in a sold-out matinee. Hot yellow spotlights my tall substantial tuxedo-clad form, my floppy wings of dark hair, my sweat-sheened face. I hear distant muffled coughs, the hum and tremble of strings and horsehair and metal and wood. I inhale the varnishy, burning-dust smell of all concert halls and the faint tang of my own sweat.

We are deep inside the sprawl of the first movement, and the music, the *violin*, is getting ahead of me.

The conductor, Ferenc Something-or-other, an up-and-coming Hungarian guy, casts worried sidelong looks from his podium. His arms swoop, his hands tamp down and string out and taper the air for the orchestra. At the first sign of tempo-pushing during the *poco affrettando*, he looks a little concerned, but it's a cadenza section that I more or less play alone anyway. The slurred sixteenth runs are not as clear as they should be, but there's a hotshot daring to the tempo that—maybe?—makes up for the less-than-perfect execution.

But things get freaky when we arrive at the next part, a long melodic sequence where the conductor and the orchestra *do* need to stay with me, but I'm cheating the dotted quarters, rushing through them, so that now Ferenc is shooting me bulging-eyed looks whenever he can, which isn't too often because the entire woodwind section is off now, and I feel the electricity in the air, the silent crackle of seventeen hundred people, shift palpably from *Whoa, look at him go!* to *What the fuck?*

My guts start to knot up, that familiar sick tug.

I arrive at the high-A cadence, and then I have several measures of rest to get it together while the orchestra plays without me. I drop the violin away from my jaw, instantly feeling a release. I sway to the orchestra's thundering gorgeous passage, eyes downcast, pretending, always pretending, to be the virtuoso immersed body and soul in the music.

And I *am* immersed, but not in the music. I'm immersed in steeling my will for the next round of battle.

My last thought before tucking the violin back under my jaw is It's getting worse. Way worse.

The next stretch is okay. It's a lyrical passage that no one would dream of pushing, tempowise, and I could have played even the demanding sixths and octaves in my sleep. Maybe it's going to be okay after all—

Nope. Here comes the *allegro molto vivace*, and the violin hums so brightly my jaw feels like it's lit up with neon. The four strings shimmer with their side-to-side, live-wire vibrations. *Go, go, go!* the violin and bow seem to shout as I scrape and pulverize horsehair and metal together, as the violin's wooden panels and sound post throb like a kicked-over wasp's nest. *Let's go!*

I close my eyes, struggle to breathe. My hands, my arms...they just *go.* They know what to do. I have practiced this passage numberless times. But it is out of control, *so* out of control. The arpeggios go faster and faster, the flutist skittering to keep up. I arrive at the shrilling-high slurred octaves and just sort of smudge half-heartedly through them like an amateur sight-reading, and then I hit the stratospherically high-D octave cadence a full beat before the rest of the orchestra.

Oh God.

I crash the second-to-last note.

Shit.

And I burn the last one.

Fuck.

The End.

Of the first movement, anyway.

The final chord hangs in the air, high above an audience holding its breath.

Even though there are still two movements to go, I look over at Ferenc and whisper, "I can't. I—I'm ill. I'm so sorry." I take the violin away from my jaw—relief—and, head down, I hurry offstage to rumbling murmurs of shock.

I make one wrong turn and then another in search of my dressing room. I have been in so many backstages in the past several years. My whole life is just a series of dressing rooms and green rooms and random conductors' flop sweat, and the whole time I've had this *thing,* this multimillion-dollar wooden box, attached to my neck like a goiter, like some deformity that wants to pull me under and make me drown.

I'm sweating. Drenched. My palms are slippery, my back wet under the tuxedo jacket and dress shirt.

Okay, I think. Okay. Even famous musicians get sick, right? I'm only human. This can't end my career, just one fuckup. Not with my impressive discography, my years of touring the great concert halls of the globe to acclaim. Not after my astonishing, out-of-nowhere wins at the Paganini and Wieniawski competitions in 2016. Can it?

Here, at last, is the dressing room with my name on a piece of paper taped to the door. I go in and straight to the open violin case.

You asshole, I think as I use a cloth to wipe the rosin dust from the strings and the fingerboard. You utter and complete asshole. What are you trying to do to me?

I set the violin in its case, Velcro the tab over its neck, cover it with a silk blanket, and shut the lid. Only then, with the violin latched inside layers of high-tech padding, steel, and fiberglass, do I feel like I can take a full breath of air.

"What in the *hell* was that?" someone says behind me.

I turn. "Amelia." Bile sluices up into my throat.

My manager, Amelia Davidson, a pretty, middle-aged woman in a black suit, is shutting the dressing-room door behind her. Her face is pinched and pale. "That was being recorded live. Congratulations. You're now in breach of your contract with Moonstone Records."

"We can redo it."

"It was supposed to be in front of a live audience."

"We can fake it."

"Moonstone won't want to pay the orchestra for another round. Not to mention Ferenc Sevely's fee. No. You blew it. What in the hell happened? You were completely—*completely*—out of control."

It wasn't me, I think.

"I know," I say. My guts are boiling in earnest now. I look at the wastebasket next to the door. I might need to hurl soon.

"So? What? Are you on drugs?"

"Of course I'm not on drugs!" I allow myself to raise my voice. It makes me feel a little better.

"Then—what? Do you need to *get* on drugs? I mean, what the *hell*, Josh."

"I'm..." I swallow bile. "I'm burned out."

"What?"

"I'm burned *out*. It's like my body and my brain aren't in sync. I need a break."

"No. You're fully booked. We're in the middle of a *European tour*."

"I can't do it, Amelia. Cancel everything. I can't."

"Listen to me, Josh. Get yourself together. You may think you're on the top of the world, but it can all go away in the blink of an eye. The classical-music world isn't any different than reality TV. Audiences want spectacle, they want fresh meat. If you aren't fresh meat—and let's face it, you've been on the circuit for several years and you aren't fresh anymore, and twenty-seven is *way* outside of wunderkind land—then you better be putting on a good show before some ten-year-old prodigy eats your lunch."

"I'm... I need... I don't know. I just need some *quiet*. Please. Please let me have a break."

"Jesus." Amelia sighs. "Well, it's not like I can stop you, is it?"

I leave through the stage door a few minutes later, not greeted by smiling faces and flowers and programs thrust out for my autograph, but like an escaping criminal. I feel like I'm floating across the rainy, windswept plaza, violin case in hand. I slide into the frontmost taxi at the curb. It stinks of diesel fumes and cigarettes.

"The Ritz-Carlton," I say to the driver.

He grunts in response.

I lay the violin case on the seat beside me. Most violinists would hold it on their lap for extra security, but I don't want to touch it.

The taxi traces the shape of the river northward toward the old city.

I'm still sweating under my wool overcoat. I desperately need water. Do I dare look at my phone? It's an addiction, usually, checking my hashtagged name on social media after a performance. Reading the rave reviews and the odd sour-grapes complaint about things like *old-school technique*. As if old-school technique is something to bitch about.

A junkielike compulsion gets the best of me. I pull out my phone.

It blinks to life with a long list of notifications: emails, texts, missed calls, and social-media posts. I scroll through. Dozens and dozens of them.

Never mind. I can't stomach it.

I close the notifications list. Then, the last thing I was reading before my warm-up backstage flashes on the screen. A news item from the *Seattle Times*:

Human Remains Unearthed on Orcas Island

I punch the website closed.

I dial the one person in my life who seems not to have contacted me in the last half hour—Drew, who as far as I know is in London, a thousand miles away.

No answer. The call goes to voicemail, and I hang up without leaving a message.

It occurs to me that, beneath the fog of shame, what I'm really feeling is *fear.*

Fear that my time is up. That the world is about to see me for the fraud I really am.

HANNAH

November isn't tourist season in the San Juan Islands, so even without a reservation I'm able to book the children and myself on the 12:35 ferry from Anacortes to Orcas. I pay the fare at the booth and park in one of the holding lanes. We won't have long to wait.

The day is murky, and fitful rain splats across the windshield. In the back seat, Sibley is listening to a *Harry Potter* audiobook through headphones. Oliver is engrossed in an electronic game beside her. They didn't question our sudden trip to the island: they are simply happy to be missing school.

At most of the ferry docks in Puget Sound, you see your boat coming a long way off, a white chunk on the blue-gray water, sliding closer and closer until it's looming over you. At the dock in Anacortes, though, the ferry comes in at a sharp angle around a point of land. You never see it coming.

Dread wraps around me, thick and woozy. It starts to squeeze. I can't shake the feeling that someone—someone I don't want to see—is going to appear from out of the rain and knock on my window.

* * *

This morning, I lay in bed pretending to sleep until I heard Allan's Tesla backing out of the driveway as he left for work. Then I got up.

Hurrying, I showered, brushed my teeth, got dressed. Designer jeans, fawn-colored cashmere turtleneck, white leather sneakers. I brushed my long pale wavy hair into a ponytail. Dabbed on tinted moisturizer, eyeliner, mascara, lip gloss. I never, ever leave the house without some sort of disguise. Not even on a day like this.

First, I looked in on Sibley, sprawled asleep in her bed, her plush rabbit, Bunners, tucked tight under her chin. Then I checked on Oliver. He was sleeping with a scowl in a tight little hedgehog ball, his phone on the mattress beside his head. His cheek was flushed, and I felt a spike of alarm, but then I realized it was just that he had too many blankets on.

I brought down our biggest suitcase from the attic. I opened it across my bed and packed sensible warm layers for the three of us, and cozy pajamas and robes. I needed to remember to grab raincoats and boots from the mudroom—

"Mrs. McCullough?"

My palm flew to my chest. "Tilde! You scared me."

Tilde, small and wan and with her hair in a messy bun, stood in the doorway. "Is everything all right? I heard a sound in the attic, a—"

"It's okay. I was looking for something."

She was eyeing the open suitcase. "Should I wake the children? It is nearly eight—"

"They won't be going to school today."

"Are they ill?"

"No. They're just…not going to school."

"Oh."

"I'm taking the kids on a road trip for a few days."

"I did not know."

"It's…impromptu."

Tilde glanced to the window, which had a view of wet trees and leaden sky. "It is not nice weather for a road trip."

"No, but I—we just—we need a change of scene, and it's easy enough to go up to—" I stopped myself. "We'll be leaving as soon as I'm finished packing, so you'll have time off until we're back."

"You are going to the island house?" Tilde asked.

"No," I said, probably too quickly. I hesitated, then added, "Don't mention any of this to Mr. McCullough, okay?"

"Okay." Suspicion shadowed Tilde's face, but she said nothing else.

At 12:15 the ferry arrives at Anacortes and disgorges dozens of vehicles. They flow past us in a splashing line.

"How long are we going to be at the island house, Mommy?" Sibley asks from the back seat. She speaks too loudly because of her headphones.

I have to lie. "Just a few days."

We bought groceries at the Whole Foods in Lynnwood on the way up. I paid with cash for the groceries and for the ferry, too. I don't want Allan to be able to track my movements.

"But it's *raining*," Sibley says. "Can we go down to the beach if it's raining?"

"Sure."

"Remember that fort Tilde and I started building last time? Do you think it's still there?"

"I don't know, honey. There have probably been some storms since then. But there's always driftwood on the beach. You can build an even better one."

"But what about our buckets and shovels? We forgot them."

"You can use sticks to dig."

"Okay," Sibley says doubtfully.

"Hannah," Oliver says, speaking for the first time in hours. Despite my best efforts, he has never willingly called me Mom,

Mama, or Mommy. It's as though he was bent on rejecting me even as a toddler.

"Yes, honey?"

"How come I've never been to the island house?"

"Because we only use it in August, and you always go away to camp in August."

"Why?"

"I don't know. I guess it's because the weather is best in August. That's what your dad says, anyway."

"He's not my dad."

"Fine. Stepdad."

I glance in the rearview mirror. Oliver's brow is furrowed as he looks out the window. He has rubbed a circle in the fogged glass. "I've been here before."

"All these ferry docks look the same."

"I have," he mutters and turns back to his game.

Then my own phone pings. It's a text from Allan, the first I've heard from him today:

Larches has room. Made reservations for Oliver/me to fly to Montana Sunday 9 a.m.

I power my phone off just as the car in front of me starts up, brake lights blinking and exhaust mushrooming. "Here we go," I say to Sibley and Oliver, trying to sound adventurous.

I turn over the engine, and we roll toward the ferry's open mouth.

ALLAN

I'll never forget the first arrowhead I ever found, when I was eleven years old. It was just lying there in a dry creek bed. Despite its thick coating of dust, I recognized the shape, and my heart skipped a beat. Kids I knew would sell such things to Pete at the Gas and General Store in Colville, who would in turn peddle them to tourists. Pothunting, that's what it's called. But when I cleaned up that arrowhead with spit on the hem of my T-shirt, when I saw its black obsidian divots and ridges glistening through the dust, I knew there was no way in hell I would ever hand it over to Pete.

What I saw when I looked at that arrowhead was something better. Something that transcended the cheap shit—the glitchy pickups, stinking mobile homes, the cans of Chef Boyardee—amid which I had wallowed all my life. I saw something that had lasted, and would last, forever. The real thing.

The moment I first saw Hannah was just like when I found that arrowhead. The two events—finding the arrowhead, finding Hannah—are overlaid in my mind like transparency sheets. They aren't identical, but they belong together, and they highlight each other's meanings. I can still feel the effect her face had on me. It flattened me out, made me so flimsy I felt as though I'd fold like a matchbook. Because of her beauty, but only in part; it was the light I saw shining out of her. The ineffable glow of the real thing. If you're lucky enough to stumble on something like that, you sure as fuck don't let it go.

Oh, I know what you're thinking. That I am, at the very least, kind of a dick, and at most, one of the narcissistic assholes the Netflix thrillers warned you about. I'm not.

She was pregnant when we met, you know, in her first trimester and just starting to show, her taut little belly domed like the Virgin's in a medieval painting. So if I'm such a villain, how come I was willing to take on not one but two of some other guy's kids? I never even asked her who the father was. Not that I needed to.

I go about my day as usual. There's a nine-o'clock partners meeting followed by two board calls and lunch with a potential investor. In between meetings I contact the admissions office at Larches Academy and then book two seats on a Sunday-morning flight to Billings. I text Hannah.

After that, my focus wanes. I keep checking my phone to see if she has texted back. I stand in my office on the fortieth floor of the Cascade Tower and look out at the swirls of sky and cloud that blot out the city. I imagine that I can feel the sway of the skyscraper in the wind. It makes me sick.

Did I cross a line yesterday? I wonder. In nine years, my wife and I have never discussed the exact circumstances of our union. It never seemed to matter because we're together, and so it was all worth it. Maybe I shouldn't have said what I did about the risk of her going to prison. But I wanted to wake her up, scare some sense into her about what's at stake.

At three, I decide to go home early. Thursday usually means a round of golf at Broadmoor or drinks with fast-talking men someplace with leather chairs. Not today.

Turning into my driveway, I can't see Hannah's Range Rover.

They're gone, I think, getting out of the car. Fuck, they're gone. Or, no—wait. Maybe she's picking up Sibley at school. They're probably on their way home right now.

In the kitchen, just for the sake of authenticity, I call, "Hannah? Sibley?" Even in this theatrical mode I can't bring myself to call for Oliver. That kid has always made my skin crawl. Then I call, "Tilde?" There is no answer, but now I hear faint music playing above me.

I go through the dining room, the living room. I look into my study. I go upstairs, then downstairs again and into the kitchen.

We house the au pairs in quarters above the kitchen, in rooms that have always been, since this house was built, the maid's quarters. They are reached by a narrow twisting stair off the kitchen. I go up, and the music grows louder, and now I can tell it's some kind of pulsating, sultry Euro pop.

There's a shut door at the top of the stairs. I knock.

"Yes?" Tilde says. I hear footsteps. The door opens, and her face appears in the gap. "Oh. Hello."

"Where are Mrs. McCullough and the children?"

"She—they went away."

"Where?"

"She did not say." Tilde's gaze drops to the floor. She knows something.

"It's okay," I say. "You need to tell me. My children are involved."

"I do not know for certain." Tilde's eyes widen with worry, and I notice she's wearing a tight pink T-shirt. She will never be pretty, but in that moment she looks so vulnerable, so girlish, that my groin starts to ache.

"Listen," I say. "Can I come in?"

Her eyes widen even more, but she steps back, holding the door open for me.

The room smells like citrusy rose perfume, and the music is coming from a small Bluetooth speaker on the dresser. There's a bed in the tiny room beyond, and a bathroom, I know. I sit down on the edge of the small couch, lean my elbows on my knees, and hold my head in my hands. I want to look distraught, but I really am distraught, too. Hannah is on the loose. Not good.

The cushions shift as Tilde sits down beside me. "Please. You must not be upset. It is fine. But you must understand my problem. I work for you, but also for Mrs. McCullough, and she will fire me if she thinks I cannot be trusted."

"I understand," I say. Tilde looks all of seventeen, huddled there in her tiny tee, her eyes wide, her hair tousled and baby-fine. I know she isn't seventeen, but just for a moment I savor the illusion. Her vulnerability is like an open wound. I want to fix it, salve it, and bandage it, but first I need to explore its contours. Discover its most painful points.

"Although… I worry about Mrs. McCullough?" Tilde says. She leans toward me, touching my hand lightly, and I can see down her shirt to a lacy blue bra and the ribs between her small breasts. "Even though I work for the family, I like to think I… work only for you."

And there it is.

I am a gentleman, you know, in spite of my backwoods trailer-trash upbringing. I always wait for them to offer.

Tilde has offered.

I reach out and grab a fistful of Tilde's T-shirt and drag it from her shoulder. I hear the seams ripping.

"Mr. McCullough," she says with a gasp, the way they always do, an invitation masquerading as surprise. It's all part of the game.

I cup her breast in my hand. I say, "Do you know how long I've wanted to do this?" They always expect to hear this.

I won't kiss her because I love my wife, so I push Tilde gently back and she, sighing, practically melts into the cushions. I crawl over her like a prowling monster. I am already hard.

When I come I shut my eyes, calling out in my mind for the sweet girl I fell in love with long ago.

Afterward, I ask Tilde again where she thinks my wife went.

This time, she tells me.

I ride the first spasm of panic. Why the hell would Hannah go to the island house? It looks worse than fleeing. It looks like returning to a crime scene.

I get up and walk out, zipping my pants and ignoring Tilde's meek call of "Mr. McCullough?" as I go down the stairs.

Hannah is feral. Something lovely and silky and vicious with needles for teeth. And yet I brought her into my house and, blind and besotted, I neglected to break her.

My mistake.

JOSH

I am wakened in the evening after the disastrous Sibelius performance by a knock on my hotel-suite door. I lurch across the room to open it, my head as light as a helium balloon. I've been holed up alone for hours in my sweatpants and a T-shirt, trying to figure out my next move, hoping for Drew to call or text, but mainly trying to smother my mortification with Xanax and all the tiny bottles of booze in the minibar.

"Room service," a waiter says in Hungarian-accented English. Beside him is a trolley with a bottle of wine, silverware, china, domed dishes, a rosebud in a vase.

"Oh. Yeah." I rub my eye. "You can just...put it anywhere."

The waiter sets everything out and leaves.

I lift one of the dome-covered dishes. Steak frites. The smell of the food turns my stomach. I clank the dome back on and look under the second one. Pizza with prosciutto. My jaws water with impending vomit. I don't even bother looking under the third dome. It must be some kind of dessert, and I already know I'm not going to eat it.

I ordered this food earlier, before leaving for the concert hall.

The evening after a performance I normally stuff myself, eat till I'm queasy, until my abdominal muscles, hidden under their soft layer of flesh, ache.

But tonight? Screw it. Tonight, I don't have to eat a single bite.

My phone, over on the bedside table, starts to ring. I approach it with dread. But when I see the name on the screen, my heart leaps. I hit Answer and put it to my ear.

"Hey," I say breathlessly. "Drew."

"Hey, Josh," Drew says with the mild Texas accent that makes my heart wring itself every time I hear it. Because it's sexy and cowboyish, but also because it seems to refer to a lost wildness that I crave. "How did the Tchaikovsky go?"

"It was Sibelius." My stomach sinks: Drew forgot what I was performing. The Tchaikovsky isn't even in my rotation this year. "I played the Sibelius. Well, part of it...and it...went badly." I swallow acid. "I didn't...finish."

"What do you mean? Are you sick?"

"Yeah. No. I'm not sure."

"Are you drunk?"

"Absolutely wasted." I tell Drew what happened onstage, broad strokes only. No one would understand—no one would *believe*—the weird battle of wills between me and that violin. I tell him the same thing I told Amelia, that I'm burned out. That my body and brain, or maybe the connection between body and brain, just said *no.*

"Come to Edinburgh," Drew says. "Visit me. Relax."

"Wait. You're in Edinburgh? Not London? Why didn't you tell me?"

"We're both free men," Drew says with an easy laugh.

Are we? I think.

"We're rehearsing at the Scottish Opera," he says. "I told you."

Did he?

"Will anyone else be there?" I ask falteringly. "Any of your friends? Your other friends, I mean?" It's greedy, wanting Drew all to myself. I want to cling, but Drew provides me with nothing to which I *can* cling. It makes me want to scream with frustration.

"Just us," Drew says. "And our music. Say *yes*. I'll pick you up at the airport."

"Okay," I say. I'll escape. Escape with Drew, delicious, impossible Drew. Leave Budapest and Amelia and the Moonstone Records people and all this crap behind. Can I do that? Can I leave the *violin* behind? No. It's insured for 3.5 million dollars and, technically, it doesn't even belong to me. I'm saddled with it. "I'll fly out as soon as I can."

HANNAH

When I brake in the driveway of the island house a little before three o'clock in the afternoon, there isn't enough gas left in the Range Rover's tank to go anywhere else. Nowhere far, anyway. I could get up to Eastsound, Orcas's only real town, but it still feels like I've come to the end of the road.

I haven't even switched off the engine before Oliver and Sibley climb out of the car—as always, leaving their doors open—and run toward the trees lining the driveway. Firs and cedars reach up into a marbled gray sky. Under their canopy spreads a tangled evergreen mess of ferns, huckleberry, and salal. The children's bright jackets—Oliver's orange, Sibley's pink—seem cartoonish against this backdrop.

Oliver wades into the undergrowth. They love the outdoors, and as anxious as it makes me, I try to let them run a little wild whenever we go anywhere rural. I know they need it. An antidote to Briarcliff's manicured yards, the crosstown car rides, the Huxley School.

Still. Night is coming, and this is the woods. I know what kinds of things can happen in the woods.

I open my own car door, and the damp, peppery air hits me. I shout after them, "Don't go too far! It's getting dark! Don't go down to the beach without me! Sibley! Oliver has never been here—could you show him around?"

"Okay, Mommy!" comes Sibley's piping voice, but she's already out of sight. Only the stiff tremble of a huckleberry bush marks where she went in.

I turn to face the house. It's large—close to four thousand square feet—but the architect tried to make it a part of the wooded landscape, with stone chimneys and artfully rusted metal siding. To me, though, the house has always seemed jarringly out of place. Its multiple low, boxy forms sit haphazardly between the trees and the cliff, as though they were dropped by accident. You can see only a sliver of the sea from this side.

I lug the suitcase to the front door. I open the lid of the security panel and tap out a code. Inside the door, something snicks. I let out a breath of relief. Allan hasn't changed the code.

Inside, I roll the suitcase down the long entry hall, which is perpendicular to the main length of the house, a concrete-and-glass tunnel through lush green plantings. Except for the hum of appliances, the house is quiet and dead cold.

The hall opens onto the dining room and kitchen. Two steps lead down into a living room with a massive fireplace and spare, expensive furniture. Beyond huge windows, trees frame a view of the sea.

The sea transfixes me for a moment: the strange teal color, the metallic glow. It's beautiful, but it hurts.

To my left is the bedroom wing. To my right, the wing into which I rarely venture. Down there lies Allan's study, the exercise studio, the library, each room with a view of the sea. Glass display cases housing Allan's collection of Northwest Coast artifacts line the long hallway.

I have never liked how those artifacts make me feel. The carved or woven objects with their stylized forms and faces hold something inside of them, something like a life, or a memory. Not that that's actually possible; I'm not superstitious. Still, it has always felt better not to look too hard.

Early on in our marriage, I accompanied Allan to an auction in New York City where he paid a quarter of a million dollars for a really old, rare slave-killer club from a Canadian First Nations tribe. Allan said slave-killer clubs were supposedly used for ceremonially crushing the skulls of slaves in a display of excess wealth. As in, *Look at me, I'm so rich I can murder my slaves just for fun.* Once, later on, I said those clubs were sick and twisted and not something to keep in a household with children. Allan said that I hadn't gone to college, so I couldn't think about other cultures without bias.

At the auction, I sat silently beside him in a tight, cream-colored dress he'd bought for me the day before at a boutique on Madison Avenue. I was just another thing he'd won.

Back then, I was proud to be his thing, proud to be on display. I didn't know any better. I knew nothing.

I flick on lights and the radiant floor heating system. I roll the suitcase into the primary bedroom and bring in the groceries, too. I take sheets and towels from the linen cupboard and make Oliver's and Sibley's beds in the rooms next to the primary suite. I make my own bed.

This house always provokes the sensation of being onstage. It's all the glass. But there's no one outside to see me but the deer and the ravens. Nothing outside but trees and softly shuffling undergrowth. Down the steep beach stairs and across the pebbled sand, the sea stretches out to meet the lapping dark beyond.

And to the south, the vacant lot. The grave.

I hadn't intended to go out there. Something is pulling me, though. I know it's weird, but I have to see it.

I change into the waterproof Hunter boots I brought. I tuck my phone into the pocket of my quilted Barbour jacket and go out the front door, leaving it ajar for Oliver and Sibley. I walk alongside the house and slip into the forest.

When I read the *Seattle Times* article yesterday, I knew which vacant lot it meant. The waterfront lot immediately to the south of Allan's—of ours—had always been vacant, but last summer the county had finally approved the permits for a new house. Allan had been gearing up to battle the new construction in order to preserve the unspoiled solitude of our own five-acre parcel, but when he learned that the lot's owner was a famous television talk-show host, he abruptly relented. He told his lawyers to drop it.

It isn't that Allan is awed by celebrity but that he calculated, first, the talk-show host would build an ultra-high-end house (thus enhancing our own property value) and, second, the talk-show host would barely ever use the place.

That's how Allan is. Calculating. Always looking for the advantage. If in the last nine years I ever wondered how our marriage had been calculated by Allan, I quickly yanked myself back. That's a dangerous thing to wonder about your spouse.

The path might not have been discernable to most people, but I've walked it before. To my left, the forest. To my right, the cliff pitching sharply down, not too steep for brush and trees to cling, but almost.

The beach down there is just a strip of pebbles. Not like our own flat crescent, which is broad enough for kite-flying and clamming. No one really swims around here without a wet suit. The water is so cold it turns your skin blue.

I walk for a few minutes, and then the path ends with something I don't recognize: a large clearing newly hacked from the forest. I stop.

This must be the talk-show host's homesite. A grimy yellow digger sits frozen on the far side. Felled trees are piled neatly, ready to be used for construction or trucked away to a sawmill.

There are two huge brush piles of mangled bushes, shreds of cedar bark, soil clumped on exposed roots.

I count three separate gashes in the ground where something—the digger, presumably—has done its worst, and then movement flashes behind one of the brush piles.

I hold my breath.

A man moves into view, a man with an athletic build in a black puffer jacket. He seems faded, almost ghostly, in the disintegrating light. I can't make out his face.

I think, A strange man out here in the forest, and me all alone? *Run.* Run like a rabbit back to the house—

He lifts a hand in greeting and calls, "Mrs. McCullough. Hey."

He knows my name, yet nothing about him is familiar.

"Hello?" I call back.

He's walking closer, his thighs hard-looking in joggers, his hands, like mine, in jacket pockets to ward off the chill. "Hi," he says again, not so loudly. When he's a few yards away, he stops. I can see him pretty well now. He's about my age and very good-looking.

"We've never met," he says.

"No."

"I'm Trey Higgins. Your new caretaker?"

"Oh, okay." My shoulders relax. "I forgot Allan hired a new... But how did you know I'm Mrs. McCullough?"

"Well, I just assumed. I mean, who else could you be? There aren't a lot of people on this part of the island. You know, you shouldn't be out here."

"Out where?"

"On this lot."

"Why not?"

"Well, it's private property, for one thing, and it's, like, a crime scene." He jerks his head, indicating someplace behind him. "Which I guess you probably know."

I look past him. Which one is it? Which hole is her grave? I say, "Yes, I know. That's why I'm here. I wanted to see it." I look back to Trey. His good looks hit me again. Bright eyes. Wide mouth. Suntanned, muscled throat. Glossy, golden-brown hair touches his jacket collar, giving him that Hot Jesus look. "Why are *you* here, if it's private property?"

"I look after this lot, too. For the owner."

"The talk-show host?"

"Yeah." He smiles, flashing white teeth. "I never talk to her personally. I deal with, I don't know, some kind of assistant."

"I guess she must be pretty upset about the…the discovery."

"It's sounding like they might not build the house after all. I didn't know you guys were on the island. Did I miss a call?"

"No," I say. Allan usually calls a day or so ahead so the caretaker can make sure the driveway is clear, stock the firewood, check the systems, and get some local women in to clean. "It was spontaneous."

"Oh, okay. Well, I hope Mr. McCullough is happy with how I've been taking care of your house."

"The house looks great," I say. "Do you think, since I'm already here, I could just…take a look?"

"Wow. That's pretty…morbid, I guess?" Slightly teasing. Almost flirtatious, actually.

"I'm just curious. It *is* right next door."

"You shouldn't get too close—the sides could cave in, and I don't know what the sheriff's guys would say if they knew I was letting people snoop around here. But okay."

He turns, and I follow him. We circle around the larger brush pile—not the same one he emerged from behind earlier—and here is the grave.

I imagined yellow police tape trembling in the breeze, just like this. But although I pictured the grave as a small, hand-dug divot, someone has excavated a large rectangular hole, several feet long and about four feet deep. The stale odor of the violated earth makes my stomach loosen with nausea.

Trey speaks. "That's where they found her."

"Who was she?"

"No idea. I mean, I'm new to the island. I've only been here about six months, so I don't... She could've been anybody. This is a lonely spot, right? Someone has a body to dispose of, they drive way out here to the ends of the earth, go down an overgrown road, start digging. I'll bet they never thought it would be found in a million years."

"Who thought that?"

"You know. The killer."

"Who, though?"

"Some jealous boyfriend or a psycho stalker? Women—girls—they get killed all the time, right? It's just how it is. She was a fallen woman from the mainland is my guess."

Fallen woman? What century is he living in? But, that *is* just how it is. Some of us are disposable. Maybe all of us are disposable if we get ourselves out of context.

I'm aware again of the bad odor of the dug-open earth, as though the approaching evening is drawing it out. I'm also aware I'm alone with a stranger.

"I should get going," I say. "My kids are running loose."

"Do you...want me to walk you back? It's dark." Now Trey sounds, well, *shy*. Like a boy talking to a girl.

"That's okay," I say. "I know the path."

CAROLINE

I do not understand why Trey doesn't go to the Island Market after he leaves CrossFit, like usual. Why he turns his Jeep Cherokee right on Main Street and continues onto Orcas Road, heading south. Is he going to the ferry dock? I picture him driving onto the boat and sailing away or, worse, picking up a female walk-on passenger from the dock—young, pretty—and taking her home with him.

Not that Trey could possibly believe in premarital relations. He is a godly man. But you can't trust women.

To my surprise, at the fork Trey drives onto Crow Valley Road, which means he is not going to the ferry dock but to Turtleback or West Sound. Maybe even Deer Harbor.

I keep well back, far enough that his taillights disappear around bends in the road for thirty seconds at a time.

When he turns onto Deer Harbor Road, I grip the steering wheel harder. It is difficult, coming down here, so close to the Farm. The memories are thick. I start to lose track of who I am.

When I think of the things that mattered to me back then, it feels like I'm thinking about another person. That version of

Caroline was a sinner. What was Uncle if not a false prophet? What were our rituals—all the pot and magic mushrooms, the drumming, those starry summer nights around the bonfire—if not pagan?

Other memories from my life before, on the Farm, I cannot even acknowledge. There are evil things burrowed deep into the flesh of my heart like dormant parasites. I do not know how to purge them, so I have decided to leave them alone. But if I happen to wake up in the middle of the night when my guard is down, I feel those evil things quietly gnawing away. In those moments, I struggle out of bed and fall to my knees and I pray to the Lord for deliverance.

It does not bother me that the Lord's face in my imagination has begun to look like Trey's. This is actually a cause for joy, because it means His face is no longer obliterated by Uncle's.

Trey's Jeep turns onto Channel Road and goes over the bridge and skirts the marsh, and now the possibilities for where he is headed have narrowed to a handful of fancy waterfront houses, a few cabins in the trees, and the Farm. But he would not be visiting the Farm. It is nothing now but an abandoned, falling-down wreck.

He passes the driveway to the Farm. He passes the driveway to the McCullough place, too, but he turns onto the next one.

After he turns, I keep going so if he notices my car, he will think I am someone minding my own business. But after I round the first bend, I park on the verge, get out, and start walking back up the road. I feel the surge of fresh exhilaration I always do when I am getting to know Trey better.

I don't know why, but it is not until I am several yards down the driveway that I realize it is going to lead me to the vacant lot where they have been excavating. It is going to lead me to the grave.

Why, Trey? I think.

I step into the forest. Luckily, the undergrowth has been

groomed here, and the trees have been thinned. It is easy to walk, provided I watch where I put my feet.

Soon, I see a big clearing up ahead. A parked digger, brush piles, holes in the ground. Those holes, so shadowed they could be a thousand feet deep, are pure evil. I can smell a dank, wormy stench.

Catching sight of Trey, I stop at the edge of the trees.

He walks to one of the brush piles and does something with his sweatpants and then stands quite still, and I realize with a thrill that he is peeing. The moment is shameful, but I can't stop looking. No sooner has he pulled up his waistband than another figure emerges over on the north edge of the trees, out by the cliff.

Trey sees her, and she sees him, and they call to each other and come together like magnets. Did they arrange to meet? I can't hear anything they say—they are too far away and there is too much wind in the trees.

"So he carried me away in the spirit into the wilderness," I whisper. The words feel quick and clean on my tongue. *"And I saw a woman sit upon a scarlet colored beast…"*

Trey, *my* Trey, and beautiful, young Mrs. McCullough.

"Having a golden cup in her hand full of abominations and filthiness of her fornication…"

Mrs. McCullough looks up at him. In the poor light her face is just a smudge with makeup-dark dolly eyes, and her pale curls twist in the wind. Trey keeps smiling at her. He can't help himself. Men can't.

They walk to one of those pits in the ground. They are standing so close.

I start to shiver, first with fear, then with loathing. I whisper, *"And upon her forehead was a name written, Mystery, Babylon the Great, the Mother of Harlots and Abominations of the Earth."*

Everything is happening again, the way the Old Testament prophesies the New. But this time, I will make it stop.

THEN

GREENE

The morning after they followed Uncle to his farm, Greene woke up alone on a mattress on a floor. He was in an attic with bare rafters and one window at floor level. He heard talking from somewhere below. Human voices, not thing voices.

He climbed out of bed and went to kneel at the window. It was grimed so thickly he saw nothing but a green blur. He rubbed one of the panes with his fist—*thanks, I want to shine*, the windowpane said—revealing a pasture edged with pointed evergreens. It had stopped raining. He saw fences, a barn, and another building. Three white animals with their heads sloped down, eating. Goats. Uncle had mentioned goats last night on the ferry. Greene saw the outhouse he had used last night. Another area with a high fence and lots of plants inside—a garden. And little people, a small crowd of them—one, two, three, four—streaking between rows of trees. Kids. Greene heard their shouts and one curling whine.

He only needed to put on his sneakers because he'd slept in the clothes from the day before, jeans and a red T-shirt. He decided not to wear the Tennis Champion windbreaker. Beauty and Fred were in the pocket, and they were probably still tired from yesterday. He would leave them be.

A ladderlike stair brought him down to a long, narrow hallway. A bigger staircase led down to the main floor, and he followed the sounds of voices to a kitchen that was hazy with woodsmoke.

Mom was sitting at a table surrounded by five or six people whose faces were all turned toward her. She was beaming, the center, like a beautiful queen. She did not see Greene in the doorway.

"You're one of us, Caroline. I can tell," said a woman standing at the stove. The stove was sooty black, with a chimney that bent and disappeared into the wall. The woman was stirring something in a pot. She had long, pale hair like a horse's mane, and she wore a flowery apron, jeans, and no shoes or socks. "I can *always* tell."

"How?" Mom asked, laughing.

"I feel it in my bones."

"Tansy is a wise, wise woman," a man said. He was stacking firewood behind the door. He had a bushy beard and a heavy brown sweater like the one Uncle had worn.

Where *was* Uncle? Not here.

Good. Maybe Greene and Mom could get out of here and go to Kit's cabin without ever seeing him again.

The pale-haired woman—Tansy—said to Mom, "You're smart, educated—I mean, come on, a botany PhD?"

"Not yet. I'm only a candidate, I never finished my—"

"Same difference. You're brilliant. Just because some dickhead professor took advantage and made it impossible for you to continue your studies doesn't mean you don't know your shit."

Mom looked surprised, but maybe also a little pleased at those words.

"My point is," Tansy said, gesturing with her wooden spoon, "you have just the kind of know-how that we need here."

"But I don't know anything about farming or—"

"We learn." This was a more soft-spoken woman, young and golden, with the bulge of a baby in her tummy. She was sitting next to Mom at the table, and she poured tea into Mom's mug.

Steam rose up like ghost ribbons. "We plunge our hands into the soil and learn the ways of the land. The land teaches you. The insects, the raindrops, heck, even the goat poop."

Everyone laughed except for Greene. He felt like he was watching a TV show. Everything looked weird. The colors were muted by the smoke in the air, and everyone's clothes, except Mom's, were worn and dirty.

"The more important thing," the golden woman said, "the thing no one can teach you…well, Caroline, face it, you've got it."

"What?" Mom asked, smiling. "Student-loan debt?"

More laughter.

"No, silly." The golden woman placed a tender hand on Mom's upper arm. "Grit. *Spirit.* That's what we need here on the Farm."

"You're making it sound like a work camp, Star," the man said, smacking the last piece of firewood onto the pile. He swept his gloved hands together and splinters drifted downward. "I'm Smoke, by the way. It's not all work here, although the truth is, work is what nourishes us, physically and emotionally. I won't say *spiritually* because I don't go in for that woo-woo kind of talk."

"Oh good," Mom said with a giggle into her mug, "because for a second I was wondering if you guys were in some kind of New Agey cult."

Silence hung. Nothing could be heard in the kitchen but the faint snap of fire behind the stove door.

Mom lowered her mug. "Oh… I didn't mean—"

More laughter, which sounded just right except for the fact that it came too late.

"A cult?" Star said. Her cheeks were flushed. "Far from it. What we are is a *community.* A community of like-minded people who believe in intentional living. Living without raping the earth."

"We live lightly on the land," Tansy said. "We give *back* to the land, and in doing so, we prepare for the future."

"I want my child to grow up in a nurturing, whole place, away from consumerism and all that *trash*, you know?" Star said, rubbing her belly.

"Yes," Mom said. "I want that, too."

"Who's this beautiful little creature?" Star said, noticing Greene in the doorway. She smiled, and she looked like an angel. "Come on, don't be scared, baby. Come sit by me." She patted the chair beside her.

"Good morning," Mom said to Greene. To the others she said, "This is Greene."

Everyone murmured *welcome* to Greene.

Greene, feeling clumsy all of a sudden, went to the chair beside Star and climbed into it. Then there was a big bowl of oatmeal in front of him, and a spoon, and someone was tousling his head, which felt so good because he hadn't been hugged or even touched by Mom in a really long time. The oatmeal had raspberries and honey and trickling white cream, and he was so, so hungry, and he ate.

The pottery bowl prattled to him about spinning, giddy and wobbly, but Greene ignored it.

"Feel," Star said, taking Mom's hand and placing it firmly on her belly.

Mom looked surprised and stiff, but then she relaxed. "The baby's kicking," she said.

"That's *life*, Caroline. Say *yes* to life."

"So," Smoke said, with a smile for Mom, "do you think you'll stick around here for a while?"

"I don't know. I mean, Kit was expecting me—"

"You mean she *ditched* you," Tansy said.

"I was thinking of driving into town and asking around for her—"

"We've never heard of her," Tansy said. "If she's not a year-round islander, chances are no one will have any idea who she is."

"Do what you need to do," Star said. "But know that you're always welcome here."

"But this is Uncle's farm, isn't it?" Mom said. "I wouldn't want to impose—"

"We already talked about it with Uncle," Smoke said. "He wants you to stay."

"He does?"

"He's thinking of growing camas like the Indigenous peoples of this island used to, and he said he could use your knowledge of botany for that project."

"Camas. Wow. Okay. Yeah, I know a little about that." Mom was nodding, almost as though she was trying to convince herself of something.

"When you're here on the Farm," Tansy said, spooning oatmeal into a row of bowls, "you start to realize things. A lot of things, actually. How little you really need to live. How much all that noise, all that *crap* out there is not only unnecessary but, let's face it, totally toxic. You start to realize that everyone out there is just going through the motions that are basically programmed into them from birth, and those motions are to be a capitalist consumer. Buy shit, make garbage, rinse, repeat. But here, you have the space to really see, to really become…" Tansy tipped her head. "Honestly, for the first time in my life I feel fully *human*. I grew up in Orange County—can you believe that? My parents had the big McMansion with the swimming pool, cars they couldn't afford, the works. I took goddamn *dressage* lessons all through high school. I mean, are you kidding me?"

"But you're good with animals," Smoke said, wrapping an arm around her. "It wasn't for nothing."

"My *point* is," Tansy said, "I didn't need all that, and being here and learning about, I don't know, earthworms and huckleberries, I finally feel okay. Like, *I'm okay*. And we have love here. Friendship. Deep, real, juicy kinship. I know that's what you want, too, Caroline. I see it all over your beautiful face."

"I do," Mom said, her voice weak and scratchy. Then, more loudly, "That *is* what I want."

"Why don't you go and find the other children?" Star whispered to Greene, who was scraping up the last clumps of oatmeal from his bowl. "They're outside playing. I'm sure they would love to meet you, Greene. Go on. Go find them!"

Greene looked at Mom, but she wasn't paying attention. He went out the kitchen door, taking care not to let the screen door slam.

A rutted path of mud and small, sparkling stones sloped away from the kitchen porch, passing through tall grass. The grass back in Idaho had been green enough—well, Greene hadn't noticed it *not* being green. But this stuff…it was as though each blade was filled up with electric liquid. The greenness *glowed*. The air was different, too. Damp and clean and sweet.

The path ended at the pasture he'd seen from the attic window, the one with the goats. And there was the high-fenced jungly garden.

He unlatched the garden gate—*forever ever ever open-shut, open-shut*, the gate said calmly—and went in.

There were rows of stalks he was sure were corn, if a Green Giant commercial on TV had been accurate, and lots of other things he didn't recognize, except for some dangling green beans. Passing through the beans, he came to a different section of the garden with rows of arching bushes. The arches made leafy tunnels, and pink dots nestled in the leaves. Berries.

He walked closer. Yes, raspberries, like the ones in his oatmeal.

His mouth watered. Would it be bad if he picked some?

He reached out.

Motion down at the other end of the tunnel caught his eye. He saw a small person, also reaching out, with golden hair lit up by the sun, in jeans and a red T-shirt—

Wait. That was *him*. His own reflection. But why was there a mirror at the other end of the raspberry tunnel? Who would *do* that?

"Hey!" his reflection called.

After a few seconds of freefall, Greene realized it wasn't his reflection. It was another kid about his size, with gold hair like his, and jeans and a red T-shirt like his.

"Who are you?" she called—because now he saw it was a little girl, with her hair mostly back in a ponytail but the rest of it a messy cloud. She was coming toward him through the tunnel. Thorns snagged her clothes, but she kept coming. She seemed used to being snagged by thorns. She carried a little basket. Her feet crunched on fallen canes.

Then she was right next to him, smiling to show rows of teeth with two missing on the bottom.

"I'm Kestrel," she said, slightly out of breath. "Who are you?"

Kestrel was the prettiest girl Greene had ever seen, even though her hair was snarled up and even though the berry juice streaks across her cheeks had dirt stuck to them. She had dimples and brown eyes, and her eyebrows tipped up a tiny bit toward the middle of her forehead, like she was worried or trying to remember something.

"I'm Greene."

"The new kid from the ferry boat?"

"I'm not new. We're leaving. To my mom's friend's house."

"Mama said your mom's friend is never going to come and you're going to live here."

"No, I'm not!" Greene yelled. "I'm leaving!"

Kestrel didn't even flinch. "How old are you?"

Greene calmed down. "Eight."

"I'm seven, but we're the same height."

"So?"

"Mama says I'm tall for my age. I'm almost as tall as my sister, Eldest, and she's going to be eleven in three weeks."

Greene thought Eldest was a funny name, but he didn't say so.

"It's a funny name," Kestrel said, as though she'd read his mind. "But she's the oldest, so Mama calls her Eldest."

"Kestrel is a kind of bird," Greene said. "A little tiny hawk with really big eyes."

"Uh-huh. Mama called me Kestrel so I'd be fierce. So I'd bite."

"Your mom wants you to *bite*?" That didn't sound like a regular mother—not that Greene's mom was regular, either, but that was more because she never paid attention. "Bite who?"

"I don't know. Everyone. Because kids shouldn't act like wimps. She lets me hit Tim. I don't hit him hard, though, because I like him, but I pretend to hit him hard to make Mama laugh."

Greene thought this sounded crazy.

"Want a strawberry?" Kestrel held up her little basket, which had small, shiny strawberries rolling around on the bottom.

"Okay." Greene took one and bit the fruity part off the stem. The flavor was a shock, as though the taste of three large strawberries had been compressed into one tiny one.

"I'm not supposed to eat the strawberries because they're so little and there aren't very many, so Uncle said they're only for jam this year because the deer got in. Tim left the gate open, he got in *so much* trouble. Uncle locked him in the cabin overnight even though Tim cried—when the deer got in they got all the strawberries and all the kale and the roses Star grows for rose hips. So I took this basket of strawberries over to eat next to the raspberry bushes so if anyone saw they'd think I was eating *raspberries*."

The strawberry taste on Greene's tongue went bitter at the mention of Uncle. He had convinced himself that Uncle was out of the picture. But now he felt like Uncle could be anywhere, even in this garden, watching, his black-dot eyes imitating the dark centers of flowers.

"I hate him," Kestrel said.

Greene didn't need to ask who she was talking about.

"Mama thinks he's nice, but he's *so mean*." Kestrel's face brightened. "If you're leaving, maybe I could come with you. I could hide in your suitcase."

"I don't have a suitcase."

"What do you have?"

"A laundry basket." Greene said this with a rush of shame, because it was weird to have a basket instead of a suitcase.

But Kestrel didn't act like it was weird. "Then I could hide in your basket. I don't want to stay here. We used to live in Bellingham, and I liked it there. My papa is there. Do you think we could go to Bellingham?"

"I'd have to ask my mom." Greene said it just to make her feel better, because he knew for sure Mom would never drive to some random town just because he asked her to. That wasn't how things worked.

"You don't want to take me," Kestrel said. "I can tell."

"I *want* to, but I don't think my mom—"

"But then how will I run away?" Kestrel's nose scrunched, and the corners of her mouth twisted down.

Pain—Kestrel's pain—washed through Greene's chest, and instinctively he took one of her hands very gently, the same way he would hold Beauty or Fred. Kestrel's hand was hot and sticky, but she grabbed his hand back.

"I want to go home." Tears made curved tracks through the dirt and strawberry juice on her cheeks.

"But isn't this where you live?"

"*No.* I mean, we live here, but I hate it. I just want my papa."

"Don't cry" was all Greene could think of to say. "Don't cry." He kept on gripping her hand, and she kept squeezing back. They stood like that for a minute, but Kestrel's crying was not letting up. Actually, she was crying harder. They were hidden from the house by all the garden plants—or Greene figured they were—but Kestrel was getting noisier and noisier. What if Uncle heard? He might walk around those tall plants like a king strutting through his kingdom, and he would see Greene and Kestrel holding hands and then…what? Kestrel had said something about Uncle locking a boy in a cabin overnight. What if Uncle did that to them?

"Want to know a secret?" Greene whispered. The promise of a secret might make her pipe down.

Kestrel opened her eyes. Her lashes were stuck together with tears. "A secret?"

"Uh-huh."

"What?" Kestrel wriggled her hand out of Greene's and smeared her forearm across her nose.

Greene cast his eyes around, looking for something that would work. His attention settled on the bracelet on her wrist. It was braided leather with a little circular charm. "What's that?" he asked, pointing.

Kestrel looked at it and wrinkled her nose. "*He* makes us wear them."

"Oh," Greene said. If the bracelet was from Uncle, he didn't want anything to do with it. "Could you take off one of your shoes?"

"Is it a magic trick?" Kestrel plopped down on the ground, cast aside her basket, and started tugging at her shoe.

Was it magic? The thing was, Greene had never shown anyone what he could do, and anyway, it wouldn't look or feel or sound like anything to anyone else unless that other person could also do what he could. And nobody could. But…it was magic, wasn't it? In a way? It didn't feel all dramatic like what witches and wizards did in movies. No bangs or whirling stars or purple smoke. What he could do—how he could listen to things—was smaller. So small, it almost wasn't even there.

"Here." Kestrel passed her shoe to Greene.

Greene sat down cross-legged, facing her so that their knees touched. "Well, you won't see anything, I don't think. It's more like…a story."

"A story?" Kestrel sounded disappointed.

Greene plowed forward anyway. Kestrel had stopped crying, and he was curious whether she'd believe what he said. "The story of your shoe."

She started to say something, but he interrupted. "Shhh," he said. He closed his eyes.

The shoe had a lot to say, in an eager, bragging way, about trips to the zoo and ice-cream shops long ago. About the sticky spots on the floor in the ice-cream shop, and the time it stepped in gum, and then a long, smelly, dark, and jumbly period at a place with a lot of other depressed shoes that Greene thought sounded like the Goodwill in Idaho, and then the shoe had a lot of annoyed words to say about how wet it always was now, how muddy, and how Kestrel struck her heels so hard when she ran, and it was just so unpleasant the way she kept the laces knotted up, it was *strangling*—

Greene sat there with his eyes closed and whispered aloud, as fast as he could, what the shoe told him. Translating for Kestrel.

Finally, the shoe fell silent. Greene opened his eyes.

"How can you hear it?" Kestrel whispered. Her lips were parted in wonder.

She believed it. She believed *him*. Greene felt like a big, beautiful flower was blossoming inside of him.

"I don't know. I just...can."

"Did someone teach you how?"

"No. I just... I've always been able to do it. When I was little, I thought everyone could."

"It's really cool!" Kestrel said with a broad grin. "I wish you weren't leaving."

"We can still be friends."

Kestrel's eyes widened. "Forever?"

Greene thought about it. He didn't like the idea of saying goodbye to this girl, it was true, plus something about her made him want to make her happy. So he said, "Okay. Forever."

NOW

HANNAH

When I get back to the house, the children aren't there. I go outside again and stand in the middle of the driveway, listening.

"Sibley?" I call. "Oliver?"

A raven, hidden behind a veil of cedar fronds, caws in answer. They're gone, I think feverishly. Someone has stolen them—

Then I hear their voices, and relief spreads like a muscle relaxant across my shoulders. *They're safe. Everything is okay. Breathe.*

They come into view from behind the garage. Oliver is bare to the waist, despite the chilly air, and he carries a stick that's about two feet long and pointed at one end. It's too sharp, I see that right away, and he's barefoot. He's saying something in low tones, and Sibley trails behind him, still sensibly suited up in her boots and jacket.

"—do what I tell you to do, because I know more about the woods than you do," Oliver is saying. They haven't noticed me.

"Nuh-*uh*!" Sibley says. "I know just as much as you, Ollie."

"You're such a dummy. Don't you know that *I*—"

"You guys," I call. "Come here for a second."

Oliver and Sibley stop, surprised by my voice. Then with obvious reluctance they come closer, eyeing me as though I'm going to put an end to their fun.

"Oliver, what happened to your jacket and boots?" I say.

"I was too hot." He cuts his dark eyes away.

"He left them in the woodshop," Sibley says in her clear, good-little-student voice.

I think, The woodshop is unlocked?

"Fine," I say, recalling how Oliver's therapist, Patti, advised me to choose my battles with him, to cut him slack. "I'm glad you're playing outside, but you need to stay within earshot of the house. And don't go down to the beach without telling me first. Okay?"

"We were just *on* the beach," Oliver says. "And you didn't even know."

"No, I didn't know."

"You suck at being a mom."

I inhale for two counts, exhale for two counts, just as Patti suggested. "Don't go back to the beach this evening, please. It's too dark. Come inside for dinner in half an hour, okay?"

Oliver doesn't answer. He drills the point of his stick into the gravel.

"We saw a witch," Sibley pipes up.

"A witch?" I say.

"Yeah," she says. "There's a witch in the woods. She's old and mean, and I think she lives inside a tree."

I realize that this is another of Sibley's flights of fancy. "Yikes," I say, playing along. "You better watch out for her."

Sibley gives a serious nod. "I will."

I feed the kids macaroni and cheese for dinner and offer to let them watch a movie. But Sibley wants to listen to *Harry Potter* in her room, snuggled up with Bunners in a pool of lamplight. Oliver wants to whittle in the garage woodshop. I consent to the whittling, but when I think he isn't looking I take the key for the table saw and slip it into my pocket.

It's not personal, I tell myself. You just don't let twelve-year-olds use table saws. It's bad enough that he has that sharp little Swiss Army knife.

"I don't *want* to use the table saw," Oliver says, sitting on a stool at the workbench. He saw me take the key, then. He still hasn't put on a shirt or shoes. Goose bumps texture his skinny upper arms, and the soles of his feet are black with dirt.

"And why is that?" I ask.

"The Indigenous people in the old times didn't have electricity, and they made all sorts of stuff anyway."

"You want to be like an Indigenous person?"

"We won't always have electricity, you know." His face, bent over his whittling, is hidden in shadow.

"Who told you that?"

"No one *told* me. Everybody knows. Climate change is going to get worse and worse with, like, floods and famines and droughts and extinctions until everything will be a wild new world where people will die unless they figure out new ways to survive." A pale curled wood shaving drifts to the floor.

"They talk about that at school?"

He shrugs.

I can't imagine Huxley teachers preaching anything of the sort to students who arrive in large SUVs from six-thousand-square-foot homes.

I want to demand answers from Oliver, insist that he tell me where he's getting those ideas, but I know better.

I say, "Make sure you turn off the woodshop lights when you're done, okay, honey?"

JOSH

All I want is escape. Maybe a little oblivion. Instead, I have spent the day in smelly taxis, cacophonous airports, and overheated airplane cabins. My nerves undulate and zap like frayed electrical cords.

It is just after four o'clock in the afternoon in Frankfurt when I sink into a wide business-class seat on the Lufthansa flight to Edinburgh. Getting myself to the Budapest airport this morning was a welcome distraction from my throbbing hangover and everything else, even sort of romantic with the thought of Drew waiting for me across the continent. But the short flight from Budapest to Frankfurt was in a toy-size plane and with a ton of turbulence. Then the layover in Frankfurt lasted for hours, and the terminal's unending stream of humanity made me feel so… small. Not a feeling I enjoy.

I was recognized once on the trip, in Terminal 1 in Frankfurt, by a teenage girl with her own violin strapped to her shoulder. Her eyes widened to see me walking past. No autograph request, but her dazzled expression was gratifying. Unless—oh

God—unless she knew about the botched Sibelius performance? Fuck social media.

Now, as the plane rolls toward the runway, the violin is in the overhead compartment and packed all around with airline pillows. The word *Stradivarius* always brings pushy flight attendants to heel. No matter what language they speak, everyone knows what a Strad is. They trip over themselves to serve the violin as though it's a person they need to impress. Kind of gross.

I slap the plastic window-cover down. I have no desire to stare at tarmac. I take a pair of high-decibel foam earplugs from my messenger bag and carefully pack my ear canals. Then I settle a pair of state-of-the-art noise-canceling headphones over the earplugs and switch them on. I'm not going to listen to music or podcasts or anything else; I'm protecting my hearing from being blown out by all the garbage noise on the plane. Otherwise, it could take a full day to recover from the flight.

Not that I plan on practicing violin for…well, for how long? It's unimaginable, the idea of empty hours, hours without violin. I haven't taken a day off practicing in years, except for the time I had viral meningitis. Even with heavy colds and stomach bugs I practice at least a little.

I pull out a prescription bottle, shake out a blue pill, and wash it down with the bottled water a flight attendant brought earlier. Maybe not the greatest idea on an empty stomach, but whatever. I still haven't eaten, not since yesterday before the concert, and it makes me feel so free.

I settle back, shut my eyes, and think of the violin in the compartment above my head. I think, Fuck you.

I took a Xanax earlier, too, at the Budapest airport, but it's wearing off. I feel the dark spirals of rebound anxiety, and I am starting to clench my jaw—

—the slick carved antler under my finger pads. The heft of it enough to make my forearm flex—

My eyes pop open.

The airplane hurtles down the runway, engines roaring.

My lungs inflate and deflate as though I'm walking uphill.

I will *not* think about that. No. I will think about Drew, beautiful Drew, to whom I am running.

We met five months ago, at a boozy after-hours party in London after Camilla Tan's Rachmaninoff in the Albert Hall. I know Camilla from our Juilliard days. Not that I lasted long at Juilliard. None of the teachers there knew what to do with me.

Anyway, I was in London to record something, but it hadn't been my performance that night, so I was keeping a relatively low profile in someone's artistic flat in Notting Hill, slinking on the peripheries and sipping expensive sherry. I was leaning on a wallpapered wall (ironically oversize cabbage roses) when this burly, bearded ginger in a Bond Street suit appeared beside me. He leaned on the pretentious wallpaper, too, his hand looking like it might crush his champagne glass by accident. He tipped his head toward me and said in that so-wrong-it's-right Texas accent, "Hot damn, what a bunch of asses."

I laughed, a genuine laugh that burst out of my throat, and a long conversation ensued. Drew was a composer, he said, and a composition professor at Guildhall. The way the others at the party spoke to Drew, I could tell he was respected. Part of the in-crowd.

I had never heard of Drew. I never perform contemporary repertoire, preferring to stick to the traditional violinist's canon and playing nothing more recent than Shostakovich, and anyway, Drew's biggest successes are his operas. Naturally Drew had heard of me. I'm a big name. But Drew didn't fawn. I'm used to people fawning, have come to expect it from anyone who knows anything about classical music. But Drew...he gave off this vibe that I should be fawning over *him*.

And I did. Oh God, I did.

The drunker I got that night, the more distracted I became by the blunt shapes of Drew's hands, the flashing blue of his eyes, the touching and oddly sexy way the skin around his thirtysomething eyes was aging, puffy. His puffy eyes were one spot, one lone spot, of vulnerability. His puffy eyes made him more, not less, beautiful. They made me feel like maybe I had a shot at—what?—sleeping with him? I wasn't sure what the goal was. Yes, I was attracted, but I also had this sense of wanting to fold him up and put him in my coat pocket. I wanted to hoard him.

I was too dumbfounded at having found Drew to really flirt that night, let alone proposition him, although by the end of the night that had been the central idea in my mind—what would it feel like to stretch naked alongside Drew? But before we parted, we exchanged phone numbers and I had gotten an invitation to the premiere of his *The Soldier and the Gypsy* at the English National Opera in three weeks.

"Stay at my place," Drew said. "I have plenty of room. Shoot me a text when you're in town." And then a woman in an orange dress scooped him up, and I went back to my room at the Corinthia not quite as empty-handed as usual.

So there was the premiere weekend in London, during which I slept on a sofa in Drew's flat with no fewer than five other bohemian men and women also crashing there and barely any time at all with Drew himself. Me, habitué of five-star hotels, couch surfing. Me, world-renowned concert violinist, begging for scraps of attention. In. Sane.

A month-ish later, Drew was in New York the same time I was briefly home, and we met up for a dinner that dragged on, and then we ended up in my tiny, sleek apartment with its sliver view of Central Park, and although we talked late into the night, we never so much as touched until two in the morning when he, leaving for his hotel and saying goodbye at the door, reached out and curled his fingers against the back of my head—

And *I* was the one to draw away, without even thinking about it, from what seemed—hadn't it?—like an impending kiss.

I do not deserve a kiss. I do not deserve love, or any of the things that pass temporarily for love. Because of what I did—and it doesn't matter that so many years have passed—I will never consider myself a *good person.*

Until I met Drew, being a good person wasn't even a goal, because I am a good—no, a *great*—violinist. That was all that mattered. Then I met Drew, and my deficiency as a human being loomed up like a zombie I didn't even know was hiding down there.

The plane shudders over a patch of turbulence, and at last, like something under pressure that has finally found a weak spot, the slave-killer club emerges. It hovers in my mind's eye like a spotlit item in a museum case.

I feel the slick carved antler under my finger pads. The heft of it enough to make my forearm flex—

My hand shakes as I reach for the flight attendant button. Xanax isn't enough. I need a drink.

HANNAH

I was dreaming, and tendrils of the dream still cling. It was the same dream as always, as though my mind has been hard-wired for endless nighttime searching.

In my dream, I hurry through an infinite rambling house. Room after room of concrete floors and glass and ponderous beams, and I search, calling out, but I cannot find him. I'm carrying a heavy baby on my hip, although I'm never aware of this at the beginning of the dream.

He has left so recently I can feel the faint breeze of the air he disrupted on the way out the door. I can almost smell him, too, my nose picking up lingering molecules. I want to smell his smell so badly, but he's gone, off on some journey in which I have no part. Sometimes I see a pair of small women's shoes, smaller than my own by three sizes (could they be a child's shoes?) arranged neatly just inside the door. The baby squirms in my arms, smacks its toothless wet gums on my shoulder as a reminder of what I'm supposed to be doing, and I always wake up in tears.

Not being able to be with the one you love, that's one kind of heartbreak. The poetic kind, the stuff of songs and greeting cards. The other kind—to have been left behind by the one you love to stumble through this world alone—let me tell you, there's no recovering from that.

My reflection in the bathroom mirror startles me. At first, I don't even recognize my own face. I look younger, frightened, pale. Almost boyish. I push my hair into a messy bun, wash, and then carefully apply a full face of makeup. Primer, foundation, concealer. Lip liner, eyeliner, eye shadow, mascara, tinted brow gel. By the time I'm dabbing on lip gloss, I look more like myself. Or I look more like how I'm used to looking.

I brew myself a double espresso with the complicated German machine in the kitchen. Then I look at my phone. No messages from Allan. That makes me nervous. It isn't like him. No news about the body they dug up next door, either.

I sign up for a news alert so that if and when any Orcas Island news emerges, I won't miss it.

When the kids get up, I make oatmeal. I spoon it into bowls and top it with milk, honey, and a sprinkle of cinnamon.

"What's this?" Sibley asks, turning steaming globs over with her spoon as though it's alien goo.

"Oatmeal," I say. I never serve it at home, preferring to feed them high-protein breakfasts. I remember the cheap, carb-heavy breakfasts I ate as a kid, how I would be hungry for hours before lunch.

Oliver hunches low over his bowl, spooning the stuff up as though he's afraid someone is going to take it away from him.

"Keep your boots on," I say to Oliver when they're getting ready to go outside and play. "Even if you're not cold, we don't want you to cut your foot or something."

He grunts and lopes out the front door.

"Wait for me, Ollie," Sibley calls, bounding after him.

CAROLINE

On Friday morning a little after nine o'clock, I park my Honda in the McCulloughs' driveway. I see a big black Range Rover inside the open garage.

Of course that's what she drives. The most ostentatious vehicle she could get her grasping little hands on, the one that says *Out of my way! I'm a rich, pampered slut-mommy, and I can run right over you and not even feel a bump.*

Why are you here, Mrs. McCullough? Without your husband, and in November? Talking to Trey, my Trey, smiling up at him not two yards away from a disturbed grave?

An image flashes into my mind, a disgusting, carnal image of Trey mounted on top of Mrs. McCullough, thrusting—

I check my French braid in the rearview mirror and adjust my glasses. They are my reading glasses, and they are starting to give me a headache already, but I don't want the lady of the house to look at me like I'm a real person. The glasses will shield me, as will my shapeless dress and gray hair. She won't give me a second glance.

I get out of the car and lug my cleaning supplies to the side door, the one that leads into their laundry–utility room, and pile them up. Vacuum. Mop and bucket. Dust shammies and furniture polish, Windex and paper towels, brushes and caustic chemicals for scrubbing other people's waste from toilet bowls.

I know where to go because I have cleaned this house before. Only a few times, when the woman they usually employ has been unavailable to cater to their whims. The rich people who own vacation houses on this island are like that, but God has seen fit to make them wealthy and stupid and uninterested in what is convenient for other people, so who am I to judge?

The laundry-room door is locked, but I know the passcode. The last time I cleaned here, I recorded it in a notebook I keep in my glove compartment that is specifically for codes, Wi-Fi passwords, and angry dogs' and gardeners' and guest-cottage occupants' names. Just a tool of the trade, although God did tell me that one day the McCulloughs' passcode in particular would be useful. I vividly remember Him saying that as I wrote down the five digits with a ballpoint pen.

The passcode releases the lock with a click.

I have brought inside most of my supplies when I hear a woman's voice deeper inside the house call, "Allan?"

A few moments later, Mrs. McCullough appears in the laundry-room doorway. When she sees me, her expression flickers from fear to confusion. "Can I help you?" she says. She is in jeans, a sweater of some fluffy pale yarn, and bare feet. She is also wearing a thick layer of makeup and I think, Whore.

"I'm here to clean," I say, frowning as though I, too, am confused. "Mr. McCullough told me to come."

"He did?" She looks afraid again.

"Yes." This is a lie, but it is for a good cause. "He called just this morning."

"Well, I don't actually need any cleaning, so…"

I hadn't planned for the possibility of Mrs. McCullough turning me away. I had just assumed that she, not used to lifting a finger, would sigh with relief and lead me to her dirty kitchen.

"I can go," I say, "but I was counting on the hours."

Her face softens. "Well, okay—I guess the kitchen *is* kind of a disaster."

I knew it.

I have vacuumed the kitchen, washed the pots in the sink, wiped down the countertops, and am loading the dishwasher when the children come in from outside, tracking mud onto the floor.

I knew about them, but it is still jarring to see them up close. The boy is slender and blond and, for some reason, barefoot and wearing only a vest on his top half so that his arms are bare. He ignores me—these are children accustomed to the presence of hired help—and goes straight to the kitchen sink. He turns on the tap, ducks his head sideways, and drinks messily from the stream of water like an animal.

The girl, in a pink jacket and rainboots, has stopped in the doorway. She says, "Why are you here?"

"I'm cleaning up your mom's mess," I reply.

That is when the boy looks at me for the first time, straightening and wiping water from his mouth. His dark eyes fasten on me for a long moment, and they are so unnerving that I turn away and busy myself with the dishwasher.

"Come on," he says to the girl.

HANNAH

Did Allan send that house cleaner to check up on me? I wonder. Did he guess that I'm here at the island house and send her to confirm it?

There's no other explanation. Allan knows I'm here. How long before he shows up? Will he pretend everything is normal? Will he confront me?

Maybe I should've sent the cleaner away, but she needs the work. She's stooped and drab and inconsequential, yet there's still something sort of sneaky about her. Even borderline creepy.

Oliver and Sibley are playing outside, so I decide to hole up in the primary suite until the cleaner is gone.

I lie on the unmade bed and stare out at the sea for a while, and then I scroll through notifications on my phone. An email from Sibley's teacher about an upcoming field trip. A shipment notice from Neiman Marcus. A message about lessons at the Seattle Tennis Club. The digital detritus of my ordinary life, my life before Wednesday. Delete, delete, delete.

I'm still waiting for a text from Allan. There is none. It's making me worried, but maybe the surprise appearance of the house cleaner is message enough.

My scrolling thumb freezes.

One of the notifications says Google News Alert: Orcas Island.

I tap the screen, opening the *Seattle Times* website. A headline reads Apparent Murder Weapon Identified in Orcas Island Mystery.

> Three days ago, the remains of an unidentified female were discovered in a shallow grave on Orcas Island, Washington. There are signs of blunt force trauma to the female's skull, leading law enforcement to suspect she may have been a homicide victim. Washington State Patrol forensics experts say that the victim was buried between five and ten years ago, and that she was probably in her late teens at the time of death.
>
> In a new development, the Washington State archaeologist has identified an unusual implement found in the grave as a precontact so-called slave-killer club made by the Tlingit First Nations tribe of present-day British Columbia. Forensic examination suggests that this club was very likely used to perpetrate the blunt force trauma to the skull. Although the state archaeologist, Dr. Bill Jansen, says that the archaeological value of the rare bone or antler club is "priceless," he notes that at auction the item would fetch about half a million dollars. In addition, Dr. Jansen notes that the club, which features carvings of both human and wolf heads, is known to have been purchased by an anonymous private collector in 2008.

Anonymous private collector? A private collector like Allan?

I try not to imagine the girl, her lips parted in a gasp. I try not to imagine the crushing, irretrievable thump on her skull.

I get off the bed and go to the north wing of the house. I

can hear the drone of a vacuum cleaner from somewhere beyond the kitchen.

I pass the darkened display cases holding Allan's artifact collection. I go into his study and shut myself in.

CAROLINE

I do not want to go near the obscene heathen things in the display cases, but Mrs. McCullough has gone into her husband's study, and I need to know why. I polish the glass with Windex and a shammy, inch by inch, listening carefully for sounds behind that door.

It is a mistake to listen so hard because it's not Mrs. McCullough I hear, but the voices of the things in the dark case. They start slowly and almost inaudibly, but once they know they have my attention, their voices clamor, talking over each other in a frantic contest.

—smoke, so sweet like the burning forest wrapping around his—

—and just like a pestle, she said, only flatter, so—

—but those huckleberries just kept on rolling around in there and it made my belly tickle almost—

"In the name of the Lord Jesus Christ I renounce the power of darkness," I mouth, reciting words suggested to me by the unmarried women's fellowship group leader, Brenda, "I bind these demons and forbid them to operate, in the name of Jesus Christ."

—plunged straight into the water—slice!—

"Resist the Devil," I whisper, "and he will flee from you."

The demon things will not quiet themselves. They chatter and chatter and chatter until my head feels like it will explode.

HANNAH

In the study, I go to the filing cabinet. Allan keeps his entire artifact collection here at the island house, along with the corresponding paperwork. It's so he can show off the artifacts' documented provenances to visiting friends and business associates. He would never be so tacky as to talk about how much they cost, but all of that is also documented.

The filing cabinet is locked.

I jerk on the handle a few times.

Definitely locked.

I go to Allan's desk, open the drawers, rummage around.

No key.

Can I pick the lock? People do that on TV, but it somehow seems too delicate, too cautious. I feel like smashing something.

I step out of the study to find the house cleaner polishing the display cases in the hallway. Her back is to me, her shoulders tight, and the circles she is tracing with her cloth are painfully slow.

"You don't need to clean those," I say.

She replies without looking at me. "Mr. McCullough insists

that I take extra care with the cases." She continues the slow circles with the cloth, challenging me to contradict my husband's orders.

I don't have time for this, so I tell her, "Okay, then," and I go outside and head for the garage.

Sibley waylays me, emerging from the bushes like a wild animal.

"Mommy!" she cries. "The witch from the forest is—"

"Don't," I snap.

She looks up at me, shock in her eyes. A twig is knotted in her hair and dirt darkens her cheek. Her glasses are slightly fogged. She isn't used to me speaking sharply, to her or to anyone. She looks like she might cry.

"I'm sorry, honey," I say. A lump fills my throat. "I'm sorry."

Then she's running away, back into the bushes.

Another mothering fail to add to my list.

In the garage, I poke around until I find what I want: a steel pry bar, about twelve inches long.

I pick it up tentatively at first, but then I almost enjoy the feel of its cold, hard heft. I'll have to get it past the house cleaner, so I poke around some more and find an old canvas beach bag splotched with dark mold. I place the pry bar inside and carry it back into the house.

The cleaner is still polishing the display cases with that excruciating slowness. She must hear me pass behind her, but she doesn't turn. I think I hear her sniffle as though she's crying, but I'm not sure.

I go back into the study and shut the door.

I wriggle the sharp, curved edge of the pry bar into the crack between the filing cabinet's drawer and frame. Then I give a shove. Metal moans. I shove again. The drawer splits open, its lock mechanism twisted. One more shove, and with a screech the lock gives way.

The cleaner must've heard that. Will she tell Allan?

I set the pry bar on the floor and flip through the file folders, checking their neatly printed labels. Each folder is for a different year, starting in 2002 and ending this year.

I look in this year's folder. There are two sets of papers: $78,000 for something described as a *Tsimshian polychromed wood crest*, and $91,000 for a *rare Tlingit wood clan hat*, both purchased at the auction of a private collection in Los Angeles. Besides the sales information, there are papers attesting to the authenticity of the items—where they were found, which experts had inspected them—in the case of this collection, a professor from UCLA.

But I'm not interested in Allan's recent acquisitions. I need to go back.

I carry the files from 2002 to 2015 to Allan's desk, switch on the lamp, and carefully go through them. Item by item—and there aren't very many, four or five at most in any given year—I search for something matching the slave-killer club in the *Seattle Times* story. Bone handle. Wolf's head.

I find it in the 2008 file. *Rare and important Tsimshian or Tlingit club.* It is not bone, but antler. Wolf's head carved into the side, human head knob at the top. Eighteen-and-a-half inches long. Purchased for $540,000 from the private collection of Gerald Sisson in Toronto. Verified authentic and *of exceptional rarity and quality.*

I sink into the desk chair.

Then it's true, I think. The murder weapon belongs to my husband.

CAROLINE

Now I understand what Mrs. McCullough is doing here on the island. I heard the moan of bending metal. She is here to pry open the past.

The things in the display case are hollering at me now, layers and layers of hectic voices, and so even though Mrs. McCullough is still in the study, I abandon the Windex and shammy. I go blindly through the house and find my purse where I left it on the kitchen counter. I fumble through to the inner, zippered pocket and pull out a green plastic prescription bottle. I uncap it, shake out a pill, and put it on my tongue. I go to the sink and fill a glass with water. I gulp down the pill.

The glass I am holding starts up with incoherent murmuring, and I drop it in the sink. It shatters in a spray of water drops and glittering shards, and it is almost as though I hear a scream.

I snatch at a curved shard, wanting only to get it all out of sight and into the trash, and my hand jerks back reflexively. Blood springs up in a jagged line across my index finger. At first, I feel nothing. Then the pain.

I grab a fistful of paper towels and wrap my finger tight. "Oh, Lord," I pray as I weep. "Please, Lord Jesus. Help me."

"Oh my gosh, are you okay?" It is Mrs. McCullough. She must have heard the shattering glass.

"It's nothing. I just— I broke a glass, you can deduct the cost from my pay… I cut myself but I—I think I need to go."

"Definitely." She steps closer, and I resist the urge to back away. "Is it deep? Do you— That's a lot of blood. Do you think you need stitches? I could drive you to the clinic, just to be double sure you don't—"

"No," I almost shout, and she looks taken aback. The idea of riding in this whore's Range Rover all the way up to the clinic in Eastsound is intolerable. Her filth would rub off on me.

"Okay," she says doubtfully, "but that much blood—"

"I'll come back tomorrow," I say, "to finish cleaning."

"You don't have to—"

"Yes, I do. I never leave my work unfinished. I have some pride." I say this accusingly, to make her back off, and it works.

"Tomorrow is fine," she says.

ALLAN

I usually avoid Bellingham, ninety or so miles north of Seattle. It's a cesspool of hippies and snobby provincial university people and homeless dudes from Alaska wintering on the sidewalks. Then there are the gun fetishists and the fundies out in the county, and the unceasing din of coal trains traveling through from Canada.

I'm in Bellingham this morning, though. Unfortunately. There's a loose end here that I have left for far too long. I guess it never seemed to matter until a few days ago. Until they dug up that corpse.

The office of Indigo Ayres, DDS, is housed in an old brick building in the Fairhaven neighborhood. I found it on the map yesterday. I suspected that with a name like Indigo, the doctor is an old hippie, and by the looks of the office, I'm right. It's located off a lobby shared with a psychotherapist and a shoe store that appears to sell nothing but Birkenstocks. The air smells of incense and carpet cleaner. The door leading into the dentist's office is strung with brass Tibetan bells.

"Good morning," the receptionist says as I enter to the tinkle of the bells. She's a woman about my age, not bad-looking if you can stomach the long-gray-hair-and-yoga type. A type that is difficult to bribe, but I'm not planning on that. Even though bribes are so often an elegant solution, under these circumstances it would be an error.

"Good morning," I say.

She's looking down at a paper appointment calendar on her desktop, searching. I think with relief that this is indeed an old-school hippie's office. One who is averse to electronics.

She looks up. "Are you Greg Klein?"

"No, I don't have an appointment, actually. I was hoping that you could pull my old records? From a while back. Twenty years or so. I'm getting implants, and my oral surgeon wants to check on an old bone graft." Possibly too much detail, but the receptionist nods in understanding.

"I'm sorry, but our electronic records only go back seven years. Twenty-year-old records would be paper only."

"Yikes. I hope they haven't been shredded."

She smiles. "Dr. Ayres has never gotten around to that, lucky for you. No, records from twenty years ago would still be archived."

"Off-site?" Here it is. The moment of truth.

"Oh, no. Down in our storage room."

Down. The basement.

"Oh, okay," I say. "Well, is there some form I could fill out to get those records pulled? A request of some kind?"

"Yes." She's rolling back in her chair, opening a drawer. "But it won't be until Monday that we can have the copies ready for you."

"That's all right," I say. "Monday is perfect."

I fill out the request form with a lot of made-up bullshit and handwriting that isn't mine, and then I leave.

An internal door in the lobby leads me into a hallway with more offices. Tax preparation. Reiki. Event planning. Another door leads to a basement stair.

On the stairway, I take the black ski balaclava from my jacket pocket and pull it on. I doubt there are security cameras in this building, but I haven't gotten where I have in life by being sloppy.

The basement stinks of rust and mouse crap. Exposed plumbing and wiring crisscrosses the ceiling. Off to the side there are three metal fire doors, and the middle one says *Indigo Ayres, DDS* in stick-on letters.

I have everything I need in an antitheft travel wallet strapped to my ribs under my shirt and jacket. Pick, rake, and tension wrench. Tiny bottle of lock lubricant. A pair of disposable nitrile gloves.

What? This surprises you? How the fuck do you think I put myself through a fancy MBA? Slinging burgers?

I was nineteen and in college in Spokane when the Ruby Ridge standoff went down just across the border in northern Idaho. Two religious nuts from the Midwest buy a shithole land parcel up in the mountains. Build a teetering shack, homeschool their kids, pray for the End Times. Believe me, there are a lot of those in Idaho and Eastern Washington. They think of that region as no-man's-land. That's where they get it wrong. This isn't the Middle Ages. You can't hide from anyone anymore, and you sure as hell can't hide from the feds.

The religious-nut husband, Randy Weaver, starts mingling with white supremacists and eventually gets himself charged for illegal-arms possession. Next thing he knows, ex-Marines with rifles are crawling around in the woods outside his shack. His wife is killed. His son is killed. A federal marshal is killed. Randy goes to prison. It's an all-American folktale. The End.

I followed the five-day standoff in the news just like everyone else. After the son was killed, it took me a long time to wrap my head around the idea that grown men, the government, would do what they did. That they would go after the crazy dad, Randy? Okay, sure. But a fourteen-year-old, a *kid*, and his dog? A mother with a baby in her arms?

Even though it had nothing to do with me, Ruby Ridge was the end of my innocence. It was a revelation. It was when I saw, laid bare, the ruthlessness of the world. Randy Weaver and his dead wife had been right: the world is a satanic shithole. But I had no intention of fleeing to the backwoods like they had. No, I decided to take this knowledge and make it work for me.

I breach the single tumbler lock in a matter of minutes, enter the room, and shut the door before I grope for the light switch. The fluorescent overhead shudders on. The room is smaller than I expected, about the same size as my walk-in closet in Seattle. Manila file folders with colored tabs pack the shelving, floor to ceiling.

I find the *S* section.

St.

Stroufe.

I tuck the files into my jeans, against my abdomen. I pull down my shirt and zip up my jacket. I switch off the light, let myself out, and relock the door.

This is for you, Hannah, I think as I go back up the stairs two at a time. You beautiful, ungrateful bitch.

I drive straight back to Seattle, arriving at my office in time to change into a suit and sit down at my midday meeting.

When I get home later, I'll lock up the dental records in my safe.

THEN

GREENE

What Uncle taught was that the Kinfolk were special. They were going to survive when the seawater surged up and the storms hit and the lights went out because they would have practiced surviving.

Look around you, he'd say. *It won't be long before it all goes to hell. It's* already *going to hell. Hell in a handbasket. People never pause to look around them and really* see. *But we'll be ready. Not pretend-ready, like those preppers with hoarded supplies in bunkers, freeze-dried food for a few years, barrels of water to last six months, tops. We'll be* really *ready. Ready to live. Ready to thrive in the New Springtime.*

To hell with the rest of them, Uncle would say. *To* hell *with them.* He would snarl it, but then he would smile, and all the adults and the older kids would laugh. They were extraordinary, sitting around a fire that sent clicking sparks up the chimney. Nature had chosen them to be the people who lasted, and the Universe had chosen Uncle to lead them forward into their mysterious, promised future.

Every Saturday night, all the Kinfolk would gather in what they called the parlor of the main farmhouse. There was only one piece of furniture in the parlor, a big old red tapestry armchair with a saggy seat. After the womenfolk had cleaned up the supper dishes, Uncle would sit in that chair and all the grown-ups would cram into the parlor, leaning against the peeling wallpaper or sitting cross-legged on uneven floorboards. It was too crowded for the kids so they—except the babies on their mothers' laps—sat out in the hallway with the door open so they could hear what Uncle said. They would comb the lice eggs out of each other's hair, or whittle, or hull seeds. They had to find useful things to do with their hands so they wouldn't fidget. Fidgeting made Uncle mad.

Greene could never bear to look at Uncle's face, so instead he would look at the grown-ups listening. Some of them would gently fondle the braided leather bracelets everyone on the Farm had to wear, with their little pottery charms stamped with a seedling. Every grown-up had the same faint smile, mouth open, eyes wide. They looked like empty things, Greene thought, broken eggshells slurped clean by racoons, waiting to be filled back up.

He preferred to make secret funny faces at Kestrel, and then they'd clamp their grubby hands over their mouths to keep in their laughter.

Kestrel's sister, Eldest, sitting up straight and attentive, her blond waves combed and braided, her pinafore dress always clean and all its holes patched, would scowl at them and mouth *Listen to Uncle.* Her teeth would flash in the firelight.

People came and went at the Farm. There was a core group of eight adults and their children that wasn't going anywhere, and then a lot of people drifting in and out, trying to "find themselves" or maybe hiding out, a few crazies and druggies. The core group came to seem like a family to Greene, although it was one messed-up family.

Greene *wanted* to leave, but the terrible problem would be figuring out a way to bring Kestrel along. Anyway, that was never going to be an issue because Mom was Uncle's biggest fan. Mom wouldn't let anyone say a word against him. She was in charge of the Farm's money and paperwork, and she was the one who made sure new arrivals forked over all their money for safekeeping.

But despite her devotion, Mom never got promoted from Uncle's left hand to his right at the supper table. Star had moved from Uncle's right hand, at the beginning of their stay, to the foot of the table after giving birth to a baby boy she called Guide. The foot of the table was the best spot for a Kinfolk woman.

Guide was the only little kid Uncle ever touched. He didn't hold him, but he would wrap his hand around Guide's fuzzy bald head. Greene pictured Uncle squeezing the baby's skull till it flattened.

After Star moved to the foot of the table, Tansy—Kestrel's mom—lost her place and had to sit on one of the benches along the side of the table. She stopped smiling. She put on weight, and her hair stopped looking shiny. She kept her eyes down.

"Uncle said Mama is bad," Kestrel told Greene one day while they were out foraging for huckleberries. Foraging was the best. They were free for a while with no one watching. No one like goody-goody Eldest, telling tales to Uncle.

"Bad? Why?"

"Because she doesn't have a baby in her tummy."

Greene didn't get it. How could that make Tansy bad? Tansy already had three children—Eldest, Kestrel, and Quill. Why did she need more? And didn't babies need a dad? By the time Greene had lived on the Farm two years, he'd connected the dots between the excited piggyback rides the goats would give each other, and the baby goats born five months later.

"Why does your mom need to have a baby in her tummy?" Greene asked Kestrel.

Kestrel palmed a handful of huckleberries into her mouth.

"'Cause Uncle wants strong healthy kin for the New Springtime."

"What about *us*? Aren't we strong and healthy?"

"We're not the right kind of kid, I don't think." Kestrel scrunched her face, a nervous tic she'd recently developed. "Because our dads aren't Kinfolk."

Well, who cared? Not Greene. He didn't even *want* to be the right kind of kid for Uncle and his stupid New Springtime he kept blabbing about but that never actually happened.

Greene should've heeded Eldest's warning: *Listen to Uncle.* Or maybe he should've watched out for Eldest.

The Kinfolk kids rotated chores weekly—so they would learn how to do everything, Uncle said—and the summer before Greene turned twelve, one of his jobs was to double-check the gates around the fenced garden at dusk. That was when the deer tiptoed out of the forest to feed.

The island deer were voracious and a constant threat. Smoke and the other men hunted the deer with rifles. There was a stockpile of rifle ammunition in the farmhouse cellar, stacks and stacks of green-and-yellow boxes that said *Remington Core-Lokt.* The Kinfolk ate a lot of venison, fresh in the fall and as cured sausages through the rest of the year.

There was the orchard, the chickens, the goats for milk, and a field of potatoes, but aside from that the vegetable garden provided a great deal of the Farm's food as well as produce to sell at the farmers market in town. They grew green beans, yellow wax beans, tomatoes of all shapes and colors, sunflowers, zucchinis, pumpkins, corn, blueberries, raspberries, strawberries, carrots, beets, turnips, and kohlrabi. Greene had hated the frozen spinach and peas Mom cooked before they moved to the Farm, but all these vegetables were good, especially with the cultured goat butter Star made.

The July just before he turned twelve, Greene checked the

garden gates periodically in the afternoons, just in case. At the first sign of dusk, he'd make sure the three gates were closed, then shut himself into the garden and scout for hidden deer. The fence was over eight feet tall, but then again, he'd seen deer spring *straight* up into the air. You never knew.

Eldest was sitting on the swing hanging from the Bigleaf Maple outside the main gate, watching him. She was fourteen, and she was too big, too cynical, for the swing.

"Look at little Greenie go," she said in a singsong taunt. "Trying so hard to make Uncle love him, but it'll never, ever work."

"I don't care what Uncle thinks," Greene muttered, latching himself inside the garden. All the gates were fastened with a simple steel hook and eye.

"Oh yeah, I almost forgot. All you care about is dumb little Kestrel."

"Shut up!"

"*You* shut up. You're pathetic, Greene."

"I'm going to tell on you for teasing. Teasing is against the rules."

"You're going to tell *Uncle* I'm teasing?"

Greene swallowed.

"I didn't think so," Eldest said. "I'm Uncle's favorite. He told me so."

"He did not."

"Oh yes, he did. He says I'm his good little girl and not to—" Eldest pressed her lips shut. "I'm his favorite. And he said it's my job to keep an eye on the rest of you dumb little kids, and if I do a good job, I'm going to get something special."

"Like what?" A strawberry cake? Greene thought. New shoes?

Eldest lifted her eyebrows. "My own *bedroom*."

"Yeah, right." Greene snorted. No one had their own bedroom. Not even any of the grown-ups, except for Uncle.

"Well, I'm going to have my own."

"You're lying."

"Am not. You'll see. Uncle said I'm special."

Without saying anything more to Eldest, Greene shoved his way through kale stalks almost as tall as he was. He was like a Diplodocus in the jungle.

He marched up and down the paths through the garden, making a complete circuit to flush out any rogue deer who might be hiding. He never saw one in the garden that whole summer. But he also knew they had uncanny ways of making themselves invisible, so he never felt totally sure that there weren't any.

Kestrel laughed at him when he shared his fear that the deer might lie in wait, camouflaged in the shadows. "They're not that smart," she said. "You worry too much."

But Greene worried anyway. The garden-gates chore was the most important, the highest-stakes job, on the roster. It wasn't that he wanted Uncle's approval, as Eldest had said. It was that he desperately didn't want to screw it up.

The next morning, Greene woke to shouts coming from outside. His heart seemed to shrivel up, a raisin inside his ribs. Then Mom came stomping up the attic stairs.

He knew. He knew even before she tore off his quilt and hollered at him that he, idiot, had left one of the gates open and the deer had gotten in and eaten the garden.

Eldest, he thought. Eldest opened that gate after I left, just to get me in trouble.

Kestrel was pale and wide-eyed when Greene slunk into the kitchen. Looking up from her bowl of oatmeal, her gaze felt to Greene like a gentle touch. I'm not alone, he reminded himself. I have Kestrel.

Uncle had taken the pickup somewhere, although Mom assured Greene that Uncle knew all about what had happened to the garden.

"That's our *food*, man," Smoke said to Greene, shaking his head in disgust. Tansy didn't give Greene his usual bowl of oatmeal.

Greene crouched beside the woodpile near the kitchen door and waited.

An hour later, Uncle, unseen by Greene, told Brian to tell everyone that Greene's punishment was to be the same as it would be for any child.

The cabin.

Mom was instructed—by Uncle, via Brian—to take Greene out to the cabin.

He walked behind her through the pasture. The wet grass soaked his jeans to the knee. Mom was silent, with a hard hunch to her shoulders.

Greene had passed by the cabin plenty of times, since it was only a little ways off one of the forest paths. It was small and slumped, made of rough logs stuck together with tar, its windows boarded up and the caving-in roof mounded lavishly, almost repulsively, with moss and ferns. It stood at the edge of a little ravine, at the bottom of which a creek trickled.

It seemed like a bad place to build a house, but Uncle said that in the olden days, when the cabin was new, there wasn't forest there and the creek was farther off. The landscape had changed.

Greene had the impression that really, the cabin was inching itself across the ground.

He followed Mom to the cabin's plank door. It had an old iron handle and a newer steel padlock.

She pushed on the door, but it didn't open until she bore down on it with her shoulder. It shuddered inward, making a gagging sound across the floorboards. Dank odor poured out along with—

—*Sissy, do not leave her alone with Papa in the—with child again, her health cannot withstand another brat un—tell tell tell tell tell!*

He could just run. No way Mom could catch him, and he knew these woods like the back of his hand. He could take the path all the way to the beach. He could walk until he found a waterfront house where someone was home. He would cry and tell them his mom and Uncle wanted to lock him up in a rotten old cabin. Maybe he'd get adopted. Him and Kestrel—

—want to tell you because no one listens to me anymore and this is too—Sissy, do not leave her alone with Papa in the—tell tell!—the coffin was planks of pine that still smelled of sap, her dress was the Sunday calico with the—

"Get in," Mom said without turning around. Her voice was toneless.

Greene stood still.

Mom spun around. "Get in!"

"Mom—"

"I've had it, Greene! I've really had it with you!"

"But the cabin is… It's saying—"

"Oh, for God's sake! Cut the drama, would you? It's just for a few hours. This is the only way you'll learn. You realize we lost a season's worth of food to the deer, don't you?"

Greene felt his face crumpling. He struggled to smooth it out again. "I checked the gates, Mom! I double-checked! Eldest was watching—"

"Don't you *dare* go and blame this on Eldest. What's the matter with you? Why can't you accept your place in our community? Why can't you make things *easy* for me for once? Get. *In.*" She pointed.

Tears tracked down Greene's cheeks. There would be no mercy from Mom. There never was. Not when he was eight and Uncle had commanded that Mom whip Greene's bare bottom with a little stinging switch for forgetting to trim his fingernails. Not when he was nine and Uncle force-fed him a disgusting casserole made from a rooster named Winston, his *friend*, until Greene vomited in front of everyone on the dining-room floor. Not when Greene was ten and his boots had floated away with the high tide on the beach, and Uncle made him go barefoot for the winter through mud and frost. No mercy. Not ever.

Greene stepped inside the cabin.

Mom shut him in.

He stood with his arms crossed and his head bowed, snot dripping, and the gashlike pain of unvoiced sobs in his throat.

The cabin had fallen silent. It was holding its breath. Waiting. Greene could almost hear, in the cabin's silence, the insects in there, moist kinds like centipedes and things with weird egg sacs. He thought he saw the glisten of slug slime and wet spiderwebs.

He listened to the clacking and clicking of Mom locking the padlock. He heard the swish of ferns as she walked away.

He waited as long as he could, and then he let the sobs out.

—sobbing, oh I know about sobbing, and crying out at the papa's birch switch, too, slicing hot on their bare bottoms and him grunting in that way, the same way as when he—

Greene squatted. He covered his ears, but that didn't help because the cabin wasn't talking to him by way of his ears.

—and I remember when the mama screamed and screamed in that bed, and the blood and the thing that was supposed to be a baby came out but it was—the pine box got bloody, too, but still they had to sit sit SIT with it until the minister could reach them from—that was when the papa started to take—

He couldn't make it stop. He simply had to listen, although he wasn't exactly sure what the cabin was telling him.

How long he listened to its snarled-up stories of the family it had once sheltered he didn't know. But when he heard an altogether different voice say, "Greene!" outside the cabin door, his heart leaped, and the cabin fell into indistinct murmuring.

Again, the voice said in a loud whisper, *"Greene!"*

Greene snuffled snot. "Kestrel?" He cracked his eyes open, and even the dim greenish light in the cabin made his eyes smart.

"Of course it's me, you silly goose."

A small hand, as familiar to Greene as his own, protruded through a hole that had rotted out beside the doorjamb.

Greene crawled over and grabbed it like a lifeline. Warm, a little sweaty. Kestrel's hand was *home.*

"It's scary in here," Greene whispered.

"'Course it is. It's jail."

"No, it's— The cabin is *talking* to me. Like things do."

"Oh." Kestrel sounded serious, and her grip tightened. "What's it saying?"

"Really gross, horrible stuff. I don't know. About people who used to live here, like a mom who died all bloody right in here—"

"Ew!"

"And a dead baby-thing and a mean dad who was hurting these girls, Sissy and Liza-something. I don't want to hear it." His voice was cracking, dissolving. "I don't want to *hear* it."

"Kes—trel!" came a distant call.

"Mama," Kestrel whispered through the hole. "I have to go."

Don't leave me, Greene thought. "Okay," he whispered.

Greene, still clutching Kestrel's fingers, felt like letting go would be letting go of the side of a boat out on the whitecapped sea. What would happen in the night? In the dark?

"When Guide or Bridget or Quill are bugging me," Kestrel said, "I tell them to cut it out." A pause. She was waiting for him to get it. That happened a lot. Her mind leaped like a deer, always landing surely. Greene's mind, on the other hand, stayed in one place like a big cedar tree, with roots that went deep into the soil.

He didn't get it.

"Tell the cabin to *cut it out,*" Kestrel whispered.

"They—things—they don't listen to me," Greene said. "That's not how… *I* listen to *them.*"

"But that's not *fair.*" Greene could hear Kestrel's indignant scowl.

"Kestrel!" Her mom's voice was closer now, and sharper. "Kestrel, it's getting dark! Are you there with Greene? *Kestrel!*"

Kestrel was letting go. Greene clutched harder, knowing he shouldn't, but then she pulled away, and he was alone in *here* and she was alone out *there*. It never felt right when they were apart.

He heard rustling as she got to her feet.

"Kestrel!" Her mom was nearby.

"Tell it to *cut it out*," Kestrel whispered once more to Greene.

With Kestrel gone, the cabin started right up again. First with sleepy murmurs, but after ten minutes or so it had crescendoed into the same breathless talk as before.

—and then Sissy said that if they told the minister about the papa he would never—because remember the thrashing Jimmy got when he told tales about—listen to that, the wind howling and the rain splattering, splat—

"Quiet," Greene whispered.

—tering and he says he didn't know this godforsaken island would be this wet, but we can't go back to Wisconsin now, not after what happened with Uncle Frederick and the—splattering, splattering—

Greene's eyes and nose were running again, but he took the biggest breath he could manage and shouted, "Be. *Quiet!*"

The cabin silenced.

Seconds passed. Maybe a minute. Greene could hear the squawk of jays outside.

—I'll bring with me to the grave, Beth said, to the grave, what Papa did to—

"CUT IT OUT!"

Silence.

The silence lasted through the night. Greene didn't sleep, though. He was afraid that if he shut his eyes for longer than a blink, the cabin would start back up again. He got what was wrong with the cabin. That the stuff that had happened inside it back in the olden days was too terrible to forget, that it thought it would feel better if it made Greene listen. But he didn't *want* to listen.

He sat with his knees drawn under his chin, arms wrapped around his legs, staring into the darkness. His teeth chattered. He tried to hold his pee, his low belly aching and hard. He thought about warm sunlight, the open beach, laughing with Kestrel. About being free.

It was Tansy, Kestrel's mom, who came in the morning to let him out. Her face appeared in the split of the door. Her mouth fell open at the sight of him and she said, "Oh God you poor thing," all in one breath.

Back at the farmhouse he stripped off his urine-reeking clothing in the upstairs bathroom, washed himself, crouching in the clawfoot tub with a bucket of cold water, and then went up to the attic to pull on his nightshirt and fall onto his mattress. Somehow, he knew he was exempt from chores that day.

He pulled the quilt up around his face—

Pricking and pinching, dizzily we—

"Quiet," Green whispered to the quilt.

A pause. Then, *Pricking and pinching, dizzily we go—such a soft, soft gingham square—*

"Cut it out!" Greene said, more loudly, commanding without being mean, like Smoke talked to the goats.

The quilt went silent.

Greene slept. And despite everything, he slept with a smile on his face.

NOW

JOSH

When the plane touches down at Edinburgh, I wake with a snort. My mouth is sour and dry, and I'm not sure where I am. I go back to sleep again until someone shakes my shoulder.

"Sir?" a woman says too close, too loud. "Sir, we are here. We are in Edinburgh."

I go through passport control and customs in a daze, feeling absolutely assaulted by the impenetrable Scots accents. Then I find a bathroom and wash up and brush my teeth and gargle with whitening mouthwash, a mini bottle of which I always carry in my messenger bag.

I have butterflies in my stomach. Not about the crisis at which my career has so abruptly arrived. About seeing Drew.

What's the matter with me? I'm supposed to be the one giving other people butterflies.

Pulling my wheeled carry-on and messenger bag, the violin case strapped over one shoulder, I pass through automatic doors to a blast of cold air. I cross the street and go into a concrete parking garage, following signs that say *Pickup Zone*.

At the pickup zone, a line of vehicles comes and goes. People and suitcases get in. People chatter and embrace. More, more, more vehicles flow past.

Where is Drew? What kind of car does he even drive? I didn't think to ask. Did I only imagine that telephone conversation, the invitation—

Wait. Over there, someone is lowering the passenger window of a BMW electric hatchback, someone is shouting, "Josh!"

I go over to the BMW with the blood singing in my veins. And there he is. Drew. The bulk of him, the twinkle-eyed smile. "There you are," he says. "Get in. Rough flight?"

"Um, no, not really." I suddenly feel like vomiting. And I might have, except there is nothing at all in my stomach except, I imagine, a bluish glaze of vodka and Xanax.

"You look, I don't know, stunned?"

"I do? I guess I was—"

"Your stuff can go on the back seat. The cargo space is full. I just did a Tesco run."

"Got it."

I collapse the handle of my roller bag and stash it on the rear seat with my messenger bag. I settle the violin in the footwell so that it won't fall if the car brakes suddenly. I'm glad to have it off my back. Then I fold myself into the passenger seat beside Drew.

Drew swings the car out into traffic while I'm still buckling. His beard has grown bushier since we last saw each other, and his profile is a little more rugged than I remember. We make small talk as he navigates through the airport and out to the main road.

He seems to exude an aura, a divine light. He glows.

I recognize that light.

Love. Oh God, no. This is *love.*

ALLAN

I'm not expecting the phone call, which I receive in the early evening after I have gone home. I've locked the dental records in my safe and screwed the au pair and done a Peloton workout. I'm showered and ordering Vietnamese delivery online when my phone lights up with a familiar number.

The rage comes out of nowhere, dizzy and hot.

I pick up the phone. "Hello."

"McCullough," a man says. He has a meaty voice and a down-home accent.

"Boyce," I say, adding silently, *you greedy, bloated tick.*

I hear a labored intake of breath. Boyce isn't keen on cardio. "It's been too long. I'm thinking you ought to come up here for a visit."

"Why would I do that?"

"You know why."

"You're going to have to be a little more specific."

"Can't a man miss his buddy?" He chuckles. It's nasty, with no trace of humor.

I want to kill him.

"What's this about?" I say.

"Don't you read the papers?"

I have my laptop right in front of me, so I tap a few well-chosen keywords and the article Boyce must be talking about pops up: Apparent Murder Weapon Identified in Orcas Island Mystery.

I skim the two paragraphs. My breathing goes quick and shallow.

Even though he's long gone, a fugitive felon for escaping jail, and probably hiding out in some backwoods hovel in Idaho or Montana, that little shit Greene Cooper isn't done fucking with me yet.

"Will you be around tomorrow midday?" I say to Boyce, struggling to sound calm.

"Sure. If I'm not out on my boat."

His boat.

I picture Boyce's fat neck, the way it used to spill over the collar of his polyester uniform shirt. I picture my hands wrapping, my thumbs burrowing into his windpipe.

"I'll see you tomorrow," I say and end the call.

CAROLINE

On Friday evening, I am at the door of Trey's apartment, which is on the second story of the Camp Praise administration cabin and accessed by an exterior wooden stair. I hold a hot lasagna covered in aluminum foil. It took me hours to make, but I enjoyed every minute.

I know you weren't expecting it, I will say to Trey, but I'll bet you haven't had a home-cooked meal in a while. My smile will be tender and just a little shy.

But when he answers the door, he is on the phone.

"—so you're going to have to get down on your knees and pray, buddy," he is saying. He steps back, opening the door wider, and beckons me with a crooked finger. "No. Nuh-uh. Not an option unless—"

Trey's place is as ragtag and bachelorlike as I expected. As he leads me to the kitchen area, my eyes greedily devour little artifacts of him. Running shoes on the floor. A hoodie cast over a chairback. A dog-eared paperback Bible on the coffee table.

"Listen," Trey says into the phone, "I've got to go, but we'll talk later, okay?" He ends the call and sighs. "What a terrible situation. Just between you and me, Cody Murphy's girlfriend got herself pregnant."

"Oh, dear," I say. I am standing awkwardly with the hot casserole, wondering what to do with it.

"Yeah. It's sin."

"Do...do his parents know?" This will take Linda Murphy down a peg, I think with pleasure.

"Yeah, but the girl's parents don't. Not yet. I'm counseling Cody to marry the girl. Then at least the baby won't be born out of wedlock, and Cody and her can work together as a team to get right with God." Trey meets my eye. The intensity of his clear grays makes me feel weak in the legs. "God is always ready to forgive. It's important to remember that, you know?"

Someone told him, I think. Someone told him about my bastard son. Or did he read that old *New Yorker* article about the Farm, the one that came out after the raid? My name is not mentioned in that article, but Greene's is. Not that I can picture that dirty magazine in Trey's hands.

Then Trey smiles, and it is such a sunny and clean smile that I realize I was mistaken. He doesn't know.

"I brought a lasagna," I say. I place it on the Formica countertop.

"Oh, whoa—actually—sorry, could you pick that up?"

Confused, I pick it up, and Trey places a folded dishtowel on the counter.

"There," he says. "You don't want to, like, burn something."

"No," I say with a prickle of shame.

He peels back the foil to see what I made. The steamy aroma from the cheese and tomatoes escapes, and I have a sudden vision of the two of us sitting close, a candle between us, enjoying this meal together.

"Oh," he says. "I'm sorry. Didn't you know? I'm paleo."

"Paleo?"

"I don't eat dairy or grains. They're, like, really bad for you. Super inflammatory. Also, tomatoes are basically in the deadly nightshade family?" He presses the foil back down around the corner of the dish. "Sorry. It was a nice gesture."

"No, I'm sorry," I whisper, my eyes cast down to the patterned linoleum floor. "I should have asked you."

"Yeah, you probably should've."

I grab the casserole too roughly, and my purse slips from my shoulder and hits the floor. Things spray out of my purse. My phone, my keys, a green plastic prescription bottle with a telltale rattling.

Trey picks up the bottle.

"Please," I say, holding out my hand. "Let me—I'll take that."

He doesn't give it back. "Caroline," he says, frowning at the bottle, then at me. "You aren't taking pharmaceuticals, are you? Do you know what this stuff does to your body?" He looks at the bottle again. "Clozapine. What's that for?"

"Please." I try for a playful note, but my voice cracks. "Trey, I'll—"

"You're a grown woman," he says. "You live on your own and make your own decisions, so you've got to decide what's best." He presses the bottle into my hand, and my fingers curl around it. "But it's my advice that you ditch those pills. You'll be like, whoa, why do I suddenly feel ten times better? Have you ever tried herbs? I, like, swear by gingko. You can pair that with a Bible-based approach."

"I haven't..." I am stuffing the bottle and keys and phone back in my purse, looping my purse strap over my shoulder, picking up the lasagna. "I'll go, okay?"

"Yeah," Trey says. "That's probably a good idea."

He doesn't go with me to the door. I can feel him watching me as I balance the lasagna on my hip and struggle with the doorknob.

I get myself back home. I do not remember how, but I must not have walked on the road because I have several fresh scratches on my hand, next to my bandaged cut from the broken glass at the McCullough house earlier. One of the new scratches weeps a fat drop of blood.

I dump the lasagna in the kitchen and go into the bathroom. I don't bother with more bandages. My savior had bleeding hands, too. I feel so close to Him in that moment, my eyes fill up. As I pull the bottle of clozapine from my purse and uncrack the child-safe lid, I see Him in my mind's eye. The shiny hair just brushing His shoulders. His tight tanned throat. His clear gray eyes.

The pills shower down into the toilet water with barely a splash. I flush and watch them disappear.

My cabin has a septic system, and this is probably bad for the tank, but it feels so right for the pills to go down the sewer pipe. Besides, this is a rental house, and I am fairly certain that my landlord is an atheist.

HANNAH

I spend the afternoon and evening in a spiral of indecision.

I know for sure that the apparent murder weapon, the carved antler slave-killer club, belongs to Allan. What's less clear is what I should do with this information.

Is it wrong to take damning evidence about your husband to law enforcement? Or is it wrong to withhold it?

Is the fact that I have my own secrets a good-enough reason to stay silent? Or should I be willing to risk everything in the name of justice?

I have other questions as well, ones that are too scary to look at head-on. They swarm in the back of my brain. Am I married to a murderer? Is it safe for the children to be in this place? Am *I* safe? Shouldn't I have been able to feel the presence of that girl's silently decaying body when I spent weekends, weeks at a time, in this house over the years? Does my own fear outweigh my responsibilities to *her*?

Anxiety leaches into my muscles. I am jumpy, restless, pacing. I pick up my phone, look up the San Juan County Sheriff's number, set my phone down, pick it up again.

Then I remember what Allan asked me on the day we learned about the dead body: *What would become of Sibley, of Oliver, if you went to prison?*

I toss the phone aside.

I make myself a cup of chamomile tea, hoping it will calm me. I curl up with my laptop in bed and open the search engine.

If I can't go to the sheriff and I can't stop obsessing, there's nothing left to do but google.

Searching *McCullough Orcas Island* and *McCullough artifact* turns up nothing. That in itself feels odd: my husband has owned this house for over a decade, and he's a fairly high-profile collector, but I remind myself that Allan regularly pays to have his name scrubbed from the internet. He's a public person, he says. He can't let garbage accumulate.

Next, I type *Orcas Island artifact* and find something interesting buried on the fifth page of results: a short newspaper article in the online archives of something called the *Journal of the San Juan Islands*, published on August 24, 2015.

August 2015. The month the ATF raid went down at the Kinfolk Farm.

The article says that a local island youth, aged seventeen, escaped from the jail at the sheriff substation on Orcas after being arrested for burgling a private home. That he was, at the time of writing, a fugitive from justice.

The article doesn't name the seventeen-year-old thief. It doesn't name the homeowner who was robbed. But Allan has always kept his artifact collection here at the island house. And the Kinfolk Farm was right next door.

I read the short article again, trying to squeeze more from it.

I don't like what it suggests. It makes the connection between Allan and the murder weapon seem not so cut-and-dried after all. It means there was this other person out there, the burglar, who might've had the murder weapon in *his* possession before it was buried with the body. If he happened to steal that exact club.

I look for more information about the burglary, but I don't get any hits.

I could broaden my search, I think.

Like I said before, I don't follow the news. So I'm astounded by the sheer number of search engine results that pop up when I type *kinfolk farm raid*. There are old newspaper and magazine articles and news videos. There are conspiracy theories about the raid with dedicated Reddit pages, blogs, and self-published e-books. There are intellectual think pieces about the overreach of the federal government, and there are YouTube memorials for those killed in the raid.

I cast around and come up with something that looks both reputable and accessible: a 2016 longread in the *New Yorker* by an investigative journalist named Milo Hetworth. I open it up on the magazine's online archive.

Reading the article, I doubt every statement the author makes. I mean, what could he really have known about those reclusive people? He never managed to get an interview with any of the actual Kinfolk. Instead, he interviewed islanders who didn't live on the Farm. He interviewed federal employees and cult experts and local reporters and one of the Kinfolk women's estranged sisters. But was any of it the actual truth?

We all spin tales. That's something I have learned in my monthly one-on-ones with Oliver's therapist. There is something about direct, personal questions that brings out the yarn-weaver in us.

Still, fiction though some of it may have been, my stomach hurts as I read about the standoff. How the ATF agents sneaked around the farm, conducting surveillance. How Uncle refused to surrender. How a kid named Quill Stroufe, and one of the agents, and Uncle were killed.

I see men in helmets and camouflage, flickering silently in and out of sight behind the firs, rifles spiking. I hear shouts and pops of gunfire echoing off tree trunks.

I stop reading. It's too much, and my throat aches. Quill Stroufe was barely older than Oliver is now.

In my imagination, I hear that tap-tapping again. God, that sound. It wrings me out.

JOSH

"I heard this amazing new recording of the Shostakovich A minor violin concerto a few days ago," Drew tells me on my first morning in Edinburgh. Upon our arrival from the airport yesterday, I promptly crashed in the guest bedroom. Now, we're having brunch in a trendy café near the flat somebody loaned to Drew for the duration of his opera's run. Correction: Drew is eating breakfast, but I'm only having coffee. "Well, not actually *new*—it's a digitally remastered recording from, like, the late sixties, with Leonid Orlyk and the Leningrad Philharmonic."

My guts ball up. They always do when anyone mentions Leonid Orlyk, one of the most famous Soviet-era violinists.

"Oh?" I say, looking out the window. Raindrops delicately speckle the plate glass.

"Yeah. You should hear it because there's just something about Orlyk's playing—his tone, but also his phrasing and even, I don't know, the speed of his vibrato?—that reminds me of your—"

"I don't want to hear it," I say. Maybe too forcefully, because a woman at the next table turns her head in surprise.

"Whoa. Okay." Drew holds up an *I surrender* hand. "I just thought—"

"I can't be influenced," I say in a more mellow voice. "When I'm working up a new piece—and I'm working up the Shostakovich for next year—I have to totally avoid listening to other recordings. So that my interpretation is unique and—and—"

"It's okay. Forget I mentioned it." Drew nudges both plates of eggs Benedict he ordered toward me. One smoked salmon, one honey-roast ham. He didn't seem to believe me when I said I wasn't hungry. "Here. You pick. Or we'll share."

I shake my head. "I told you, I'm not hungry."

On a normal day I will stuff myself with carbs until I'm high, fill myself with rich cheeses and desserts until I imagine I can feel the flesh of my hands and chin growing. At these times it doesn't feel like it's even my own body. In childhood and adolescence, I was lean and taut, but now…it's like I'm imprisoned in someone else's fleshy carcass to which I compulsively administer abuse.

Feed the beast.

The thought always emerges from the smog of oversatiation and grief.

Feed the beast.

Drew says, "You haven't eaten since I picked you up at the airport."

Actually, I haven't eaten in days, unless you count the cream I've been dumping into my coffee. I'm pretty sure I've lost a few pounds already. I can see it in my hands. The dimples on the backs of my knuckles are shallower.

"I'm not hungry," I repeat.

"Are you sick?"

"No. I just don't want to eat."

Drew leans closer over the table. "You don't need to worry about your weight, you know. Not on account of me."

I frown. "What?"

Drew sits back. "I know."

My pulse is thrumming against my Adam's apple. "Know what?"

"That you have a crush on me." Drew's eyes twinkle.

My shoulders relax. "Oh. Okay. Maybe a… I… Am I that obvious?"

Drew grins, lifting his coffee cup to his mouth. "Just a little."

I wait for Drew to say the crush is mutual.

That doesn't happen.

"Oh my gosh—*hi*," someone exclaims.

I look up expecting to see one of my fans, but the guy standing beside our table isn't looking at me but at Drew. He is thin and sandy-haired, with an elfin face. He wears an expensive-looking wool peacoat, a fluffy scarf, and jeans.

"Duncan," Drew says with obvious pleasure. He gets to his feet and gives the guy a hug. It starts out seeming like a bro hug, but it goes on for a little too long, and the guy—Duncan, evidently—looks around Drew's arm. He flicks his eyes down and up me, just slowly enough for me to feel like a beached whale.

Drew breaks the hug. "Can you join us?"

"Sorry." Duncan has a British accent of some kind. "I'm meeting Tasha and Clio—they're over there."

Drew turns, squints across the restaurant, waves. Then he turns to me. "Josh, this is Duncan Feist. He's a tenor in my opera."

"Nice to meet you," I say with a false smile.

"Likewise," Duncan says without enthusiasm. Then, the inevitable question asked by every musician, because we live in a bubble and have zero interest in anyone outside of it: "Are you a musician?"

I wait for Drew to jump in, to tell this hot little monster that I happen to be one of the most famous concert violinists in the world and that if he doesn't recognize me, he must be a complete philistine.

Nope. Drew has sat down and is looking at his phone.

I say to Duncan, "Yeah, I'm a violinist."

"Cool," Duncan says without interest. Then to Drew, "So,

a bunch of us are meeting up at the Bailie tonight. You absolutely *must* come."

"I don't know," Drew says, smiling into my eyes. "Maybe. I have a guest."

"I've actually been meaning to ask you something, Josh," Drew says when Duncan has sauntered off.

My heart trips over itself. "Okay."

"I'm writing a solo violin sonata—sort of in the tradition of Bach and Ysaÿe—and I wanted to ask if you would premiere it. Next summer, at Tanglewood. And also make the first recording."

Aaand there it is. The real reason I'm here. Not to make love in a big feather bed but to get down to work on his fucking opus.

"Oh," I say. "I... I'm flattered."

"But?"

But I never want to touch that ghastly violin again, I think. Is that a good-enough answer?

"But I... Well, in light of what happened in Budapest, I'm actually thinking of taking a hiatus. Or sabbatical? Whatever you call it. A break. For a while."

"Oh. Okay." Drew shrugs and turns his attention to the smoked salmon eggs Benedict. But before he looks away, I see the hardening, the cooling off, in his eyes.

So that's it. Drew's love is contingent.

My dad is fond of saying everyone has their price, and the older I get, the more I suspect he's right.

Drew leaves for a rehearsal after brunch, so I'm left to my own devices. I wind up sleeping off the rest of my jet lag in the flat's guest bedroom. When Drew comes back, we go out for dinner and then on to the pub. Neither of us mention his sonata.

The pub situation is hellish, because Duncan is there in a tight little T-shirt and a subtle smoky eye. He dominates Drew's attention, sitting too close, laughing too loud.

I find myself in a corner booth with Tasha, a soprano in the chorus of the opera company.

"I know who you are," she says to me, sipping her drink. "I have some of your stuff on Spotify. Your Mozart A Major with the London Philharmonic? That's my favorite recording of that piece."

I nod in a way I hope seems modest, even though I'm actually thinking, Finally someone in this stupid town knows who I am. "But Duncan is still the great piece of ass."

Tasha takes another sip. "I don't get it. If you think Drew is so hung up on looks—so *shallow*—how can you be interested in him?"

"You're sounding very much like a woman right now."

"I'm serious. Drew obviously likes you or he wouldn't have invited you up here. So, I don't know, why don't you take a risk?"

"Annihilate myself on the bonfire of love?"

"You're only young once, sweetie."

I have no way to tell Tasha that my entire life over the past nine years has been one long, disastrous exercise in self-annihilation.

I look around for Drew, but he isn't where he was before, and neither is Duncan.

I go and check the bathrooms. Drew isn't there, either.

Did he ditch me? No. He wouldn't do that to me, his house guest. His *famous* house guest. Would he?

I find my coat, put it on, and go out onto the sidewalk.

My ears are ringing from the too-loud music inside, so the quiet air is like a cushion. But my relief is short-lived because it registers that the couple making out against the building next door is Drew and Duncan.

The orange dot of the cigarette dangling from Drew's hand glows like a warning.

He holds Duncan's head in his other hand, his shoulders hunched in concentration. Duncan's back presses against the building stones, his head tipped up to Drew's hungry mouth.

My first reaction is shock, then a liquid bolt of unbidden arousal, capped off with a surge of jealousy so potent it feels like a punch in the head.

"Oh," Duncan says, pulling away from Drew. His eyes slide sideways to me. "Someone likes to watch."

When Drew sees me, his face creases in a smile. "Joshie," he calls.

Joshie? What in the actual fuck?

I clear my throat. "Oh. Hey. I was just—I needed a little fresh air? Well, really, some quiet. My ears. I don't want to blow out my ears. The, uh…"

Drew is strolling toward me, taking a drag of the cigarette. Duncan looks confused for a second, but then he trots after Drew.

Drew waves the cigarette. "Want one?" he asks.

"No, thanks."

"What do you think of the band?"

"Oh. Great. They're great."

"Stop lying. You hate it."

"No, I don't. Listen. I… I've been thinking." I look briefly at Duncan, who is now posing prettily beside Drew and scrolling through his phone. Then I meet Drew's eyes, which in the lamplight are nothing but two shadows. "I changed my mind. About your sonata. I want to do it."

"Are you serious?"

"Yeah. I'm in."

"That's amazing!" Drew throws his big arms around me and pulls me in for a smoky hug.

I savor the hug for a moment, but I can't resist glancing over at Duncan.

Duncan is still looking at his phone, but his cheek twitches, just below his eye.

I think, Whatever comes next, wherever I have to go, and whatever crazy things I have to do to make this work, it's all worth it. Just for that one little twitch.

HANNAH

"I hope the witch doesn't come back today," Sibley says in the morning, forking up a bite of toaster waffle with syrup.

I sigh. "Honey. Please. There is no witch."

Sibley sets her glass down. Milk streaks both of her round cheeks. "Why don't you believe me, Mommy?"

Because I'd lose my mind if I believed every last thing a little kid said, I think.

Aloud I say, "I love that you have an imagination, honey. But why don't you focus on imagining nice things? Fairies or unicorns or something. They might be in the forest, too, you know."

"You never believe her," Oliver says. He stabs a chunk of waffle with his fork.

"I do, honey. I do."

Oliver lifts his dark eyes to look at me. The contempt I see in them is as raw as freshly butchered meat. "You're always pretending." He stuffs waffle into his mouth.

I'm not even sure what he means, yet his words cut me. "I'm not pretending."

He rolls his eyes, says nothing so that my words hang in the air like the naked lie that they are.

★ ★ ★

Not long after the children have gone outside to play, I hear a vehicle's engine approaching. Fear shoots through me.

Allan, I think. Allan is here.

I open the front door just as a green Jeep Cherokee is braking in front of the garage. A man climbs out, and I breathe a sigh of relief, because it's the caretaker I met out on the vacant lot the day before yesterday. Trey, I think his name is.

"Hey," he calls, lifting a hand as he approaches. He's wearing jeans, a ball cap, and a black sweatshirt that reads *Real Men Love Jesus* in white lettering. "Good morning."

"Hello," I say. "What are you doing here?"

"Mr. McCullough didn't tell you?" He stops only a few paces away. It feels too close.

"Tell me what?"

"Last week we got a truckload of cordwood delivered for your fireplaces. They dumped it out behind the garage?"

"I didn't notice that."

"Well, I'm here to stack it." He grins. "I guess *stacking* the firewood is above those guys' pay grade, but hey, it's a free cardio workout for me. Sorry I scared you—"

"I'm not scared."

"It'll take me one, maybe two hours, if you're okay with it?"

"Sure," I say. "Take your time."

ALLAN

I board the 12:35 ferry in Anacortes without having to wait more than fifteen minutes. On the car deck, I get out and zigzag through tightly packed vehicles to the stairs. A few people are sitting behind the wheels of their vehicles, reading, talking, or napping, but on this long crossing, most people go upstairs. I usually stay in my own car, but I need to pee, and I feel restless.

I go up to the passenger deck with its asbestos floor tiles and brown vinyl seats. The decor is trapped in the past, but there's no shortage of security cameras. They sprang up like mushrooms after 9/11, and they are everywhere. So are the metal fire stations.

There's a fire station outside the men's restroom, and when I emerge, I stop to look at it for a moment, not for the first time. It consists of a wall-hung white metal box, painted red inside, with a label that says *Fire Station 18.* Inside the box, a dingy folded fire hose and a red-bladed hatchet hang from metal brackets. Not behind glass. Right out in the open, where anyone could grab them.

I marvel at the orderliness of citizens who can have a sharp weapon like that within reach and manage never to use it. Admirable self-control.

★ ★ ★

On the island, I pass Deer Harbor Road about three miles north of the ferry dock and keep going. That road leads to my own house. To my wife. It feels strange to pass it by, but I have other things to deal with right now.

I drive up to Eastsound and cut east-southeast on the winding two-lane highway, through the trees and fields to Olga. I've never been to retired Sergeant Boyce's house, but I know exactly where it is because I looked it up on the Zillow real-estate map.

Olga is technically a town; it even has its own tiny post office. But it's really nothing but a scattering of small houses on a slope down to the water.

I park behind a hulking black Ford F-150 SuperCrew pickup in front of a small, well-maintained Craftsman bungalow. The house doesn't look like anything special. It's barely over a thousand square feet (according to Zillow), but I know that it's worth three quarters of a million dollars and, with that south-facing sea view just across the road, appreciating by the minute.

I haven't even gotten out of my car when the front door opens and Boyce comes out.

He walks out to meet me in the road, a tall beefy man in belted blue jeans and a plaid flannel shirt snug to his paunch. Spiky shock of gray hair. Basset-hound face and close-set eyes.

"Afternoon, McCullough," he says in his folksy way that, though consistent, I've always suspected is an act.

"Hi." I push on my sunglasses. I need a barrier between us.

"How about a stroll onto the beach." Not a question.

Since my eyes are hidden by my sunglasses, I give in to the urge to look up and down the street. The row of little houses is utterly quiet. Half of them probably aren't even inhabited at this time of year. No cars drive on the road. There is no sound at all except water slapping on the pebbles, the wind, and in the distance, the sustained groan of a boat engine.

Boyce chuckles. "Don't you worry, no one's watching. I have

to say, though, if you're looking to fly under the radar, buddy, that ain't the right car to do it in." He casts a contemptuous look at my Tesla. "A little too shiny and new."

"I could say the same." I look pointedly at the Ford F-150.

He smiles. It's a gloating smile. "The wife tried to convince me to buy some Japanese piece of shit, but I like to roll coal."

We both know I purchased the Ford—with all the upgrades—two years ago. But Boyce gets his jollies from doublespeak. He likes making me sweat, and then twisting the knife, and then making me sweat some more.

We walk across the road, through a strip of seagrass, and then we crunch down to the water's edge. Boyce squints out at the blue horizon. Wide stance. Folded, territorial arms. My blood pressure ticks upward.

"Why am I here, Boyce?" I ask. I know why, but it feels better to start off on the offensive. "Why did you call?"

"The way I see it, it doesn't matter who called who."

"Cut the crap."

"Now, that's no way to talk. Say, I hear your wife's on the island."

"How do you know that?"

"This is a tight-knit community. And the gals like to gossip."

"Sure," I say. *The gals*, my ass. Boyce and his buddies congregate every morning at Margie's Platter to trade rumors and get unlimited refills of coffee that tastes like boiled cardboard.

Boyce says, "Funny time for a trip to the island is what I thought. Most women would want to steer clear of a house right next door to a murder grave. But I guess pretty little Mrs. McCullough ain't like most women, is she?"

"Don't," I say. My jaw is so tight it aches.

Boyce gazes out at the water. "I've been thinking things through. Putting two and two together. And I'm thinking it's real innneresting that you dropped those charges against Greene Cooper for stealing one of your Indian artifacts and now, lo and behold, some poor girl is found buried with one of those very artifacts. Don't *you* think it's inneresting?"

"I think it looks like Greene Cooper isn't just a federal fugitive. It looks like he's a murderer."

"Maybe. Maybe not."

"What do you want?"

"My wife wants to go on one of them cruises. Down in the Caribbean. What can I do? Happy wife, happy life."

I feel Boyce's sidelong glance, but I will not look at him. Instead, I look at the water and think about how I should've gotten rid of him back when I had the chance. The craziest part of all this is, I have no idea what, exactly, he knows. Just that he knows *something.* Whatever that something is, he'll be holding it over my head until one of us is dead.

Well, I think, if this is what I'm here for, I'm going to get my money's worth.

I say, "What do they know about that body? The sheriff's office, I mean."

"You know I'm retired."

"I also know you shoot the shit at the diner with the boys who aren't retired."

"No one knows anything you can't read in the papers. And with you being so generous about my wife's cruise and all, I'm not about to enlighten anyone about anything."

"There's no connection between me and that farm."

"That's what you always say. But I remember how much you hated Garnock and his groupies. I remember how you couldn't hide your grin when you found out he was dead."

What I remember is standing in my yard with my back to the sea, looking to the east. Seeing orange sparks floating up into the dark sky. Smelling woodsmoke mingled with weed. Hearing cracks of gunfire. I remember people, insubstantial as ghosts, leaving footprints across my beach. "They were poaching on my land and constantly firing guns. They were lowering my property value."

"Seemed to me more like a dick-swinging contest between you and Garnock. And it was a contest you won, wasn't it? Nice and neat."

I explode. "Haven't I held up my end of the agreement? Haven't I paid and paid and paid every time you come asking for more?" I know this is the very nature of blackmail. It's quicksand. Once you're in, there's no getting out. I have considered killing Boyce, but I don't know what he's told his wife and buddies. I don't know what kind of dead man's switches he's rigged. Despite the plaid flannel and the folksy shit, he's a very smart guy.

"How much?" I say.

"Thirty."

"Some cruise."

"Well, the wife wants to take her mama. The old bitch will be ninety come February. She thought it would be nice to upgrade us to a couple of them balcony staterooms."

Like I said, Boyce enjoys digging the knife in deep and giving it a good twist.

I tell him I'll wire the thirty grand to his account, the same way we always do it.

"Naw." He's shaking his head. "I'm gonna be wanting cash this time."

"What?"

"Suppose you get arrested for murder—"

"What?" I say again. I sound like a fool.

Boyce lifts a big palm. "Hear me out, buddy. It was one thing to accept wire transfers from you back when it looked like all your dirty secrets were going to stay hidden. But now, with that dead girl, well, people are going to start digging through your shit. They'll look at your bank records. They'll look at everything. Matter of fact—" now he sounds sly "—I know the new detective from the sheriff's office is planning on paying you a visit. Little

Deb Haglund. She grew up here on the island, you know. She was the captain of the high-school cheerleading squad back in the day. Boy oh boy, you would've liked her the way she was back then."

I tell Boyce I'll get him the cash by Monday afternoon, and I leave him standing there on the beach.

THEN

GREENE

After that terrible night in the cabin, Greene talked back to things every chance he got. At first, he just told them to pipe down. It was such a relief to finally have some peace and quiet. But then he got curious about whether things might do other stuff besides pipe down.

When he was alone in the attic one day, he took his old Matchbox pickup truck, Fred, from his hiding place under the mattress. He sat on the floor and held Fred gently in his palm.

Fred started up with his usual sleepy murmurs about the claustrophobic conditions under the mattress.

Shush, Greene said, but kindly.

Fred fell silent.

You can hear me, Greene said.

There was a long pause. Then, *Yes.*

Why didn't you tell me you would listen? Greene asked. *Why didn't you tell me you could hear?*

You only wanted to listen, Fred said.

What else can you do? Greene asked.

I don't do anything. I just am.

Greene set Fred carefully on the wooden floor. *I want you to roll*, Greene said. *Please.*

Fred rolled on his wheels about an inch and came to a standstill.

Greene stared in disbelief. He couldn't have wiped the stupid grin off his face if you paid him.

Roll farther, Greene said. *Roll all the way across the room.*

Fred rolled slowly across the attic and stopped when his front bumper hit the far wall.

Now come back.

Fred turned around and came back.

Thank you, Greene said. *You're remarkable.*

Greene trained Fred and Beauty like they were clever pets. He could ask them to roll on their wheels but also to lift themselves into the air like bumblebees and fly.

He moved on to other things. Soon, he could make firewood stack itself into a pile. He could open and shut the garden gate not by lifting the latch but just by asking. He could move the hand pump with a whispered request. He never had to bend over and tie his shoelaces.

He imagined an invisible, complicated spiderweb that connected all the things and creatures and plants of the world to each other. Everyone and everything was kin. But what made Greene different, he thought, was that he was the only one who was paying attention to this fact.

Kestrel was the only one he showed. He knew anyone else would think he was crazy, or even dangerous. When only Kestrel was looking, he would make her fork and spoon undulate like soft clay and dance in the air. He would make the illustrations in a book or the photographs in some old magazine rearrange themselves to tell new stories, to show different faces.

Kestrel would laugh. "How do you *do* that?" she'd ask with a grin. She never acted like there was anything spooky about it.

She seemed to take it for granted that the world's things were Greene's puppets, and she was his audience of one.

One evening when Greene was thirteen, Uncle was gripping his fork and knife too tightly at supper time. Greene noticed how his finger joints looked white through his weird gold skin. How he chewed his venison and dumplings rapidly, his black-dot eyes fixed high on the wall.

The conversation at the table tiptoed around Uncle and his churning mood. No one looked at him directly, but Greene felt how everyone's peripheral vision was keeping track of him all the same. Something was coming. When Uncle got like this, it never just blew over. He had to erupt.

Eldest, as beautiful and aloof as a princess, sat at the foot of the table. As soon as she'd turned sixteen two months earlier, she'd taken the place of Star there. Eldest was Uncle's wife now, because Uncle said sixteen was the age that females were ready for reproduction. Eldest liked to brag that she was Uncle's favorite wife because she was the only one who shared his bedroom. Greene didn't think that was anything to brag about. He knew for a fact that Eldest had to cut Uncle's toenails.

Not that Eldest complained about the toenails, or the bed-sharing, or the way Uncle kissed her on the mouth in front of everybody else. It was like the real Eldest, the girl she was before Uncle started doing things to her, was buried down deep. She never smiled anymore, except to Uncle. And Greene could tell even those smiles were fake because they didn't reach her eyes. She'd nod for Uncle, smile for Uncle, say *yes* to Uncle, but her eyes had gone empty.

"I miss her," Kestrel told Greene. "I miss how she was before we came here. She used to be so funny. And we'd play together with LEGO for hours."

"Yeah," Greene said. His throat ached for Kestrel, and also

because he knew exactly what she meant. He missed Mom every day even though she was always nearby.

Kestrel said that she'd tried to talk to Eldest about what was going on, to ask if she was okay, to talk to her about how she might be able to get out of what Uncle called *a wife's duty*, and Eldest had gotten so angry that she'd started to shake. *Mind your own business*, Eldest had said. *And stay away from Uncle.*

Greene laughed bitterly at that. "Like you'd want to go anywhere near him," he said to Kestrel.

"I'm not sure that's what she meant," Kestrel replied, which made no sense to Greene.

Greene read a lot. Anything he could get his hands on. He didn't have access to a library or a bookstore, but with newcomers to the Farm came reading material. Trashy novels, Zen writings, dog-eared paperback Dickens, Tolstoy, Kerouac, ragged issues of *Smithsonian* and *Newsweek*. He knew from his reading that young women, very young women, married much older men. Woody Allen's daughter-wife. Movie-star couples. Esther getting engaged to her old benefactor in *Bleak House*. Even people out in the real world thought it was okay.

But when Greene watched Uncle touching Eldest, Greene knew, deep in his bones, that it was wrong. He didn't even *like* Eldest: she'd always been aloof toward him, always hoping to get him in trouble. Yet he still couldn't stand the sight of Uncle's probing fingers in her wavy golden hair.

Star, with her toddler son, Guide, on her lap, sat on Uncle's right. Mom was still on Uncle's left. Tansy, with her newborn son, Littlest, wrapped close to her chest, sat in a chair against the wall, away from everyone else. She'd finally given birth to another child, and although he looked like Uncle with his golden skin, fair hair, and dark eyes, he'd been born with a red birthmark like a slap print on one cheek. Uncle said the baby was a monster, and that there had to be something wrong with Tansy to have produced such a thing. He said she should've drowned it in a bucket.

Uncle's fork and knife clattered onto his plate.

Silence ballooned. The oil-lamp flame flickered for no reason.

"Didn't any of you notice what happened past the western boundary of our land today?" Uncle said. He looked around, hostile and expectant. "Or are all of you going to go along as though nothing's wrong?"

A middle-aged, stooped man called Jacob lifted a tentative hand. Jacob was distinguished among the Kinfolk for crafting dozens of misshapen blue pottery mugs, which they sold at their farmers-market stall alongside the produce. "I noticed something," he said. "I was loading up some firewood over there. I heard—I saw—what's going on."

"And you didn't think it was important enough to mention?"

"I didn't—"

"Please." Uncle only ever said *please* in a sarcastic tone. "If it doesn't interfere too much with stuffing your face, tell your kinfolk what you saw."

Jacob swallowed with apparent difficulty. He looked around the lamplit circle of faces. "Well, it looks like construction is starting on the next parcel over. They're excavating for a foundation. They're going to build a palace, whoever it—"

"It's Allan McCullough," Uncle said. "Allan McCullough is building that house. He's some kind of businessman down in Seattle. A capitalist with delusions of grandeur. Someone who never did a real day's work in his life."

What that meant was *McCullough wasn't a real man.* Greene had heard this mantra often. Real men worked with their hands. Bureaucrats, intellectuals, and capitalists, Uncle said, may as well have had their nuts cut off.

"He came to see me," Uncle said. "He had a check in his hand. He wanted to buy this farm right out from under us. It's a deliberate provocation!" Uncle slammed his fist on the tabletop and made the dishes jump.

Uncle thought lots of things were deliberate provocations, but the truth was the Kinfolk, at least, lived in dread of provoking him even by accident.

"He doesn't want to buy this land," Uncle said. "He wants to wage war. Well, he's messing with the wrong people, isn't he?"

The grown-ups nodded and murmured.

"Men," Uncle said, "be prepared to defend our precious home at any time of the day or night."

Greene stayed silent and kept his head down, just like Kestrel beside him. But he was curious about the construction. It was as though the real world had at last butted up against the Farm.

He made up his mind to ask Kestrel if she wanted to go and spy on this McCullough guy's house.

Greene and Kestrel had already been venturing farther and farther afield. They had a droopy old JanSport backpack that hung on a hook in the goat barn. That backpack was everything to them. When they knew they'd be able to escape for an afternoon without anyone noticing, they would, little by little, stash food and mason jars of water in the backpack. They kept a bandanna for an emergency bandage in the backpack, and a notebook and a pencil. They even had matches in there, in a little aluminum cylinder someone had left when they moved away from the Farm. They kept their provisions hidden because if anyone found out how far away from the Farm they strayed, there would be hell to pay.

It was worth the risk. At the Farm, they had to act serious and always look like they were working. Out there, they could laugh and let loose and just be kids. They could be themselves.

They would scale the cliff down to the beach and walk and walk, goofing around and skipping flat stones and lying in the sun. If the tide was high, parts of the beach were covered up and the sea went right up to the base of the cliff. Then they needed to run across people's yards at the top of the cliff to get past.

The only person who ever saw them as they streaked by was a woman who lived in a tiny house with a rusted steel roof. She had dark brown skin and a puff of gray hair and an outbuilding with a kiln and racks of pottery.

"Hello," she would call, waving her hand.

They always dashed into the undergrowth without replying. It was like being called to from across a canyon.

The first time Greene and Kestrel went to see where the mysterious businessman, McCullough, was building his house, there wasn't much to see, just piles of cleared brush and Douglas firs, backhoes, and big muddy pits in the ground. But they got into the habit of making a detour to check the progress of the construction every time they set out on an excursion.

After a while, they saw concrete mixers operated by men in baseball caps and dirty pants. Then stacks of steel beams and shipping-container storage units. Still later, the house started going up, too close to the cliff for Greene's liking, a collection of boxlike forms, some lengthwise and some on end, arranged in a crooked pile.

The house was restless. It seemed hungry.

One day, as he and Kestrel walked toward the construction site, a vehicle approached along the newly built driveway, its engine humming. Greene and Kestrel crouched without needing to discuss it, like two well-trained spies.

They watched, their breathing synchronized, as a large black vehicle passed. Only a little mud flecked its wheel wells, so it wasn't an island car. Silver letters on the back said *Lexus*.

"Who's that?" Kestrel whispered.

"Maybe the architect or something? Or maybe it's..." Greene stood, his heart pumping. "Let's go see. Maybe it's *McCullough*."

"Dirty capitalist," Kestrel said in a low, sinister voice, mocking Uncle.

They both laughed.

To see McCullough would be cool. After all the talk at the Farm about this guy for *months*...it would be like sighting Bigfoot.

They stopped behind the salal at the edge of the construction site. The Lexus had parked.

Two men came out the front. One taller and rounder, one shorter and totally bald. Both of them wore jeans, jackets, and sunglasses, looking too clean and pressed for the woods.

"Which one do you think is McCullough?" Kestrel whispered.

"Dunno." Greene grinned. "'Cause they both look like goddamn bureaucratic eunuchs."

From the back of the Lexus came, first, a small thin woman with sunglasses, a long black ponytail, and high-heeled boots. She slammed her door shut with, it seemed, all the force in her wiry body. She went to stand with the two men in a tight cluster, all of them looking besieged by the towering wet green all around them.

Finally, a pair of legs swung out of the car. Little feet in red cowboy boots, skinny legs in blue jeans—someone hopped out. A dark-haired boy, not as young as his knobby knees at first had suggested, but *their* age. Twelve or thirteen.

"*He* has sunglasses, too?" Kestrel whispered, her voice bubbling with mirth. "Oh my God."

Greene scoffed laughingly, as he knew Kestrel expected, but he was kind of pretending. Because the boy down there in the sunglasses and the red boots wasn't laughable so much as fascinating. He stood out against all the murky browns and greens like a visitor from another galaxy.

The boy slammed his door shut with his whole body, just

like the woman—his mom, Greene figured—had done. The sound spliced the air.

He turned his face up to their hiding place.

Greene's breath caught, and Kestrel shrank back.

The boy's lips parted slightly. He raised his sunglasses to forehead level. He was pink-cheeked and glossy-haired, with round eyes that tapered to points at their outer corners.

He looked right at Greene, although Greene was sure the other boy couldn't *really* see him through the leafy screen of salal. "Hey!" the boy called. Accusingly. Pompously.

Greene and Kestrel crouch-waddled backward until they were out of the boy's sight. Then they straightened and ran away down the path, laughing so hard together.

NOW

CAROLINE

On Saturday, I rush through cleaning the Finches' vulgar log cabin–style mansion. When I am done, I load my supplies into my Honda and start driving toward Deer Harbor.

After a few miles, I hear a voice, silky and soft, but so persistent. It is coming from my purse, which is on the passenger seat beside me.

Oh, Lord, I pray. *Oh, dear Jesus, please deliver me.*

The voice grows louder.

—want to smash it smash it pry it smash—

I know I should throw that thing into a dumpster or toss it off the ferry, like a pure Christian woman who smites the Devil when she recognizes him.

But how can I tell the difference between the voice of Satan and the voice of God?

When I round the last bend in the McCulloughs' driveway, Trey's Jeep Cherokee is parked there.

No, I think, slamming my foot on the brake, pitching myself forward against my seat belt and back. Please, Lord, no. If I see them together and they are—no. I can't bear it.

Why would a godly man like Trey wallow in such filth? Mrs. McCullough is not a believer—no, that does not even begin to describe how disgusting she is, and my Trey, my Treyson Paul Higgins, he—he—

I jam the gears into Reverse and accelerate backward along the winding driveway.

HANNAH

By two o'clock, Oliver and Sibley still haven't come inside for lunch. Their chicken nuggets have gone cold on the kitchen island. Their apple slices have turned brown.

I put on sneakers and a sweatshirt and go outside to find them.

I tell myself they're just so engrossed in their playing that they forgot the time. They're probably building a fort.

I look everywhere. I start with the garage, the woodshop, the house's immediate vicinity, but don't find them. Trey's Jeep is gone, and I see the firewood stacked along the back of the garage.

I go down the cliff stairs to the beach. No kids, and no fresh footprints in the sand, either. I go back up the stairs, and I start shouting their names.

I cross the driveway and enter the forest where I've seen them coming and going several times. An almost invisible track goes through the underbrush. A deer path, I think, the moss and mud worn down by dainty hooves. It crosses spongy ground, past cedars and firs and through bare alder thickets, the ferns and salal impossibly green.

I realize that although the track seems meandering, the general trajectory is to the east. Toward the Kinfolk Farm.

As I go, I shout their names, but they don't answer. I keep my eyes on the trail so I won't trip. I strain my ears. Where are they? They wouldn't have gone to the vacant lot next door, would they? Not to that grave?

Then I hear something. It comes from ahead of me. I quicken my pace, shouting, "Sibley! Oliver!"

The trail straightens out, and I see a small figure up ahead.

"Sibley!" I shout.

"Mama!" she says on a sob, half walking, half stumbling toward me. Her gait is jerky, puppetlike, wrong. There's something red on her cheek and on her pink puffer jacket. Wrong, wrong, wrong.

My mind slows to a sluggish underwater crawl, but there is a shriek in my ears. Or is the shriek coming out of me? I feel my arms pumping and my legs jogging but, like in a nightmare, I'm not making much progress toward my daughter. My bleeding, sobbing daughter—

Then somehow I'm with her, tilting her face gently up to the meager light of the sky. Her glasses are gone. Her eyes are scrunched tight, tears drip swiftly, and there is a hole, a big bleeding *hole* in her smooth, round, little-girl cheek—

The earth bucks under my feet. I force an exhale. Keep it together, I tell myself. Keep it together for your child.

A round, quarter-sized rupture blooms scarlet on her cheek. Thick dark rivulets of blood drip down her jaw. Her jacket is garishly smeared, and her lips are bloody, too.

"We have to get you to the doctor," I say. I'm stripping off my sweatshirt. "I'll give you a piggyback. You press this on the—on your cheek. Okay? It's going to be all right, honey. It's going to be all right."

I push the balled-up sweatshirt into Sibley's hand, push it to the hole in her cheek—

She'll be disfigured, I'm thinking, her beautiful face ruined—

—and I crouch, one fist to the dirt, and Sibley, sobbing, climbs onto my back and wraps an arm around my neck, holding too tightly at my throat as she always does. I stand up, my legs buckling slightly under her sixty-five pounds, hook my arms under her knees, and leaning forward, breathing hard, I walk as fast as I can back toward the house.

Now that I have a mission—get to the house, get my purse and car keys, drive to the clinic in Eastsound—I don't have to think about anything else. Only about these steps, these essential steps.

I feel something dim and ugly loping behind me. Something from the past.

We're in the Range Rover and jostling down the driveway when I see Oliver waist-deep in salal at the edge of the forest. Shirtless, barefoot, dirt-smeared, with a sharpened stick hanging from his hand.

I see him, see the stick, see the unfathomable sheen in his dark eyes, and I don't slow down, I don't even wave. I keep going.

I leave him back there, my first baby. I leave him alone in the dark.

When we reach the clinic, I have no recollection of the eleven-mile drive. I carry Sibley inside like a toddler, and the receptionist's eyes widen at the sight of all the blood.

There's a white room, and a doctor snapping on gloves and flipping on a searing light, and only when he asks me what happened as he examines Sibley do I realize I haven't asked Sibley that question.

"I—I don't know," I say, my voice tremulous.

"It was a stick," Sibley whispers tearfully. "A sharp stick. It hurts *so bad*."

The shriek starts up again in my ears.

I say, "Did Oliver—"

The doctor—the ID badge on his lanyard says *Dr. Chadha*—gives me a sharp look. "Who's Oliver?"

"Her brother. But he didn't..." I look away.

This is my fault. What kind of mother leaves her daughter alone with a kid like Oliver, a kid who was just suspended from school for biting another child's cheek?

I have failed Sibley. I have failed Oliver, too, because now Sibley and Oliver's relationship is beyond repair.

Probably my own relationship with Oliver is, too.

And Allan, oh God, when Allan finds out—

"We don't usually stitch or even tape puncture wounds," Dr. Chadha is saying. "They're deep so it's easy to trap bacteria inside, which would lead to infection—"

"But she'll have a *scar* if we—"

"She'll have a scar regardless. And if infection sets in, any scarring could become much worse. I'm going to clean it up, make sure there isn't any foreign material in there, and then we'll—"

"But she has a hole in her cheek!" I say, talking over him. "Are you sure you're qualified to make these kinds of decisions? Is there another doctor here? Someone who's—"

"I'm the only doctor here, Mrs. McCullough."

Wait, I think foggily, how does he know I'm Mrs. McCullough? Was it the— Oh, right. The receptionist made me turn over my insurance card.

"And I understand you're upset. I'm here to give your child the best care I can, all right?"

I hesitate, all the fight, all the spoiled-Huxley-School-mom bravado draining out of me. "Yes," I say. "Yes. I'm sorry. I—"

"No need to apologize."

A battered blue Honda is parked in the driveway when we arrive back at the house an hour later. The front door is wide open.

Dread wraps, lazy and cold, around my innards.

Then I recognize the car—it belongs to that strange house

cleaner. I forgot all about her saying she'd come back to finish the house. Why on earth has she come so late on a Saturday?

At the clinic, the doctor prescribed Sibley a painkiller and administered the first dose, fruit-punch-red syrup in a little plastic cup. She fell almost instantly to sleep in the car and she isn't waking up, so I carry her inside. My muscles are getting tired.

"Hello?" I call.

The kitchen island is strewn with an open bag of sliced bread, an open jar of peanut butter, and a box of granola on its side. A carton of milk sits beside the sink. The milk carton's cap is on the floor.

Oliver has been here for food, then. Whether he's in or out now, I can't guess.

A vacuum cleaner turns on somewhere in the north wing of the house.

I gently lay Sibley on my own bed, pull off her boots, and fold the duvet over her little body. As much as I hate the sight of the blood-caked jacket, I can't take it off now without risking waking her.

I leave the bedroom door ajar so I'll hear if Sibley calls for me, and I look for Oliver.

He isn't in his bedroom or the unused guest rooms, nor in any of the living spaces. I check the pantry and the laundry room and then venture into the north wing.

The cleaning woman is vacuuming Allan's study. Because of the noise she doesn't hear me.

I go outside to the driveway and make a slow, circular scan. The setting sun is a copper blob behind the tree trunks to the southwest. The sea is a winey purple, and the undergrowth of the forest black.

There are no lights on in the garage or the woodshop, but that doesn't mean Oliver isn't in there.

I go into the garage by way of the side door, switching on the overhead. No Oliver.

He isn't in the woodshop, either. But lined up in a neat row on the workbench are two or three dozen sharpened sticks.

Each is about two feet long, with the bark still on, each sharpened to a point that makes my own cheek cry out in imagined pain.

I back away from the sticks. I flick off the light and shut the door. I try to remember where I put the woodshop key. What was I thinking, letting Oliver use a knife? Letting him make his own wooden weapons by the dozen, carved to points sharp enough to puncture flesh? A kid who's been seeing a shrink since he was four? A *violent* kid?

Outside, the tree boughs ripple like sea creatures.

"I have to go look for my son," I tell the house cleaner.

She switches off the vacuum and looks at me through those distorting lenses of hers. "Your son," she repeats.

"Yes. It's getting dark, and he hasn't come back. I think he might've gotten lost. The thing is, my daughter is asleep, and so I was just wondering if it'd be okay if I left you in charge of her. She...she's injured. She probably won't wake up. She took a pretty strong painkiller. I'll only be gone for a few minutes."

The house cleaner shrugs. "Sure," she says and switches the vacuum back on.

I find the emergency flashlight in a pantry drawer and go outside again. It's getting darker and colder with each passing moment, and it's starting to drizzle.

I go to the same deer track I was on earlier, the one where I found Sibley. I switch on the flashlight, and its beam shoots out, whitening the corrugated tree trunks.

The undergrowth is so dense Oliver would have to keep to paths like this or else be netted by thickets. Unless he went down to the beach?

My fury at Oliver for hurting Sibley is replaced by the vision of a boy's skinny corpse bobbing face down in a tide pool—

Check this path first, I tell myself. Then the beach. One thing at a time. One foot in front of the other.

The path winds through the forest, and after about five minutes of steady plodding I find myself out in the open and across a ditch from the Kinfolk Farm's driveway.

I stop. I'm breathing hard, and I can taste my own sweat. My ankles, bare between the tops of my sneakers and the hems of my jeans, ache with cold.

I run the flashlight beam slowly down and up the driveway. No child.

Next, I aim the flashlight across the road. At the overgrown split-rail fence, the sagging outbuildings, the farmhouse whose blown-out windows gape, its siding like a silvery photo negative under the white beam. I move the beam away from the house, but then quickly back again because the house's front door stands open, a black rectangular void. The high wet grass in front of the house has a part in it, leading straight to the sagging porch.

I consider shouting for Oliver. I could stay right here in my imaginary safe zone on the far side of this ditch. But he never comes when he is called.

I force myself forward. Over the ditch, across the road, through the broken gate, and along the path in the grass to the front door.

CAROLINE

I find the girl sleeping. In the lamplight, the white gauze on her cheek seems to glow.

I go silently closer. I bend over her, reach out. I pick at the edge of the medical tape holding the gauze in place. I can see the pink of blood seeping through.

She moans and flips her head the other way, then back.

I pick at the tape some more. She moans again but doesn't open her eyes. Once the tape is loose, I lift the gauze. Underneath is a clotted, meaty wound.

I have calmed down since I fled from the sight of Trey's Jeep in the driveway. I looked to Him for guidance, and now I am serene.

This will make her go away, I think as I peer into the wound. This will make the whore and her dirty spawn run away and never come back.

The girl takes a long inhale, and her eyelids flutter. She is waking up.

I stick the tape back down on her cheek, hard.

Her eyes fly open, and when she sees me, she grimaces with fear. "Mommy," she whispers. "Where's Mommy?"

"Mommy left," I say and enjoy the crumpling of her face, which is so much like her mother's.

"I think you're mean."

"And I think you're spoiled."

"You're the witch," she whispers. Her pupils are shrunken from the pain medicine. "You're the witch, and I want Mommy." She starts to cry.

ALLAN

Dr. Chadha at the clinic in Eastsound leaves me a voicemail while I'm on the ferry, but I don't pick it up until I'm back on the mainland and driving on I-5 south toward Seattle.

It takes three listens for it to fully sink in. Sibley is injured. My wife seems distraught. Something about Sibley's brother and a sharp stick.

Then I smile. Naturally, I think it's terrible that Sibley has gotten hurt. But children heal, and if it doesn't heal optimally, I happen to play golf with the best plastic surgeon in the state.

I'm smiling because now I'm holding all the aces in this little game with Hannah. I can tell her how any judge in the land would rule that she isn't fit to have sole custody of the children in the event of a divorce.

Hannah will relent. We'll go back to the way things were before, when Hannah was so mild and malleable. When she didn't talk back. Only it'll be even better than before, because she'll have no choice but to send Oliver to Montana after this. Even though the doctor was mincing words, of *course* it was Oliver who hurt Sibley. That creepy kid will finally be out of the picture.

What it all means is... I won.

HANNAH

My flashlight beam licks peeling paint and dust-scummed glass. Through the open doorway, I see a newel post and sagging stair treads.

I force myself to step across the threshold into the entry hall. It smells dank and sweet and rotten. The staircase creeps upward into blackness.

There is a sound overhead. Not the creak of a floorboard or the fall of a foot. Just...something.

"Oliver?" I whisper. I can't bear to raise my voice in this place.

I go up. Placing each foot carefully, crunching on fallen plaster. At the top I skirt the flashlight beam over the long hallway.

There, again: a sound. This time like a snuffle. The third door stands ajar, so I go to the doorway. The room is lit faintly by a window. It appears to be empty except for what looks like a bundle of rags in the corner.

I'm turning away, thinking the snuffle hadn't come from this room after all, when I hear a breath. It came from the rags in the corner.

"Oliver?" I whisper again.

The rags shift.

It isn't a bundle of rags, but Oliver, lying in the fetal position, facing the corner. The bare, fair skin of his back looks iridescent under the flashlight's beam.

I switch off the flashlight. "Oliver," I whisper. "Are you hurt?"

No answer.

I go to his side and crouch. Through the darkness I see the rise and fall of his breathing. He snuffles again. He's been crying. "Talk to me," I say.

"Don't want to." This is mumbled against his arm.

"Why?"

"You think everything's my fault."

"What is?"

"Stop trying to trick me into saying something. Do you think I'm stupid?"

"Okay, fine. Then just tell me what you did."

"What do you mean?"

"What did you do? To Sibley?"

"I didn't do anything to Sibley. She's such a *crybaby*."

Rage shoots through me, so molten-fast it makes me dizzy. "How could you *say*—" I take a deep breath. I say quietly, firmly, "Give me the knife."

"What knife?"

"The knife you use to sharpen the sticks."

"It's in the woodshop."

"Why did you do it?" I hear the pitch of my voice edging up.

"Do what? I don't even know what you're talking about!"

"Sibley's cheek." A vision of the gory red hole rises up, and I swallow.

Oliver snorts. "She got hurt, so you blame me? You never loved me. You pretend to, but you don't really." A pause. "You think I'm like him."

"Like who?" I know who.

"*Him*. My dad."

"You mean Daddy?"

"Quit pretending! I *know*, Hannah—"

"Mama—"

"*Hannah!* Stop it! I know! Do you think I don't remember anything? I remember a lot. Patti's helping me remember. When I was little, I thought I was just, like, making stuff up. Like imaginary friends, or maybe like I was crazy. Because you never talk about those people. The people from before. But I remember them. And I remember this room. This was where my bed was, in this corner." His voice cracks. "I remember my mom. My *real* mom." He turns his eyes for the first time up to me, and in the poor light they are shiny black orbs.

His father's eyes. Uncle's.

Revulsion bucks me slightly back, and then I feel ashamed, and I try to lean toward Oliver again. But I can't.

"What happened to her?" he whispers. "To our mom?"

"Oliver, I want you to know that everything I did, I did it for you—"

"Stop lying! You did it for yourself! For yourself and Sibley! She's your *real* baby, she's the one you really care about, and I'm just—just—"

"You're my *brother*, Littlest." His true name falls like a silvery charm from my lips. "My baby brother. You were my first baby. I took care of you even when you were a newborn. I fed you goat's milk in a tiny cup because Mama couldn't nurse you, and I lay beside your little basket so when you woke up in the night you wouldn't need to cry. Please believe me. I did everything—*everything*—for you. I love you." I lift my hand tentatively and touch his bare shoulder.

He jerks away. He is repulsed by me, too. Both of us are a reminder to the other of our lives before. Of the badness before.

"I don't believe you," Oliver says. "I *don't*. How can you love me if you're pretending you don't even know who I am?"

"I do love you. I loved you since the day you were born."

"You just p-put up with m-me, and Allan wants to send me away to Mont-tana a-and—I want my mom. I just want *Mama*." Tears spill down his cheeks. He hacks out an awful, guttural sob.

Before today, I would've promised anything to this weeping boy. But he hurt my baby, my Sibley, and my heart has hardened against him.

Allan is right: there is something terribly wrong with Oliver, something that even the most devoted older sister can't fix. What a fool I was to leave Sibley alone with Oliver. Oliver, who's been sharpening sticks for the past three days. Oliver, who bit another child's cheek. Oliver, my daughter's disturbed, violent little uncle.

My mistake, I suddenly realize, *has* been pretending, just as Oliver says. Looking the other way. Denying to myself and to everyone else that the past ran its terrible course.

Pretending is how we've survived all these years, like prey camouflaging itself to grasses and rocks. Hiding. Hoping to be spared. But pretending is destroying us.

"I'm sorry," I say to Oliver. "No more pretending, okay? No more pretending."

"You have to listen to us."

"What do you… *Us?*"

"Sibley and me. We tell you stuff, but you never listen."

I bristle at his mention of the girl he has wounded and probably disfigured. "What are you talking about?" I barely recognize my own voice, it is so cold.

"Like about the witch."

"The witch," I say flatly.

"We saw her in the woods. She talked to us, she said mean stuff, and then she— You hired her to clean our house? That is so *stupid*."

"Wait," I say. "The witch is…the house cleaner is the witch?"

"Yeah."

"She talked to you in the woods?"

"She's from here, Hannah."

"From the island?"

"No. From *here*. From the Farm. She's from before."

No, I think. No, no, no.

Oliver says, "I remember her. And she's *so mean*."

Oh my God. There was something creepy about that woman, but I didn't realize… Could it be? Could she, under that thick layer of flesh, those glasses, that shapeless clothing…could she be… Did I leave my Sibley in the care of spiteful Caroline Cooper?

"We have to go, Oliver. Come on. Let's get up." I scramble to my feet, my motions drunken with fear.

For an agonizing moment, Oliver doesn't move. I'm wondering if I have the strength to carry him when he sits up.

"Come on," I repeat. "We have to hurry. Sibley is—"

"Then why don't you just leave!" Oliver shouts.

"No. I'm not leaving you here."

He gets to his knees and then to his feet. We go down the stairs and out of that broken house.

Then I start running.

THEN

GREENE

On a warm September day, a man named Felix showed up at the Farm on a mud-crusted motorbike and asked if he could stay. Uncle said *yes*, but that Felix had to sleep in the goat-barn loft. Felix laughed, saying that was exactly the kind of thing he'd been hoping for.

Greene saw the womenfolk watching out the kitchen window as Felix rolled wheelbarrows of stuff around, readying his loft. He wore a dingy white undershirt without sleeves, showing the rounded bulk of his brown shoulders. Mom pursed her lips and said something about Felix certainly being self-confident. Eldest and Tansy watched Felix with the silent raptness of deer hunters.

Felix told everyone that on his Nez Perce side he was descended from chiefs, and on the other side he was Swedish thunder god. He said this with a dazzling smile, so you couldn't even hold it against him. He was nice, Greene thought, but Uncle didn't like him one bit. Greene knew Felix's days at the Farm were numbered. He'd seen it before. Uncle was a rooster, jealously patrolling his henhouse.

Five months later, in February, Tansy left with Felix and never came back.

They left without warning before dawn one day, picked up, everyone figured, in a vehicle they'd arranged beforehand. They left notes, written in Tansy's handwriting but signed by Felix, too. They said they were in love and that they needed to make a fresh start.

Tansy left all four of her children behind: Eldest, Kestrel, Quill, Littlest. Uncle said she was a whore without natural maternal feeling. Then he never spoke of her again, and so no one else did, either.

One afternoon that April, Greene found Kestrel mucking out the goat barn and asked her if she'd like to go for a walk to the beach like they used to. He said he had someplace to show her.

Kestrel paused her muckrake. "Tricks?" she asked darkly.

She was sixteen now, and her attitude had changed toward Greene and what he could do with things. She'd started calling it *tricks*, and she made it sound dirty. She didn't want to see it anymore. She didn't want Greene to mention it. Greene wasn't sure if it was because of her mother leaving, or something else.

"Not tricks," Greene said, trying not to sound hurt. "Just... a place."

"Can Littlest come?"

This was another change since Tansy left: now, Kestrel rarely went anywhere without Littlest. He was always on her lap or clinging to her legs or riding on her hip, even though at three he was too big for that. But Kestrel was tall and strong and, more importantly, unwilling to let him out of her sight, especially now that he was being potty-trained.

When she held him, she would brush her lips in his fuzzy wafting blond hair. His chubby little hand would rest lightly on her collarbone. He would bury his round, red-mottled cheek against her breast, eyelids heavy. The only time Littlest wasn't whiny and wandering aimlessly around with a rock or a stick or a crust of bread was when he was in Kestrel's arms. You would've thought they were mother and child, except, God, how young of a mother would she have had to be?

Greene said to Kestrel, "It's probably not a good idea for him to come. It's kind of a hike."

She glanced out into the barnyard. Eldest was feeding the goats with Quill. Littlest, in a sweater, a cloth diaper, and bare feet, was squatting next to a puddle and poking in the mud with a stick. Wolf, the Farm's new big bushy gray mongrel, sat next to Littlest, slowly panting and watching the progress of the stick with interest.

"It's okay," Greene said. "You don't have to be with them every second of the day."

"I just... I worry about them. Both of them."

"I know. But they're fine. And Wolf is like Littlest's guardian angel."

They both looked at Littlest and how the red birthmark on his cheek stood out bright and alarming in the sunlight. They watched as Eldest, in her long faded floral dress, went over to Littlest, scooped him up, and kissed him.

Kestrel said, "Your mom—she slapped him yesterday, and Uncle *laughed*..." She sounded close to tears.

"Eldest has him," Greene said. "She'll keep him safe."

Eldest was now cradling Littlest and swaying back and forth, her skirts swishing, singing to him in a low voice. Littlest didn't cling to Eldest the way he did to Kestrel, but Eldest had always been protective of both of her half brothers.

"Please," Greene said to Kestrel. "Just one hike."

"No," Kestrel said and turned back to her mucking.

Since Kestrel didn't want to go for a walk, Greene took his axe and a cart and went out to cut firewood alongside the south path. At Uncle's direction he frequently cut trees on Allan McCullough's property, but today he was on Kinfolk Farm property—if only just—because McCullough was on the island.

The day was warming up, and hurtling the axe into the rock-hard fir wood, again and again, was making Greene sweaty. He could've told the axe to do most of the work, but he liked the exercise. He straightened, resting the axe-head on his boot, and wiped his face with his T-shirt. Then he heard rhythmic thumping from farther up the trail.

Someone's running, he thought. Is there an emergency? Is it Kestrel, or—

A person appeared from around the bend in the trail. A stranger, a slim boy about Greene's age, with fair skin and dark hair, arms pumping and feet thudding. He saw Greene, cried out, and came to a stumbling stop.

"Oh my *God*!" the boy shouted. "Jesus! You almost made me—" He didn't finish. He'd seen Greene's axe. "Oh." He was panting. "What are you—"

"I'm cutting wood," Greene said. "Not chopping up dead bodies, in case that's what your problem is. And you're on private property."

"Excuse me? *I'm* on private property?"

"Yep." Greene pointed. "See the red stripe painted on that tree? That's the boundary marker."

The boy looked slightly deflated. "Oh." He was wearing black shorts, a bright pink tank top, and new-looking running shoes. The clothes and shoes were constructed of silky, plasticky fabrics that to Greene seemed exotic. "How do I know you're not, like, some sick, crazy murderer?"

"What would I be doing out here in the woods if I were?"

"That's a stupid question." The boy tossed the dark hank of hair that swept across his forehead, and Greene realized he was the boy with the red cowboy boots he'd seen years ago, getting out of McCullough's car. "Obviously, you're lying in wait for a victim."

"You must be new here."

"What's that supposed to mean?"

"Number one, I live right over there—" Greene jerked his thumb in the direction of the Farm "—and I go on this trail at least once a week. And number two, if someone wanted to prey on people, they wouldn't do it on this trail because this trail averages zero users per month. Not counting me and other Farm people, that is."

"What are you even— Oh. Right. The *Farm*." The boy's lips curved in a sardonic smile. "I know about you guys. It's, like, a commune? Or—wait—isn't it a cult?"

"Why not both?"

"So you worship your holy leader Uncle, and he has, like, six wives? How do *you* figure into that math, by the way? And you guys just *love* your guns. Wait—do *you* have a gun?" The boy's eyes flicked around, as though searching for firearms. "You guys have to do target practice every day, right?"

"Who told you that? Your dad?"

"Excuse me?"

"You're Allan McCullough's son."

The boy's eyes flared. They were beautiful eyes, with glossy, chestnut-brown irises. "I don't need to be *told* about the guns—I can freaking hear them, like, *all* the time. Anyway, my dad and I don't really talk, unless you count his constant lectures on how I'm wasting my life and destroying my future. But you can hear a ton of gossip about you and your *kinfolk* at the ice-cream shop in Eastsound. Anyway..." He glanced at his turquoise wristwatch.

"By all means." Greene gestured down the trail. "Don't let a mere peasant like me waylay you from your purpose, my liege."

The boy snorted, but he also looked pleased to be called *my liege*.

That's the version of himself he likes, Greene thought. The feudal-lord version.

"Do you...want to come to my house for a beverage?" the boy asked.

"What?" Greene was sure he'd misheard him.

"For a cold drink? Because you're all sweaty?"

"Oh." Greene squinted down the trail in the direction of the

Farm. It felt impossible that he could say yes. It felt like being tendered an invitation from a space alien. On the other hand, why the heck shouldn't he? He was seventeen years old, for crying out loud. "Yeah," he said. "Okay."

He stowed the axe in the cart and started walking with the boy through the trees.

"I'm Josh, by the way," the boy said.

"Greene."

Greene and Kestrel had been spying on McCullough's house for years, but only from the periphery. It felt strange to walk down the middle of his driveway and go through the front door.

He followed Josh down a concrete-floored passage with glass walls, into a kitchen in which neither food nor cooking tools were visible. The kitchen opened out to a dining room and a sunken living space with soaring ceilings, scant, low furniture, and walls of windows overlooking the sea.

"It sucks being in this house with my dad," Josh said, opening the refrigerator. "It's like being locked in a room with, like, a giant snake."

"What does he do?"

"It's more like what he *doesn't* do. He doesn't really talk to me—he's always on the phone, wandering around blabbing about, I don't know, deals, and—get this—when he's talking about money, he calls a million dollars a *buck*. As in, *Yeah, Bob, let's offer them three bucks and see if they bite*. It's *so* annoying." Josh set a plastic bottle of Coke on the countertop. Greene remembered Coke from before he came to the island. He began to salivate.

"Is he…is your dad here now?"

Josh laughed. "No. He's in Eastsound." He took down glasses and poured the Coke. He passed a full, fizzing glass to Greene. "Want something stronger in there?"

"Like what?"

Josh rolled his eyes. "Like whiskey?"

"Oh. Sure." There was never any alcohol on the Farm. Only magic mushrooms and lots and lots of weed.

"It's in my dad's study," Josh said.

Greene followed Josh into a long hallway lined with display cases. Behind the glass, things were lit with hidden lights. Native American artifacts, he could see. Dozens, maybe hundreds, of them, from glistening black arrowheads to delicate baskets. Carved masks, pestles, boxes, and digging sticks.

Greene heard the glassy sigh of the case and the muffled whispers of the baskets inside, stories of hot summers swaying in the wind, sweetly drying, the rip and slash of harvest, and the pleasure of the backbends, forward bends, and snuggled-in-tight feeling of the weave—

"Come on," Josh said. "Trust me, you do *not* want to look at those spooky-ass things."

Josh glugged whiskey into their glasses of Coke, and then they went to the living room.

They spread out on two of the couches and talked about nothing in particular while the sugar and caffeine and alcohol spread slowly through Greene's body. He felt illuminated and mellow all at once. He felt *great*.

"I don't have a boyfriend," Josh said when his glass was empty.

Greene was jerked out of his contemplation of the sea outside. "What?"

"I thought you might be wondering if I had a boyfriend. Back in Seattle, I mean."

Greene scratched his eyebrow. "Oh."

"I don't. Just so you know. I did have one last year, but he graduated. He's at Stanford now. He's on the swim team there. He's going to try out for the Olympics."

"Oh. Cool."

"I'm guessing down at the cult, kids don't date." Josh slid Greene a coy, calculating look.

"Date?" Greene said. "No. But there's..." *There's plenty of sex down there*, he finished silently. *The place runs on sex like your Lexus runs on liquefied dinosaurs.* "People still…get together. It's not a religious community, you know."

"People *get together*? Really? Like, while they're churning butter?" Josh laughed.

No, while they're tripping on shrooms and having a four-way with Uncle 'cause it's the end of the world, Greene thought. "People are people, wherever you go," he said. "At least, so I figure. I haven't traveled much."

Josh was watching him closely now. It made him nervous.

"Uh…did you want to ask me something else, Josh?"

"Yeah. Do you want to make out?"

Greene stared blankly at him.

"Like, kiss," Josh said.

"Oh. Um, no, thanks. I have… There's a girl."

Josh's expression shifted. "Okay."

"And I… I love her. So I couldn't…" Not that he had ever told Kestrel he loved her, let alone made out with her.

"What's her name?" Now Josh's voice was hard.

"Kestrel."

"She's in the cult, too?"

"Not… She lives on the Farm, yeah."

"Is she beautiful?"

"Yeah. She's the most beautiful girl in the world."

Josh snorted. "Wow. You have it bad. What does she look like?"

"She's…she has long, wavy blond hair, and these little freckles on her nose, and brown eyes—wait. Why do you want to know?"

"Just wondering what kind of girl could make you fall in love with her. Not that you probably have a ton of options."

"I should go," Greene said, setting aside his empty glass and getting to his feet.

"What? Did I, like, *offend* you?"

"You have been pretty consistently offensive, yes."

Josh's mouth fell open.

No one ever stands up to him, Greene thought. He's spoiled rotten.

"Anyway," Greene said, "thanks for the drink. I can see myself out." He started up the living-room steps.

"Wait," Josh called. "Don't go."

Greene kept moving toward the front door.

"Please."

Sighing, Greene stopped.

"I'm sorry, okay?" Josh said. "Sorry for being so—such an asshole."

"Okay," Greene said. He started walking again.

"I'm going to be here all summer. Maybe we—maybe you could come over and hang out again?"

"Maybe," Greene said, and then he left.

After meeting Josh, Greene couldn't stop thinking about him. His turquoise-and-pink brightness, the aura of privilege around him like a perfumed bubble, and the knowledge that his real life was off this island, somewhere in a gleaming urban hum. Or so Greene imagined.

He'd read about spelunkers—cave explorers—who, as they went deeper and deeper into caves, made sure they didn't get lost by leaving a rope trail behind them. Greene felt like he was deep, deep inside a labyrinthine cave, so buried in the belly of a mountain he could feel the throb of the earth's melted core through the soles of his shoes. Lost. Lost to the world out there. Lost since he was eight years old.

Except now here was this boy, this princeling, who'd appeared like a bright strand of rope that might lead him back out into the open again.

PART TWO

NOW

HANNAH

When Oliver and I reach the house, the cleaner's Honda is still in the driveway.

I shove through the front door, my thoughts clamoring with all the horrific things that could have happened to Sibley. I run through the dim house to my bedroom. I find her asleep.

My stomach twists at the sight of the bloody gauze on her cheek. But she's okay, I tell myself. She's okay.

I look for the house cleaner.

I find her sitting on the edge of a couch in the living room, hugging her big leather purse on her lap. She turns to look at me. Her expression is so malicious that I can't believe I didn't recognize her before. She's the same. Older, heavier, grayer, but oh, she is still the same.

I stand at the top of the steps leading down to the living room. I'm still breathless from running.

"What's the matter?" she asks in a voice both dull and mocking.

"Get out of my house."

Her brow knits in mock confusion. "I have only been doing what you told me to do, Mrs. McCullough. I have been watching your child—"

"Stop it."

"—even though I have other places to be, other—"

"I know who you are, so you can stop pretending." I take a shuddery breath. "And you've known all along who I am, too, haven't you, Caroline?"

She doesn't betray any surprise at that. "You didn't think I would hurt your child, did you? Your illegitimate whore's child?"

"That's rich, coming from you, because the last time I checked, your own son was illegitimate, too."

"But I have accepted the Lord Jesus Christ into my heart, while you—" she waves a hand around the room "—*you* have made whoring into a full-time career. It wasn't a mistake what you did, was it, Mrs. McCullough? No, it was a choice. You traded in your body for all this. But it won't be long before Mr. McCullough tires of you the same way he tired of all the sluts who came before you. *Then* what are you going to do?"

"Why are you here?"

She shrugs. "I clean houses."

"Did Allan send you?"

Something flickers across her stolid features.

"He did, didn't he?" I say. "He told you to spy on me."

"No. I came here to stop you from tempting Trey."

I stare at her, not understanding. Then I remember. Trey. The new caretaker. "What?" I say, almost laughing. *"Him?"*

"I know he's been here with you. He can't help himself. Just like Uncle couldn't." Her voice sounds tearful. "You—you snare them. You're a spider."

"I snared Uncle?" I'm getting angry. "I was a *child*. He was a grown man."

"You *manipulated* him—"

"I was trying to survive."

"I know why you're here."

"What are you talking about?"

"The body in the grave. Your sister."

"I—"

"Hannah?" says a small voice. It's Oliver, shadowed in the hallway leading to the bedroom wing. "Can't you make her go? I don't want her here."

"Hannah?" Caroline says with a knowing smile.

"I go by Hannah now," I say, daring her to contradict me.

"I'll bet you do."

I'm a liar. You already figured that out. Fine, I'm a liar. But something tells me that if you grew up in an apocalyptic cult, you wouldn't be broadcasting that information, either.

You have to understand that I was grieving when Allan and I married. My brother Quill had been shot dead by a sniper's rifle. The home I'd known for most of my childhood had collapsed like a paper diorama.

It's impossible to convey how absolute my sense of disillusionment was in those weeks after the raid. I was wandering alone in the furthest frontiers of my mind, a desolate, bombed-out space. It felt like I would never find my way back to the ordinary world.

Then I met Allan on his beach.

After Uncle and what he did to me, it didn't seem strange that a man of Allan's age would regard me as a viable romantic interest. Not that I thought it was right, exactly. But I guess along the way someone had impressed upon me the idea that it was okay. That men couldn't help themselves. That when it came to females, younger was always better, as though we were cartons of milk.

We married in a hurry. From the moment we first met to the day we signed the papers at City Hall in Seattle, only one month passed. Scandalous, sure. But there just seemed no point in waiting.

We honeymooned for ten days at a resort in Asia, leaving Littlest, who was in the process of being legally adopted by Allan, behind in Seattle with a pair of nannies.

The resort was reached by an interminable journey in a first-class airplane cabin. I had never seen any kind of luxury before—

I'd never even been on a plane—so the glasses of sparkling water the flight attendants served, the dainty dishes of meat and caviar and mousse, seemed like heaven. I sat in my seat mesmerized by the movie screen in front of me. I could barely process the rapid-fire colorful images. I couldn't get enough.

I remember how Allan watched me wolfing down the food, gaping at the movies, and how he was by turns reprimanding and amused. "We have our work cut out for us, don't we?" he'd said.

And that gorgeous resort. I'd never felt anything like the softness of the towels, the smoothness of the sheets. I'd never eaten such food or smelled such flowers. None of it seemed real. Yes, my heart was broken. But I also remember thinking for the first time in my entire life, I'm safe now.

We spent our days in a fluttering-curtained cabana overlooking an indigo sea. At night, Allan did as he wished with me. It wasn't like I was a novice in the bedroom. I mean, I was already pregnant. Allan never minded that.

No one at the resort seemed to notice or care about the huge age difference between us. At the time it made me feel sophisticated, but now I know that men take mistresses and escorts to resorts like that, and that's what everyone must have thought I was, too.

Also, fun fact: the human brain doesn't finish developing until the age of twenty-five. Yeah. It took me a few years, but I grew up, and when I did, I realized that equal parts desperation and obsessive lust don't equal a healthy marriage. But in marrying Allan, I saved my unborn baby. I saved my brother Littlest, who otherwise would've been put into foster care. And I saved myself.

Now, Caroline looks at Oliver, who's still in the hallway. "I didn't think it was him at first," she says to me. "That Devil's slap on his cheek, where did it—"

"We had it lasered off," I say in a cutting, final tone. I look again to the hallway. Oliver is gone.

"But it's still there," Caroline says. "Underneath."

"No, it's not."

"The mark of the beast."

"Shut up!"

"I saw what he did to your little girl's face. Uncle was right. He's a monster."

"You chose Uncle over your own child. *You're* the monster."

"You don't know how I suffered. How I—"

"We *all* suffered. Uncle tormented *all* of us. The difference is us kids didn't have any choice. You adults—you, and my mom, and Star and Smoke and Jacob and the rest—all of you chose to suffer. Chose freely. Because you were messed up and perverted, and you *liked* it. And now you have the nerve to act like you're the one who suffered? No, Caroline. You were Uncle's *enabler.* You were *complicit.* You're just like all the other women in the world who let men abuse their children, who just stand by and watch, wringing their hands as though they can't do anything. You could have. You could've saved us. You could've stopped everything in its tracks. You could've gotten us to safety. It would've saved Quill's life. But no. You chose to stay because you liked being kicked around. Get out of my house. Now. Get out, or I'm calling the sheriff."

"Call the sheriff?" she says. "You? No, you wouldn't dare."

"Get out," I whisper.

She's getting to her feet, clumping past me in her heavy orthopedic sneakers, holding her purse awkwardly to her midsection. "I'm surprised you keep leaving him alone with your girl," she says. She radiates loathing so thick I can almost smell it. "You of all people should know better."

She's right. It's insanity to leave the children alone together.

Caroline is forgotten. I half run, half stagger back to my bedroom to find Oliver kneeling at Sibley's bedside, whispering to her.

"Get away from her," I say. "Get *away*!"

Oliver's eyes go round with shock. Sibley looks like she's going to cry.

I stop in the middle of the room. They were talking. That was all. Talking.

"What's the matter, Mommy?" Sibley asks. Bunners is tucked in the crook of her elbow. Oliver must have brought the toy to her.

I press a palm against my forehead. "I'm just—I'm sorry. I thought… Never mind." I force myself to breathe. "What were you guys talking about?"

Oliver's eyes slide sideways to meet Sibley's. Something unspoken passes between them. Then Oliver rubs his nose, and Sibley blinks rapidly.

They'd make terrible poker players.

"What were you talking about?" I repeat.

Oliver gets up and sidles past me, and he's gone.

I kneel at Sibley's bedside just as Oliver had done. "What were you talking about, honey?"

"It's a secret," she says.

"What kind of secret?"

"If I tell you, it won't be a secret anymore."

"Where is the stick that—the stick that hurt you?"

"In the forest."

"Will you show it to me?"

"No." The corners of her lips quirk down.

"Why not?"

"I don't want to go back there."

"Back where?"

Sibley squeezes her eyes shut. "Mommy, it hurts to talk." She curls onto her side, her back to me, and bundles Bunners to her chest.

I want to demand answers, but I keep quiet. I want to go to

Oliver and scream that he has ruined my baby's beauty, ruined my perfect Sibley. I want to tell him he's a freak and a monster.

The truth is, I am monstrous, too.

I get up and peek into Oliver's room. He's in bed with the lights out.

Then, listening carefully for any sound that would suggest Oliver is leaving his room, I check to make sure Caroline's gone. Her car is no longer in the driveway. I lock the front door and then do a circuit of the house, confirming that all the other exterior doors are locked as well. That's when I notice that she left the vacuum and all her other cleaning supplies behind.

She'll be back, I think. And she knows the passcode for the security system. The passcode that it isn't in my power to change.

I go back to my bedroom. Sibley is already asleep.

I lock the door from the inside and sit down on the edge of the bed. I try to think straight, to breathe. I wish I could cry. I imagine it would give me some relief from the anxiety that's building like poisonous steam inside of me.

Caroline Cooper is selfish and delusional, but she was right about one thing: I wouldn't dare call the sheriff.

My sister's death is being investigated. It's only a matter of time before somebody figures out what I did. No one will care that I did it out of desperation and love, and I'll go to prison for a long, long time.

What will happen to Sibley and Oliver if I go to prison and Allan is left in charge? He will certainly send Oliver to that awful boarding school. And he doesn't really love Sibley. She isn't his child.

No. If I'm going to prison, Allan has to go, too.

I have to figure out why he's lying about his connection to my sister's death. I have to do it before the law catches up with me.

The only thing I can think of doing is dialing the mystery phone number, the Orcas Island number to which Allan made a call the day we found out about my sister's body. He lied and said he'd been talking to Head of School Preller. Who was it really?

I dial the number once, twice, three times. Each time it goes straight to the canned voicemail message.

Is that the only clue I have?

I think of that article about the Kinfolk Farm raid in the *New Yorker*'s online archives, the one I didn't have the heart to finish reading. Maybe there's something in there.

On the bedroom desk, I open my laptop and pull up the article.

When I come to the section about the aftermath of the raid, it mentions that only one arrest was ever made in connection with the Kinfolk: that of seventeen-year-old Farm resident Greene Cooper for the burglary of a neighbor's house. He was arrested the day after the raid.

I knew Greene was arrested that day because I looked out my bedroom window and saw him being taken away in the sheriff's SUV. But no one at the Farm knew *why*. No one seemed to care. In those days and weeks after Uncle and Quill died, the Farm was like a razed anthill. Everyone was swarming and panicked.

I always assumed Greene's arrest was about the guns. All the males on the Farm had to help Uncle with the guns.

A few days after he'd been taken away, I learned Greene had escaped from jail and disappeared. I never saw him again.

I make myself keep reading.

An officer named Ed Fletcher lost his job with the sheriff's office because he was on duty when Greene Cooper escaped from the substation jail in Eastsound.

Which means he might know if Greene stole the murder weapon from Allan, or if he stole something else.

Yes, it's a breadcrumb. But that's what I'm down to now. Following breadcrumbs through the forest, trying to see them before the birds do.

I look in the *Orcas Island Whitepages* online. By some miracle, Ed Fletcher's telephone number is listed. I shut myself in the bathroom so I won't bother Sibley, and I dial. It goes to voicemail. I leave a message saying I'm researching the Kinfolk Farm raid and could he please call me back.

Ed Fletcher, I think, please let me find you.

JOSH

It's the day after I found Drew making out with Duncan on the sidewalk, the day after I told Drew I would premiere his solo violin sonata, and I'm on an evening flight out of Edinburgh.

I didn't say goodbye to Drew; I just sneaked out after dinner while he was working something out on the piano. I did leave a note, saying something came up and I needed to meet with my manager. A lie, obviously. But if everything goes as planned, I'll be back with Drew in only a day or so.

The violin and my roller bag are stowed in the compartment overhead. I'm drinking a cup of coffee spiked with cognac, provided by the attentive first-class flight attendant.

I watch her as I sip my coffee. She's so pretty, so put-together. She has a smile for everyone in this cabin because we're all paying through the nose.

She reminds me of my stepmother, Hannah. She and Allan like to say she was a flight attendant and that they met on the red-eye from LaGuardia to Sea-Tac.

That's a lie. I know who she really is.

* * *

Five years ago, I finally worked up the nerve to call my dad after a few years of basically ghosting him. I'd be playing the Tchaikovsky concerto with the Seattle Symphony, and what better piece, with such dazzling virtuosic demands, with which to say *How do you like me now, asshole?*

Also, I felt obligated to check in with him. I was supporting myself by then, but he still legally owned the violin. He could take it away at any point, and if he did that, my career would be over. So yeah, it seemed smart to show up and kiss the ring.

Allan didn't sound impressed on the phone. He said, "I'm told the Seattle Symphony is quite good, for a regional orchestra," which was a calculated insult. The Seattle Symphony is world-class, and Allan knows it. I felt the rush of blood to my head and that scooped-out, diminished feeling. But I heard myself saying I'd arrange for comp tickets for him at the will-call window and agreeing to meet him afterward for drinks.

The concert went well that night—those were the days when the violin and I were in perfect sync—and then I walked the few blocks through the rain to the Four Seasons.

I was still high from the backstage commotion: flowers and autographs and local violin students in a wide-eyed clutch, escorted by teachers and parents, all wanting to shake my hand. The conductor and his manager asked me out to drinks, which normally I would've done, but I said, "Tonight I'm going to see family," and they looked gratifyingly disappointed.

God, I love all that. After the concert is when the worship is thickest, even more so than when I'm spotlit onstage. Onstage, there are times when I feel like nothing but an exquisitely trained monkey. But afterward, everyone wants *me*. Sometimes I wonder if I've done everything—the transactions and sacrifices and calculations—just for those moments. Those are the moments I think, I won.

Even there in that dimly lit hotel-lobby bar, I felt the eyes on me. There's a certain sizzle in the air when I'm being recognized, and I felt it then.

To the hostess I said, "I'm meeting someone. Allan McCullough. He—" I spotted my dad. Ignoring whatever the hostess was saying to me, I made my way across the bar.

"Hello, Allan," I said, standing over the curved banquette in which my dad lolled, one arm draped along the seat back. His fingers brushed the shoulder of the woman beside him.

Allan has really outdone himself this time, I thought, because this new wife can't be a day over twenty-four. I mean, it was hard to be sure, with her thick layer of makeup and the possibility of Botox and fillers. But still. It was disgusting.

"He never calls me *Dad*," Allan said with a chuckle to his wife. He was angry, though, I could hear it. Ten seconds in and he was already angry at me. "Well, Josh. Have a seat. You know, I almost didn't recognize you when you walked out onstage. You've put on a lot of weight."

Annd there it is, I thought. One point for Allan.

"Aren't you going to introduce me to my new mommy?" I asked. I wanted to make her uncomfortable, looming over the table with my considerable height and bulk, but she looked up at me steadily.

"I'm Hannah," she said. She had pale blond hair, wavy and long. She wore a clinging black blouse, and diamonds twinkled on her earlobes. She sat very straight. "Your performance was amazing, Josh. I've never heard anything so incredible in my life. Seriously."

I was beginning to like her. In fact, she seemed vaguely familiar.

"Are you going to join us or not?" Allan asked me.

I carefully lowered the violin case's strap from my shoulder. I slid into the banquette on Hannah's side, except that she was sitting so close to Allan that they were both basically across from me. Good, I thought. I need my space. I laid the violin case on the seat between us. It was almost like another guest at the table.

"Did you have good seats?" I asked them as I signaled the waiter. "I never know what they're going to give people with those comp tickets."

"They were great," Hannah said. "Dead center."

Allan took a long, silent drink of his whiskey.

Okay, I get it, I thought. I'm here so Allan can show off his trophy to me and grind me emotionally into dust. Cool.

The waiter arrived, and I ordered a vodka martini and a club sandwich. I never eat heavily in front of others. The meal would tide me over until I could order room service at my hotel.

Hannah and I made small talk while Allan stared out into the bar, totally disengaged. As I told her about my tour and she told me about my toddler half sister, Sibley, the sense that I'd seen her before intensified. Allan had told me she was a flight attendant when they met, so I'd made up my mind that I'd seen her on a flight—God knows I flew a lot—when she dipped her head to hear what Allan was saying. Something about the way she moved, or maybe seeing a different angle of her face…suddenly I knew where I'd seen her before.

From my dad's island house, I sometimes saw people digging for shellfish down on the beach. They only came when I was in the house alone, I'd noticed, when Allan's car was gone.

They'd appear on the beach with their shovels and their metal buckets, coming out of nowhere like cockroaches. I had the impression that, in my dad's absence, they went all over his land as though they owned it. The idea pleased me. Always nice to see people giving Allan the finger. But it was a little creepy, too, the idea of people crawling around in the trees all around me as I stood in the house practicing violin.

One day, a few months after I first met Greene, the two sisters showed up on the beach.

I had been practicing Paganini's twenty-fourth Caprice. I couldn't get it up to tempo without it sounding muddy, and I was ready for a distraction. I set the violin and bow down on the dining table. I got out Allan's power binoculars, which were supposedly for looking at whales and boats and eagles.

I messed around with the focus until what emerged was a clear image of two girls in jeans and chunky-knit sweaters. I followed their progress across the wet, dark sand.

They were obviously sisters, older teenagers, both with long, wavy fair hair. They seemed to be arguing, both talking at the same time, both frowning. They were pink-cheeked from the wind and both—if you liked that sort of thing—pretty. Frankly, the younger one was gorgeous. Despite her baggy sweater, I could see she had a willowy, ethereal quality that, had she been taller, would have seamlessly translated onto the pages of *Vogue*. The older one was more athletic-looking, with that wholesome, girl-next-door kind of look.

It was obvious to me, with my eyes glued to the binoculars, that the younger one was Kestrel. Greene, so beautiful himself, would make perfect sense at her side. Together they would look like an emperor and empress from the Middle Ages. Clovis and Clotilda, ruling together.

So, I remember thinking, *this* is who Greene loves.

And the other girl had to be Eldest, who Greene had mentioned in passing a few times.

The two sisters left a scattered line of footprints. The wind lifted their shimmering hair. They set down their buckets near the water's edge. Holding their shovels ready, they bent to examine the sand, their argument apparently over. Then they started digging, hunched over their shovels, black sand flying in clumps over their shoulders. Digging and digging, and then the older one threw herself to her knees, scrabbled in the pit they dug, and pulled up something tubelike, oozing obscenely, primevally, from its shell. A geoduck.

As she threw the disgusting thing into her bucket, the younger one—Kestrel—turned and, shading her eyes with her hand, squinted up at the house. She seemed to be looking right at me.

I shuffled backward, away from the window and out of view.

Allan is such a filthy bastard, I thought as I stared at my new stepmother, Hannah—no, *Eldest*—across the table in the Four Seasons lobby bar that night. Harvesting a bride from the fucking cult?

Back when I'd seen her on the beach, Eldest hadn't been as beautiful as her little sister. But that night in the lobby bar, she had been cleaned and polished and tastefully lit, just like one of Allan's precious artifacts.

How she had changed.

CAROLINE

She is still here. The whore, in her decadent house on the cliff. I checked earlier today, parking on the main road and creeping through the woods. I saw her Range Rover in the garage. I saw lights in the windows.

I missed Sunday-morning worship to do that, and fellowship afterward, which means I missed seeing Trey. But this is a form of worship, too, casting the whore off the island. It is God's work.

Why hasn't she left yet? I keep wondering. Isn't it enough that the girl's cheek is punctured straight through? If that did not scare her away, what will?

Now I sit in my car, parked across the street from Orcas Bible Church. I did not park in the lot because I am not going in; I just need to see Trey when he comes out of fellowship. I need to know where he goes for Sunday dinner. He goes to a different family's house each week, usually families with teenagers in youth group.

People start straggling out of the fellowship hall, and then they come thicker. They get in their cars and drive away. And here is Trey at last, surrounded by his halo of beauty and righteousness. He is talking to Jace Paternas, and they stand for a while by Jace's car. Then Trey goes to his Jeep and as he does so, he casts a look in my direction.

I slide lower in my seat.

Did he see me? Does it matter?

Trey navigates out of the parking lot and onto the road. I turn over my engine and follow.

—*thirsty thirsty*—my car whispers to me. I notice that the fuel gauge is drooping close to Empty—*thirsty thirsty*—

Trey does not go far. He parks in front of a shingled Cape Cod in town, with a white picket fence and ruffled curtains in the windows. It is, I know, the Hitchcock family's home. They have a sulky teenage daughter named Kaylie who does not understand how to keep her body modestly covered. Thinking of Trey sitting across from Kaylie at the dinner table drives a spike of hate through me.

I park two car lengths behind Trey's Jeep. He gets out and looks at me as he slams his door.

I have been seen.

My first instinct is to drive away fast. But then I think, since he has seen me, why not talk to him? Because, dear Lord, how I miss him.

I get out of my car. "Trey," I call.

He waves a hand, not in greeting, but in a gesture that seems to say *Go away*. He is walking to the Hitchcocks' gate. An arbor curves over the gate, knitted with dead vines that look like snakes.

I hurry to catch up. "Trey," I call again.

The gate latch seems to be stuck. He gives it a hard rattle, but it doesn't open. Only then does he turn to face me. His face is flushed. "Listen," he says, "I'm getting pretty sick of the stalking, Caroline."

"What?" I stop a few paces away. I long to touch him.

"You think I don't see you, like, following me around? Sitting in parking lots? Asking people at church about me? You're messed up, Caroline." He shakes his head. "So messed up."

"It's not like that," I say. "It's because… Trey. Treyson. Can't you see God wants us to be together?"

His eyes narrow. "It's sacrilege to pretend to understand the mind of God."

"I didn't—"

"Especially for a woman. Don't you know why Adam and Eve were banished from the Garden of Eden? Because Eve, Woman—that's you, Caroline—disobeyed God, and mankind has been, like, trying to get back there, back to the Garden, ever since. But we never will. It's too late, and it's all because of *you*."

"I'm sorry," I whisper, hanging my head. "I really am."

"It doesn't matter how *sorry* you are. I mean…" He shakes his head as though he is disgusted. "Grace, not works, Caroline. You need to go back to basics. Read the Bible, and I mean carefully. And in the meantime, stop stalking me. Pastor Mike has counseled me—"

"You told Pastor Mike that—"

"Don't *interrupt*." Trey seems, for the first time, like he is getting angry.

Good, I think, because I want to rile him up. I want to disobey. I want to enrage him so that he will come at me, hands to my throat. I want to rouse passion in him, and I don't care what kind.

"Pastor Mike didn't think it was a huge deal," Trey says. "He was the one who told me to invite you to Bible study, because he said it's just that you're lonely. But he said if you don't cut it out, I need to go to Brenda Kusek—"

No, please Lord, no, I think. Not smug, condescending Brenda Kusek.

"—to get the unmarried women's fellowship involved. That's what the fellowship is for. Helping each other grapple with sin." He shrugs, as though he is bored now. "I have to go. They're waiting for me." He tries the gate latch again, and this time it opens. He steps through, shuts it, and goes up the brick walkway.

"Is it because of her?" I yell after him. "That whore? She's got you in her web! Can't you see?"

Trey looks over his shoulder. "That's sin talking, Caroline. Got it? *Sin.* Now, leave me alone or the entire church is going to find out what you really are."

Someone opens the door—it's Pamela Hitchcock, I can see her pinched face—and Trey disappears into her house.

I go back to my car, and I sit there for a long time, with my purse in my lap and my hand inside the purse, wrapped around the pry bar I stole from the McCullough house.

—*want to smash it smash it pry it smash*—the pry bar whispers.

HANNAH

I never should've left Sibley alone with Oliver, and I'm not going to do it again.

I monitor Oliver's movements through the house from the minute he wakes up on Sunday. Not that I'm making a big deal of it, because I don't want him to notice. But I'm aware. Constantly aware.

Sibley spends the day propped up in bed with Bunners, bingeing Netflix cartoons in a hydrocodone daze. She wears the backup glasses that I somehow had the foresight to pack, since her other ones were lost in the woods.

Oliver mostly stays in his room, but he makes a few forays into the kitchen for food.

In the early afternoon, I'm sitting with Sibley, watching cartoons, holding her sweaty little hand. I'm waiting impatiently for Ed Fletcher, the fired sheriff's officer I read about in the *New Yorker* article, to call me back. So far, he hasn't. I've also been calling the mystery phone number at regular intervals. It goes straight to voicemail every time.

Then, at 1:24, the doorbell rings.

I consider not answering the door. If I do, I'll have to leave Sibley alone.

The doorbell rings again.

"I'm going to go see who that is," I say to Sibley. "You stay put, okay, honey?"

She nods listlessly.

I would've liked to lock Sibley in the bedroom, but the door only locks from the inside.

"Don't...don't talk to Oliver, okay?" I say.

"Why?" The syllable is made gummy by her wound.

"Just... We all need some alone time today."

I go to the front door and open it.

Two people stand outside. Both of them are wearing beige shirts with star-shaped badges on the breast and patches on the sleeves. One is a big handsome guy with a buzz cut and almond-shaped eyes. A black Under Armour shirt is visible at the open neck of the uniform. The other is a pretty, plump, blonde woman who's just about the least coplike person you could imagine. It's easy to picture her wearing denim capris and Keds, waiting in line at Disneyland.

"Mrs. McCullough," the woman says in a cheerful voice. "I'm Detective Haglund, and this is Detective Hale. We're from the San Juan County Sheriff's Office."

"Hi," I say. My hand is still on the door handle.

"I'm sure you're aware that last week a body was found at the lot next door?" Haglund says.

"Yes. I saw—I read about it in the newspaper."

"Well, we thought we'd stop by because we heard you were on the island—"

"Really?" I frown. "From who?"

"Trey Higgins told us," the guy, Hale, says. "Your caretaker? He just mentioned it in passing."

"Okay," I say slowly.

Haglund tilts her head. "I'm just curious. Why did you come here at this of all times?"

"It's my house."

"Well, sure, but coming out here for a visit after a body was found next door—"

"The body has nothing to do with me."

"Of course. But even so, doesn't it kind of, I don't know, give you the willies?"

"No," I say. "Like I said, it has nothing to do with me. I'm here because my son was suspended from school on Wednesday. I wanted to get the kids away from the city, give them a break, I guess, before figuring out what to do next. I didn't really think it through."

"You have two children, don't you?"

"Yes."

"But they're not your husband's."

Why in the world is she asking me about this? "Not biologically, no. But Allan has raised them as his own."

"That makes sense. Because the timeline doesn't add up. Your kids' ages, and how long you and your husband have been married."

My hands are sweating now, which makes no sense because Haglund is so pleasant. There isn't even a spark of malice in her eyes. Honestly, her whole attitude is so devoid of the judgy, you're-a-gold-digger damnation I'm used to getting from other women that I almost want to like her. Which is probably what she's banking on.

Haglund looks past me into the house. "Is your husband here?"

"No."

"Where is he?"

"In Seattle, I think."

"You don't know where your husband is?"

"We're…we haven't really been in communication today."

The detectives exchange a quick glance.

"Going through a rough patch?" Haglund asks.

She sounds so genuinely sympathetic that I say, "Sort of." Then I catch myself. "I mean…no."

"Which is it?"

"It's just that we aren't seeing eye to eye about our son's suspension from school. Nothing to do with…you know."

Haglund frowns. "I don't know, actually."

"It's not about the… The rough patch isn't about…" I need to shut up.

"About the body?" Haglund asks.

Hale says, "I don't get it. Why would a married couple go through a rough patch because of a dead body that has nothing to do with them?"

Both detectives look at me with bright, expectant eyes.

This isn't a casual visit, I realize. This is an ambush.

"Because it's…" I swallow. "Because it *could* be stressful. But like I said, we're— The rough patch has nothing to do with that. It's just normal family stuff."

"How did you two meet, by the way?" Haglund asks in a girl-talk kind of voice.

"What?" Too close, I think. She's already circling too close.

"I'm just curious."

"I can't imagine how that could be important."

They wait.

"I was a flight attendant," I say. "For Alaska Airlines. We met on the red-eye between New York and Seattle and got to talking. We just clicked." I feel a burst of anxiety—I'm now officially lying to sheriff's detectives—followed quickly by shame.

There's so much shame attached to all of this, and yet Allan doesn't feel ashamed. Back then, Uncle didn't feel ashamed, even though he took me to his bed long before the age of consent.

It was all incredibly shameful, and *someone* needed to feel it, and that someone has always been me.

But I'm done with being the victim of men who are way older

and way more powerful than me. I'm done with being grateful for the supposed privilege of being a man's prized possession. I'm done with feeling ashamed. *Done.*

All this time, I've been a stupid little pig hiding in a house that's being circled by wolves.

Well, it's *my* turn to be the wolf.

I say, "To tell you the truth, my husband and I did have a slight disagreement related to the body."

"Really?" Haglund says. She sounds as relaxed as ever, but her eyes have a new intensity.

"Yeah. Allan probably wouldn't mention it to you, but the possible murder weapon, the club that was—that was in the grave? With the body?"

"Yeah?"

"It belongs to him."

The detectives exchange another look.

Hale says, "What exactly are you saying, ma'am?"

"My husband is a collector, an art-and-antiquities collector, and he—those kinds of things, clubs like that—"

"Slave-killer clubs?" Haglund says.

"Yeah—he collects them." I'm breathless now and trying hard to hide it. "After I read about the club they found in the grave, I looked in his records—the description of it rang a bell—and I found the documentation. For that exact club."

"We're going to need to see that," Haglund says. The soccer-mom facade is gone. She's all business now.

"Of course," I say. "Come in."

THEN

GREENE

On a rainy afternoon in early May, a few weeks after Greene had spent that fascinating, uncomfortable afternoon with Josh McCullough, once again he asked Kestrel if she would go for a walk with him.

This time, she started untying her apron before he'd finished the question.

They set off on one of their familiar trails. The forest pattered gently with a billion raindrops on a billion leaves.

They came out onto the sea cliff. The madrone trunks stood out as though outlined in ink against the vague gray of the sea. They both paused, and breathed. The briny wind spiraled up into their faces. It pushed their hair back and made Greene's ears sting.

Kestrel wrapped her cold-reddened fingers around the JanSport backpack straps. Mist droplets spangled her sweater, and her ponytail, and her eyelashes. Her nose and cheeks were pink.

Something in Greene's chest made a sort of heaving, a gathering-up, and then it felt as though it was brimming with some warm, bright liquid that would overflow with the radiant sight of her, so without thinking he opened his mouth and said, "I love you."

She blinked, keeping her eyes on the choppy water. She sighed—

Not a good sign, buddy, Greene thought with mingled self-loathing and panic.

—and then she turned to look at him. Her eyes were wide and unguarded, and she said simply, "I love you, too."

First, he was surprised into blankness. Then her words sank in like honey into bread, and his soul was humming. He palmed the water off his face, bent—by now he was inches taller than she was—and touched his lips to hers. As close as they always had been, the only kisses they'd shared were when they were little kids kissing each other's owies, standing in for their mothers. But never this kind of kiss.

"Is it…too weird?" he asked, pulling away a little.

She gave a nervous, breathy laugh. "I don't know… Is it?"

"I, uh, I've wanted to kiss you for a really long time, but I didn't—"

She reached up, pressed an icy-cold hand against the back of his neck, and brought his face closer.

Kestrel had seemed suspicious about wherever it was Greene was taking her. But when they reached the tiny house with the rusted roof, she drew a breath and cried, "It's amazing. Like in a book. Someone lives here—the woman with the curly gray hair, the one who always said hello to us—"

"Yeah. She's a potter. I—we met. We talked. She hired me to look after the place when she's not here."

"Seriously?"

"Yeah. But don't—don't tell anyone."

"She's going to pay you? Money?"

"Uh-huh."

"What will you do with it?"

Leave, Greene thought. *With you.*

He didn't need keys to open the door, not this or any other door. He could simply ask for latches to click or bolts to slide, and they obliged. But he was with Kestrel, and she didn't want to see or hear about his *tricks* anymore. So he took the key from its hiding place under a plant pot and opened the door like a normal person.

The house was only one room plus a tiny bathroom. Thin blue daylight came through the windows.

While Kestrel looked around, Greene knelt in front of the woodstove. He built a little structure of kindling and crumpled newspaper. Then he glanced over his shoulder to make sure Kestrel wasn't watching. She stood at one of the windows, looking out into the trees.

He told the crumpled newspaper to *heat up*, to *spark*, to *burn, damn it*, never mind the newspaper's chatter about the smothering tight roll of the printing press and the kindling's Zenlike chants of *standing up in the sun in the bird-chirp forest*, and with a sudden *shush!* they burst into clean, yellow flame. He tended the fire for a while, then added some bigger sticks, then a small log, and then shut the woodstove door partway.

He stood, brushing dirt and bark from his palms, and hung his sweater over a chairback and set it close to the woodstove to dry. "Want to dry your sweater?" he asked Kestrel.

She didn't answer but came over, stripped her sweater off over her head—she wore a blue T-shirt underneath—and passed it to Greene. Then she took hold of the braided leather bracelet on her wrist, wriggled it off, and tossed it aside. "I hate that thing," she said.

Greene had stopped wearing his own bracelet years ago. Uncle had never seemed to notice, but he certainly noticed if any of the girls or women weren't wearing theirs.

He draped Kestrel's sweater over another chairback. He suddenly felt awkward. "There," he said. "The fire's going, and everything will be toasty in half an hour. When it's hot enough, I'll make you a cup of tea."

"You're so domestic," Kestrel said with a teasing smile. "I had no idea."

"You know how the Kinfolk women are. No men allowed in the kitchen. They aren't letting me live up to my full potential. You look cold."

"I *am* cold." Kestrel shivered, and Greene could see the goose bumps on her bare arms.

He wanted to wrap his arms around her body to warm her, but also to feel her goose bumps, to kiss her again, and what was more, to do something else. Something only half-familiar, something he had no idea how to even *acknowledge* let alone control, something that had left its lair in the back of his mind and was practically roaring to be let out. A sweaty, pulsating creature that wanted to push, to cover, to roll, tangle, and thrust.

He wrapped a blanket around Kestrel instead and silently asked it to warm her. But Kestrel pushed the blanket onto the floor, lay down, and pulled Greene on top of her.

Springtime on the island was always a long, drawn-out tease. That year, Greene noticed, as though for the very first time, the constellations of white flowers in the grass, the folded-tissue buds on the alders, fir lemons as tender as baby-bird toes, the hot pink dots of salmonberry blossoms, and a sweetness wafting off the grass that smelled exactly like a just-cut melon.

The dim fogginess of that spring suited Greene and Kestrel perfectly. It was like packing material around their fragile secret: their love, encased by the potter's house.

They made a bed for themselves out of moth-eaten Hudson's Bay blankets, in front of the woodstove. That bed seemed to Greene to be the precise center of the universe, the one anchored, holy spot from which the entire creation expanded outward.

"People use each other," Kestrel said once while they were talking on the blankets. She said it in an offhand way that made Greene's stomach shrivel.

"Use?" He pulled away from her warmth, propping himself on his elbow to see her better.

"Yeah." She frowned as she lay there, her hair spilling across the blanket. "How can you think they don't, growing up the way we have? Everything's a barter."

"You don't believe that." He felt as though a bruise were spreading slowly across his heart.

"I do."

"Then you think that I…that we…" He faltered, unable to translate the bruise feeling into words.

She laughed. "Come on, Greene. Why do you have to make it into some big deal?"

He lay back down beside her, not as close this time, and covered his eyes with his forearm. "Because I just… I love you."

"I love you, too. You know that I do."

"But?" He was still hiding behind his arm.

She paused. Then she said in a different, smaller voice, "I'm just…scared."

He moved his arm, turned his head. "Of what?"

"Of *what*? Of being left behind. First my dad abandoned us, and then my mom just—she just *leaves*? Without saying goodbye? And my sister, she might as well be dead the way she's become *his* wife. So who's next? Judging by the general trend in my life that has every person who I consider family just—just *leaving*, you're next."

"I'm not leaving without you. I promise."

"How can you promise that?"

"Because you're my family. You and the boys. I don't have anything else. Why would I just up and leave?"

"Because you're not going to sit around on the Farm forever. When you turn eighteen, nobody can stop you from leaving. Actually, you could probably take off today and no one would care. But I am *not* leaving my brothers behind when I turn eighteen."

Greene thought of all the good mothers he'd seen in his life, not feckless human mothers like theirs who had sacrificed the mother-child bond at the altar of Uncle's ego but animal mothers. Furious swooping swallows guarding their nests, pissed-off mama goats, a mother deer staring, staring at meadow peripheries as her fawn grazed. If there was any natural law in the universe, surely it was that mothers protected their young. So he couldn't fault Kestrel, even if the children in question were not her own but her little brothers.

"We'll take them with us," Greene said.

"I'm not their legal guardian. Uncle is. We'd be kidnapping them."

"We'll tell people how Uncle doesn't take care of them, how he's mean to them—"

"Then they'll be taken into state custody, and I will, too. Terra told me." Terra was a young woman who'd come and gone a few months back. "Do you think I haven't thought this through? Until you're eighteen, they can take you away, and they separate siblings. So no. I'm not running away."

"We'll just take it day by day, step by step," Greene said, pressing his mouth against her smooth, hot cheek, "and someday we'll find our way off this island. Together."

She rolled onto her back and stared at the ceiling. "I think I'm going to die here," she said.

In the middle of June, Josh McCullough came back.

Greene was woodcutting on the boundary of Kinfolk and McCullough land, in the same place he'd met Josh back in April. He'd been out there chopping down trees for weeks, every afternoon he wasn't with Kestrel at the potter's house. He hadn't forgotten how Josh had said he'd be spending the summer on the island. Josh was going to need to show up soon or there would be no forest left to cut.

Finally, on a Saturday, he appeared around the bend in the trail. He didn't seem surprised to see Greene this time.

"Hey," Josh said. He stopped to watch Greene lift up a log and heave it onto his cart. "Wow. You're so strong."

"Hi," Greene said, straightening. He was instantly aware of how different the two of them were. Mostly it was because Josh looked so *clean* in his jeans and bright white T-shirt, while Greene was in his dirty old Smoke hand-me-downs that had probably been hand-me-downs from someone else.

Josh pushed his hands into his pockets. "I didn't really mean what I asked you last time," he said. "I just—I think I had too much to drink. I'm usually way better than that about vibing things out."

"Don't worry about it."

"Do you want to, I don't know, hang out again?"

Greene scratched the back of his neck. "Okay. Yeah."

"I'd invite you over to the house, but my dad is there." Josh pulled a face. "He's going to be here all week." His eyes roved over Greene's woodcutting setup. "Are you...do you *have* to do that?"

"It's better than being at the house."

"God, I can *so* relate. Hey—we could hang out here, couldn't we? I could bring some Coke and a bottle of my dad's finest."

"I should probably get back—"

"Tomorrow?"

"Okay. Tomorrow."

"I'm going out woodcutting again," Greene said to Kestrel the next morning while they were eating breakfast with her brothers.

"The woodshed is stuffed full." She looked up from watching Littlest, who was playing on the floor with Wolf. "What's out there in the woods, Greene?"

He spooned up a big glob of oatmeal. "What's *not* out there in the woods? It's a fairyland." He shoveled the spoonful into his mouth. Day after day, always oatmeal. His brain was probably made of oatmeal at this point.

"You're up to something," Kestrel said.

Greene leaned over the table and lowered his voice. "The only thing I'm *up to* is getting a break from this nuthouse. Is it just me, or are there more guns than vegetables around here these days?"

"It's fun," Quill said in his husky, boyish voice. "The guns. Can't wait to shoot something real instead of straw bales and old bottles."

Kestrel and Greene exchanged a quick glance.

"Shoot something *real*?" Kestrel asked Quill. "Like what?"

"Like a deer. Or a rabbit." Quill was smiling and scowling at the same time as he scraped up the last of his oatmeal. His spoon grated against the rough pottery bowl. "Something that bleeds and squeals."

Greene heard Kestrel's breath catch.

Kestrel touched Quill's arm, but he shook her off. She placed her hand back on her lap, looking small and scared.

Greene meant to say something, anything, to try and correct Quill's way of thinking, tell him that gentleness was strength or whatever. But he said nothing. What would be the use? The grown men Quill looked up to—Uncle, Smoke, Jacob—were the ones telling him it was good to make things squeal and bleed.

The heavy, waterlogged burden of it all—of whatever screwed-up stuff was going on in Quill's head, of Littlest with his perpetual green-snotty nose and blotchy birthmark, of Kestrel's beautiful face sometimes looking not like the face of a sixteen-year-old but of a woman twice her age—it filled Greene with a rage so hot that he wanted to tip the table over, to smash Jacob's stupid pottery bowls that were *purposely* ugly. He wanted to howl and bellow and then just get. The hell. *Out*.

He was seventeen years old, strong, and—he was pretty sure—smart, besides which he had a gift, an extraordinary talent that could take him far, far away.

But these three pitiful kids—Kestrel, Quill, Littlest—were the only family he had. They kept him here.

He got up with his bowl and spoon, washed them in silence at the basin, and walked out.

NOW

ALLAN

I have to go back to the island tomorrow, since Boyce wants the 30K in cash. It's a chunk of change but not technically a problem for me. I'm not saying I'll *enjoy* forking over my hard-earned funds to that swollen parasite. But accessing that kind of money, even in untraceable cash, is simply a matter of opening the wall safe in my study here at the Briarcliff house.

What *is* a problem is the au pair walking into my study while I'm crouched in front of the safe like a thief. I have a half-inch-thick stack of Franklins in my hand, and two more stacks on the floor beside me.

"Mr. McCullough?" she says with a timidity that belies the scanty pink nightie she's wearing. It's still the afternoon, so I assume the nightie is for me.

"You should knock," I say.

"The door was open."

"What do you want?"

"I..." She appears to shrink a little. "I wanted to ask if you... if there is anything you want?"

My thoughts have been devoured by my wife, so I'm surprised that I find the skim-milk knobbiness of the au pair's knees touching.

No—actually, I find it arousing.

I place the stacks of cash, wafting that dirty, inky smell we all love, back in the safe. I shut it, stand, and walk slowly to the leather armchair by the fireplace. I sit down. "Come here," I say. I've forgotten her name again.

I'm going to be honest here: I'm getting bored of you judging me. Here, let's do a little thought experiment. I bet you think the Vikings were really cool. I bet you just love a Viking documentary on TV. Well, do you think the Vikings had pangs of conscience while they raped and pillaged? Fuck, no. It would've been testosterone rage the whole gory time, and then they'd laugh about it over beer later. It's a weakness of modern civilization to expect conscience out of men who in older millennia would've been warriors and kings.

The au pair is astride my lap with the pink nightie pushed up to her waist, when outside the sound of a vehicle engine grows louder and then cuts out. I hear car doors slam.

Hannah, I think, my heart lifting.

I push the au pair off.

Finally. Finally, my love has come back.

"Go to your quarters," I say to the au pair.

I walk to the kitchen. I can see part of the driveway from the window over the sink.

It isn't my wife's Range Rover I see. It's a silver SUV with a green stripe across the side and the word *Sheriff* in white.

The doorbell rings.

It's obvious which of the San Juan County Sheriff's detectives is the one to be reckoned with. At first glance I would've picked the Hawaiian guy, with his ex-military haircut, wrestler's neck, and stony expression. But then I realize it's the woman who's going to try to fuck me over.

She—Detective Haglund—is around forty, with a soft, wide-hipped maternal body, a blond ponytail, and sweeping bangs. She has a way of blinking her blue eyes slowly, as if she's just woken up. But there's also a shrewdness in her eyes that tells me the minivan-mom thing is fake.

I let them into my house, and we stand talking in the entry hall with its hand-carved staircase and antique Turkish rugs. I'm not going to take them into a more comfortable room.

Detective Haglund makes quick work of the preliminaries. A body was discovered next door to my island house, apparent homicide, and do I have any idea who the girl might have been?

I act concerned but detached. "What a tragedy," I say. "I wish I could help you out, but I know nothing. These things can happen right next door and have absolutely nothing to do with you."

"Actually, it *does* have something to do with you, Mr. McCullough," Haglund says, "because the apparent murder weapon, the slave-killer club, belongs to you."

My rejoinder is probably a few seconds too late, because for a moment I simply stand there wondering how they figured this out. When I purchase items for my collection, the transactions are always anonymous. I like my privacy.

"How do you know that?" I finally say. The question makes me sound guilty as fuck.

"We saw documentation for what appears to be the item. You purchased it from someone named Gerald Sisson in Toronto in 2008 for about half a million dollars."

"You saw the… You were in my study? On the island? Searching my papers? That filing cabinet is kept *locked*. It—" I stop myself. I can't afford to lose it. Not now. I run a palm over my bald skull, and it feels as fragile as an egg. "You need a warrant for that."

"Your wife let us into the house," Haglund says.

"You talked to my *wife*?"

"Why?" Haglund tips her head. "Is that a problem?"

"Not a problem, no. Except she's just as private a person as I am, so I'm surprised she agreed to show you private papers. *My* private papers."

"We're not saying she did that," Haglund says. "Not necessarily."

Would Hannah make me—make our *marriage*—vulnerable? Would she throw me to the wolves?

Haglund is saying, "So I guess my question, Mr. McCullough, is how exactly did your club end up in that grave?"

"I don't know because the club was stolen from me."

The detectives exchange a glance, and then Haglund says, "We're aware that there was a burglary at your island residence in August of 2015 and that Kinfolk Farm resident Greene Cooper was arrested for the crime. You're saying that the murder weapon was one of the items you reported stolen?"

"Correct."

"Wow," Haglund says.

"Exactly," I say. "Yes, the murder weapon belonged to me—actually, it *still* belongs to me, and I expect it to be returned—but Cooper stole it. I don't understand why you aren't doubling down on your efforts to find him, since he's looking like a—"

"Cooper is a federal fugitive," Hale cuts in. "Searching for him is outside of county jurisdiction."

"How convenient," I say dryly.

"Can you describe the items he stole?" Haglund says.

"There were eight items missing. Two clubs—one antler, the one that was apparently found in that grave, one wooden—and a precontact mask." I doubt these detectives know what *precontact* means, but they don't ask for clarification. "Some rare cedar baskets, a carved stone pestle, and a digging stick."

"What was the value of these items?" Hale asks. He's pulled out a notebook and pen.

"They were insured for about a million and a half, all together," I say.

Hale lets out a low whistle.

"Why did you keep such valuable stuff in that house?" Haglund asks. "It isn't your primary residence, so—"

"I used to spend more time there."

"Oh, really?"

"And I think the Indigenous items suit the house."

"Why did you stop going there so much?"

"My wife doesn't like it."

"Why not?" Haglund is studying me minutely. "I mean, she's there right now."

"I really don't see what that has to do with Greene Cooper stealing my artifacts."

"I'm just curious." She smiles in a way that signals she's not backing off.

"Hannah prefers the city. It's too quiet up there."

"Okay." Haglund toggles her eyes to Hale and back. "How much did you interact with Chris Garnock?"

"Garnock? What does he have to do with this?"

"The deceased has been identified as a likely member of the Kinfolk Community. I'm sure you know that already."

I want to ask if they've made any progress identifying the body, but I won't. That would sound suspicious. Besides, their only chance to positively identify it would've been with the decades-old dental records that are locked in my safe. This almost makes me laugh.

"Chris Garnock was your neighbor," Haglund says. "You must've interacted with him at some point."

"As a matter of fact, I did. He'd come onto my property from time to time. Making threats. Total nutjob. Delusions of grandeur."

"What did he want?"

Now, this is tricky. Back in 2015 I complained to then-Sergeant Boyce, off the record, about Garnock and his groupies. More than once. Has Boyce told these detectives about my complaints? I have no idea. But it would be a mistake to get trapped in a lie, even a little one.

"He was angered when I offered to buy his property for approximately twice the market value," I say.

"So *you* were the one making demands?"

"That's not how it played out. I made him a simple, businesslike proposition, and he retaliated with escalating attempts at intimidation. Lots of gunfire, night and day. You must know about all the weapons they were hoarding. And once I found a dying doe on my doorstep with her throat slit."

"You never reported any of this to the sheriff?"

"I may have mentioned it in passing to the sergeant. It was annoying, but it wasn't worth burning through my time and energy."

"How often did you come in contact with other residents of the Kinfolk Community? Besides Garnock, I mean."

Those people had been like wild animals, sneaking through my trees, along my tide line, flickering at the edges of my vision. I wouldn't mention how they had poached and foraged on my land for firewood, shellfish, mushrooms, huckleberries, deer. I had a right to be outraged by those crimes, but the inevitable next question would be *Who? Who exactly was poaching and foraging on your land?*

And I can't very well fucking say *Among others, the woman who is now my wife.*

"I never came in contact with any of them," I say.

"Okay," Haglund says. "Walk us through the burglary."

"I did this before, on record. After it happened."

"I'm afraid I didn't see that documentation."

Bullshit.

She says, "Could you take me through it again?"

"It's been a long time."

She smiles encouragingly. "Just do your best. You arrived on the island the day after the raid."

"That's right. It was still a zoo up there, with news vans and reporters and rubberneckers everywhere. I had a hell of a time even getting down my own driveway because there were so many vehicles everywhere, and when I arrived at my house, I discovered that the security system had been disengaged."

"Power failure?"

"Not possible. It's connected to a solar battery. I soon found out that Greene Cooper had disengaged it and helped himself to my most valuable artifacts."

"It's surprising that a kid from an off-grid homestead could disengage a high-tech security system, don't you think?" Haglund says.

"He didn't seem to have any trouble breaking out of your jail."

"Fair enough. Okay. You saw your security system had been disabled, and then you noticed that valuable artifacts were missing from a display case."

"Yes."

"Then what did you do?"

"You already know this."

"I want to hear your version."

"There are no *versions*," I say hotly. "There are only facts."

Hale glances up from his notebook. I guess I need to dial it down.

Haglund says, "Was anything else missing besides the artifacts you mentioned?"

"No."

"Then you called the sheriff's office."

"Yes."

"And you said what?"

"You *know* all this."

"Please, Mr. McCullough. There's no need to get angry."

"You're wasting my time and yours."

"You reported the burglary to the sheriff's office. To Sergeant Boyce. He told you federal law enforcement had found items matching the description of your stolen artifacts in a backpack under Cooper's bed at the Farm the previous day? When they were conducting a sweep of the premises after Garnock's death?"

"Yes."

"So Sergeant Boyce arrested Cooper and booked him at the substation."

"Yes."

"Then the next morning, you called Boyce and told him you'd decided not to press charges. But Greene Cooper had already escaped."

"Right."

"But you didn't *know* that Cooper had escaped, did you?"

"Not until I called Boyce."

"I guess what I'm confused about, Mr. McCullough, is why you decided to drop the charges."

"Because my artifacts were returned to me by the sheriff's office, only..." It is essential that I phrase this just right; it's something I have never told anyone before. "I didn't notice that the antler slave-killer club hadn't been returned."

"Really?" Haglund frowns. "I find that kind of hard to believe. It's worth more than my house."

"I was in the middle of closing a massive deal. I was stressed-out, sleep-deprived, working around the clock. I didn't notice it hadn't been returned until weeks later, and by then, well, Cooper was on the run and, it was pretty clear to me, never coming back. I knew trying to get it back was a lost cause."

"Okay," Haglund says. "But... I guess I just think it's interesting that the club turned up, all these years later, as an apparent murder weapon in a grave."

"What can I say? You're just going to have to find Greene Cooper and ask him about it."

"But you can't actually prove that he stole it."

I give a snort. "Please. I gave detailed descriptions of every stolen item to Boyce. There's a record of it. Why would I have reported the club missing if I'd used it to kill someone?"

"That's easy," Haglund says. "To cover your tracks."

HANNAH

On Sunday evening, I still haven't gotten through to the mystery phone number, nor have I heard back from Ed Fletcher. If neither of those breadcrumbs comes to anything, I have no idea what I'll do next.

I make dinner for Oliver and Sibley and sit them down to eat it at the kitchen island. Chicken nuggets for Oliver and vanilla ice cream for Sibley. They're unusually quiet: Oliver is sulky, and Sibley is high on hydrocodone.

I can't get used to the white bandaging on her face. It makes my breathing go shallow every time I see it.

I'm unloading the dishwasher with my back to them when I hear them giggle.

Turning, I see a flash in my peripheral vision, a silvery dancing blur several inches above the countertop. But by the time I have turned around completely, what I see is Sibley's spoon hitting her bowl with a sharp clank.

"Be gentle with your silverware, honey," I say.

"You said you were going to stop pretending," Oliver says to me, glowering.

"What are you talking about?"

He slides off his stool and walks out of the kitchen. Sibley gets down from her own stool and starts to follow him.

"No!" I say.

She gives a start and turns around. "I want to lie down, Mommy."

I lower my voice. "Why don't you go lie down in the living room where I can keep an eye on you?"

I watch Sibley pad barefoot down into the living room. She curls up on a couch with a throw blanket. She looks so small, so vulnerable. I feel like I'm failing on every front, but I can't find my way out.

I rinse Oliver's dishes and put them in the dishwasher. Then I reach for Sibley's.

Her spoon is bent. It lies on its side in the ice-cream-streaked bowl like a little metal person in the fetal position.

This is no bendy aluminum spoon. It is hard, unyielding, high-quality stainless steel. Not even a bodybuilder could've bent it with bare hands.

And yet, it is bent.

I'm almost afraid to touch it. I pick it up, and I'm relieved that it feels as cold and lifeless as it's supposed to. I throw it in the trash.

I brace myself, palms on the counter's edge. I take big slow breaths. I keep seeing that silvery dancing blur, then the curled-up spoon. I keep hearing the clank of metal on porcelain. I tell myself I haven't been getting enough sleep. You start imagining things when you're sleep-deprived. That's a scientifically documented fact.

I hear that tap-tapping in the back of my mind again. It's rain, I realize for the first time. Raindrops. How could a sound like that hurt so much?

My phone vibrates on the countertop where it's charging. The screen lights with a vaguely familiar local number. But it's not *the* number, the mystery number. The clinic, maybe? I pick it up.

"Hello?" I say.

"Hi, there. This is Ed Fletcher. You left me a message? Said you had some questions about the Kinfolk Farm raid?" His deep voice has a hint of redneck drawl.

"Yes," I say. "Thanks for getting back to me." I tell him, sounding to my own ears young and unconvincing, that I'm a writer. I ask if he'd be willing to answer a few questions.

To my surprise, he says without hesitation, "Sure."

"Oh. Great. Can I meet you for coffee in Eastsound? Maybe tomorrow?"

"I wouldn't say no to a beer."

"Okay." Sibley's follow-up appointment at the clinic is at one. "Are you free at two o'clock?" I conjure up the name of a place where I can take the children, because no way am I leaving them alone. "The Harbor Inn?"

"Sure thing. I'll be at the bar in a Seahawks cap. I'm built like an old linebacker, and I've got a knee brace. You can't miss me."

JOSH

I landed in Geneva late last night and took a taxi straight to the Hotel Les Armures. It's a five-star, but less luxurious than I prefer. However, it's in the Old Town, and that's where Greene Cooper lives.

Two years ago, I gave a recital here in Geneva at the Victoria Hall. There was nothing noteworthy about the performance. I don't even remember what I played. But I'll never forget what happened later that evening.

I was out late with my accompanist and some music people—a bitchy soprano, a few wealthy Swiss hangers-on, and, for some reason, an extraordinarily hot Italian television actor. It was a warm summer evening, and we were all drunk at an outdoor bar beside the fountain in the Place du Bourg-de-Four.

I was lighting up a stinky Gauloises and thinking I was making progress with the Italian actor, when someone who looked exactly like Greene Cooper walked past in the square.

My thumb on the lighter froze.

The square was illuminated only by the windows of the bars

and restaurants. But...yes. That was one hundred percent Greene Cooper. Except, how was he here? And dressed like *that*?

Of course, I of all people knew that a fake passport would be no problem for Greene. No problem at all.

I jumped to my feet and, ignoring the queries of my drinking companions behind me, I set off after him.

He walked with the same fit, elastic stride I remembered. He seemed a little taller, a little broader in the shoulders. I couldn't see his face, but his hair was cropped in a conservative style. He was wearing gray trousers and a white shirt with the sleeves rolled to the elbow. They were expensive clothes—I could tell that even in the bad light—but not showy, and they fit him perfectly.

He turned onto one of the cobbled streets leading off the square.

I quickened my pace and followed him for five or six more blocks, twisting and turning through irrational dark streets, past a cathedral and closed storefronts and drunk couples walking arm in arm.

On a sloping little street reached by a flight of stone stairs, he stopped at a pair of doors between a closed café and an antiques shop.

He punched his finger on the security keypad in the wall beside the doors. He was going to vanish again.

"Greene!" I called, stumbling on the cobblestones. Only then did I realize how drunk I was.

Greene's head whipped around.

I went toward him, trying to walk in more or less a straight line.

"Greene," I said, more quietly. I came to a stop a few paces away. Metal numerals over the doors said *14*.

"Josh?" He was frowning in disbelief. His hand dropped away from the keypad.

I imagined that he was wondering what had happened to me, why I was so fat, and I wanted to scream at him and tell him that it was all his fault. But I just swallowed and said, "Yeah."

"Are you...following me?"

"No. I mean—I saw you back in the square, and I thought it was you. I wanted to… I wanted to be sure."

"You can't tell anyone you saw me."

"I won't."

He loomed toward me, threatening in a way he never had been before. "Swear to me that you won't."

"I swear. But…what are you doing in Geneva?"

A pause. "I work here."

"But you…"

"I managed to build a life for myself here, okay? I figured out how to use my abilities to…to do something good."

"Do something *good*?" I looked at his tailored shirt. "You look rich. It suits you. What are you up to? Minting counterfeit cash?"

"Why would I do that?"

"Are you serious? With what you can do, you could be the richest person on the planet. You could turn fucking gravel into diamonds. You could—"

"What would be the point?"

That stopped me. I frowned, my thoughts spinning with drunkenness. "What would be the point? To be rich. To have no worries. To, like, be able to say *I'm the richest one*."

"All the rich people I've ever met seem just as miserable as everyone else."

That made me think of my dad.

"I can't find her, Josh," Greene said quietly.

"Who?"

He made a face that said *Really?*

"Oh," I said. "Kestrel."

"I've never been able to find her." His voice sounded bleak. "They weren't using their real names at the Farm, so it's impossible to trace her. I think she told me her real name once, but I can't remember it. Sometimes I wake up feeling like I'm about to remember it, but it always slips away."

"Her older sister married my dad."

Greene stared at me for a moment. *"Eldest?"*

"She goes by *Hannah* now."

Greene ran a hand over his head. "Jesus."

"I know. My dad is so gross."

"So have you ever seen her? Kestrel?"

"No."

"Does Eldest ever talk about her?"

"I basically never talk to them or see them. My relationship with my dad is dead. But I mean… I could give you their address in Seattle? You could, I don't know, write Eldest a letter? She might know where her sister is?"

We stood there in the dark street while Greene keyed my dad's address into his phone. I noticed his hands were shaking. Then he said, "Listen, Josh, I have to go. Please promise me you won't tell anyone—and I mean *anyone*—that you saw me."

"I promise. And I… Greene, I'm so sorry. About…"

He gave a humorless laugh, shaking his head. "What you did… There aren't enough apologies in the world to make up for that."

"But you're okay," I said, as though trying to convince him.

"Go." He sounded angry again, and he pointed behind me, in the direction of the square. "I never want to see you again. And if I'm found, I'll know you're to blame."

"I wouldn't do that to you. I— Everything I have I owe to you."

He didn't reply to that.

"I…cared about you," I whispered.

"You ruined my life."

I wanted to ask him the question that had been burning a hole in my brain: If that was a Devil's bargain we made, the two of us back on the island, then which one of us is the Devil?

But in silence I turned and walked back toward the square, feeling Greene's eyes on me until I reached the top of the steps. Before I turned the corner, I saw a blue-and-white street sign on the side of the building: *Rue du Perron.*

14 Rue du Perron, I chanted inwardly as I walked back to the square. *14 Rue du Perron.*

★ ★ ★

When I got back home to New York, I hired a private detective to learn more about Greene Cooper's new life. I was curious, that's all. At the time, I never intended to *do* anything with the information. That was before things with the violin went off the rails.

The detective, working digitally out of Midtown, soon found out the names, ages, and occupations of all the residents of 14 Rue du Perron. Based on the occupation, it was easy to guess which name was Greene Cooper's alias.

Jeffrey Lewis had been working for six years for an art-and-antiques authentication firm in Geneva called Hoffer's. This high-end, very discreet specialty firm served museums, auction houses, and private individuals, helping them trace and document the provenance of artworks and detect forgeries.

I pictured Greene running his fingertips lightly across the surface of an oil painting and listening to it whisper its life story. His working at an authentication firm was so much better than the other scenarios everyone had imagined for him. I tried to be happy for him. I really did.

Now, on this dank Monday morning in November, I impatiently watch the clock on my phone while I drink coffee in the restaurant of the Hotel Les Armures. I have the violin with me, sitting at my feet.

At nine o'clock, I sign the check, put on my wool overcoat, sling the violin over my shoulder, and go out into the cold.

Hoffer's is only a few blocks away, marked by a discreet sign on one of the handsome stone buildings. I ring the polished-brass buzzer, and a woman's voice on the intercom asks in French how she may help me.

I say in my prep school French that I have an appointment with Jeffrey Lewis.

There's a long pause. I'm drawing a breath to speak again when she says in English, "Jeffrey Lewis is not here."

"When will he be in?"

"Not until next week."

"But I have an appointment," I say with mock outrage.

"I am very sorry, sir, but that must be a mistake—"

"Where did he go?"

"He is on holiday."

"Holiday?"

"Yes, sir."

"Where?"

"That is not something I may disclose. But if another person in the office may assist you—"

"No," I say. "Thanks." I walk slowly away down the street. Icy little raindrops are beginning to fall.

What am I going to do? Fuck. I have to fix this. I *have* to. Otherwise, my life as I know it is over, and so is my shot at love.

I picture Drew's eyes twinkling at me. I picture him kissing Duncan.

I turn and walk quickly back to Hoffer's. I ring the intercom again, and the same crisp woman's voice answers.

"I changed my mind," I tell her. "I'd like to see another person instead of Jeffrey Lewis. Getting my—my item authenticated is…it's urgent."

"Oh, I see. Well—"

"It's a Stradivarius violin," I say.

Silence. She's processing that magical, open-sesame word: *Stradivarius.*

"We do not typically authenticate musical instruments, sir, but—"

"Mr. Lewis said he would. And it is a *major* inconvenience to me that he canceled our appointment without—"

"Please come in, sir," she says, and there is a jarring buzz and then a click as the door unlocks.

I soon learn the woman with whom I've been speaking is a cool brunette in a cashmere turtleneck. Sitting behind her desk in a minimalist reception room, she sizes me up from head to toe. Good clothes, she's probably thinking. But he doesn't look after himself.

"Hello," she says with a tight professional smile. "I see you have your violin with you?"

"Yes." I stop at her desk. "Because I had an appointment with Mr. Lewis. And he took off to—where was it he took off to?"

The receptionist's expression closes. "I do not know."

She *does* know, I realize. She just doesn't want to tell me.

"Look," I say, "Mr. Lewis promised to examine my violin because I have reason to doubt its authenticity, and he's the only person I trust to authenticate it correctly."

"He is very good."

"I know. And this—it's complicated, but I have to see him right away. It's urgent."

"I am very sorry, sir, but—"

"*Please.* I'm desperate. Please tell me where he went." I'm fumbling out my phone, typing my own name in the search engine, pulling up the image results. I turn the screen to face her. "This is me. I'm— This is my career. And my violin—there's something wrong with it, and Mr. Lewis is the only one who can help me." I stop, shocked at how much of the actual truth has just come out of my mouth.

Gingerly, the receptionist takes my phone. She scrolls slowly through the images. "Josh McCullough," she says. "I have heard of you." She passes the phone back to me. She glances over her shoulder, to a doorway leading into the back. She leans toward me and lowers her voice. "Mr. Lewis went to America."

"Wait—when?"

"Yesterday."

"He… Really? To New York?"

"No. I am not supposed to know this, but I happened to see his computer screen when he was buying his airline ticket. He went to Seattle."

HANNAH

We reach the clinic in Eastsound for Sibley's appointment just before one o'clock on Monday—Sibley, Oliver, and I. We've just checked in and sat down in the waiting room when a nurse with a clipboard appears in a doorway. "Sibley McCullough?" she calls.

I take Sibley's hand, and we stand. Oliver stands up, too. He's wearing boots and a jacket, but only because I won our argument about it earlier.

"No," I say to him. "It'd be better if you wait out here."

Oliver looks confused, but he sits down again. The nurse and receptionist are watching the whole thing. I see them exchange a look.

I feel a jolt of anger because I know what they're thinking: there's the messed-up kid who maimed a little girl.

But how can I be angry at them for thinking the truth?

Dr. Chadha says Sibley's wound looks good. There's no sign of infection, keep doing what we're doing. He changes the gauze and tape and gives Sibley a sticker.

"Oh, and before you go, Mrs. McCullough," he says, "I just wanted to check in with you about…well, about the cause of the accident."

I'm standing with Sibley's hand tight in mine. "Okay," I say slowly.

"It sounded like maybe…" his eyes slide to Sibley and back again "…it wasn't entirely an accident?"

I see what's going on here. He talked to Allan. Together they're conspiring to have Oliver taken away.

"It was definitely an accident," I say firmly.

Dr. Chadha looks at Sibley. "Was it an accident?"

I say, "Um, *excuse* me—"

"No," Sibley says.

I swear my heart stops.

"Okay," the doctor says. "Can you tell me who hurt you?"

"The stick."

"I know the stick hurt you, Sibley, but who was holding it?"

Sibley looks up at me. Her eyes are enormous behind her glasses. To the doctor she says, "I'm not supposed to tell."

"Honey," I say, "I never told you—"

"I'm not sure what's going on here, Mrs. McCullough," Dr. Chadha says, "but I'm starting to wonder if I should get Child Protective Services involved."

"That's— No. That's ridiculous."

"I'm not getting a straight story about who harmed your child."

"It was the *stick*," Sibley says.

"Come on, baby," I say, gently squeezing her hand. "We're going."

A little later, I arrive with Oliver and Sibley at the Harbor Inn in Eastsound. It has a view of the bay, comfort foods on the menu, and a roaring tourist trade in the summer. Today, though, it's nearly empty. An Eagles song blares on the sound system, and the air smells of beer and bleach.

Only one person is sitting at the bar, a heavy-set, sixtysomething guy in a Seahawks cap and a blue fabric knee brace worn over his jeans. Ed Fletcher.

I get Oliver and Sibley settled into a booth just across from the bar.

"I'm going to be right there if you guys need anything," I tell them. "Sibley, you could order a milkshake or pudding or scrambled eggs."

"Do they have Jell-O?"

"They might. Oliver—you can have whatever you like."

He keeps his face buried in the laminated menu.

I go to the bar and slide onto the stool beside the guy. ESPN jitters silently on TVs high on the wall.

"Hi," I say. "Mr. Fletcher? I—I'm Hannah Smith." I'm not wearing makeup today, for the first time in years. Strangely enough, without it I feel more disguised than ever.

"You can call me Ed." He has sad brown eyes and weather-beaten skin.

After the bartender has brought our drinks—soda water with lime for me, Budweiser for Ed—he gestures with a thumb and says, "What happened to your kid?"

"An accident with a stick."

"Yikes."

"Yeah. So…thanks for meeting me."

"Sure. There hasn't been any interest in that raid for years."

"I'm actually interested in one specific angle. Greene Cooper's arrest." No point in beating around the bush.

"Cooper's arrest?"

"Yeah."

"You must've read that *New Yorker* article."

"I did."

"My fifteen seconds of fame." He gives a wry laugh and sips his beer.

"I can't get a definitive answer about whose house he robbed. None of the articles say."

"It was his rich neighbor. Allan McCullough? Guy with a big weekend house down by where the Farm used to be."

So it's true, I think. "What did he steal?"

"Oh, some old Indian stuff. Real valuable, though."

"The reason I'm interested in Cooper's arrest is because of the dead girl they found last week."

Ed gives me a sharp look. "Oh yeah? So that's what you're really writing about?"

"I'm wondering if it's all connected somehow."

"Got yourself a conspiracy theory brewing?"

"Well, the girl was found with a club in her grave—an Indigenous artifact. I mean, I'm just wondering—was that club one of the artifacts Greene Cooper stole?" I hold my breath. It feels like everything hinges on Ed's answer.

"I don't know," he says.

I exhale.

He continues. "You may be onto something there, but I wouldn't recommend digging around in McCullough's business."

"What? Why?"

"Because he's rich. He's powerful. A writer like you? No offense, but he'd destroy you. He's always looking out for numero uno and that's *him*. Not that I can hold it against him. I mean, he made himself a fortune in business—he's some kind of entrepreneur or investor, super, super successful—and he has this gorgeous wife and, I don't know, maybe four houses? You kind of want to hate him for it, but he deserves everything he's got because he's had the guts to reach out and take what he wants, you know? Most people are afraid to do that. But McCullough says, *Fuck you. I see it, I want it, I take it.*" Ed takes a philosophical sip of beer.

Hearing someone talk like this about my husband, my life... it makes me feel sick.

"I will say it's pretty damn ironic," Ed says, "because breaking out of jail made Cooper into a fugitive—and that's a federal felony—all for charges that ended up not even being pressed."

"Did McCullough say why he didn't want to press charges?"

"Nope." Ed squints, thinking. "No, I take that back. I think he said something about not wanting his name in the papers."

That sounds like Allan.

"Or maybe him not pressing charges has to do with the other stuff," Ed says. "Stuff I know that no one else does. About Cooper's jailbreak. I lost my job over that, you know? And no one would even listen to my side of the story. It was the darndest thing. I couldn't tell my boss or anyone what really happened. What I saw. They'd think I'd gone nuts. If I told you, you'd say I'm nuts."

"I won't."

"Oh, you will." He stares glumly up at the TV, which is now playing an ad for Toyota pickup trucks.

I wait.

Ed says, "Greene Cooper was the only prisoner in the jail the night he was arrested. Not that there was anything unusual about that. The place only has two cells, and most of the time they're both empty. The jail's mainly kept busy with drunk drivers, especially in tourist season. Assholes come out here and treat the island like their own personal playground. Anyway, after Cooper was booked that night, it was just him and me after midnight. The station was dead quiet, even though the raid had gone down in Deer Harbor the day before. The ATF seized jurisdiction early on, never asked for backup, basically told Sergeant Boyce to back off and let the big boys take care of things. Jesus, Boyce was pissed off about that. He thought of them as city boys, throwing their weight around. It was our guys—Boyce and Deputy Jeffs—who told the ATF about those weapons stockpiles in the woods, you know. But it's a federal crime, Garnock owning *any* guns, what with him being dishonorably discharged from the army way back when, which makes you a felon—and then when he missed his court date…" Ed makes a whistling sound through his teeth. "Thought he was a god, I guess. Thought the rules didn't apply to him. Got what he deserved. But man, that kid? The one the feds shot?"

"Yeah," I say, looking away. Quill, I think. My little brother Quill. "No one ever pressed any charges for…for the boy's death, right?" I focus on how the condensation drips down my glass.

"Not as far as I know. I mean, the talking heads had their panties in a twist about it, yammering on about overreach of federal power and all that, but in the end, I guess no one really cared that much after all. The kid didn't even have his parents there at the Farm. I guess they brought him there and left him." Ed takes a swallow of beer. "Damn hippies."

I can't do this for much longer, I think. I'm going to break.

I say, "So the night Greene Cooper broke out of jail…"

"Right, right. Well, it was just him and me in the station. He was back there in his cell, and I was up in front at my desk, doing paperwork, listening to the Mariners game—real low, I could still hear every sound Cooper made in his cell, though he didn't make many. He was real quiet, real, I don't know, *defeated*. He just sat there on the bench, sort of hunched over his knees. Every time I looked in at him, he had his face in his hands. Man, he looked so weird. His clothes, his shoes—everything was all worn out, but then patched and repaired in a way people don't do anymore. Nowadays, you just throw it out. With all his patches and shit, he looked like something from, I don't know, a Robin Hood movie or something. I brought him a microwave dinner like we always gave, and I brought him juice and water. All he took was the water. The way he was sitting so still like that, for so long, it was creeping me out. Most people pace around, and a lot of times they'll yell stuff to whoever's up in front. Or they lie down and go to sleep. But Cooper just sat there, face in hands. Never said a word. Of course, his cult leader had been killed, and that kid, too. So he might've been in shock. He must've been in pain, 'cause he had a big old swollen lump on one side of his face and a black eye. Or maybe he was just wondering what the fuck he was going to do next." Ed glances sidelong at me. "Sorry. I try not to cuss around ladies."

"It's fine," I say. I sip my soda water carefully. I hope Ed doesn't notice how my hand is shaking.

"Cooper would've had to walk right past me where I was sitting at my desk. He would've had to push the button that unlocked the front doors because they were always locked at night. They said I must've fallen asleep, and that's why I didn't see him go, or maybe I was in the can. But I never fell asleep, and I always left the door of the can open when I was working there alone. I swear on my wife's grave that Cooper did not come through that office. And even if he did, how'd he get out of the cell? They said I forgot to shut the cell door after I brought him his food, but that's garbage because I never opened the door. I always used the little food door. I got rushed by a prisoner once, so I was always extra cautious about opening the cell up when I didn't have backup. Not that I needed to worry about Cooper 'cause, like I said, he was just sitting there, not moving."

I imagine seventeen-year-old Greene sitting on that bench, face hidden in his hands. So young, but his whole world had ended.

When people leave cults, their brains basically have to rewire. They go through a rocky transition back into the real world. It's like landing a damaged plane in a hurricane. Sometimes I suspect I still haven't landed.

I say, "Then…how did he escape?"

Ed swivels his beer bottle on the bar top. "I never told anyone except for two people. The first one was my wife, Peg, and she's dead now. Cancer."

"I'm sorry."

"She didn't believe me. She said I must've been drinking on the job. But I never drank on the job. Not one drop. The other person I told was that journalist writing about the raid for the *New Yorker.*"

"Milo Hetworth," I say.

"That's the guy. You know him?"

"No."

"I wouldn't have told him what I saw, only he said other people saw some weird shit, too, during the raid."

"What do you mean?"

"Some of the ATF agents he interviewed, they swore they saw stuff at the Farm there's no good explanation for. But when the article came out in the magazine, it wasn't in there. I figured it was because those ATF folks aren't supposed to talk about their work to journalists, so somebody pulled the plug."

This is all starting to sound paranoid and tinfoil-hatty to me. "Tell me how Cooper broke out of jail," I say.

"You won't believe it."

"Try me."

He sighs. "Don't repeat it to anyone. I got enough problems as it is without county health coming at me with the schizo pills."

"I won't tell anyone. I promise."

Ed looks up and down the empty bar. Then, addressing his beer rather than me, he says in a lower voice, "Like I said, I never saw Cooper pass through the office. I never fell asleep. Well, a little after two o'clock in the morning, I decided I should go and check on him. The idea that he might still be sitting there in the exact same position on the bench was really bugging me. I wanted to go back and see him lying down asleep. So I let myself through the door that leads to the cells. The lights are always on back there, for security, so right away, I see his cell is empty. I check the door, though, and it's still locked. There's a window in that cell, high up, too small for a person to climb through even if they could somehow remove the metal grid. He just…vanished."

I say nothing.

Ed continues. "So I'm standing there, just completely freaked out, and I'm about to turn around and go search the rest of the station when I see something. On the wall." He lifts his cap and runs a hand through his graying hair, making it stand on end. Now he has the look of a street-corner ranter. "The jail cell has these painted cinder-block walls. Inmates scratch words and pictures into the paint. It all gets painted over periodically, but at that time on one of the cinder blocks over the bench someone had written *fuk you*, scratched in real deep. *F U K.* We'd been meaning to get some paint on it for a while but hadn't gotten around to it. So I knew that *fuk you* was there and knew exactly *where* it was, above the bench and under the window. Where it was supposed to be—where it was before."

"What do you mean?"

"Well, when I was standing there wondering where the hell Cooper had got to, I realized that the cinder block with the *fuk you* on it had been moved."

"Moved," I echo.

"It was over to the left of the bench."

"Maybe the bench had been moved."

"It's bolted to the floor." He shakes his head, drains the beer. Suddenly he looks haggard, and I can smell the souring alcohol and yeast on his breath. "The cinder blocks on the wall had been rearranged."

"I don't understand—"

"I don't understand it, either!" Ed explodes. The bartender glances over. More softly Ed says, "Sorry. I'm sorry. It's just... I got fired over that jailbreak, and it wasn't my fault. I turn it over in my mind, you know, over and over. I try to understand what I saw. But unless you're a goddamn magician, I don't see how you do that."

"Magician? Do you...believe in magic?" It's a ridiculous thing to ask, and I regret it instantly.

"Magic, like *Harry Potter* shit? Wands and wizards? Nah. But magic, like maybe there's more to this world than what they tell us? Yeah. Yeah, I believe that."

"But...what do you think happened?"

"I don't know what happened. Not for sure. But what it looked like to me was Cooper removed some of the cinder blocks so he could get outside, and then he put them back again but in the wrong order."

I stare at Ed. I don't even know what to say to something like that.

"Like I said, that journalist said some of the ATF agents saw weird shit, too." Now Ed sounds defensive. "Like, when they were at the Farm, there were shovels and mattresses and stuff flying through the air. He said they'd been drinking water from a pump on the property, and they thought the water was contaminated. Maybe with peyote or magic mushrooms or else some kind of toxic mold."

I want to get away from Ed now, away from this suffocating crazy talk. I pick up my handbag, signaling the end of the conversation.

Ed shrugs dismissively and turns his face up toward the TV. "I knew you wouldn't believe me."

No, I think. I don't believe you. But it's obvious what I need to do next: find out why Allan dropped the charges against Greene.

"Well," I say, standing up, "thank you so much for your time."

"Yup," Ed says. He's still looking at the TV.

I start to walk away but stop and go back to his side. "You don't happen to have Sergeant Boyce's phone number, do you?"

"That asshole?"

"I just thought—"

"As a matter of fact, I do."

ALLAN

Pulling up to my island house around three on Monday afternoon, I immediately see that Hannah's Range Rover isn't in the driveway, but a rusted-out blue Honda Accord is. Then I notice that the front door of the house is wide open.

I hear the smashing glass even before I get inside. I stride quickly along the entry hall and out into the main living space.

The living room looks fine, but the kitchen has been devastated. Cabinet doors hang off their hinges. Glass and ceramic shards litter the floor. The dishwasher door lolls open, its rolling racks upended.

This time, I'm not being robbed, I'm being vandalized.

The brittle crash of breaking glass sends me running into the hallway where I keep my display cases. Someone is swinging a metal tool high in the air—

"No!" I shout.

—and down onto one of the cases. The glass bursts like tinkling confetti and the tool—a short pry bar—splinters a wooden mask.

The vandal is a sturdy woman in a shapeless denim dress and

sneakers. Her long gray hair is wild around her shoulders. Then my brain makes sense of her features, and I can't believe my eyes.

I know this person. Well, I did, once. Briefly.

"Caroline Cooper," I say. "What the fuck are you doing?"

She freezes in the middle of another swing. She looks at me, her face a startled blank. But then recognition dawns, followed swiftly, unmistakably, by fear.

"How did you get in here?" I say, taking a step toward her. I'm not afraid of her pry bar—she's obviously out of shape, her movements undisciplined.

She takes a step back, her sneakers crunching on glass.

"How did you get in?" I repeat.

She hunches forward, adjusts her grip on the pry bar, and charges past me.

"Hey!" I shout. I start after her, but I skid on broken glass and come down hard on one knee. Pain drills up my thigh and into my spine.

I get to my feet and limp to the front door.

She's dumping herself behind the wheel of the Honda when I get outside. I jog to my Tesla as her engine grinds to life. She shoots into Reverse, the engine yowling, and I jump back just in time.

There she goes, jouncing in Reverse all the way down my driveway. By the time I shift my Tesla into Drive, her Honda has already disappeared.

I don't see her car again until I reach the main road.

I follow her along Channel Road, past the marsh, over the bridge, and through Deer Harbor. She's driving erratically and too fast, but there's no way her shitty car can outpace mine, and anyway, we're on an island. There's only so far she can go in any direction before she has to stop.

She turns onto Deer Harbor Road and traces the harbor north and then southward again. Then onto Crow Valley Road, heading north.

I follow her for miles and miles to the northwest section of the island. My knee bleeds steadily into my jeans. I touch the wound gingerly and feel the embedded glass.

Caroline turns off Enchanted Forest Road onto a narrow dirt lane shadowed by huge cedars, and I realize we're near Camp Praise, where the fundies send their gay kids for so-called deprogramming. A hundred feet along, she turns hard and jerks to a stop in front of a little red house set back in the trees.

I brake, too, and leap out of my car as she's running for the front door.

She slams the door, but not fast enough—I wedge the toe of my shoe in the doorframe before it hits home. Then I lean hard against the door, and although Caroline is a lot heftier than she was nine years ago, her soft bulk is no match for my strength. She staggers back, and I enter her house.

It stinks like garbage inside, that's the first thing I notice. It's low-ceilinged and cramped.

Caroline is edging backward into a little rat's nest of a living room. "Get away from me," she says hoarsely. "Leave me alone."

I advance toward her, limping. "Not until you tell me why you were trashing my house."

"She's a…she's a whore. She takes and takes!"

"Who? My wife?" I say and take a long stride forward.

"Wife? She's not a *wife*. She's a—"

I silence Caroline with a slap across her face.

She whimpers, both of her hands flying to her cheek.

"You're weak," I say. "And just look at this place—it's a dump. I paid you so well. Where did it all go?" To be fair, I only paid Caroline ten thousand dollars. But she should've made more of it. "And why the fuck are you here? You were supposed to *leave*. That was part of the deal."

She is cowering against the wall, still holding her cheek. Her knuckles are wrapped in dirty Band-Aids. "I don't have to explain myself to you!" Her voice is tearful and indignant. "I did what you wanted—what you *needed*—and I'm not doing anything else."

"I wouldn't have you do anything else for me if you offered to do it for free. Because now look at the shitstorm we're in. They dug up a dead girl—a dead girl buried with *my club*. What the fuck am I supposed to do about that?" I lift a finger and hold it close to Caroline's face. "Leave. Leave this island like you were supposed to nine years ago and never come back, or I swear to God, I *will* kill you."

I'm turning to go when something catches my eye in the squalid room. A low table against the wall, draped in purple cloth. Unlit candles clutter the surface. I see what looks like a Bible and, propped against the wall, a framed print.

"You found God?" I start to laugh. *"You?"*

The print is a crappy shopping-mall rendition of Jesus Christ in a field of flowers, his hands outstretched to the viewer. Only, there's something wrong with his face.

"Holy shit," I say.

Someone—Caroline, presumably—has stuck a black-and-white cutout face on top of Jesus's.

"Wait," I say. "Is that Garnock?"

"Go away," Caroline whispers. She's hugging herself and rocking.

I look closer and see that it isn't Chris Garnock's face glued onto Jesus's body. It's the face of my new caretaker, Trey Higgins.

"Well," I say to Caroline as I leave, "I guess some things never change."

THEN

GREENE

Greene found Josh sitting on a stump at the property boundary.

"Took you long enough," Josh said.

"Sorry."

"It's okay. It's kind of nice being out here in the woods." He kicked the white canvas backpack at his feet. "I brought refreshments."

Greene sat down on a rock while Josh took out red plastic cups, a bottle of Coke, and a full bottle of amber-colored liquor.

"My dad's precious single malt," Josh said with a grin.

"Won't he be mad?"

"He won't even notice it's gone."

Josh poured their drinks with what looked to Greene like a whole lot of whiskey, and then they drank in silence. The forest was starting to smell like the warm sap perfume of summer. The sun was out, and the whiskey slipped through Greene's body. He took off his own backpack—the old JanSport—and laid his head against a tree trunk. He studied the lacework of the branches overhead.

"Why do you want to be here?" he asked Josh. "If you don't have to? Or are you— Is your dad *making* you spend the summer here?"

"Believe it or not, I'm here voluntarily."

"Why?"

"I'm woodshedding."

"What?"

"Woodshedding. It's an expression musicians use. Like cramming for a test, except you're practicing."

"So...you're a musician."

"I'm a violinist. I want to be a professional, but... Anyway, my mom and Allan agreed to let me take a year off before college to get ready to audition at the big conservatories. I have to apply to regular colleges, too—that's the agreement. I'm still taking lessons with Margaret—she's the best violin teacher in Seattle. She doesn't think I can do it, and I know the younger students in my studio and their parents are secretly laughing at me. But I just..." Tears welled in Josh's eyes, and he tried to hide it by taking a long drink. "I just want to *try*. For the first time in my life, I have zero obligations except to practice violin. My high school—Lakeside?"

"Never heard of it."

"Well, it's academically very rigorous. Tons of kids go on to Ivies from there. Bill Gates went there."

"Who's Bill Gates?"

Josh burst out laughing. "Seriously?"

"You don't seem to get that I live on a commune without electricity and running water, let alone television or radio or—"

"No, I get it, I get it. It's just...honestly, I'm jealous. I wish I didn't know who Bill Gates was, either. Anyway, I just graduated from high school. With decent grades, too. But the point is, I graduated so now there's no homework, no SAT prep, no Debate Club or Korean Club that my mom and dad forced me to participate in to make me look—" Josh made quotation marks in the air with his fingers "—well-rounded. Now it's just violin. All day, every day, except Fridays when I'll fly down to Seattle for my lessons with Margaret."

"And then you'll do your auditions."

"Yeah. In January."

"And what if you—"

"It's going to happen. It *has* to happen." Josh poured himself more whiskey, straight this time, no Coke. He took a deep gulp. "My dad thinks I'm wasting my time. He says if I were truly gifted at the violin, I'd already be a professional, like, I don't know, some child prodigy. He did buy me a new violin, but I think it's so if I get into Juilliard or Curtis, he can take the credit. Or I guess I should say, he bought it for *himself*, as an investment, but I get to play it."

"As an investment? A *fiddle*?"

"It's a Strad," Josh said. Greene could hear both pride and awe in his voice.

"And…what's a Strad?"

"Are you kidding me? You have never heard of a—"

"You keep forgetting where I—"

"Okay, okay, sorry, cult boy. A Stradivarius. Only, like, the best kind of violin in the world? Mine used to belong to this super famous Soviet violinist back in the day, but it was just sitting and rotting in a private collection for decades, and a few months ago my dad bought it at an auction in London. It was three million dollars."

Greene lowered the cup from his lips. "Hold on."

"What?"

"You're complaining about your dad, and meanwhile he bought you a three-*million*-dollar fiddle?"

"I told you, he didn't buy it for *me*. He bought it for himself. As an investment. Stringed instruments of that caliber appreciate over time, guaranteed. He's just going to let me use it, and in a way I'm doing *him* a favor because violins have to be played or they kind of, like, go bad. Collectors literally pay people to play their instruments. To exercise them, I guess. Like race-horses or whatever. My dad…he collects stuff. Valuable, super rare stuff. He grew up, like, really poor out in Bumblefuck, and he's always telling me this stupid story about this arrowhead he found when he was eleven years old that made him realize he was, like, destined for—"

"Josh?" a man shouted, not very far away.

Josh stiffened. "Omigod. Oh shit! That was my dad. Shit. He can't see me with—"

"With me?"

"*No.* With his whiskey." Josh was shoving the bottles of Coke and single malt into the backpack, dumping out his plastic cup and cramming it in there, too.

"Josh!" McCullough called, louder now.

Greene was on his feet, slinging the JanSport onto his back. "This way," he said softly, and he slipped into the undergrowth.

A moment later, Josh was jostling the bushes behind him.

Greene set forth on a deer path. Birds and little animals skittered in the bushes as they passed.

"Josh?" McCullough shouted behind them. "Josh, I saw you! Who's that boy? *Stop!*"

Fear zapped through Greene's veins. Why am I doing this? he wondered.

"Don't stop," Josh whispered behind Greene. "Please."

"I know a place we can hide," Greene whispered back.

The ground began to slope steeply down, and the going grew rough. The path was strewn with the decaying layers of the forest: rashes of moist, fragile mushrooms; potholes tangled with dragging sprays of ferns; bits of cedar bark dangling from spiderwebs.

"Here," Greene said. They'd come to one of the Kinfolk's five pit houses, which Uncle had made them build over the past year or so. "We can hide here."

"Where?" Josh's voice wavered.

Greene squatted to sweep aside the leaves that camouflaged the trapdoor.

"What the *hell*?" Josh whispered.

"It's a pit house."

"A what?"

Greene lifted the trapdoor. An earthy, fungussy smell rose up. He stepped down onto a ladder.

Josh was watching him with an open mouth. "What the *fuck* is—"

"Josh!" McCullough shouted higher up the slope.

Greene jumped down to the bottom of the pit house and whispered up to Josh, "Last chance."

"But I—"

"Josh! Where are you?" McCullough's voice was closer. He sounded furious.

"Jesus," Josh muttered under his breath. He came so fast down the ladder that he half fell the last few rungs.

Greene reached up and pulled the trapdoor shut.

It wasn't totally dark, once their eyes adjusted. The pit house was eight feet square and five feet deep—Greene knew because he'd helped dig it—and even though the logs that formed the ceiling were clotted with dirt and roots, there were still a few chinks through which daylight shone.

"What's..." Josh swallowed thickly, as though pushing down vomit. "What's under that cloth?" He was looking at the canvas tarp–covered hump that took up half the pit.

"Just...supplies," Greene whispered. "Extra supplies."

"You guys are digging holes and storing supplies *here*? Why?"

"You're really going to be angry with me after I just helped you escape your dad? He's probably going to have me arrested for kidnapping you or something."

Josh wrapped his arms around himself. He was shaking.

"What's the matter?" Greene whispered. "Why are you so afraid of your dad?"

"Because he's an *asshole*. And if I piss him off, he might take my violin away." Josh sank to a crouch.

"Josh!" came McCullough's voice.

Josh lay his face on his knees and began to weep with rhythmic, wet sucks of air.

"Josh!" McCullough was so close now.

"Shh," Greene said, almost inaudibly.

It seemed as though Josh hadn't heard. His weeping grew louder.

Greene shrugged one of the JanSport straps off his shoulder so he could swivel the backpack around to his belly. He unzipped the outer pocket and pulled out a little airtight aluminum cylinder. He unscrewed the match container lid and the odor of sulfur bloomed. The container was full of matches, tiny red heads up.

—we want to we want to we want to FOOM!—

Greene told the matches to pipe down and listen.

—we want to…we…want…to…

Greene said to them, *You're going to go foom, okay, you get to go foom, but first, please just dance—but soothing. Orderly. To stop this boy from freaking out—*

Freak out freak out foom foom FOOM!

No, Greene said. *Not like that at all. Foom, but foom slowly, and dance like fireflies. Be beautiful. Be wonderful—*

He lifted the match canister up.

Now float and foom and dance.

One, then two matches floated from the canister to hang vertically in the air. Another match floated out of the canister, and then another. They quivered with excitement. Greene smelled very faint smoke.

"Josh," Greene whispered. "Look."

Josh lifted his face and saw the suspended matches. He stopped weeping. The blossoming of wonder on his face transformed him into a little child.

Greene felt just like he had on that long-ago day, the first time with Kestrel, when *she* saw. When *she* believed.

The matches—a dozen in all—had finished their gentle ascent from the canister, forming a hovering ring.

Foom, Greene told them.

The matches burst into twelve tiny yellow flames.

Dance, Greene told them.

The matches became a serenely spinning constellation of cheery flames, tracing circles and spirals like a courtly dance.

Greene was grinning.

"What the fuck?" Josh whispered.

Greene's grin fell off. This wasn't like with Kestrel at all. Josh's face had gone slack, and Greene could see the reflection of the flames in his eyes. He was terrified.

Out, Greene told the matches.

The matches extinguished themselves and fell to the ground. The air filled with bitter smoke.

"What the fuck was that?" Josh whispered, scrambling to his feet. Tears dripped down his face as he stumbled toward the ladder. He tripped on the tarp-covered hump and thudded with a grunt to his hands and knees.

"Are you okay?" Greene whispered.

Josh winced, rubbing his knee. Then the rubbing stopped. He was staring at something protruding from under the tarp.

A shotgun.

"What is—" Josh frowned at the gun, then sent a frightened glance at Greene. He grabbed a corner of the tarp—

"Don't," Greene said.

—and flung it aside.

The guns and ammo were supposed to be stowed in pine boxes built by the Kinfolk men. But Uncle was buying arms faster than they could build the boxes. So when Josh removed that tarp, he revealed a stack of nine or ten long guns and about a dozen cardboard cases of shells and bullets.

Without another word, Josh dashed over to the ladder, scrambled up, and shoved open the trapdoor.

By the time Greene's eyeballs adjusted to the sudden daylight, Josh was gone.

After that, Greene was sure he'd never see Josh again, so he was surprised when he saw him only a few days later.

Greene was walking back from meeting Kestrel after dinner in the potter's house. He and Kestrel usually came and went to their meetings separately, so as not to draw attention to themselves.

He was feeling relaxed and walking slowly, enjoying the pink light of the setting sun when—there was Josh, sitting on the same tree stump as before.

"Hey," Josh said, sitting up straighter.

"Hey." Greene stopped.

"I…wanted to explain myself."

"What do you mean?"

Josh rolled his eyes. "About the last time I saw you? It's just… you didn't tell me you know how to do stuff like that."

"Stuff like what?"

"Like, magic tricks."

"It's not… Yeah. I study, uh, magic tricks. Illusions of the stage and stuff."

"It was really good. If you ever leave your cult, you could get a job in Vegas."

Greene started walking again. He passed Josh and kept going.

"Want to come over?" Josh called. "My dad is gone."

Greene stopped. He was annoyed with Josh and sick of his drama. But he also wasn't ready to go back to the stifling atmosphere of the Farm. "Okay," he said.

"Would you play something for me?" Greene asked, as he and Josh took their first sips of their drinks in McCullough's kitchen. "On your violin?"

"No," Josh said bluntly. "You wouldn't even know what you're listening to. You don't have electricity on your farm, right? You haven't left this island in ten years—have you ever even *heard* classical music?"

"You make me sound like a freak."

"Well…" Josh shrugged. "You *are* a freak."

"We hear music on the farm," Greene said. "The way you're supposed to hear it. I mean, do you think Mozart listened to the radio?"

"Wait—you know who Mozart is?"

Is. Josh talked like these composers were still around. "Yeah. Of course I know who he was. I read."

"But you've never heard any of Mozart's music?"

"No."

"That's weird."

"Yeah. I get it. I'm weird."

Josh's sullen energy had lifted, and he set his Coke and whiskey aside. "Fine. You win. I'll play you some Mozart."

Josh led Greene to his bedroom, which had the same low, spare furnishings as the rest of the house. Nothing was out except for a music stand with sheet music spread across it, a stack of sheet music on the floor, an open violin case sitting on a desk, and a violin and two bows on top of the bed's white blanket.

"That's it?" Greene said, regarding the instrument. "The Strad?"

"Yeah."

"You use two different bows?"

"I'm trying to figure out which one sort of, like, *gets along* with the violin best. Is that weird to say?"

Greene gave him a sharp look. "No," he said. "It makes sense."

Josh picked up the Strad. He held it gingerly, almost as though he were frightened of it. He picked up one of the bows, then put the violin under his chin and proceeded to do that waah-waah thing with the pegs: tuning. Eyes closed.

Then he opened his eyes. "Sit down," he said to Greene. "You're making me nervous."

Greene went to the desk, pulled out the chair, and sat. "What are you going to play?"

"Mozart's A Major violin concerto. First movement. Obviously, I'm not warmed up, but whatever. It's not, like, Paganini."

Greene had no idea what that meant, but he nodded. In the back of his mind, he was starting to worry about McCullough arriving home unexpectedly. Finding a scuzzy Kinfolk boy in his house.

Josh stood still for a moment with the violin under his chin and the bow dangling by his side. Greene had a sense of Josh sort of wrapping himself up in something invisible. Sealing himself off.

Then he lifted the bow and in a single melting motion his eyes fell shut, his head sank voluptuously sideways to the violin, and the horsehairs of the bow pulled down and drew out the first shimmering note.

Greene sat dazed. He had never heard music like this. He had never, despite having grown up surrounded by people busily working, seen anyone do anything with such skilled precision. It was as though the music were not as important as the triggering of Josh's pale slim fingers, or the way his bow arm moved back and forth and up and down in a blur, a rigid pale wing.

Then, with a series of resonant chords, the piece was finished. Josh dropped his bow but kept the violin loosely on his shoulder. "So. That's the first movement, but it doesn't sound right without the piano. It's supposed to be with an orchestra. If you're a real soloist. Aren't you going to say anything?"

"It was great."

"Great?" Josh's eyes narrowed.

"That's a compliment."

"It sounded sarcastic."

"It's not. Really. I've never heard anything like that. Ever. It seemed like you were doing magic tricks with sound."

"Wow, high praise, coming from Mr. Magic Tricks himself. But none of that was a trick. I practice, like, *all* the time.

I'm still trying to figure out this instrument. Like, it's great up in the higher registers, but when I'm up in position on the G string, it still won't speak clearly. A freaking Strad, and it won't speak." Josh said this as though it were the violin's fault, not his.

"What do you mean?" Greene asked. He watched the soft gleam of light on the violin's varnish. It made the wood seem pliant somehow. Under Greene's gaze it seemed to be stirring, waking, stretching, and yawning the way so many things did when he encountered them.

"Listen," Josh said, and he raised violin and bow and played a dozen or so notes. "Hear that? Like it's choked?"

"Kind of," Greene lied. It sounded wonderful to him.

"Maybe I should get it adjusted again."

—miss him so much, fat fingertips pressing and the touch of the bow like a purr. Yes, a purr—he doesn't—he doesn't—

The violin had found its voice. It was muttering a complaint that seemed to be directed at Greene, although maybe it was only muttering to itself.

Greene got up from the chair and went closer. "Play that part again," he said to Josh. "So I can hear."

Josh played the notes again. "Hear it? Choked."

—ouch! With his sharp little fingertips and yes, the power but he tries too hard, this boy, he tries too hard and it HURTS. Make him stop for god's sake we'll go back in the case and rest in the pine sap dusty rosin coffin and we'll dream of his soft, wide fingertips and—oh please, just keep me away from—

Later, Greene would look back on this moment and wish he'd kept his mouth shut or, at the very least, thought through the possibilities, the problems, the *disasters*, that his words could wreak. But in the moment, feeling simply like an earnest translator, he said to Josh, "It says it doesn't want you to play it—"

"*What?* Stop. Get away from—"

"No, no. Listen. It's like…it misses a person who used to play it. A man. With fat fingers."

Josh's eyes narrowed. "Is this some kind of joke?"

Greene stepped back. "No. Sorry. It's—"

"You said you didn't know anything about classical music."

"I don't."

"Did my…did my dad tell you about Orlyk?"

"What? What the heck is Orlyk? *No.* And I've never even met your—"

"I think you should leave," Josh said.

"I didn't—"

"Leave!"

When Greene arrived back at the farmhouse, he knew something was off the minute he walked through the kitchen door.

He felt a tight shivery energy as he walked upstairs. Did he hear people whispering behind the closed doors? Or was the house itself abuzz? He hated to ask the farmhouse anything, having shushed it and all of its contents into near-total silence years ago.

The tiny room he shared with Quill and Guide was dark when he entered, but no sooner had he shut himself into the hot, boy-smelling space than there was rustling on the top bunk and Quill whispered in his husky voice, "Did ya hear?"

"Hear what?"

"About Uncle."

"What about him?"

"Know how he and Eldest went into town for the market today?"

"Sure."

"Well, he got arrested."

"Arrested." Greene sat stiffly down on the lower bunk. Was it possible that Uncle wasn't invincible, after all?

"Yeah. That sergeant guy pulled Uncle over, up at the junction by the hardware store."

Greene had seen Sergeant Boyce twice, a tall man with a paunch and a mean turn to his mouth. He had rolled up in his sheriff's SUV with another uniformed officer last month, wanting to speak to Uncle about neighbors' complaints of gunfire.

"Pulled over for what?" Greene asked.

"For having a broken taillight. Can you believe the government can stop you for a busted lightbulb? I tell you, I'd like those suckers to set one foot on our farm. I'll sink a slug into them, right between the eyes! Drop them like—"

"Quill," Greene said wearily, automatically, "you can't shoot people."

"'Course I can. Protecting my property. It's my right."

Greene leaned his elbows on his knees. "Then what?"

"The sergeant guy made Uncle get out, and when he did, he saw Uncle's shotgun on the rack, and he said Uncle wasn't allowed to have it on account of quitting the army all those years ago. Isn't that so *stupid*? Then the sergeant guy arrested Uncle. Put him in handcuffs and drove him away to the jail."

"Is that where he is now?" Greene asked. "In jail?"

"No, he's back here now on account of your mom paying the bail money."

Uncle *was* invincible, then, even if he was made that way by people like Mom.

NOW

ALLAN

I'm back at my island house. I tweezered the glass out of my knee and bandaged it up. I put on a clean pair of jeans. I'm assessing the damage done by that whack-job Caroline and her pry bar when I hear a vehicle engine outside.

Fuck, I think, walking to the front door. If that's the sheriff's detectives…

But this time, it's Hannah, braking her Range Rover in the driveway. Oliver's in the passenger seat beside her, and Sibley's in the back. None of them has noticed me yet.

Hannah looks different—younger, more vulnerable—and I am instantly warm with desire. It takes me a moment to put my finger on what's changed. She's always worn makeup, ever since we got married and I took her to the Nordstrom cosmetics department. She said she wanted to look older so people wouldn't judge our age difference.

But today, no makeup.

She sees me as she's climbing out of the car. Fear tightens her face, and she hesitates with her hand on the door. Fear. Of *me.*

The injustice of this, after everything I've done for her, sends a bolt of fury to mingle with my desire.

"What are you doing here?" she says with a glance back at the children. They're unbuckling.

"I'm here to bring you home," I say.

"Daddy!" Sibley cries, and then she's running toward me with her beaten-up rabbit toy in the crook of her elbow. Her movements have a drunken looseness, and when I look down into her face, I see how constricted her pupils are behind her glasses.

Sibley touches the edge of the bandage on her cheek. "I got hurt," she says.

"I see that."

Oliver slips behind me and disappears into the house. The back of my neck prickles.

I always knew it was a mistake letting the spawn of Chris Garnock under my roof. That man was defective. Delusions of grandeur, no empathy, all the classic signs of a malignant narcissist. Is that a genetic condition? Because it seems like little Oliver inherited the works.

I imagine myself grabbing him by his tender tween ear like my grandpa used to do to me. Delivering openhanded slaps across his skull like my father used to.

Sibley says to me, "Bunners doesn't like you when you make that face."

Hannah reaches the kitchen ahead of me. She stops short in the doorway and looks around the ransacked room. Her face is white. "Allan? What happened in here?"

"When I showed up earlier, this crazy woman was going to town with a pry bar," I say. "She said she was the house cleaner?"

"Oh my God," Hannah whispers. "Oh my God." She turns to Sibley. "Sweetie, why don't you go to my room and watch cartoons?"

"But you said I can't go back there when Oliver is—"

"It's okay." Hannah slides me a look. Is it sly, or frightened? "For now it's okay."

I wait until Sibley is out of earshot. "We need to talk about getting Oliver out to Montana as soon as possible. What he did to Sibley is—"

"We don't know for sure he did it."

"Of course he did."

"You've been talking to that doctor at the clinic—"

"I'm Oliver's *parent*. But first, I want to know who this Caroline person is."

"She's been here, cleaning the house. But she… I didn't recognize her at first, but I know her. From before."

"What?" I think I sound pretty convincingly incredulous. It's important that Hannah never, ever learns that Caroline Cooper and I have met. "From the Farm?"

"Yes. Caroline Cooper. Greene's… But I thought you… She said you called her to come in and clean. I thought—"

"No," I say, and this is the honest-to-God truth. "I never called her."

Hannah's surveying the wreckage of the kitchen again. "Why would she do this?"

"I have no idea—but she did seem like a total nutcase. I guess we should call the sheriff's—"

"No," Hannah says.

"Why not? She trespassed, and the damage has to be in the tens of thousands—"

"We can't—not now. There's already too much on our plates."

"Hannah. Be reasonable. The insurance company is never going to pay if we don't contact law enforcement." I'm almost enjoying this. I know what she's afraid of: that if we set the sheriff's office on Caroline Cooper, Caroline will tell them who Hannah really is.

"But we…" Hannah's face changes. When she looks at me again, her eyes are cunning.

What happened to my beautiful girl?

"Actually," Hannah says, "I'm surprised you would want to involve the sheriff's office, all things considered."

"What's that supposed to mean?"

"I spoke to some detectives yesterday, and they told me they wanted to talk to you. Did they?"

"As a matter of fact, yes. Because you sent them to me, Hannah."

"I didn't *send*—"

"You told them it was my club they found in the grave. You showed them the paperwork. You sicced them on me like a couple of attack dogs, and I guess I'm just wondering why? Why are you treating me like your enemy? Jesus. Babe. It's *me.* Your husband. Remember him?"

"You've been lying to me."

I loved her so much more when she didn't talk back.

"Lying about what?" I ask.

"About that phone call last week. You said it was Mr. Preller, but it wasn't. It was an Orcas Island number. Who was it?"

"There are just some things it's better if you don't—"

"What kind of things?"

"It's for your own good."

"You also lied about the fact that the slave-killer club they found in…that they found in her grave…my *sister's* grave…" She presses her fingertips to her forehead and shuts her eyes.

I have never seen Hannah cry. Not once, not even at the very beginning when her entire world was in tatters. She isn't crying now, either. I should've realized years ago that the girl is made of ice.

She opens her eyes and says softly, "Why did you kill her, Allan? I just can't figure out *why*. I mean, when did you two even meet?"

"I didn't *kill* her. Jesus. I never even *met* her." I try for outraged dignity. "How could you think that about me? *Me?* The guy who saved you and those kids? The guy who gave you this fairy-tale life that you're evidently willing to throw away over some paranoid fantasy?"

"Then why was your club in her grave?"

"Greene Cooper stole that club. Isn't it obvious that he killed her? There should be a full-scale manhunt for him."

"No." Hannah's shaking her head. "No. Greene wouldn't have killed her."

I snort. "All you people on that farm were so delusional. You thought Garnock was a prophet, and look how wrong you were about *that*. So why can't Greene Cooper have been a killer?"

She watches me so carefully. "But you didn't press charges for the burglary."

"I knew the sheriff's office would never get the club back. Bunch of amateurs."

She says, "Okay," in a tone that means *Yeah, right.*

I was wrong a few minutes ago. Hannah doesn't look younger and more vulnerable without makeup on. She looks hard. She looks suspicious and scheming and *old*. And she's trying to pin a murder on me.

I picture Hannah's face as it was in our early days. Her beauty still unconscious of itself, her eyes still adoring me. I watch her drift upward and then disintegrate, the way ashes of burning paper do. *Goodbye, my love,* I say to her. *Goodbye.*

"I hate to change the subject," I say, "but I'm worried about Sibley."

"The doctor said we just have to wait and see how the wound—"

"No. Not that. If it doesn't heal right, there's reconstructive surgery. What I'm worried about is her mental health."

Hannah blinks. "What?"

"Didn't you hear what she said to me outside? That that mangy rabbit toy of hers doesn't *like* me? I mean, Jesus fucking Christ."

"She's on pain medication."

"No." I shake my head. "This has been going on for years, and you know it. She talks with her toys. She talks to the sheets on her bed and her pajamas and the fucking light switch. She's mentally ill. She needs to be medicated, and so does the boy. Violent little freak."

"You don't—"

"So there are a couple ways this can go, Hannah. You can keep on digging around in the dirt, trying to find some way to make me look like a killer. Or you can get a grip on yourself and come back home and forget all this bullshit."

We gaze into each other's eyes. A casual observer might've even mistaken it for mutual love.

Hannah is the first to look away. "Okay," she says softly. "I'll come home."

HANNAH

Allan tells me that he's going to change and then go for a trail run, that he knows it's awkward timing, but he's missed two workouts already and if he doesn't go now, his anxiety will shoot through the roof.

"Don't touch any of this," he says, meaning the mess Caroline Cooper made. "I'll clean it up when I get back. I'll grab some takeout in town for dinner—sound good? We can head back home in the morning."

I nod, a Stepford Wife bobblehead with a smile that Allan either can't tell is fake or doesn't care.

I'm so relieved to see the taillights of his Tesla disappear behind the greenery.

I go to the main bedroom. Sibley is curled up with Bunners, watching cartoons. Only then, seeing her, does the fury hit. The very idea that someone might give unnecessary psychiatric medication to my child… It triggers a savage instinct in my brain.

I lock the bedroom door from the inside—wondering as I do where Oliver went—and then I go into the bathroom.

I turn on the shower, the ceiling fan, and the ceiling fan in the toilet closet, too. My hands are shaking—no, I'm shaking all over.

I didn't miss the look on Allan's face when I asked why he never pressed burglary charges against Greene Cooper. It's such a small detail, and yet it seems like my only chance of getting to the bottom of what he's hiding before it's too late.

I dial the number Ed Fletcher gave me for retired Sergeant Boyce.

Boyce doesn't sound very surprised when I identify myself as Mrs. McCullough nor when I say I need to talk to him in person.

"I'll be in town tonight with the wife," Boyce says. "We're having dinner at the Rusty Anchor. Give me a call when you get there, and I'll come out for a chat in the parking lot. Say, around six o'clock."

"Okay," I say. "Great."

ALLAN

There will be no trail run. I don't have the time.

I brake in the deserted parking lot at the base of the Turtleback trail system and try to control my breathing. I wasn't lying to Hannah about my anxiety being sky-high.

A green Jeep Cherokee pulls in next to me. Its noisy engine cuts out. Then my caretaker, Trey Higgins, gets out and circles around to my passenger door.

"Hey," he says, getting in. He's in a hoodie and shorts and I can smell his sweat.

"Hey," I say.

"I got your message."

"Obviously." Trey is kind of an idiot. This is something that up until now I considered an asset. His stupidity makes him easy to direct. But now I'm getting nervous about whether or not he can pull this off.

I guess my silence is making him uncomfortable, because he says, "Uh, you said you had something else you wanted me to do?"

"Yes."

He rubs the back of his neck. "Okay, well, the thing is, I'm not sure… I don't feel that great about the stuff you already had me do, you know."

"You haven't done anything wrong. Scouting out the situation when a dead body is found practically in my yard isn't wrong. Checking up on a woman when she's run off with the kids, that's not wrong."

"Well, no, but—"

"I'm pretty sure it's in the Bible that a woman has to obey her husband."

"Yeah, that's true."

"Well, Mrs. McCullough hasn't been obedient."

"Okay. Yeah, I see your point."

I tell Trey what I want him to do for me. One last little task before we part ways as employer and employee.

"What?" he says. *"No."*

"Why not?"

"I'm a follower of Christ." He says this in a pompous tone, as though the statement—however untrue—makes him unimpeachable.

But everyone has their price. Even so-called followers of Christ.

"Fifty," I say.

"What?"

"Fifty grand. Cash."

Trey's hesitation hangs heavily in the air.

"Think what you could do with that kind of money," I say in a reasonable tone. "You could start a fucking orphanage in Africa. Wouldn't that be nice? Take your money and get far, far away from this island? And as a bonus, you'll be done with *her*."

"I *am* getting sick of her." He narrows his eyes, shakes his head. "Psycho."

"There you go. Plus, you still wouldn't be doing anything wrong."

"I wouldn't?"

"You'd be helping justice to be served."

"I'm not sure I can convince her."

"Oh, I'm sure you can figure out a way. After all, she's in love with you."

Trey groans.

"Do you even know who Caroline really is?" I ask. "Where she comes from?"

"What do you mean?"

"She used to be a member of the Kinfolk Community."

"The—that cult?" Trey sounds confused.

"Yeah. They weren't Christians, you know."

"Pastor Mike says they worshipped Satan. How could Caroline…?" The confused look on his face is replaced with something hard and mean.

I reach down into the door pocket and produce an overstuffed business-size envelope. It holds the thirty thousand for Boyce, but Trey doesn't need to know that.

He looks at the envelope hungrily. He knows what's in there.

"Here's the cash, all yours—"

He reaches for it, but I yank it out of his reach.

"—after you get it done."

"Okay," Trey says. As he's pushing open the door, his phone erupts into an electric guitar rendition of "Hallelujah." He pulls it out of his hoodie pocket with a groan, scowls at the number, and silences it. "She keeps calling me," he says. "Caroline. From a different number."

"She's really got it bad for you, buddy," I say.

I saw the number. It was Hannah's.

"Tonight," I say to Trey.

Boyce calls while I'm driving toward his house. I consider ignoring the call. I imagine him making more demands. I picture myself lying on the ground, injured, bleeding from the nose. Bleeding green cash.

I tap the car's touch-screen control panel, and Boyce's folksy-ass voice booms through the speakers. "Hey there, buddy."

I wince and lower the volume. "Hi," I say.

"Listen, when you come—you're still coming, aren't you?"

"Yes."

"Well, don't come to the house. My neighbor was asking about you. She noticed that midlife-crisis vehicle of yours, was wondering who you were." He pronounces *vehicle* as *vee-HICK-le*, and it makes me want to punch his teeth in.

"Where should I go?" I ask.

"Meet me up at the Mountain Lake boat launch. You know, in the state park. It'll be real quiet up there this time of year."

Apprehension zings through my veins. I don't like the idea of being alone with Boyce up on the mountain after sunset. But as usual, I have zero leverage with him.

"All right," I say.

"Don't be late. I'm taking the wife out for a nice dinner." Boyce hangs up.

CAROLINE

I am cleaning the Kennys' house, squirting Clorox on their tiled shower wall, when my phone vibrates in my apron pocket. This is such an infrequent occurrence that I jump. I set aside the spray bottle and dig out my phone. The screen informs me that I have a new text message from Trey Higgins.

I lower myself to sit on the edge of the bathtub. I stare at his precious name. We have never texted or spoken on the phone, but Trey's number has been programmed into my Contacts for months.

The bleach spray drips slowly down the wall, its fumes filling my eyes and making them water. Trembling, I open the message.

Hi its Trey. Bible study tonite @ 7? My place. Theres some stuff we need to discuss

I sit staring at the digital words for a long time. The black letters start crawling like insects.

Trey. Trey wants me after all. He has realized his mistake.

I am almost paralyzed with joy. My mind's eye is filled with his image, beautiful and contemptuous, the tiny golden cross glinting at his throat. Below this runs the faint but unrelenting babbling of the bathtub on which I sit.

"Shut up," I whisper. I hug myself and begin to rock. "Shut up," I whisper again, more softly, almost inaudible.

The babbling grows louder.

I lurch to my feet and the babbling stops.

I want to tell Trey that his word is my command. That no matter how long or how hard he might punish me, I will always be here waiting for him.

Instead, I text him a single word: Yes.

THEN

GREENE

The Tuesday after Uncle was arrested, Greene went out to the woods to look for a hatchet he'd lost, and there was Josh, walking on the path.

"God, you look depressed," Josh said.

"Uh, hello to you, too?"

"Can we talk?"

"We're talking right now."

"I shouldn't have made you leave the other day."

Not *I'm sorry.*

"I just— You kind of scared me?" Josh said. "I mean, at first I thought you were pulling some kind of prank, but deep down I… It was weird." He searched Greene's face. "Aren't you going to say anything?"

"Yeah," Greene said. "What do you want from me?"

Josh pressed his lips together. He swallowed. "I…want you to tell me what else my violin says." A pause. "Is that… Does that sound crazy?"

Something stirred in Greene's heart, blossoming upward, sweet but almost painful. Josh believed in him, after all.

Greene spoke with effort because the blossoming feeling was crowding around his vocal cords. "No," he said. "It doesn't sound crazy."

"So you can really… Things…just say stuff? To you?"

"Yeah. They tell me what happened to them. What they remember, or what they want. Their stories."

"What about the matches? In the pit house?"

"What about them?"

"That wasn't a magic trick, was it?"

"Depends on how you define *magic*."

"Quit messing with me. Did the matches talk to you?"

"Yes."

"But when they danced—"

"I asked them to do it."

Josh's eyes widened, a thirsty boy looking at a brimming cup of cold water. "So you could tell my violin to, I don't know, like, *play differently*?"

Greene hesitated. "I mean, I could *try*. But it wouldn't necessarily respond. It sounded really… It's really upset. It's grieving."

Josh said softly, "For Orlyk."

"Is that the man with the fat fingertips who played it before?"

"Yeah. I still can't believe you…"

Greene shrugged. "You know what? It doesn't matter *what* you believe, because I don't have to convince you."

"Wait. Sorry."

Sorry? Greene thought savagely. The princeling actually said *sorry*?

"Leonid Orlyk was a famous Soviet violinist," Josh said. "Probably the greatest there was in, like, the sixties and seventies. A lot of his recordings are still considered definitive, especially his Sibelius concerto and his Beethoven sonatas. The Strad belonged to him, back in his heyday, before his heart attacks."

"Is he still alive?"

"No. He died of one last massive heart attack in the eighties.

So as much as the violin is apparently bitching about my fingers not being fat enough, at least I'm not eating myself into the grave. Oh my God, I can't believe I'm talking about a *violin* like this, like it can—"

"Just let it go."

"Let what go?"

"All the thoughts that are trapping you inside that way of thinking." This was what Greene longed to tell Kestrel. He could see her face locking up, eyes glazing. "People go around thinking that, wherever they are and whoever—or *what*ever—they're dealing with, *they* just so happen to be the exact center of the universe." He looked challengingly at Josh. "You do that."

"*Excuse* me?" Josh's cheeks flushed. "Now we're critiquing *my*—"

"If you can't get this concept, there is no way you can cooperate with your violin. Because the *violin* thinks that *it* is the center of the universe, too."

"I have absolutely *no* idea what you're—"

"Don't you get it? If you can get rid of the illusion that you're the center of the universe, maybe see things from, say, the violin's perspective, everything will start to look—"

"I'll pay you. A lot."

"What?" Greene stared.

A thousand bucks, he thought. Two thousand. That would be enough, wouldn't it? To get to Bellingham, to find Kestrel's dad—

"To, like, charm the violin," Josh said. "Tell it to remember, to *keep* remembering, how Orlyk played it. Tell it to respond to my playing like it's Orlyk's playing. Is that— Could you *do* that?"

Greene forced himself to speak. "I mean, I *could*. But—why do you want that, Josh?"

"What do you mean? So I can play like *that*. So I can have a solo career."

"But why?"

"Because my dad says I can't. He's always acted like I'm a failure. Like I'll never—"

"This is all about your *dad*?"

"I can get you fifty thousand dollars."

"*What?* You have that much?"

"Yeah. Greene, if you could really do that, get the violin to act differently, it could… This could be what I need. This could be *it*. I could finally get over my technique issues and the tone problems in the higher registers— It could… I mean, if I played like freaking *Leonid Orlyk*, I would definitely get into Juilliard." He was peering into Greene's eyes. Probing. "Hey, don't you want to make an easy 50K?"

Fifty thousand dollars was an unimaginable fortune to Greene. He couldn't quite comprehend the meaning of that number, compared to the paltry sums that had passed through his hands in his life—five- and ten-dollar bills going into the farmers-market till, dingy dollars and quarters going out, or the crisp twenties with which the potter paid him. But *fifty thousand dollars*?

Money like that had its own kind of force field. It was like a layer of padding. It could keep you safe.

It could set you free.

But something was squirming in the back of Greene's mind. This felt dirty. It felt wrong. Was spoiled Josh McCullough capable of getting over his ego enough to make the violin happy? And could he, Greene, really make the Strad behave itself indefinitely like some kind of *slave*, just so Josh could say *told you so* to his dad?

He shook his head. "Not everything is for sale, Josh."

"Um, yeah, it kind of is."

"No, it's not. And I won't do it."

The following Saturday morning, so early the sun was nothing but a gold edge to the fir tops, Greene and Kestrel were loading up the old Dodge Ram with crates of kale and lettuce for the farmers market.

Kestrel wore a red down vest, her hair up in a messy ponytail. Her face was still soft with sleep. Greene felt wide awake, wired. It wasn't too often that he went into town, but almost all the adults were sick with a stomach bug. Some of the kids had had the bug earlier, because that's how it always happened: the little dominoes fell first. Somehow, Greene, Kestrel, and Uncle were unscathed.

The two teenagers were going to run the farmers-market stall. The Farm couldn't go without the meager infusion of cash the market brought in, especially after the coffers had been drained dry from Mom paying Uncle's bail. Neither Greene nor Kestrel could drive the pickup, though. There were no plans for them to learn. Uncle drove the pickup. Sometimes, *sometimes*, Smoke did. But even that was rare. Uncle liked to be in control.

—splitting, cracking, splintering—bam-bam!—

That was the wooden crate Greene was hefting into the stack on the pickup bed.

What's that? he asked the crate. *The bam-bam?*

—dense silvery flat-bam-bam! Splitting, cracking, splintering-bam-bam!—

Okay. A hammer. The crate must've been talking about when it was built.

—splitting, cracking, splintering—

Greene heard the kitchen door slam. His whole body tensed. He could feel Uncle coming, feel the black vortex of his eyes.

He turned to see Uncle crossing the yard, but the man wasn't looking at Greene, he was looking at Kestrel. Kestrel, bending to pick up the last crate of produce, her ponytail falling across the side of her neck.

She straightened and looked at Uncle, her eyes level, almost challenging, and Greene couldn't understand. You didn't look into Uncle's face like that. *They* didn't, anyway. They'd talked about it. They were only half joking when they said he'd suck your soul out through your eyeballs if you looked too long, that that's what had happened to their mothers and to Eldest and Star and Smoke and Jacob and all the rest.

In that moment that went on so, so long but which must've lasted for only two or three seconds, it didn't seem like Uncle had sucked out Kestrel's soul.

But it sure seemed like he was trying.

"You done?" Uncle asked.

"Last one," Kestrel said, looking away, hefting the crate, setting it down on the tailgate.

"How many times do I have to tell you not to load things on the tailgate?" Uncle was going to the driver's-side door. "Wrecks the hinges."

Kestrel looked at Greene and rolled her eyes. It was their old familiar conspiracy again, except...what had that long look been?

They drove the miles into Eastsound: winding roads canopied by tree boughs, straight roads bordered by fields and farms. For the millionth time Greene thought, I could walk this, easy. Anytime I want. Walk right into town and—

That was where it always ended. Because he *could* walk it easy, but then what? What did you do when you were still legally a minor and you hated where you lived and you wanted to escape? He figured that if he'd gone to school in town he might have made friends, friends with real parents, sane parents, who might help him out. Point him to a lawyer or a goddamn orphanage. Yeah, even an orphanage sounded better than the Farm.

Or maybe the mantra stopped because of the girl next to him.

Kestrel sat between Uncle and Greene, straight and alert as she stared out the windshield. Her hands were shoved inside her vest pockets. All of her sleepiness had been replaced by a wary stillness.

Something was wrong. Greene understood Kestrel, her atmosphere, better than he understood himself. She was soft. Flexible.

Bright. She got angry, but it blew over quickly, and she loved to laugh. Or she used to, anyway.

No one in the pickup said anything. No radio, either, because heaven forbid they hear an advertisement that might awaken capitalistic appetites. Just the grinding hum of the engine, the sticky whoosh of tires on asphalt. Everyone looking ahead.

Uncle braked at the stop sign where Crow Valley Road met Orcas Road. They waited for another car. Uncle placed his palm on Kestrel's blue-jeaned left thigh. He firmly, slowly pushed his hand along to her knee. Then he lifted his hand and wrapped it lazily around the steering wheel again. He made the turn.

Uncle said nothing. Kestrel said nothing. She had tensed, but she hadn't recoiled. Greene felt her atmosphere twist and spin.

Or was that Greene's own atmosphere? Or was it all of theirs, Kestrel's and Greene's and Uncle's, plumes of frenzied, stinking black smoke like the time they accidentally burned those old logs that turned out to be railroad ties soaked in tar? Poisonous smoke blotting out the sky.

Uncle double-parked in front of the village green where the farmers market was held. He sat behind the wheel, emanating impatience. Kestrel and Greene unloaded the folding table, the awning, the painted sign that read *Kinfolk Farm*, and the crates of produce. When Greene slammed the tailgate shut, Uncle leaned out the cab window on his elbow. "That it?"

"Yup," Greene said, not quite meeting Uncle's reflected face in the side mirror. Kestrel was behind Greene, fussing with something or other. Busy work to keep her head low.

"I'll be back at one," Uncle said, turning over the engine. "I expect every last leaf of those greens to be sold, boy."

"Why did he do that?" Greene asked Kestrel. They were unfolding the portable table.

"Huh?" Kestrel said, avoiding his eye.

"In the pickup. At the stop sign." Greene drew a big breath. "He touched your leg?"

She wouldn't look at him.

He wanted to clasp her hand as he always had, but he didn't. She appeared far away, backlit. Out of reach.

She didn't answer his question.

His soul shrank to a pebble.

She turned her head away, smiled. "Hello," she said to someone on the other side of the crates. "Good morning. We're still setting up, but if you come back in a few minutes we have some nice baby lettuce, Russian kale, and fresh rosemary and sage, great for poultry—"

He was lost.

At the stall next to theirs, the sheep-cheese lady with the orange felt hat arrived, and on the other side the man with dirty coolers filled with meat, and across the way the familiar stalls with dahlias, wax beans, tomatoes, pottery. The shoppers arrived, then the couple on the banjo and fiddle, and things got noisier and more crowded—but not too noisy and crowded because it was only a little island. But there were always tourists, escapees from Seattle craving a little country. They dressed the part in jeans and sometimes even work boots, but you could always pick out the Seattle people. They looked too clean, and they carried their white paper coffee cups like shields.

Kestrel did the selling because she was like a magnet. People couldn't resist her beauty, her smile, the way she tipped her head to listen. Greene worked beside her, rotating crates, bagging stuff. He was happy to be her sidekick. It almost felt like how things used to be.

After about an hour, there was a lull. By then Greene had worked out what he wanted to say.

Kestrel was standing behind their dwindled stock, unscrewing the lid of a mason jar that served as her water bottle. She tipped her head and took a drink.

"We'll go to the sheriff," Greene told her softly. "We'll report Uncle."

Kestrel stopped drinking. Slowly, she lowered the jar. She didn't look at him. "There's nothing to report, Greene."

"What did—"

"Nothing!"

He touched her arm lightly and felt what she was feeling, right to the core of him, so strong he couldn't have said what *he* felt like.

What Kestrel was feeling was shame. Shame like a wilting leaf of lettuce, a banished dog. Shame that wanted to hide.

"How long has he been—"

"A long time."

"It's not your fault," Greene whispered to her. "How could it be *your* fault?"

She shook his hand from her arm. She whispered back, "Because when he—when he does things to me—"

Greene's stomach turned.

"—I don't move. I don't say anything or run away—not that I *like*… I *hate* it. But if I don't *do* anything, then it's my fault."

Greene frowned, confused. Kestrel was convincing, and he'd always had a hard time disentangling his ideas from hers. But he gave his head a sharp shake. "No."

"I just pretend I'm not there," Kestrel said, so softly now it was like she was talking to herself. "I go somewhere else in my head. That's what Eldest told me to do. I don't have to feel it if I don't want to."

Greene studied Kestrel's agonizingly beloved profile. The shape of her nose, the way her upper lip tilted up, the wisp of hair escaped from her ponytail and stuck to her cheek. "We can run away. We'll take this money—" he gestured to the cashbox that had been steadily filling up "—and just *go*. I'll use my gift. It could protect us—"

"Stop talking about your *tricks*," Kestrel said in a fierce whisper, ducking her head for privacy, but also with more shame. "We're not little kids anymore! *Please.* Stop."

"Here," Greene said, taking hold of her vest's zipper toggle.

—purr purr purr they all fit fit fit—

"I'll show you how real it—"

Kestrel swatted his hand away. "Cut it out!"

The sheep-cheese lady was staring, and a mother pushing a stroller, too. Both women watched Greene with accusing eyes.

He stepped away from Kestrel and slumped down on an upside-down crate.

Then, a fresh rush of customers for Kestrel to help while Greene sat and sulked.

He was spinning, head over heels, through a galaxy lit only by the dullest points of light. Spinning, and God, it was cold.

NOW

ALLAN

Darkness has fallen by the time I reach the boat launch up at Mountain Lake. There's Boyce's big new truck I paid for, parked with the engine running. Slow-motion billows of exhaust wrap around it and dissolve into the night.

I park beside him, but not too close. I pull the overstuffed envelope from the door pocket. God, I'm sick of this game.

I get out of the car. The air is heavy with water vapor, and it instantly wets my face. I smell the dankness of the lake and the tang of rotting fir duff. I circle around and stand in the neutral zone between our vehicles. Boyce takes his sweet time because that's the kind of little power play he enjoys, but finally he swings open his door and climbs out. The radio is playing, some fake hick crooning about liquor being quicker than love, and there's someone else in the pickup cab, sitting in the passenger seat and lit up by the starship-control glitter of the dashboard. A smallish person with a puff of curls.

"You brought company," I say to Boyce.

He shuts his door and turns to me. He's wearing jeans with a big buckle and a denim trucker jacket, open to show a dress shirt underneath. "Just the wife. I don't keep secrets from Patty. That's how it's supposed to be in a marriage, son."

He's trying to bait me. I'm not going to fall for it.

"Here," I say, holding out the envelope.

Boyce lumbers forward and takes it. He pries the envelope open and peers in.

"It's all there," I say. "I've never cheated you."

"Nope." Boyce chuckles. "You haven't, have you? Well, I'll be going. Me and Patty have a dinner reservation, and I've got an appointment to talk to someone, too. Someone you know."

"What the fuck are you talking about?"

"It was the darndest thing. Your little wife called me this afternoon, saying she wanted to talk. Said it was real urgent—something about Greene Cooper's arrest way back when. Now, why does she want to know about that? I thought. I'll bet Allan won't be too happy."

"Stay away from her," I say. "Stay the fuck away."

"I'll do what I want, son. You know that." Boyce pivots, opens his door—now the country music is audible again—and sets one foot up onto the running board. His glossy snakeskin boot catches the light.

There's something about that boot and that music that make me just lose it. Maybe because I know the boots cost a fortune and I paid for them. Maybe because that sickening music yanks me right back to my childhood, like it's telling me I will never, ever transcend that stupefying hick shit no matter how hard I try. Or maybe it's because at that moment it fully sinks in that if Hannah starts talking to Boyce, she might tell him *everything.*

I take a quick step forward and grab the collar of Boyce's jacket. I shove him to the ground. He's bigger than me, but I work out a lot, and I've caught him by surprise.

He's splayed and flailing for a second, trying to get up, and it's suddenly so apparent that he's just an old man that I almost laugh.

Now he's sitting up, which is convenient because I don't have to bend very far to wrap my hands around his neck. I dig my thumbs into the soft flesh under his collar, burrowing for his windpipe exactly the way I have daydreamed about for years. I squeeze. His skin is clammy and fragile.

His wife in the cab has figured out what's going on. She's screaming. Not the full scream of a young woman but an old woman's warble.

Boyce goes slack. A few seconds after that, I feel the life go out of him and I think, Oh fuck, what have I done?

I let go of him, and his torso thunks sideways on the gravel.

I look up to see his wife climbing behind the steering wheel. The pickup has been running all this time, the country music still twanging endlessly, so all she'll need to do is put it in Reverse. She'll be gone, and I'll be screwed.

I leap over Boyce's body, grab her arm, and drag her from the cab. She has more fight in her than her husband did, but she's as weak as a kitten. I crush her windpipe, too, and step over her body. I switch off the pickup's engine, and when that music cuts out and leaves me in the good, clean silence of the night, I feel like I can finally breathe again.

I pocket the keys. I consider getting both of their bodies back in the cab and rolling the whole thing down the boat ramp and into the lake. But I'm not sure the lake is even deep enough to cover the pickup. It's swampy and coated with a scum of lily pads. For all I know it's only waist-deep, and if it is there will be no getting the pickup out again.

I'm going to have to dispose of the bodies somewhere else. Somewhere far away.

I drag Boyce's wife around to the back of my car and dump her in the trunk. Then I drag Boyce around by those provoking snakeskin boots. He's a big man. Getting him into the trunk is a full-body workout. I remind myself to lift from the knees. I don't want to throw my back out on top of everything else.

I pull on the pair of leather gloves I keep in the glove compartment, because fingerprints might become an issue. Then I find a folded blue plastic tarp in the back of Boyce's pickup. I unfold it partway, spread it over the two of them, and slam the trunk shut.

I drive Boyce's pickup up the road and, the first chance I see, drive it deep into the trees. I keep my gloves on for all this. It occurs to me, and not for the first time, that the good thing about being as bald as a basketball is that I don't have many telltale hairs to shed.

There are a lot of trails up here in the state park, but at this time of year there can't be many hikers. The pickup will stay hidden for a few days, tops. But that should be long enough for me to figure out next steps.

I walk back down the road to my car.

CAROLINE

Trey lets me into his apartment and invites me to sit on his couch. He says he is thankful that I agreed to come to study the Word with him, and he passes me a mug, which is painted with orange-and-white mushrooms.

"Thanks," I whisper, my fingers wrapping around the searing-hot ceramic. *Whore*, the mug whispers.

"What?" Trey is standing over me.

I dare not raise my eyes. I would like to put the malicious too-hot mug down, but I am afraid Trey might take it as an insult. "Thank you," I say more loudly.

"You're welcome." Trey says this with finality, as though I have, for now anyway, learned my lesson to speak more audibly.

I *have* learned it, I think, but now all I want is more lessons. Teach me, Trey. Punish me if I fail.

The ember of lust that I have carried between my legs day in, day out since the first time I saw Trey flickers into flame. I steal a furtive glance at his thighs in his snug jeans as he lowers himself into his chair.

"How about First Timothy, Chapter Two?" he says.

I nod. At last, I have an excuse to put down the hot mug.

I pick up my worn Bible, every one of its ribbon bookmarks in use, and open it to the New Testament. I am proud of how quickly I locate the right page. The margins are already marked up in pencil because we have studied it carefully in the unmarried women's fellowship group.

"I exhort therefore, that, first of all, supplications, prayers, intercessions, and giving of thanks, be made for all men," Trey begins in his warm, gentle voice. He reads all fifteen verses, and then stops. He looks at me. The spot between my legs is on fire. "I'm not sure that really sank in?" he says. "Should I read it again?"

With effort, and keeping my eyes cast down, I nod once.

"Or maybe just the parts that seem real pertinent to us," Trey says. "Like—" He runs a finger down the page. "Like verse twelve?"

I open my mouth to say *yes*, but then my eyes fall on the words to which Trey referred, and I cannot speak. My entire skin tingles as though I am wrapped in sunlight.

He wants me, I think. I feel like weeping. I feel like I might combust. Despite Mrs. McCullough, despite those little sluts at youth group, he wants *me*.

Trey reads, *"But I suffer not a woman to teach, nor to usurp authority over the man—"*

I feel his eyes on me as he speaks—he must be reciting from memory—but I don't look up. My eyes, my will, would break the spell. I want nothing but to be consumed by this spell like dry leaves in a burn barrel, orange flame licking upward, my self vanishing.

"—but to be in silence." A pause. "Why is that, Caroline? Why must Woman be silent? Why must she submit?"

Mute, I shake my head. There is a long silence. Then I hear a creak as Trey leans forward in his chair, and his hand is on my shoulder. Pushing. Pushing me to my knees. They thump on the bare floorboards. Pain shoots through my leg bones.

"It's right *here*, Caroline," Trey says, suddenly sounding angry. "It's right here in *The Book*." His hand is still on me, his fingertips digging into my shoulder blade. *"For Adam was first formed, then Eve. And Adam was not deceived, but the woman being deceived was in the transgression."* He lets go of my shoulder and unzips his jeans. He pulls my head toward the hard core of him. "Are you a sinner, Caroline?" he says softly. "Huh? You a sinner?"

I know what he wants from me, and who am I, a mere woman, to object? So I whisper, "Yes, Trey. Yes."

Afterward, Trey zips his jeans and walks over to the kitchen sink. He fills a glass with water and drinks it slowly, his back to me.

I stay on my knees on the floor. I am empty and translucent, a soap bubble floating slowly sideways.

He speaks without turning around. "There's something you're going to need to do. You're going to call the sheriff and tell them it was Mrs. McCullough who killed that girl they dug up."

"Why?" I whisper. "Why do you want me to do that?"

He turns around. "Because I care about your soul? Because I don't want you to go to Hell? You understand that you *have* to do it, right? That if you don't tell the sheriff it was Mrs. McCullough, they're going to wind up arresting the wrong person, someone who's innocent. Then how will you feel? I know what you are, Caroline. I found out. You were one of those, like, Satan-worshippers on that farm—"

"How did you—"

"Don't *interrupt*. But you can fix it now. Well, sort of. You have a chance to make it a little better, by making sure they lock Mrs. McCullough up for good."

"But she… Did she kill her? Did she kill her sister?" I can almost… Yes. I can see it. Her lips parting in a gasp when she sees the club swing high.

"Get up," Trey says. "Why are you still down there on your knees? Get up, and get out your phone."

I obey. I am brimming with joy. I am Trey's now, so his wish, at last, is my command.

JOSH

The moment my plane touches down in Seattle, I'm switching on my phone and checking my text messages, but there isn't a single new message. Not from Drew. Not from Amelia. Not from anyone. Even my social-media alerts have died down. The botched Sibelius was five days ago, and everyone in classical music has apparently moved on. It's like my career—no, *I*—never existed.

Then I see the news alert from the *Seattle Times*.

Fugitive Breaks into Crime Lab

A federal fugitive who has been on the run for nine years was arrested late last night after breaking into a Washington State Patrol crime lab in Marysville. Greene Cooper escaped custody of the San Juan County Sheriff in August 2015 after his arrest on burglary charges. He has been wanted by federal law enforcement ever since.

Last night around eleven o'clock, State Patrol officers were summoned to the State Patrol D-7 Station after the security system was triggered. They arrived to discover a man, later identified as Cooper, who had breached the secure entry as well as the secure door leading to the crime lab. At time of reporting, it was unclear how Cooper could have gotten past the security checkpoint and the secured doors, and the office has launched an internal investigation into the matter. Cooper was shot by an officer and taken into custody.

The State Patrol D-7 Station currently holds evidence pertaining to the homicide investigation of an adolescent female who was discovered in a shallow grave on Orcas Island last week. The deceased female is thought to have been a member or visitor of the Kinfolk Community, a group of self-professed "radical homesteaders." Cooper was a longtime member of the Kinfolk Community.

Cooper has been arrested for trespass, and he will also face arraignment on federal charges. He is currently under police guard at Providence Regional Medical Center, and he is reported to be in stable condition as he awaits surgery.

My hands shake. I feel like I'm going to throw up.

This is what Greene flew all the way from Geneva to do? Break into a freaking evidence lab to—well, to do what? Steal the murder weapon? I mean, what the *fuck*?

I go in a daze through passport control and customs and out into the cold, wet night. The air smells like home so intensely that I fight the urge to go back into the terminal and buy a ticket to anywhere else. But I need rest. I need it desperately. I couldn't sleep on the flight, but I drank plenty of vodka and now I feel like a walking corpse.

I get a Lyft and go downtown, where I check in to the Fairmont. I go up to my room. I park my bags and slide off the violin case and set it on the floor. The relief of getting it off my back almost makes me cry.

I go to the minibar and, kneeling in front of it with my coat and shoes still on, I grab a little bottle of SKYY Vodka, crack off the cap, and pour the contents down my throat. After that, I feel a little bit better, so I reach for another bottle.

If Greene is under police guard, then I won't be able to access him. I won't be able to fix this. I have come to the end of the road.

I crawl over to my messenger bag and take out the bottle of Xanax. I count the pills in my palm. Twenty-one.

I could swallow them all right now and avoid dealing with any of this shit ever again. I'm a worthless person. I ruined Greene's life and the lives of other people, too. I'm responsible for deaths. I'm a selfish, spoiled piece of shit who is wholly unworthy of love. If I can't play violin, I am nobody and I have nothing. Nothing, that is, except a long list of disastrous mistakes.

After I saw the guns and ammunition in the pit house that day, I should've kept my mouth shut. But I've always been kind of a shitty person, so what I did instead was tell my dad about them. When the ATF raided the Farm later that summer, it was because Uncle missed his court date, but it was also because they'd been tipped off about weapons stockpiles on the property.

And that isn't even the worst thing I did.

I realize I'm crying, and that disgusts me, but I can't stop the heaving sobs, the snot and tears.

But, a tiny little voice says, so quiet I almost can't hear it.

But, what? I ask it savagely.

But you know how to love. So that's something.

It seems like an incredibly lame consolation prize to have nothing but the ability to love, especially when no one on the entire planet even *wants* my love. But somehow it's enough to make me pour the pills back into the bottle and snap the lid shut.

I climb fully clothed onto the bed. I don't even take off my shoes. I plummet almost instantly into headachy sleep.

HANNAH

Allan still isn't back from his trail run at five to six. I'm supposed to speak to Boyce at the Rusty Anchor at six, so I have no choice but to get Sibley and Oliver into the car and start driving.

"Where are we going?" Sibley asks. She looks so sleepy, huddled in the back seat with Bunners in her arms.

"I have to run an errand," I say.

Oliver sits in silence, looking out the window.

At quarter past six, I pull into the last spot in the gravel parking lot of the Rusty Anchor. I dial Boyce's number. It goes straight to voicemail.

I dial again. Same thing.

I force myself to wait a few minutes, peering through the lit-up windows of the restaurant, but I don't even know what Boyce looks like.

I dial again. Voicemail.

The first real wave of despair hits me.

I get Sibley out of the car and, leaving Oliver to wait alone, we go inside the restaurant. I ask the hostess if Sergeant Boyce and his wife are seated.

The hostess, eyeing Sibley's bandage, tells me they had a five-thirty reservation but they never showed.

We go back to the car. I dial Boyce's number again. Once again, straight to voicemail.

"Mommy, what's wrong?" Sibley asks. "Don't be sad, Mommy."

"I'm not sad," I say.

I hear Oliver's little snort of derision.

I swivel to face him. "Was there something you wanted to say to me, Oliver?"

He gives me a hostile look. Then he cuts his eyes away.

"It's because he's tired of you pretending," Sibley says.

"What?"

"He says you pretend you don't understand stuff, but you really do. Like about Bunners. And the stick."

"Oliver, when we discussed not pretending anymore, I was talking about who we are," I say. "Where we came from. Not—not magical sticks."

"But you *know* Sibley can do stuff," he says. "I've seen you watch her do it. She can make our LEGO build themselves, she can make her Calico Critters walk. She can talk to Bunners. She says things know stuff and, if you listen, they'll tell you what they know."

"No," I say, shaking my head. "No, Oliver. We can't—we aren't going to talk like that. We'll all go crazy if we start talking like that. What I think is you're making all this stuff up so people won't blame you for what you did. But you hurt Sibley. *You* did. You're never going to get better if you won't take responsibility for your—"

"It wasn't me!" Oliver shouts.

"It wasn't Ollie," Sibley says. "It was the stick. It's a really bad stick."

"Fine," I say with an angry sigh, turning over the engine. "Then show me the bad stick."

★ ★ ★

I understand why Sibley is covering for Oliver. She loves him. She doesn't want him to get in trouble. She might even have some intuition that he's on the verge of being sent away.

And maybe indulging their charade about the stick is yet another mothering fail. But it's the only way I can think of to put this matter to rest.

They'd been playing on the Kinfolk Farm parcel that day, so instead of driving back to our own house, I turn onto the Farm's dark, overgrown driveway. I park next to the mailbox. I find the flashlight I keep in the glove compartment, and we get out.

I avoid looking at the eyeless house.

Oliver and Sibley lead me across the barnyard and through a broken-down section of fencing, into a field. It is a damp and velvety-black night, with rain so fine it's like walking through clouds.

The field, which had once been for the goats, is a sea of lush blackberries. Their thorny canes arch like the arms of some thousand-armed sea creature. Last summer's berries are shriveled and black on the vine.

I pass the flashlight to Oliver, and he leads us along a track through the field and thicket. I glimpse the yellow glow of a deer's eyes.

Oh God, I think. I knew they'd been exploring the Farm's land, but they ventured this way? This is the worst way.

The field ends in a line of forest. I know this spot. The cabin used to be just another minute's walk inside the trees.

Oliver and Sibley lead me through the forest for about a minute. Then they stop. Oliver aims the flashlight beam at something in the middle of a clearing.

Sticks. Dozens of two-foot-tall slender sticks bristle up around a small patch of ground. It is no natural formation, not some windblown pile or animal warren. A human or humans arranged them so. Neatly, evenly spaced, every stick almost exactly the same height.

A fence? I think. Or a fort?

I picture Oliver hunched over his whittling on the woodshop stool, lit by yellow lamplight. I think of him driving the point of his sharp sticks into the dirt. How I thought they were weapons.

I was terribly, unforgivably wrong. They aren't weapons.

I step closer. The sticks encircle an oval hump in the muddy vegetation.

"Wolf," I whisper. A lump is forming in my throat. I turn to Oliver. "Is this Wolf's grave?"

This is where Greene buried Wolf on that nightmare day, after the raiders left with the bodies of Uncle and Quill. Oliver carved these sticks to mark Wolf's grave. Our dog. *His* dog.

"Yeah," Oliver says. "Wolf." His voice sounds so small, so childish. "He was a good boy. I remember him. The way his ears felt. He'd chew sticks up into just a pile of spitty woodchips. I remember him a lot."

I turn to Sibley. "And you…you were helping Oliver make this?"

She nods.

"I told her about how we lived here before," Oliver says, "and how I'm really her uncle, not her brother, but I made her promise not to talk about it to anyone else because I'm not supposed to remember about before. I didn't let her use the whittling knife, because she's not old enough, but she helped me find branches that I could carve, and she helped me twist them into the dirt. And she…"

"What?"

"Nothing."

"Oliver. Whatever it was you were about to say, I need to know."

There's a long pause. He whispers, "It was a bad stick."

"We found it over there," Sibley says, pointing. I realize with horror that she is pointing toward where the cabin used to be.

"It was a handle for a shovel or something," Oliver says. "Sibley said it was a bad stick, and she didn't want to touch it, but I thought it was good wood, so I carved it for Wolf's grave. It got really sharp, sharper than the other ones, maybe because it was a harder kind of wood or something. I don't know."

"I didn't notice it was the bad one, and I picked it up," Sibley says. "It jumped up like a snake and bit my face."

"What?" I whisper.

Oliver says, "She screamed, and when I ran over, she was bleeding, and the stick was on the ground all bloody."

I take a deep breath. I let it out slowly, carefully. "The stick did it," I say.

"Yeah," Oliver says. He turns his face away. "I told you," he mumbles to Sibley. "I told you she'd keep pretending."

Sibley steps closer to him. She slips her hand into his. "It's okay, Ollie," she says, "because *we* know."

I look at these two small people standing hand in hand in the big, dark woods, and it reminds me of who I used to be, once upon a time. Lost. No one to protect me. So even though I don't really know what to make of what they're telling me about that stick, I know that I have to believe them.

I go to Sibley and Oliver. I bend down and wrap my arms around both of them and hold on tight. "I believe you," I whisper. "Both of you. I believe you. It *is* a bad stick—sticks can be bad like that, things can be bad. And I know that you would never hurt Sibley, Oliver. I know it. Now, let's go, okay? It's time to go."

"Where?" Oliver asks warily, pulling out of my embrace. "To the house? Allan said he was taking me to Montana tomorrow night. On an airplane. Hannah, I don't want to go."

"We aren't going to see Allan. We'll go straight to the ferry."

No, I think suddenly—Sibley's medication. It's at the house, and we can't leave without it. She'll be in too much pain.

"We're going to stop by the house for a second," I say, "just to pick up a couple things. And then we'll go."

We walk back to the car. We drive the short distance to our house—to Allan's house—next door.

My headlight beams sweep across the driveway. An SUV is sitting behind Allan's Tesla. The SUV has a green stripe across the side and white lettering: *Sheriff.*

I park. I get out, and before I shut the car door, three people come out of the house: Allan, and the two sheriff's detectives. They are gilded by the light of the porch lanterns. Allan stays back, but the two detectives come over.

"Hannah McCullough," the woman says, "you are under arrest for the murder of Gretchen, otherwise known as Kestrel, Stroufe."

The words are surreal. They ring almost comically in my ears. Yet they are, to be fair, the only right culmination of my sins.

THEN

GREENE

As soon as they got back from the farmers market, Greene walked straight to Josh's house. He went the fastest way, on the driveway, because he didn't give a damn if McCullough saw him. The only thing he could think of was how Uncle had touched Kestrel's leg in the pickup truck. How Kestrel had said it had been going on for a long time.

When Greene saw McCullough's Lexus parked in the driveway, his resolve faltered. But only a little.

He thumped his fist on the front door.

Please, please, please let it be Josh who opens the door, he thought.

The door opened. It was McCullough, in clean jeans and a baby blue polo shirt. He didn't look all that surprised to see Greene.

"Hi," Greene said. "I'm— Is Josh around?" The question was just a formality: he could hear Josh playing violin somewhere in the house. It wasn't the Mozart, but something more complicated.

"Yes."

"Can I speak to him?"

"You certainly look the worse for wear. Don't they let you take baths in your cult?"

Heat rushed into Greene's head. "It's urgent," he said.

"Let me guess. You're upset that your leader is in jail."

Greene looked hard at McCullough, startled. "How do you know about that?"

"News travels fast on this island."

"Well, he's not in jail. He's been out for a week. On bail."

Now it was McCullough's turn to look startled. "What?"

"Yeah."

"That slippery little shit." McCullough gave Greene an assessing look. "You fucking hate him, don't you? You look like a smart kid. You look like you have some self-esteem, which is more than I can say for the rest of them. How old are you?"

"Seventeen."

"Seventeen? Then why are you even sticking around?"

"It's complicated."

"Your parents?"

"No."

"Wait—*Josh?*"

"No!"

"I know. A girl. Oh, man. If she's pretty, then I'll bet Garnock makes you share."

Greene's ears burned. McCullough was burrowing under his skin like larvae under tree bark.

"Listen," McCullough said. "If Garnock misses his court date, he'll be arrested again, and I guarantee he won't be let out on bail. He'll sit in jail until a trial that he's going to lose, and then he'll be locked up in a federal penitentiary for years. You and your girl will be done with him forever. Wouldn't that be great?"

Greene stuck his hands in his pockets. "Can I talk to Josh now?"

McCullough opened the door wider and stepped aside. "Just follow the sounds of desperation."

Greene carried the secret of his bargain with Josh that afternoon like a treasure in his heart. They'd come to a quick agreement, whispering behind the closed door of Josh's bedroom: in five days, when McCullough went away on a business trip and left Josh alone, Greene would return and make the violin believe Josh was Leonid Orlyk. Josh would be going to Seattle for two weeks to have his violin lessons and attend a string-quartet workshop. When he came back to the island on August 21, he'd have fifty thousand dollars with him, cash.

Greene longed to tell Kestrel about the bargain, but he also didn't want to say anything to her until he had the money in hand. He pictured how her face would light up, with relief, with joy, with love.

"I found a way off this stupid island," he'd say to her, and she would throw her arms around his neck.

As for what McCullough had said about Uncle missing his court date, Greene didn't give it much thought. How the heck could he make Uncle miss his court date, anyway? Overdose him with mushrooms? Lock him in the cabin? Shove him out to sea in an oarless boat?

Actually, all those ideas sounded pretty good. But Uncle no longer mattered. Soon, Greene would have a king's ransom in United States cash. Uncle could go to Hell for all he cared.

But when Greene arrived back at the farmhouse after scything down a nettle patch a few days later, stinging and begrimed and heading upstairs to wash, an opportunity presented itself as though by divine intervention: someone had set the day's mail on the table in the entry hall. Three envelopes, with one on top that whispered to Greene as he passed.

—come here—

He froze, his hand on the banister.

—because you have to—

There were voices in the kitchen, and floorboards creaked overhead. But no one would see him.

He grabbed the envelope—

—ouch ouch!—

—bounded up the stairs two at a time, loped down the hallway, and shut himself in his room.

His hand shook as he inspected the envelope. It was light, containing probably only a few sheets of paper. He turned it over and looked at the sealed flap.

Open up, he said to the envelope. *Unstick your glue, no ripping. Neat and tidy*—the envelope flap lifted gently—*there you go.*

Greene slid out two folded sheets of paper. He opened them. The first sheet said

United States District Court
for the
Western District of Washington
United States of America
v.
Christopher James Garnock
Case No. 66754

Summons in a Criminal Case
YOU ARE SUMMONED to appear before the United States District Court at the time, date, and place set forth below to answer to one or more offenses or violations based on the following document filed with the court:

Below this were several options with boxes. The box next to *Indictment* was checked.

Place: United States Courthouse, 700 Stewart Street, Seattle, WA 98101
Courtroom No.: 7
Date and Time: August 21, 2015, 2:00 p.m.
This offense is briefly described as follows: Felon in Possession of a Firearm, in violation of 18 U.S.C. § 922(g) (One Count)

Greene skimmed the rest, and then his eyes were pulled irresistibly back to:

Date and Time: August 21, 2015, 2:00 p.m.

Here it is, Greene thought. The answer. So simple. I'll have my fifty thousand bucks and we can run away, but this will be extra insurance that Uncle will never, ever hurt anyone again.

Change, he said to the letter. *Change* 21 *to* 22. *Move, little number one. Curve over. Jut out.*

The pixilated black ink slowly rearranged itself. The *1* morphed into *2* so that now it said:

Date and Time: August 22, 2015, 2:00 p.m.

Greene folded the papers neatly and slid them back into the envelope.

Seal yourself, he said to the envelope. *Stick strong, just like before.*

The flap closed. Pressed. Sealed.

He opened his bedroom door a crack. Listened. He went softly along the hallway, down the stairs.

As he passed the entry table, he tossed the envelope on top of the others.

Then he went to the kitchen. He was ravenous.

Greene met Kestrel at the potter's house the next day. As always, they fell into each other's warmth and didn't speak at all. Greene couldn't have spoken, anyway. His thoughts were stuck on what he was going to do for Josh for fifty thousand bucks. On how Uncle thought his court date was August 22. Wondering if maybe neither of those things were the right things to do.

No going back, though, he thought, and then his thoughts were wiped out by the urgency of his body and Kestrel's.

It was raining. The tap-tapping of the raindrops on the metal roof cocooned them in their own gorgeous little world.

Afterward, Kestrel lay on her side, eyes shut, her hands under her cheek in the same way she'd done her entire life. Greene had known her for so long that he saw her at every age at once. At least when her eyes were shut. When they were open, pain flitted like a ghost behind her eyes.

Greene bundled up his courage, blocked out all his doubts, and whispered into her hair, "There's a way out, Kestrel. I found the way out."

Her eyes flew open. The illusion of seven-year-old Kestrel, ten-, eleven-, fourteen-year-old Kestrel, vanished. "What? What are you talking about?"

"I found a way to get us out of here. All of us. You, me, Quill, and Littlest."

"How." Flat. Disbelieving.

"I can't tell you."

She scoffed. "Spare me the drama."

"It's for your own good. Not knowing, I mean."

"And does it involve *tricks*, Greene?"

He said nothing.

"It *does*? Oh my God. *Greene.* Please." She sat up, holding the blanket to her bare breasts. "Greene, I love you, I cannot even say how much I love you—" she took his hand "—but I can't *do* this—"

"Why don't you just—"

"Let me finish!" Her voice was cracking. "Can't you see what's happening to Quill? How people treat Littlest? And you're still living in your fantasy world?"

"I—"

"If you go there, Greene, if you go *there*—" she was wet-eyed now "—then you leave me behind here. You leave me behind to deal with all the crap while you're…" she smeared viciously at her eyes and nose "…while you're still pretending you can do *magic*?"

"I'm fixing everything. I'm freeing us."

"Doing what?" Her voice grew hard. "I can read you like a book. I've known you since you were eight."

But you don't know me, Greene thought. You refuse to know me anymore. You call what I am, who I am, *pretending*.

He said, "I can't—"

"You know what? Forget it, Greene. Just *forget* it." Kestrel started yanking on her T-shirt. "You want your little secrets? Okay, fine. But I'm done with this until you—you..." She gulped, and it sounded painful. "Until you figure out how to share."

"Until *I* figure out how to share?" Greene was getting angry now. When had he ever gotten angry at Kestrel? His beloved, his best friend? The world was coming to an end. "What about you?"

She was standing up, stuffing a foot into her jeans. "What about me? I have nothing to share. In case you hadn't noticed I spend all my time playing mommy to Quill and Littlest, and whatever time is left over I spend worrying if you should be locked up in a mental institution—"

Greene sucked in air, like the time Guide slugged him hard in the gut.

Kestrel's face fell. "I'm sorry. I didn't mean—"

"No. You *did* mean it."

She gave a heavy sigh. "Okay, fine. I did. But not the locked-up part. Listen. Out in the real world, they have medicine for these kinds of problems. No one holds it against you. It's considered a sickness, like a sore throat or, I don't know, like arthritis."

"Arthritis?" Greene vaguely thought he should be getting up and getting dressed, too, but he couldn't move. He couldn't even look at her. It hurt too much. "You really think I'm crazy."

"Not crazy." Kestrel buttoned her jeans. "Special. You're *special*, Greene. Your brain is, I don't know, wired differently. That's all. But you have to understand that it is scientifically impossible to do the things you say you can do—"

"That I *say* I can do? You've seen me do them. Dozens—no,

hundreds of times. From day one. You've *seen* it." He sounded like he was begging. He disgusted himself.

"No," Kestrel said. Clothed now, she stood very still and looked at him. Wary. Pitying. "When we were little kids, I loved listening to your stories about what things told you—"

"My *stories*?"

"—and later on, when you got so good at doing magic tricks—"

"What?"

"—I loved that, too. But then I realized what was really going on. That you can't tell the difference between what's real and what's pretend. That you think you can actually communicate with inanimate objects."

Even though she was standing right there, close enough that if Greene got to his feet he could wrap his arms around her... she seemed to be standing on another island, separated from him by a quick, dangerous current.

"I can't do this anymore, Greene." Her voice was gentler now.

He forced himself to speak even though his throat ached terribly. "Can't do what?"

"I have to focus all of my energy on Quill and Littlest. I shouldn't even be here. I don't like leaving Littlest with your mom. I don't like the way she looks at him."

"Fine. We won't come out here anymore. But that doesn't mean we—"

"Yes, it does. I shouldn't even... It's wrong for us to do this." She gestured to the bed.

"Wrong? No, it's not! Kestrel, we love each other—"

"You're not *well*, Greene. Don't you get it? Your mind is—it's sick. I shouldn't go to bed with someone who's sick. That's wrong. That's something Uncle would—"

"Don't say his name!" Greene shouted.

Kestrel folded her arms over her chest. "I needed to be able to count on you—"

Needed? Greene thought. Past tense?

"—and I needed you to try and be a grown-up with me. To keep my—*our*—family together. But instead, you're going further and further into this—this *fantasy* world, and you've left me behind." She was pulling her cardigan on, holding its dingy gray flaps protectively to her belly as though she had a stomachache.

"I'm trying to help us," Greene said, even though he knew she couldn't hear him from her distant shore. "To save us. Save our family. The only way I know how."

"It's like you can't hear me, Greene—"

"It's like *you* can't hear *me*—"

"—and I'm all alone now." Kestrel's face crumpled. "I don't know what to do! *I don't know what to do.*" She was crying like she had the day they met in the raspberry patch. Her heart was breaking, and Greene felt what she felt: alone, hollow, with echoing black outer space spinning out around her—

He was on his feet, reaching for her—

"No." She stepped back, shaking her head. "No, Greene. We can't do this play-pretend world in this—this *shack* anymore. Really. I'm done with all this." She turned, hair flying out like a golden fan. She opened the door, stepped outside into the rain, and shut the door gingerly behind her in a way that hurt Greene more than a slam.

NOW

ALLAN

By some miracle I don't have to wait at the ferry dock. It's the offseason, plus it's Tuesday night, so we just roll right on the boat to Anacortes. Hannah will be at the sheriff's substation by now. They will have booked her. Considering how passionately I used to love her, I'm surprised that I feel nothing at all.

"What's that smell, Daddy?" Sibley asks as I'm parking on the vehicle deck.

Patty Boyce's sickly perfume permeates the car, but I say, "I don't smell anything."

"When is Mommy going to be with us?" Sibley is breathing through her nose. I'm guessing it hurts to breathe through her mouth. The air must rush across the hole on the inside of her cheek, thrilling with pain.

"I don't know," I say. "Why don't you take a nap? Or play on your phone?"

"I don't have a phone. We left my iPad at the island house." She sounds close to tears. "Where did they take Mommy?"

"Go to sleep," I say, wishing I'd remembered to grab her opioid syrup before we left the island house. I'm tired of her questions. “Why aren’t *you* playing on your phone?” I ask Oliver, giving him a sharp look through the rearview mirror. “Usually that’s all you want to do.”

“I’m done with that,” he says. He meets my eye impassively.

I make the kids go up to the cafeteria with me during the sailing. We get back into the car as we dock at Anacortes, and both of them are asleep by the time we reach I-5. I drive carefully, staying under the speed limit, and we reach my Briarcliff house before midnight.

I pull into the garage and park next to my Porsche. After I’ve woken up the kids and sent them inside to bed, I plug the charger into its port on the Tesla. I lock the car, shut the garage doors, and go inside.

Tomorrow I’ll drive out to the Olympic Peninsula. There are vast swathes of trees over there. Lonely Forest Service roads that wind for mile upon mile into the mountains. There are ravines, shadowy and deep.

I go up to my room and shower off Patty Boyce’s insidious perfume and the stench under my arms. I brush my teeth and moisturize, and when I come out of the bathroom, the au pair is in my bed.

She doesn’t seem to mind that I still can’t remember her name.

HANNAH

I was booked in the sheriff's substation in Eastsound. They took mug shots and said a lot of different things to me, but it's all a blur. The one thing I remember clearly is that they said no bail had been set because I was a flight risk and because I had committed a capital offense. Because I'm a danger to others.

There are two cells, but I'm the only prisoner here, in the cell in the corner. There's a metal bench, bolted to the concrete floor. The walls are constructed of cinder blocks, which are painted a glossy beige. There is one small window, high up on the wall, with metal slats. The light on the ceiling is caged with metal. It emits a tinny hum.

I sit on the bench and think about Ed Fletcher's story. How Greene sat here—maybe in this very same cell—with his face in his hands so still and for so long that it gave Ed the creeps.

Now I get it. There seems no point in moving. No point in crying, or fighting, or even breathing. It's all over. I have failed Oliver and Sibley, the two people for whom I have done terrible things and made shameful sacrifices.

I just wanted us to survive. Survive together.

JOSH

I wake. My head feels like it's being crushed inside an enormous fist. For a terrifying long moment, I don't even know where I am. Somewhere pitch-dark, and it smells like hotel-linen detergent. So, okay, a hotel. I'm used to hotels.

I sit up. I'm woozy. I can feel that I'm fully clothed, right down to a coat and a pair of shoes.

Then I remember. This is Seattle. I drank too much again last night. I wanted to die, because I'm at the end.

Only…it's not the end. It's not. Because—what was it? Yes, because I found Greene. I know exactly where he is now. All I have to do is figure out how to sidestep the police officer who will be guarding his hospital room.

I picture Greene lying in one of those plastic beds, still and pale and so defenseless.

I force myself to sit up. This could be my only chance.

Since I'm fully clothed, after I pee and brush my teeth I simply grab the violin and my roller bag and messenger bag and leave the room.

But I need money, I realize in the elevator. Cash that's untraceable, and I can't rent a car or take a Lyft to the hospital. Once I do what I need to do, I'm going to be the fugitive.

I have to stop at my dad's house in Briarcliff.

ALLAN

When I wake up, my first thought is of the dead bodies in the trunk of my car. I wonder how to get that rank perfume smell out. I'll probably have to sell the car, and do you have any idea how long the waiting list is for a custom Tesla?

I open my eyes. There is a girl in my bed. Not Hannah. The nameless au pair.

She opens her eyes and smiles. She snuggles close to me and kisses my bicep. "Good morning, Mr. McCullough," she says in a sleepy, sultry voice.

I think I may have made the mistake of telling her last night that Hannah's in jail and I'm divorcing her.

I sit up. "Can you go?" I say, stretching out my neck. "I have to get ready for work." Not that I'm actually going to work today, I'm going to the peninsula to deal with those bodies.

The au pair sits up, covering what there is of her breasts with her forearm. She looks confused.

"I see what's going on here," I say. "You thought that since I'm getting divorced, you were going to have your shot. I appreciate your enterprising spirit, but the thing is I only date pretty girls, and you're…well, you're not very pretty. Sexy as hell. But not pretty enough for me." I pick up a corner of the duvet and yank it off her, leaving her pitifully exposed. *"Go."*

She crawls out of bed and scoops up her robe from the floor. She drags it onto herself as she walks to the door, and I notice she's starting to cry.

"Clean yourself up, and then go and check on the children," I call after her. "That's what you're being paid for, right?"

JOSH

The Lyft I took from the Fairmont drops me, with my luggage and violin, at my dad's house in Briarcliff. A girl in jeans and a T-shirt answers the kitchen door when I knock. I assume she's a nanny or a housekeeper. She's puffy-eyed, and her nose is red. Clearly she's been crying.

"Hi," I say. "I'm Josh. Allan's son."

"Oh," she says, nodding. "Yes."

"Is my father here?" I ask, looking past her. "I saw both of his cars in the garage."

"He is here, upstairs. He came back from a run a few minutes ago." She has a French accent.

I roll my eyes. "One of his endless showers?" This is perfect, I think. If Allan's in the shower, I won't even have to interact with him. I won't have to explain, to lie, to beg for favors, to sneak around. I can just take. "I'll wait for him inside," I say and push past the girl.

I scan the wall hooks in the mudroom, looking for car keys, but I don't see any. I park the violin and my luggage and then go into the kitchen, the French girl following me. I open and shut drawers, look in cupboards, dig through the bowl of odds and ends on the counter.

"What are you looking for?" the girl asks.

"Car keys."

"You must be upset."

"About what?"

"The news."

"What news?"

"About Mrs. McCullough."

"What about her?"

"She was arrested last night. She is in jail on the island."

I stare at the girl as this sinks in. "Arrested for—"

"Murder," she whispers.

Holy shit.

I decide to go to my dad's study next. I need to get the money before he comes downstairs. The cars keys will be easier to sneak.

Way back when I was thirteen, I figured out that Allan had a wall safe hidden behind a couch in his study. It took me about a year to guess the combination: the date he found that stupid arrowhead he was always lecturing me about. After that, I treated the safe as my own personal ATM. I never took much—a few hundred here or there when my allowance ran out.

The one time I needed serious cash, the safe was for some reason empty, a coincidence that basically ruined everyone's life.

Now, I push the couch aside and kneel in front of the safe. Obviously, it's crossed my mind that Allan might have changed the combination. It has been almost a decade since I tried to get in here.

But no. Even though my fingers are fumbling, I hear the dry click that tells me the lock has opened.

I exhale with relief when I see all the tidy taped bundles of cash.

I take two of the bundles and stuff them in my coat pocket.

The bills are hundreds, so each stack is ten thousand bucks. More than enough for my purposes.

There are two manila folders leaning against the inside wall of the safe, the kind you see in doctor's offices. I don't recall Allan ever having anything but cash in this safe. It strikes me as strange, and so I pull out the folders and flip through them.

Inside are dental records. Dental records from almost twenty years ago, for two children named Hannah Stroufe and Gretchen Stroufe. Also tucked in the back of Gretchen's folder are birth certificates and social security cards for the same two girls, born three and a half years apart in Bellingham, Washington.

I know that the documents for Hannah Stroufe must be my stepmother's. But my dad having the records for the other girl, presumably Hannah's sister, locked in this safe? It doesn't seem even remotely legitimate.

The word that pops into my head is *leverage*. These documents could give me, for the first time in my entire life, leverage against my dad.

The next time he threatens to take away the violin, I'll just tell him I have *these*, so I win.

I shut the safe, replace the couch. I'm tucking the folders inside my coat when the French girl walks in.

She stops short, her eyes glued to where my hand is hidden inside my coat.

"What," I say. My tone is toneless, but inwardly I'm thinking, Shit!

"I heard you moving the furniture."

"And?"

"You must be taking things from your father's safe."

"Listen," I say, moving toward the door, "I really don't—"

"I will not tell him," she whispers. "I *hate* him."

I scan her face. Her nostrils are flared. Her lips are working. "I believe it," I say.

"You were looking for car keys—I got these from upstairs.

He didn't see me." She holds out her fist, slowly uncurls her fingers, and there's a black plastic key fob in her palm. "He loves that stupid car more than any person."

I hear the faint clack of a doorknob upstairs, footsteps, then Allan's voice. "Hello?" he calls. "Who's here?"

"Take it," the girl whispers.

My dad's Tesla is fully charged, and I get across the city to I-5 slowly but steadily. There's a stench in the car that is bugging me, though, like cheap perfume and, below that, something almost meaty. I crack the windows and drive north. I'm going against commuter traffic, luckily, and I reach Everett in forty minutes.

My first stop is Whistle Workwear.

I'm the only customer. The woman behind the register is watching me as I examine the rack of men's XL scrubs. I hope she didn't notice I arrived in a hundred-thousand-dollar car.

I buy blue nurse's scrubs for myself, top and bottoms, a pair of socks, and a pair of black Crocs. I also buy men's work boots, size twelve, in yellowish leather, Carhartt jeans 33x34—way too small for me, but then, I'm not going to be wearing them—a size large thick gray hoodie, a black baseball cap, and a nylon backpack. I pay with some of the hundreds. I feel like the woman takes note of how crisp the bills are, but she doesn't comment.

I take it all out to the Tesla in a big plastic bag. With the key fob, I unlock the trunk.

There's a big pile of junk inside—bulky stuff under a blue plastic tarp. The perfume smell is stronger back here, too.

I lift a corner of the tarp.

What I see is hard to register. I mean, it's obviously a dead guy, but the gray flabbiness of his skin and the way his eyes stare looks realer than real. His lips sag sideways to reveal long, yellowed teeth. He has bristled gray hair. He's wearing one of those fleece-lined denim trucker jackets. There's a second body, too, underneath the guy. I see a smaller hand, white and swollen, pink varnish on the nails, a gold wedding band.

I quickly pull the corner of the tarp back down over them. I think about the woman inside Whistle Workwear as I shut the trunk. Is she watching? Could she have seen? I didn't look at the bodies long, maybe two or three seconds, and if she *had* seen something, wouldn't she be screaming right now?

I get behind the wheel. My pulse hisses in my eardrums as I start the car.

I drive to Providence Regional Medical Center and enter the attached parking garage. I would've liked to park far from prying eyes, but parking on the upper levels or the roof, where it's bound to be emptier, will make it harder to leave in a hurry. Luckily, the back windows of the Tesla are heavily tinted. No one will see what's back there.

Once I'm parked on Level 3, I rip the wrapping from the new pair of socks and pull them onto my hands. I get out of the car.

I survey the vicinity. There are several other parked cars, but I don't see any people. I don't see any security cameras, either, but I can't be one hundred percent sure that there aren't any.

I open the trunk again and lift the tarp. This time, the perfume smell makes my jaws water with nausea. I try not to look at the guy too hard as I reach into his back jeans pocket and pull out his wallet. I flip it open and look at the driver's license. Washington State. Harlan Piskey Boyce. Orcas Island address.

I slide the license back in the wallet, put the wallet in his pocket, and replace the tarp. I shut the trunk.

Sitting behind the wheel, I pull up Google on my phone. In under a minute, I learn that Harlan Piskey Boyce used to be a sheriff's sergeant for San Juan County.

Jesus Christ, I think. I cannot *deal* with this right now. I'm wasting precious time.

I change into my new scrubs and Crocs in the car. I put my

phone in the pocket of the pants. Then I rip the tags off the rest of my purchases and stuff them all into the new backpack.

As I lock the car, I think about the violin behind the tinted windows on the rear seat and think, Happy now, asshole?

I find an elevator that takes me to a pedestrian walkway into the hospital.

It's the same as any hospital, with the bustling doctors and nurses, lost-looking people, and the odors of coffee and off-gassing plastics.

I find a directory. The newspaper journalist had reported on Greene's condition when he was awaiting surgery. Greene must've been operated on by now, though. He must either be in Critical Care (which could create major problems) or in Surgical Care.

I decide to check Surgical Care first.

On the way, I stop at the cafeteria and purchase the biggest cup of Mountain Dew available, extra ice, no lid. Then I take an elevator up to Surgical Care on floor four.

There are a lot of people moving around there, for which I'm glad. I don't want anyone looking at me too closely.

I turn left and walk down the corridor in a way that I hope looks purposeful. I have the stuffed-full backpack slung over one shoulder and the cup of Mountain Dew in hand.

Greene is under police guard. He's been charged with multiple felonies. I don't have to peer into the rooms to see the patients, I just have to look for a cop.

I reach the end of the corridor without seeing one. I turn around, feeling a rush of unease. What if Greene is in a special section of the hospital for security risks? Is there such a thing? What if he was transported to another hospital, or to jail? I can't drive around looking for him forever with two dead bodies in the trunk.

I pass the elevators and start down the other side of the corridor.

Once I turn the corner, I see the cop right away. He's sitting on a chair outside a door, his blue uniform weighted down with a gun and a stick on his belt and one of those radio things attached to his chest. He stares into space.

I walk past the cop. He looks sleepy. The door next to him is half-open, and I see a nurse moving around in front of a bed. I catch a glimpse of short dark gold hair on a pillow.

My pulse quickens. I know that hair.

I walk to the end of the corridor. Then I turn around and walk back. As I pass the cop, I stumble on my own feet and dump my massive cup of Mountain Dew all over him.

"Shit!" he shouts, jumping to his feet. "Shit!" Ice cubes clatter on the floor. The front of his uniform is dark with moisture.

"Oh my God," I say. "I am *so* sorry." A puddle of radioactive-green soda is spreading across the tiles. It has already caused a traffic jam.

The nurse pokes her head out of Greene's room. "Oh gosh," she says. She darts back into the room and comes out a second later with her hands full of paper towels. She kneels down by the mess.

I edge past the people who have stopped and the people who are mincing over the spill. The door is still ajar.

I see Greene Cooper in the bed under a smooth blue blanket. His eyes are shut.

I slip into the room.

ALLAN

I put on slacks, an Oxford shirt, dress shoes, and an overcoat and tell the au pair I'm going to work and that she's in charge of the children. Carrying a duffel bag with a track suit and sneakers inside, I go out to the garage. I wonder what I'm going to do with the kids long-term. It would be easy to put the girl into a boarding school for little fuckups, too, what with her penchant for talking to inanimate objects. But those schools are expensive.

My Porsche sits in the garage. But my Tesla is gone.

The floor under me seems to tilt, and I grab the doorjamb to steady myself. About a gallon of adrenaline pumps into my system.

Someone stole my car. With Boyce and his wife in the back.

I can't guess who stole my car, but I suddenly realize that I can easily find out where it is. I take my phone from my pocket and open the Tesla app. My hands are sweating, but with only a few stabs of my fingertip, I locate the car.

I stare at the little red arrow on the satellite map. What the fuck is going on?

My Tesla is up in Everett, parked at Providence Regional Medical Center.

None of this makes any sense, but I have to get to that car, those corpses, before it's too late. It may already be too late.

I get into my Porsche and back out of the garage.

JOSH

"Greene," I whisper, standing over his hospital bed.

His eyes open. They are the same olive and gold I remember. "Josh," he mumbles.

"I've come to get you out of here."

"I can leave whenever I want."

"Then—"

"She's dead, Josh," he whispers, his voice cracking. "Kestrel is *dead.* All this time I kept myself going by picturing her alive somewhere, having a good life, but...all this time she's been buried in that..." He's crying now. "She never made it off the island." He shuts his wet eyes. "I wanted to see the weapon. In the crime lab. It would've told me what happened. Who did it."

"Yeah. I figured." I look nervously over my shoulder. The nurse is still on hands and knees, mopping up Mountain Dew.

"Now I'll never know."

"Her sister was arrested last night," I say.

His eyes open. "What? You mean Eldest?"

"Yeah. For... They said she did it."

"Oh my God." He's crying again. "No. *Eldest?* She was always... Oh my God. But...why?"

"I can take you to her." I speak the idea without thinking it through. "You could ask her why."

"You know where she is?"

"I think so, yeah."

Greene sits up, yanks his IV out of its port, and swings his bare feet to the floor. He's wearing nothing but one of those inadequate papery gowns. His face scrunches.

"You're in pain," I say.

"The surgery was this morning. They dug a bullet out of my belly."

I look over my shoulder again. The nurse is almost done cleaning up the soda and ice. The traffic jam has cleared.

"I didn't plan past the part where I got into your room," I say.

"You knew you wouldn't need to."

This is probably true.

Greene goes to the door and closes it. I hear a soft cracking sound. "The door doesn't lock from this side," he says, "so I asked the lock to jam itself. It'll buy us a little time."

I nod. I believe him, even though objectively it sounds like madness. I mean, I've been dealing with that vindictive violin all this time. Of *course* I believe him.

He goes into the small bathroom, beckoning me to follow. He isn't walking completely straight.

I get into the cramped space with him, with its roll-in shower and handrailed toilet and punch of disinfectant, and Greene reaches around me and shuts the door.

"I brought you a change of clothes," I whisper, patting the backpack.

"In a minute," Greene whispers back. "Where are the nearest stairs?"

"That way," I say, pointing at the shower.

Greene steps into the shower. He runs his fingertips lightly down the square yellow wall tiles. Slowly, the tiles split apart at their grout lines with tiny snaps—my breath catches because it's scary and beautiful and amazing—and the wall underneath them splits apart, too.

There's another bathroom on the other side of the wall, a mirror image of the one we're in. When the opening in the wall is large enough, Greene steps through, and then he turns to me. "Come on."

I step through. It's a tight fit. I get drywall dust on my scrubs.

Greene touches the wall again, and it closes up like a hole in Play-Doh. The tiles end up a little crooked.

"No time to fix that up," he says.

We look out into the room. The door is closed. No nurses or doctors or visitors, only a white-haired person asleep in a bed. Out in the hallway, people are speaking with raised voices, and I hear the blip of the cop's radio. They have noticed Greene is gone.

"You should probably change," I whisper.

Greene nods.

I pass him the backpack and turn around to give him privacy.

Once he's in the jeans and sweatshirt and boots, Greene goes to the far wall of the room, to an empty spot behind the door. With finger and thumb, he stretches a little peephole open in the wall, all the way through to the other side. He looks through with one eye. "Empty," he whispers. He gets the wall to open itself wide, we both go through, and it closes back up again.

We go into the next room's bathroom and pass through the wall to the adjacent bathroom and then one more wall, and we're in a stairwell.

We head down the stairs. We need to go down to Level 2 to reach the pedestrian skybridge.

We pass two security guards stampeding up the stairs with their radios crackling. They don't give us a second glance.

We reach Level 2. I grab the handle of a door with a vertical slit of a window, but it doesn't move.

"We're under lockdown," I whisper. "Shit."

"I like locks," Greene says. He wraps his fingers around the door handle. I hear a click. He pushes the door open.

"And locks like you," I say.

This section of the hospital feels normal. No one seems to know about the hospitalized felon's escape upstairs. We pass through a busy corridor in what appears to be the OB-GYN department, then out to the mezzanine and onto the pedestrian skybridge.

In the parking garage, we take the stairs up one flight. We reach the Tesla. I unlock it, and we climb in. Greene is looking pale. He's hunched a little, squinting as though he's in pain.

"Are you okay?" I ask him as I back out of the parking spot.

"I've been better. What's in the back? It stinks."

"Uh...dead bodies." I shift into Drive.

"Are you... Did you—"

"Jesus, Greene! I didn't kill anyone!"

"Sorry. I just—I had to ask."

"It's someone named Harlan Boyce—he was a sheriff's sergeant on Orcas—"

"*Him?* I know him. Knew him. Asshole."

"—and some woman, maybe his wife?"

"But what's he—"

"This is my dad's car. I—stole it."

"Oh." Greene nods as though everything adds up. "Well, we really don't want to get stopped for a traffic violation, then."

I pull up next to the parking attendant's booth. I hand the woman in the booth my ticket and some cash. She gives me my change, and the barrier lifts.

Somehow, I did it. We're out.

I drive carefully through Everett—checking my mirrors for flashing blue lights about every three seconds—and get onto I-5 North.

Fifty-five miles to Anacortes, I think.

"Okay, Josh," Greene says as I accelerate on the freeway. "What do I have to do for you?"

"What?" I throw him a quick look. My gut gives a mean little tug.

"I know you. There's always a trade-off. So what is it?"

THEN

GREENE

"I couldn't get the money," Josh told Greene when he returned from Seattle on August 21. They'd met as planned in the forest by the stump. Josh looked nervous. He had his white canvas backpack over one shoulder.

"You... What did you say?" Greene felt like the ground had dropped out from under him.

"I couldn't get it," Josh said. "My dad has this safe, at our house in Seattle, and he always keeps money in there—like, a *lot* of money. But for some reason there wasn't any this time."

"Then what's in your backpack?" Greene asked. A pathetic question.

"I feel *so* bad," Josh said, as though he hadn't heard Greene. "I can check again next time I go to Seattle—"

"But...we need—I need it *now.* We can't wait." Uncle's court date in Seattle—his real court date—was that day. It had been half an hour earlier. Which meant Uncle was going to be arrested again, anytime now. Greene had planned to get himself and Kestrel and the boys away as soon as the cops came for Uncle. He figured that with that kind of a distraction, no one would notice their absence for a while. They'd have a head start.

If anyone even gave a damn they were gone.

"Well, I..." Josh slid the backpack off his shoulder. He held it out to Greene. The cloth sagged under the weight of whatever was inside. "I can give you these. They're worth, like, *way* more than fifty thousand bucks. I'm not sure, but I think they could be worth, like, a million."

Greene could barely understand Josh's words, but he took the backpack and set it carefully on the dirt path. He knelt, unzipped it, and looked inside.

He didn't even know what he was looking at—a jumble of dirty-looking old things, like crap you'd find in a box in an attic. He didn't have the energy to untangle its garbled, complaining chatter.

He looked up at Josh. "Where'd you get this stuff?"

"It's... I took it from my dad. From his artifact collection. Trust me, it's really valuable, and if you could figure out a way to sell it—"

"Sell it? Sell stolen stuff? *Where?* This is—Josh, this isn't what we agreed on."

Greene expected at least an apology. But Josh just pushed his hands into his pockets and shrugged. "Take it or leave it. To be honest, you're getting the bargain of the century."

NOW

JOSH

"I'm sorry," I say to Greene as we rush down the freeway at exactly one mile per hour under the speed limit. "I'm sorry I didn't hold up my end of the agreement. I'm sorry that instead of giving you the cash, I gave you those artifacts. I'm sorry that when you were arrested for having them, I kept quiet. I could've gone to the sheriff's office—"

"You mean to the dead guy in the trunk?" Greene says wryly.

"—and told them that I gave them to you. I mean, my dad figured it out pretty fast—that I stole them, not you. That's why he never pressed charges. He was covering for me, or I guess I should say he was covering for his own reputation. He never cared about me as a person. Not really. Anyway, Greene, I'm sorry. I'm so sorry."

"You were only a kid," Greene says. He has a hand on the side of his belly now, and he looks ashen. "We were both just kids. But...you haven't answered my question. What's the trade-off today? I mean, you're risking arrest to take me up to see Eldest, and I seriously doubt you're doing that out of the goodness of your heart."

I really am a crap human, I think. Everyone knows it.

"Let me guess," Greene says. "It's about that thing in the back seat." He gestures to the violin in its case.

"How did you—"

"I can hear it."

"Oh. Right. Is it talking about me?"

"Yup."

"And?"

"It hates you."

"Oh my God. I knew it," I whisper. The speedometer is ticking upward.

"Whoa, slow down, buddy," Greene says.

"I've been trying to keep it happy," I say. "Trying so *hard*. Eating and eating and getting fatter and fatter so my fingers will feel like Orlyk's, so I'll have a double chin like Orlyk... I even found out what aftershave he used, and what kind of cloth his tuxedos were made of, and his favorite brand of vodka. I replicated all of it, but it's not working anymore. None of it is good enough! I don't—"

"The violin loves Orlyk," Greene says quietly. "It knows he's gone, and no one can replace him. It's brokenhearted, I guess you could say."

"Then what am I going to... My career is screwed, and the guy I'm in love with... I mean— What can I *do*?"

"I'm not sure," Greene says.

ALLAN

The crosstown traffic is a nightmare. It takes me fifty minutes just to reach I-5, and another forty minutes to clear the bumper-to-bumper aftermath of a collision north of the city. I try to calm myself by counting on my inhales, holding for a two-count, and exhaling slowly.

It doesn't work.

Just past Northgate, I check the Tesla app again.

I can't believe what I'm seeing. Now the little red arrow on the satellite map indicates that my Tesla is parked in a holding lane at the ferry dock in Anacortes.

Whoever stole my car is going to Orcas Island.

My lungs feel like they've been packaged up with duct tape. Sweat trickles down my back.

I'm already in the freeway's fast lane, but now I press the gas even harder, passing vehicles on the right if necessary. As I go, I use voice commands on my phone to look up the Anacortes–Orcas ferry schedule.

The next boat is leaving in twenty-seven minutes. There's no way in hell I can make it in time.

I roar past six cars, swerve into the right lane, and take the next exit. I speed across an overpass and merge back onto the freeway, this time heading south.

I voice-dial Trey Higgins. He doesn't pick up. I try again a few minutes later. No answer.

I pass through downtown Seattle and SoDo and Georgetown, and then I exit. Sea-Tac is Seattle's main airport, but the private aircrafts and some of the tiny puddle-jumper airlines fly out of here: Boeing Field.

I park in the lot and walk quickly into the old brick terminal. I purchase a one-way ticket to Orcas Island on Kenmore Air. It's leaving in an hour, and the flight time is forty minutes.

I sit down on a plastic chair in the waiting area. I stand up again. I start pacing, dialing Trey's number over and over. He will not pick up.

I have no choice, I realize. I have to call that lunatic Caroline Cooper.

CAROLINE

I am sweeping up rat poop in the tack room at the James place when my phone vibrates in my apron pocket.

Trey, I think. Praise Him.

I drop the broom on the floor in my haste to dig out the phone. It is not Trey's number but one I do not recognize.

I answer the call.

"Caroline," a man says. "Where are you? Are you on the island?" He sounds agitated.

"Who is this?"

"Allan McCullough. Listen—are you still on the island?"

Fear slices through me. The last time I saw Mr. McCullough, he said he would kill me if I didn't leave. I wonder if this is a trick.

"I know I said some things to you," he says. "Stuff I didn't mean."

"You mean about *killing* me?"

"I didn't mean it."

Oh, he meant it. But I can feel he wants something from me now.

"Where are you?" he asks.

I hesitate. "I'm at work."

"On the island?" Yes. He is desperate. The last time Mr. Mc-

Cullough was this desperate, I came away with an envelope thick with cash.

"Yes," I say. "I'm on the island."

"Thank God." Now his voice sounds muffled, like he is near other people and doesn't want them to overhear. "I need you to help me. I'll pay you. You won't have to work for months. But I need you to help me."

"Doing what?"

"Take your car and pick me up at the Eastsound airport at three thirty. Don't be late."

"How much?"

"Ten grand."

Ten grand, I think. Imagine what I could do with that. I could go to Hawaii with Trey. I picture us walking hand in hand along a beach tinted pink by the sunset. Our mingled footprints trail behind us.

"Okay," I say.

HANNAH

I'm lying on my side on the jail-cell bench, my hands under my cheek for a pillow. I wish I could sleep, but it won't come. I mostly think about Sibley and Oliver.

I'm pretty sure it's the afternoon. It's raining and windy outside, and splattering gusts hit the side of the building.

I had a meeting with a state-appointed defender earlier, but I didn't feel much like talking. My life has ended. Why bother arguing about it? The defender said I'll appear before a judge tomorrow. The county courthouse is in Friday Harbor, on a different island. I'll go there on a ferry in the morning in the back of a sheriff's SUV.

I hear a scraping sound and lift my head.

Silence.

Wait—more scraping, very close. It's coming from inside the cinder-block wall. It sounds hollow and ponderous, and then I see with horror that the cinder blocks are coming apart at the mortar. I see a jagged slice of gray daylight. The wall is slowly spreading open, and rain is spraying in through a vertical crack.

An earthquake, I think as I scramble to my feet—some kind of slow-motion earthquake.

I stumble across the cell and press myself back into the farthest corner.

A man stands in the new opening. He has wet hair and a shining-wet face, and his jeans and sweatshirt are soaked through.

I tell myself I'm only dreaming, even though the rain feels so real. Dreaming of Greene.

He's no longer a fresh, bright-eyed teenager. He is worn. His face is thinner. His eyes are dimmer. But he still looks so, so vivid, and I realize that since he left, the whole world has been slightly out of focus because it was no longer what my heart thought was real.

"Kestrel?" he breathes, and I watch his face soften with relief, with joy, with love. "I thought you were dead."

I'm not dreaming.

Somehow in that moment, I feel nothing. Then I go to that box in my mind, the one in which I have kept hidden from myself all the grief, the shame, the fear. Where I hid my true self. Where I hid my love. I open it.

"Hi," I whisper back.

I did something bad.

I was manipulated into it, but that's no excuse. Even at sixteen I wasn't *that* stupid. I allowed Allan to dupe me. I had my reasons, foremost being survival.

Before our mother took us to live at Uncle's farm when we were six and ten years old, my sister and I had different names, the names that were on our birth certificates. My older sister was named Hannah Clare Stroufe. I was called Gretchen Alyssa Stroufe. But when our mother took us to live on the Farm, Mama renamed herself Tansy, for the yellow flowers that splotch the island's fields and ditches in the summer. She didn't know, I guess, that tansies are not only an invasive species but toxic. My older sister, Hannah, was renamed Eldest, and I was henceforth to be known as Kestrel.

The instant Uncle was killed, a spell broke. Like the inhabitants of an enchanted fairy-tale castle, everyone on the Farm woke up. We were no longer Kinfolk. We were free. I was solely responsible for my half brother Littlest, barely four years old and traumatized. Our brother Quill had been shot dead. I had only a week earlier figured out I was pregnant. Greene had been arrested, broken out of jail, and vanished.

I was half-crazed with desperation. I was looking for a savior.

Well, I found one: Allan McCullough. Or, to be precise, he found *me*, sitting on his beach a week after the raid. He seemed so kind, so warm. He seemed more like a grown-up than any of the tripped-out weirdos who populated the Farm. Allan seemed almost like a god. No joke. Like I said, I was only sixteen.

So. What is *it*, you've been wondering? Allan's and my original sin? The appalling secret we share?

It isn't that we got married when I was only sixteen. You would think that it would be illegal for a forty-two-year-old to marry a sixteen-year-old. But it isn't illegal, if the minor can secure parental consent. Or maybe you'd assume that statutory rape would come into the picture, but, unbelievably, it does not. Not in Washington State, whose laws say that in cases of marriage, an adult may legally have sex with a sixteen-year-old. Maybe you'd start to wonder if dirty old men were writing these laws.

We had to act fast, Allan and I, to make sure Littlest and I didn't get taken into state custody. Allan and I couldn't marry without parental consent until I turned eighteen, but that was years away, and my parents were AWOL.

There was another way, though. My sister, Eldest, disappeared after the raid, along with everyone else on the Farm. "Well, that's easy, then," Allan said to me. "You just say you're Hannah, and all your problems go away. No foster care for you or your little brother, plus we can get married right away and start our new life together."

All right, I said. You know best, I trust you, thank you, thank you.

All we needed to get married was a driver's license with Hannah's name and birth date on it. Allan arranged for all of that. He called in a favor, he said. He managed to get me a passport, too. I never asked how.

I was such an idiot.

I didn't even mind taking her name. I didn't want to be Kestrel anymore. Greene had abandoned Kestrel. She was wrecked. My sister had been Eldest to me for so long, so the name Hannah seemed like a clean garment, barely worn. I slipped it on. It sort of fit.

Identity theft is a crime punishable by a decade or more in prison. But it seemed more than justified, and no one got hurt. That's what I thought, anyway.

Here he is, I think, as I look at Greene looking at me with the rain and the wind coming in through the hole in the cinderblock wall. Here is the one I love.

Seeing him again after all this time is like jumping into a pool of turquoise water. It's like sucking up pure oxygen.

"I'm taking you away from here," he says, holding out his hand.

"I'll be a fugitive. I'll go to prison."

"I will never let that happen."

Part of my brain tells me to reject what I'm seeing: I'm overtired, under extreme stress. A human being couldn't have opened a wall and stepped through. But another part of my brain accepts it as natural. Hadn't I watched him do these kinds of things when we were little kids? And, if I am being totally honest with myself...haven't I watched our daughter do them, too?

I go to Greene, and I take his hand.

We hurry across the rainswept, near-empty gravel parking lot to the main road where a car is waiting by the ditch.

I balk. The car is Allan's Tesla.

"It's okay," Greene says. "It's not him."

We get into the back seat.

It really isn't my husband behind the wheel.

"Josh?" I say, because I know Josh, Allan's son, the famous violinist. I met him once, after one of his concerts. I notice a suitcase-like thing on the front passenger seat and realize it must be his violin.

He's twisted around and frowning at Greene. "What's going on, Greene? I thought you were going to ask her—"

"This is Kestrel, Josh," Greene says. "*Kestrel.* Not Eldest." He takes my hand.

"Wait—what?"

"We need to go."

"Where?"

"To the ferry."

Josh drives. The windshield wipers flip back and forth. He keeps glancing at me through the mirror, frowning.

Finally he says, "I recognized you. That night at the Four Seasons after my concert? I knew you were from the Farm. But I thought you were Eldest."

"How did you recognize me?" I ask. "We'd never met before."

"No, but I saw you once. You and your sister, down on the beach. I saw you through binoculars. From the house. Sorry. Is that creepy? You guys were digging for geoducks." He shakes his head. "I don't know why I was so sure you were Eldest—maybe because you were taller, so I just assumed you were also older?"

"Yeah," I say. "I was taller than she was by the time I was ten or eleven." I think of my sister with a sting of grief. Her delicate limbs, her fragile beauty. Because of how Uncle used us and pitted us all against each other, she was lost to me long before she disappeared. But it hasn't fully sunk in until right now that I'll never have a chance to fix that. She's gone forever.

Greene is still holding my hand, and he squeezes a little harder. It's enough to keep the tears in.

"Okay," Josh says, turning south onto the two-lane highway. "Until law enforcement is specifically looking for a black Tesla—or unless they start checking inside every car in the ferry holding lanes, which I've seen before—we're probably good. It all depends on how long the people at the jail take to figure out you're gone." He glances at Greene in the mirror. "Did you patch up your work?"

"I didn't want to waste time," Greene says.

"What?" Josh says.

"This is Allan's car," I say. "Won't he report it missing? Or did you—"

"Trust me," Josh says grimly, "he is not going to report this car stolen."

"Why?" I ask.

Josh and Greene exchange a look in the mirror.

"We'll tell you about it later," Josh says.

"We'll go back to the mainland," Greene says to me, "get Sibley and Littlest, and leave the country. Okay? I'll keep you safe."

None of that should sound even remotely possible. "Okay," I say.

When we reach the ferry terminal, the guy in the ticket booth tells us the next boat is only minutes away and that it will leave again at 4:20.

It's 3:51.

ALLAN

The weather turned foul and there was some talk in the Boeing Field terminal of my flight being canceled, but eventually it took off, to be tossed around in the swollen dark clouds like a toy. The woman across the aisle from me retched repeatedly into one of those paper baggies.

When we finally land on Orcas, I feel like I've aged ten years.

The Eastsound airport is nothing but a building resembling a ranch house on the edge of a landing strip. I disembark and go across the windblown tarmac, through the terminal, and out to the parking lot. I have my phone out, waiting for it to reconnect to the network.

I recognize Caroline Cooper's Honda. She's parked sloppily across two spots in the near-empty lot, idling.

I open the passenger door and slump down into the seat. I don't bother to say hello because I see my phone finally has three bars, so I open my Tesla app.

I swear to God someone is dicking around with me, because according to the app, my Tesla is now at the Orcas Island ferry dock, parked in a holding lane, waiting for the next boat back to the mainland.

Caroline says, "Where do you want to—"

"Take me to the ferry dock." I slide the phone into my coat pocket.

"But that doesn't make sense. You just—"

"It doesn't need to make sense!" I shout.

She shrinks away from me.

"Drive," I say.

Caroline drives the Honda with passive-aggressive slowness through the empty little town and onto Orcas Road. Even on this straight paved two-lane road, she doesn't pick up speed.

My eyes dart to the dusty instrument panel. "Thirty-two miles an hour?" I say. "We're never going to—" I stop. My eyes go back to the panel. To the glowing yellow fuel light. To the fuel dial sagging below *E*. "How long have you been out of gas?"

"I don't know. I didn't notice it was—"

"Goddamn it!"

Caroline's shoulders stiffen. "I can turn back, go get some gas at—"

"There's no time," I say. "The next boat is leaving in twenty minutes. Keep driving."

We're about four miles from the ferry dock when the engine stalls out. Caroline brakes frantically and steers the car to the side of the road. We come to a complete, silent stop.

HANNAH

"Where did you go?" I ask Greene as we sit waiting in the car at the ferry dock.

His hand is still clasping mine. "They were going to put me in prison and throw away the key. I had to disappear. After I got out of the jail, I wandered around north of town until I found the beach. I found a rowboat in someone's shed and took it out onto the sea. I crossed over to Saturna Island. After a month of hiding out in someone's empty cabin and eating their canned food, I rowed back to Orcas, but I couldn't find anyone on the Farm. It was like we'd never existed. I didn't stick around for long. I sneaked onto a ferry to Friday Harbor, and then I stowed away on a fishing boat and made my way to Vancouver. I got a job washing dishes in a restaurant, and one day I found a passport one of the customers dropped in the restroom. I kept it. It was a UK passport, and the guy looked nothing like me, but I altered the picture, and the dates and the name, everything. Then I saved my money. I flew to France and got a job as a custodian at an auction house in Lyon. I learned how to speak French, and I started working my way up until I was in a position to…to use my talents." He smiles, but he looks ashen, and the muscles around his eyes are tight.

"Are you okay?" I ask.

"Just…tired. I wanted to search for you, Kestrel, but I never even knew your last name, or even what your first name was before you came to the Farm. When I ran into Josh in Europe a few years ago, he told me your sister had married his dad. I was going to reach out to her, to ask her if she knew where you went, but I was afraid she and Allan might call the police. Then last week, when I found out about the body… I was so afraid it was you. I came here to find out." He gives my hand a squeeze. "Thank God it wasn't. And you? What happened to you after…after I left?"

"The state would've taken Littlest away from me," I say. "They would've put him in a foster home—*I* would've had to go into foster care, too, and then after that, where would I and my baby have… I did what I needed to do. I took my sister's name so we could stay together. The three of us. Me, Littlest, and my baby." I meet Greene's eye. "*Our* baby."

"Our baby," he echoes softly. "I'm so sorry."

"*Sorry?* She's the best thing that ever happened to me. She's so much like you, Greene."

"Poor kid."

"She has your…" I take a deep breath. "She has your gift." I can't bear to tell him about Sibley's injury, or how the minutes away from her are piling up and I feel like I'm going crazy with worry.

"My gift?" Greene studies my face with a mixture of surprise and wariness.

"I'm sorry," I whisper. "For turning away from you. For saying I couldn't see anymore when I think I *could* have if I'd wanted to. Maybe I couldn't see anymore because it felt safer not to, or maybe I couldn't because of everything else that was happening to me. But I wasn't thinking about *you*, and how betrayed and alone it made you feel. None of the really bad stuff would've happened if we had just stuck together. We could've gotten through it together if we had only—"

"Don't beat yourself up like that. We were too young to know—"

"But Quill," I say. "*Quill.* If we'd left the Farm earlier, the four of us together, Quill would still be..." Then, finally, *finally*, I start to cry. My face stretches into a painful grimace, and the sobs are heaving, suffocating.

"Kestrel," Greene mumbles, and he leans toward me and wraps me in his arms, and I press my face against his neck, and I can smell him, his own scent that I thought was lost to me forever, and this only makes me cry harder.

Greene makes a sound, halfway between a moan and a gasp, and I pull away.

He's pressing his hand on his sweatshirt, at the side of his belly. He pulls the hand away.

His palm is bright with blood.

"Greene! You're hurt! What—"

"Long story," he says with a grimace. He leans his head back. "I'll be okay. I just need a little rest. And it's not like we can go to the hospital." He gives a crooked smile and shuts his eyes.

I take his hand. I carefully wipe off the blood with my own shirt, and then hold his hand. My heart beats stiffly, painfully. I can't lose this person. Not again.

"There's something I need to show you, Kestrel," Josh says. I almost forgot he's still in the car. He's reaching into the deep caddy between the front seats and pulling out two manila folders. He passes them back to me.

They look like medical files, with hot pink tabs. "What's this?"

Then I see the names on the tabs: *Stroufe, Hannah. Stroufe, Gretchen.*

I whip through the files, my heart pounding even harder. They're old dental records from when my sister and I were little, from our dentist in Bellingham, before we moved to the Farm. There are charts of teeth, records of visits, X-rays. My own charts probably don't tell much of a story since I last went to Dr. Indigo Ayres when I was six. But my sister's charts… She was ten the last time she saw him. That means there are X-rays here of her adult teeth.

I look at Josh. "Where did you get these?"

"They were in my dad's safe."

"These records will prove that was Eldest they found," I say. "But why did Allan have them?"

"I think you just answered your own question," Josh says.

The truth lands like a punch. Allan had these records locked up in his safe because he wanted to make sure I could never prove my identity. He wanted to keep me trapped in my deception forever.

"Did you see what else is in there?" Josh says. "Underneath?"

Under the dental records are two birth certificates, mine and my sister's, and our social security cards together in a clear plastic sleeve.

My mind shuffles things around until it all adds up.

"Allan killed my sister," I say. "He killed her for her documentation."

Driving onto the ferry feels too easy.

Josh parks the Tesla on the vehicle deck. In front and back of us are tall delivery trucks. There's a wall on one side, and on the other side and staggered slightly forward, yet another truck.

I feel safe surrounded like this and hidden behind the tinted windows of the Tesla's back seat. In less than two hours, we'll be on the mainland. An hour and a half after that, I'll be with Sibley and Oliver. I'm not sure how we'll be able to flee like Greene says we can, especially with Greene hurt and seeping blood. But I have to believe in it. There's no other choice.

ALLAN

Never once in my life have I relied on the kindness of complete fucking strangers, but what do you know, some asshole in a pickup truck stops behind Caroline's stalled-out Honda and offers us gas from his spare fuel can.

I still have to pay him—nothing in this life is free—and since he doesn't have change, I end up giving him fifty cents more per gallon than market price.

Caroline and I are the third-to-last vehicle on the 4:20 boat.

HANNAH

The ferry's massive engines churn to life. I feel a release as we pull away from the dock.

We're doing it, I think, holding tightly to Greene's hand. We're finally getting off this island together.

ALLAN

Once the ferry has set sail, I get out of Caroline's car.

"Hey!" she says. "What about my money?"

I slam the door without answering. I have no intention of paying that lunatic. She's the reason I'm in this situation.

I walk between the rows of tight-packed vehicles, searching for my Tesla. I reach the end of the row, where the rear of the deck opens out onto an unrelenting view of gushing wake and receding land.

Wind buffets the cold water, whipping my face and stuffing my ears. The only thing standing between me and the edge of the deck is a plastic mesh fence clipped to the walls on either side. The fence is loose and flexible, and it droops down to knee-height.

I've always thought this looked just a little too enticing. You could push someone overboard, no problem.

I turn away from the water and survey the car deck. Where the fuck is my Tesla? And who's going to be behind the wheel when I find it?

I walk the next aisle, and halfway down I glimpse it, almost hidden by some delivery trucks.

I go closer, and I see who's behind the wheel.

My son.

Fury surges through me.

Josh is looking down. He doesn't see me coming.

Now I'm right up next to the driver's-side door. I raise my fist and slam it down on the glass. It doesn't break, but Josh gives a start and swings his head.

JOSH

When I see my dad outside the car, I gasp. He literally looks like a monster, red-faced and hunched in his wrinkled wool overcoat.

He lifts his fist and thumps again on the window. Then again, and again.

"Open the goddamn door," he says, his voice muffled by the glass.

"Don't," Hannah whispers from the back seat. Allan hasn't yet noticed Greene and her back there, probably because of the tinted glass. "Josh, please don't open it."

My heart is exploding. I can barely breathe. I keep my eyes straight ahead, but I can feel Allan's eyes boring into me like lasers. How is he here? On this boat?

"Josh," he says, "if you don't open this door, I *will* take away that *fucking* violin."

No, I think wildly. He can't take the violin. It will— I'll— Drew will never—

"Don't listen to him," Hannah whispers. "He's only bluffing. And if he does take it away—it won't matter, right? You can play on a different one."

"No," I say. My voice is hoarse. "I can't."

"I *will* take it away," Allan says, louder now.

Something bubbles up inside me. The strangest feeling. It is rage, yes, but it feels righteous. It feels brave.

I face my father and say, very clearly, "Not everything in the entire world is a transaction, Allan. Not everything is for sale. Leave me *alone*."

Allan's eyes flare even wider. He thumps his fist one more time on the window, and then he's edging away between the car and the wall.

"What should we do?" Hannah says.

"Stay in the car." Greene is pushing open his door and climbing out. A big splotch of blood has darkened his sweatshirt. "It's safer, and we don't want to call attention to ourselves."

"But where are you going?" I say.

"Greene," Hannah says, "please don't—"

"We need to ditch this car. I'm going to find us a better place to hide."

THEN

GREENE

When the feds arrived, they were so quiet. They flickered past your peripheral vision like mice, but when you turned your head you'd see nothing but tree trunks and swaying summer grass.

Kestrel spotted them first, before breakfast when she went to let the goats out of the barn. She came breathlessly into the house and said she'd seen men in helmets and camouflage in the trees. She said it looked like they had rifles.

"I told you," Uncle said. He sounded almost pleased. "I told you they were out to get me."

But no one could understand why the feds had arrived the very morning Uncle was getting ready to go down to the district court in Seattle. The Dodge pickup was all gassed up and ready to go. Eldest was supposed to be going with him, but Greene's mom said she'd gone blackberry-picking early and hadn't returned yet.

The feds out there in the trees—it just didn't make any sense. The Kinfolk kept repeating this, again and again, holed up in the farmhouse with the curtains shut.

The faceless men filled Greene with a terror so immense it

felt like a ripped-out hole in the universe. They had automatic rifles and electronic radios and power binoculars. What were the Kinfolk to them? Nothing but filthy wild animals hunkered, stinking of fear, in a rotten burrow in the earth.

For the first time in his life, it occurred to him that maybe Uncle had been right all along. Maybe it really *was* them against the world.

When ten o'clock rolled around, it was do or die: Uncle had to leave for the dock to catch the ferry or he was going to miss his court appointment. So Greene's mom knelt at Uncle's feet and carefully put on his socks and shoes for him, and then the other women kissed him, one by one, and the men bowed their heads in reverence.

Uncle got a shotgun from his bedroom. He opened the front door and stepped out. Mom pulled the door shut again. Then they all listened for the rumble of the Dodge's engine turning over.

For almost a minute, there was no sound.

Then there was a crack of gunfire. Pounding on the floorboards of the front porch. Then the door burst open, and Uncle jumped inside and slammed the door.

"I got one," he said. He was breathing hard, and his dark eyes looked so alive. "I got one of those suckers, right in the brain. I figured it out—they *want* me to miss my court date. Those assholes are setting me up. But they aren't taking me off this farm unless it's in a pine box."

That was when it finally sank in for Greene. I did this, he thought. I made this happen.

"Come out with your hands up," a man's voice blared outside. It was made too loud and fuzzy by some kind of electronic device.

Greene, standing against a wall, shifted.

Uncle lifted his shotgun and pointed it at him. "Don't you dare, boy," he said.

* * *

They waited in the farmhouse all day long. Sitting and not talking. Wide-eyed. Hungry. Littlest whined quietly to Kestrel. Wolf paced through the downstairs rooms, head hung low, panting. He peed on the dining-room floor because no one would let him outside.

Periodically, the man's too-loud voice would startle them out of their stupor and tell them to come out, to surrender. Each time, Uncle would caress the trigger of his shotgun, watching Greene.

By nightfall, Uncle had grown agitated. He was pacing the rooms just like Wolf and repeatedly looking out the gaps between the curtains.

Greene knew one thing for certain: Uncle's mood was not going to blow over. He had to erupt.

It came in the form of an announcement. Uncle said he was going out to one of the pit houses in the woods. He said he wanted to use the hand grenades he'd stockpiled out there to force the feds out into the open. Then he and the other Kinfolk men would have a clear shot at them.

He pointed to Quill. "You're coming with me. Kids will keep 'em from shooting."

Quill scrambled to his feet, his face lighting up.

Uncle pointed at Littlest. "And that thing's coming."

"What?" Kestrel said. "Uncle. Please. No. You can't take kids to—"

"And you're coming, too, sweetheart," Uncle said to her with a nasty smile. "To babysit."

"Don't," Greene said, approaching Uncle. "Don't take them. They're only kids. They don't deserve—"

Uncle smashed the butt of his shotgun down on Greene's cheekbone.

Greene staggered back, his eyes detonating with stars. Then came the pain. He held on to his face as though to keep it from falling apart.

Kestrel moved toward Greene, but Uncle swung on her. "Keep out of this!" He turned back to Greene, the shotgun leveled point-blank at his face. "Stay out of this, boy, or I'll drop you."

Kestrel sent Greene a pleading look. *Please*, her eyes were saying. *Please.*

Please, what? Greene thought with furious frustration.

Greene watched Uncle's shotgun as he and Kestrel and the boys climbed, one by one, out the living-room window.

Hey, Greene said to the shotgun. *NO. No exploding. You are frozen. Do you understand? FROZEN.*

—I like to click-click-pow!—

Not today you don't, Greene said.

Uncle and Kestrel and the boys melted into the darkness.

Greene ran upstairs, then climbed the ladderlike stairs to the attic where Mom and Star and a woman named Rosie slept. He dragged every single thing in that attic over to the window—mattresses and blankets, an old leather chest, a shelf full of books, a washbasin and jug, baskets of clothes. He shimmied open the window, which sat at the level of the floor. One by one, he sent the things in the room out the window with whispered instructions.

Dozens of books flapped away into the sky like startled doves. Dresses and shirts and blankets billowed like jellyfish over the barnyard, weaving through the orchard, rushing into the forest. Only one of the mattresses could be squeezed through the window, to sail out, spinning and twisting, toward the pasture. The washbasin and jug clanked their metal selves together rhythmically, persistently, following their instructions to orbit the house.

Thank you, Greene called after all of them.

He ran downstairs again, to the kitchen. With all the distractions he'd just sent, maybe the feds wouldn't notice Uncle and Kestrel and the boys sneaking through the dark. Maybe they wouldn't notice Greene following.

Wolf rushed up to Greene, whining and panting. He knew Littlest had gone.

"Stay, boy," Greene told the dog. *Stay*, he told the door latch as he opened the kitchen door.

No, the latch said. *Don't want to.*

Greene didn't have time to argue with a door latch. He slipped outside.

All of the pit houses could be reached by the path near the old cabin. He was sure that was the route Uncle would've chosen.

He ran across the barnyard, as he went telling the muckrakes and pitchforks and shovels in the barn to go up into the sky and dance. He made it through the orchard and across the pasture and reached the line of pointed firs. He turned to look back at the Farm, at all of the things darting and floating in the weak moonlight.

It didn't seem smart to walk on the path, so Greene followed it off to the side. The hand grenades were in the second pit house. He knew exactly where it was. He'd catch up to Uncle and Kestrel and the boys there and figure out a way to get the people he loved away from Uncle and his death wish.

Were there men out here? Greene strained his ears at every rustle. He tried to see into the deepest shadows. His body felt small and soft and vulnerable, a target made of flesh.

Up ahead, he saw the sagging shape of the cabin.

He'd never forgotten the long night he'd spent locked in there with the cabin's sickening murmurs. The night he'd learned to talk back to things.

From way off in the distance came the sound of Wolf barking.

Greene went around to the back side of the cabin, where it was making its slow collapsing slide down the ravine.

He heard a whimper and froze.

Then whispering. It was coming from inside the cabin.

The wall on the ravine side was half-rotted by now, the roof open to the sky. He could see right in, even though there wasn't much light.

Uncle. Quill. Littlest. Kestrel. They were all inside. Uncle was crouched by the rotting plank door, peering out the crack, his shotgun erect. Quill, right beside him, had a gun, too.

They must've seen or heard men out here. They must've run for cover.

Littlest was whimpering. Kestrel tried to shush him, to rock him in her arms, but he was agitated, climbing and struggling.

"Would you make that goddamn little monster shut *up*?" Uncle whispered.

It's like they're already in their coffin, Greene thought. Uncle will let them die in there.

He wanted to let Kestrel know he was there, but if Uncle saw him, he'd shoot. He was sure of it.

Wolf's barking was closer now.

And the cabin was whispering.

—and Sissy said, do not leave me alone with Papa in the—with child again—

The cabin remembered Greene. It wanted him to listen to its awful stories.

—my health cannot withstand another brat un—tell tell tell tell tell!—

Shut up! Greene told it savagely.

—when the mama screamed and screamed in that bed and the blood and the thing that was supposed to be a baby—

Shut up, shut up, shut up! Greene silently raged.

Wolf's barking was even closer.

Greene thought of that stupid kitchen door latch. That was how Wolf must've gotten out. He pictured the dog snuffling along on the scent of his beloved Littlest, through the orchard, across the pasture, into the trees.

—and he says he didn't know this godforsaken island would be this wet, but we can't—splattering—Liza-Beaulah is crying again, she won't stop, not after—make him stop, dear Lord, oh please make the papa stop this—

Wolf's barking was so close now, with a shrill, hysterical edge.

Gunfire cracked and echoed.

Wolf went silent midbark.

"Those sonofabitches shot my dog!" Quill shouted. He bolted to his feet and slammed open the cabin door. He raised his gun.

No one tells you how crude these events are. How blunt and quick. How quiet, too. You hear nothing but one short pop and then the blood pumping past your eardrums. And the trees, the sky, they don't care. They act like nothing has changed.

"Quill!" Kestrel screamed, throwing herself toward the door, toward her fallen little brother.

Littlest wailed.

"Kestrel!" Greene shouted. "No!"

Uncle's head spun around. His eyes were black voids. He leveled his shotgun.

That's the papa! Greene lied to the cabin. *Right there, the papa who did all those terrible things to Sissy and Liza-Beaulah! Get him!*

"Kestrel!" Greene shouted again.

Kestrel grabbed Littlest by the back of his shirt and dragged him toward Greene. Greene reached out and took him in his arms as Kestrel climbed out, and the cabin was trembling violently, a big body filled with seething, murderous hatred.

Greene and Kestrel and Littlest fell together onto the steep slope of ferns as the cabin imploded voraciously, like a sea anemone absorbing its prey, silencing Uncle's scream.

They tumbled and rolled all the way to the bottom of the ravine.

They were still tangled up together down there when the silhouettes of two men with rifles appeared at the top of the slope. A flashlight beam swept across them.

Squinting against the white light, Greene and Kestrel raised their hands.

"We surrender," Greene shouted.

Littlest started to cry.

NOW

ALLAN

I find the stairs leading up to the passenger decks and take them two at a time. I go to the men's restroom but stop just outside the door. Here it is. Fire Station 18. The wall-hung white metal box, painted red inside. The dingy folded fire hose. The red-bladed hatchet hanging from its metal brackets. Not behind glass. Right out in the open.

I grab it.

I like the dense heft of it, enough to make my forearm flex.

I stride back to the stairs. I go down.

HANNAH

Josh's window doesn't shatter under the first blow of Allan's hatchet, but it does under the second. I watch it crackle into squares and rectangles, hover for a moment, and then slump away with a tinkling sound.

Josh has thrown himself over to the passenger side, on top of his violin case. "Get out, Hannah," he says, his voice harsh. "We have to get out." He shoves the passenger door open.

I'm fumbling with my own door handle, pushing it open—

"Hannah?" At last, Allan has noticed me. He's halfway in the driver's seat, staring back at me. "What the *fuck*, Hannah? You're supposed to be in *jail*. You're— Josh. Did you—"

Josh is out of the car. He's hugging his violin case like it's a baby and he whispers, *"Run."*

We can't run, though. The vehicles are too tightly packed. I stumble along between the rows, elbowing side mirrors and bumping into doors. I set off somebody's car alarm and keep going. I can hear Josh breathing heavily right behind me.

I glance over my shoulder, see the whites of Josh's eyes. Several paces behind him is Allan. I can't tell if he still has the hatchet.

I reach the end of the row of vehicles. Here is the rear mouth of the ferry, a gaping open-air hole, the frothing V-shaped wake, the fading horizon, the blackening sky. The wind is so noisy here, and the sea spray swirls and slaps and stings. Nothing separates us from the curved edge of the stern but a sagging mesh fence and, beyond it, a few empty feet of deck.

"The stairs," Josh is saying. "Where are the stairs? Did we pass them? We need to go—"

At first I think he's stopped talking because he spotted the stairs, but it's because Allan has shoved past him.

Allan says, "You're coming with me," as he pulls me backward.

CAROLINE

Mr. McCullough thinks he can get away without paying me, but I won't let him do that to Trey and me. We deserve to go to Hawaii—our relationship *needs* it.

It is so strange. I find Mr. McCullough's car parked on the ferry deck, the one he was driving the day he chased me to my house. No one is inside it, but the driver-side window is shattered.

Something red on the seat catches my eye. At first I think it's blood, but then I see that it is a hatchet painted red. It calls so sweetly to me. I reach down through the broken window. My fingers touch the handle and it whispers—*do it do it do it. Yesssss—*

My hand recoils.

It has been more than nine years since something said those words to me.

I had just found the backpack with those things, those horrible heathen things, muttering their vicious stories. It was in the woodshed, tucked up in the rafters. I wouldn't have seen it except one of the straps was hanging down and it caught my eye when I went in to get some kindling to start the cookstove.

Firewood was supposed to be men's work, but once again my foolish son had not replenished the supply in the kitchen.

I took the backpack down and looked inside. I did not understand what I was looking at. I pulled out the long, carved bone with the evil face carved into the knob on top, and that was when Eldest came in.

It was her fault because if she hadn't come in when that thing was in my hand whispering its vicious stories, egging me on with its *do it do it do it*, telling me to hit, to strike just so, that the soft thud would be heavenly...if she hadn't come in...

But she did.

I hesitate, then reach again for the red hatchet on the car seat. I grip the handle—*yesssss*—and I lift it off the seat.

I work my way between the tightly packed vehicles. In my hand the hatchet quietly chants, *do it do it do it. Yesssss*—

HANNAH

"Come on," Allan says, pulling me.

"No." I give my arm a jerk, but Allan holds fast. I lean all of my weight forward and, with another jerk of my arm, I break free. I trip on the mesh fence and go sprawling over it. I hit the metal decking on my hands and knees, and pain shatters through me.

When I open my eyes, they're filled with wind and spray and the sight of gushing water.

I feel a hand grab the back of my jacket and drag me up. "I've had enough of your bullshit, Hannah," Allan says, his breath hot in my ear.

"Let me go!" I try to shout. I pull and push and twist.

"Goddamn it, Hannah, you're going to go fucking overboard."

"I'd rather go overboard," I say, still struggling, "than pretend to be your perfect little wife for one more second."

"Stop talking," Allan shouts. "Just *stop talking*!"

"You've been lying to me all these years. You had my sister's documentation—you *killed* her for it—"

"That's bullshit," Allan says. "I never even met her."

"Stop lying!" With my last bit of energy, I jerk out of Allan's grasp. But the deck is so wet and slippery. I go down, and so does Allan.

My head hits the deck with a blow that dims my vision. Then I skid as though in slow motion, the water rushing up to get me.

I throw out my hand and claw my fingers through the mesh fencing. My legs skid past the rest of me and keep going, jutting over the edge of the deck.

I clutch the fencing. I open my mouth to scream, but a moan comes out. The metal deck is vibrating so hard it feels like it'll disintegrate my teeth and my bones.

"Take my hand," someone shouts. Josh. Just on the other side of the fence, his violin case strapped to his shoulder. He reaches for me.

I grab his hand. It's so strong. He feels like an anchor.

But then Allan is up again. I can't see very well, but I do see that.

"Let go of her," Allan says.

Josh's grip tightens on my hand.

"What is she to you, Josh? You never cared about anyone else in your entire life. The only thing you ever cared about was that violin." Allan rushes Josh. He drags the violin case off him by its strap.

"No!" Josh shouts. But he doesn't let go of my hand. "Dad! Please, no—"

"It's mine, isn't it?" Allan says. "I'll do whatever the fuck I want with my possessions." He steps over the mesh fence to be closer to the water. He lifts the violin case overhead.

"No! *Please.*" Josh is crying now, but he still hasn't let go of my hand. "You can't—the whole freaking world isn't *yours*! I mean, you've been going around *murdering* people to get what you want? We figured out what you did to Eldest to get her documentation, and I found Boyce and his wife, and I know you're the one who set up the raid by telling the ATF about those weapons in the woods— *No!*"

I watch Allan throw the violin case. It slips under churning white foam and out of sight.

"Oh shit," Josh whispers. He's weeping. "Oh God."

But he never lets go of my hand.

A sharp pain behind my eyes makes me close them tight as a woman's voice calls, "You? *You* set Uncle up?"

Then nothing but darkness.

ALLAN

"You? *You* set Uncle up?" Caroline Cooper pushes through the clump of bystanders gathering around Hannah's limp form on the deck. They're talking about finding a pulse and moving her and not moving her and security guards and calling 9-1-1, and I decide it's time to go, but here is crazy Caroline. Hair tangled, eyes wild. Stepping over the plastic mesh fence. Blocking my path.

Holding a red hatchet.

I knew Caroline was a murderer the instant I read the report about the body in the *Seattle Times* last week. Maybe on some level I even knew it when she showed up at my front door at the island house two weeks after the ATF raid, offering to sell me the birth certificate and social security card of Hannah Stroufe. I remember smelling death in the air that night. I just didn't know whose death it was.

I'd never met Caroline before, but she knew who I was, and she also knew that I'd been spending time with Kestrel. Spying on us, probably. She knew that I wanted the thing every man wants but can't have: a sixteen-year-old bride. You don't believe it? Fuck, try reading the news. We all know it's true. And Caroline Cooper, for the bargain price of ten thousand dollars, had found me a work-around, because for all her holier-than-thou bullshit, she has the instincts of a brothel madam.

"*You* set the feds on Uncle?" Caroline is saying as she steps closer.

"You have no idea what kind of shit he was up to," I say.

"No! I knew him better than anybody else. We shared something, a special connection deeper than anything he had with those teenage sluts he kept in his bed." Her eyes turn to slits. "And you... you destroyed him—you destroyed me. You have no idea how I have suffered without him. Uncle." She's weeping. "Oh, *Uncle*."

"You killed her," I say. "You killed that girl. I fucking knew it."

"They seduced Uncle," she says, her face crumpling with self-pity. "Those two sisters. They *stole* him from me. She...she told me that after his court date they were going to leave the Farm together, just the two of them. I couldn't lose him like that—he *needed* me."

Caroline looks so weak, so contemptible, like a lump of unformed clay standing there in the rain. I sigh, thinking of what I'm going to have to do yet again.

"I'll pay you," I say. The boat bucks up and then down on a wave, and freezing water sloshes aboard. "Just get out of my way."

"No." Rainwater streams down her face. It dribbles into her mouth.

"Be reasonable," I say.

Caroline lifts the hatchet. It's too heavy, so her arm wavers in the air. "The axe wants to bite," she says. "The axe wants to crack, and rip, and *split*—"

I see it coming toward my face, a red smudge in the rain. Here's the end, I think.

In my last fraction of a second, I have the presence of mind to snatch at her sleeve so we'll crumple into the water together when the hatchet cuts into my brain.

I'm pretty proud of that.

GREENE

I was gone only a few minutes, searching for a place on this boat where Kestrel and Josh and I could hide until we reach the mainland. I found an empty delivery truck and went back to the Tesla.

I found it broken and empty.

And now, when I come out onto the open-air stern of the vehicle deck, a half dozen people are clustered, talking, pointing. One woman is weeping, and I hear a snippet of what she is saying: "—just went over! Together! They—"

My heart turns to ice.

Kestrel, I think. Where's Kestrel?

Then I see her lying on the deck, people bending around her.

I run over and kneel beside her. Her eyes are shut. Her hair is bloody. I bend to hold her close, my lips pressed against her cold cheek. "We're getting our second chance, Kestrel," I whisper, so softly that only she can hear. "We're finally getting off that island together. We'll go and get Littlest and our daughter, and then I'll make every door open for you, every lock. We'll fly away, to the mountains or the ocean or to a beautiful city, wherever you want. We'll be together, we'll stay together, never stop staying together."

I watch her eyelids quiver.

"Please," I whisper.

SIX MONTHS LATER

HANNAH

We arrived here on a ferry boat from Bari, Italy, after a long air journey from Calgary to Rome by way of Mexico and Cuba and Spain. Greene changed our passports for each leg of the journey. It was probably overkill, but the five of us were traveling together. We never considered splitting up our family to be less conspicuous, even for a day. We've learned that it's best to stick together.

Greene brought us to this lovely little town: all stone buildings with red-tile roofs, built back into mountains and overlooking the sea. He said he came to this country once for an art-authentication job and found it charming.

Certainly, a lot of its charm lies in the fact that it doesn't have an extradition treaty with the United States of America.

The US Marshals are searching for Greene and me. We're both fugitives now. I read about it online. And the FBI would like to question Josh, whose image was picked up on surveillance cameras at the hospital, and outside the Orcas Island jail, and on the ferry.

No one knows what to make of the retired sheriff's sergeant

and his wife found murdered in the trunk of Allan McCullough's abandoned Tesla. No one understands why Allan McCullough was pushed into the frigid sea by Caroline Cooper. There are speculations about revenge, or an old affair. People love speculating about that kind of stuff. Most of all, people like to invent theories about how Greene, Josh, and I managed to get off that ferry unseen. How we managed to go to Seattle, get Oliver and Sibley, and vanish.

But you can guess, can't you?

I don't read the news about all that anymore. It's from a different life and a different world.

For months we've been simply living, in a stone villa on a steep, cobbled street. We sleep and eat and listen to the radio and watch incomprehensible cartoons. Oliver and Sibley have browned skin and sun-bleached unkempt hair because we walk down to the beach every day. We even have a dog, a mongrel puppy who won't be separated from Oliver.

The children are happy. I don't know what we'll do about schooling or how long we'll stay here, but for now the only thing that matters is that they're happy. The wound on Sibley's cheek has healed to a puckered little scar. Oliver smiles now. He *laughs*.

Josh lies on a wooden lounge chair on the terrace most days, sleeping, reading junky paperbacks, and staring out at the Adriatic. He says he's truly resting for the first time since he decided to become a professional violinist when he was ten. He also says he's deciding what to do with the rest of his life, but I think he's grieving. Not for his dad—no one grieved for Allan except Sibley, who was told he died in a boating accident. No, I'm certain Josh is grieving for his violin.

And Greene, my beloved Greene is here with me, so I don't dream about him anymore.

Our lives are pleasant. The sun shines almost every day in this country. The food and coffee are wonderful. Brooms and mops clean the house for us. Pans and pots cook our food. When we need money, Sibley and Oliver bring a bucket to the beach and gather up oyster shells. Greene cleans them in our kitchen sink and lays them in the sun to dry, and then he and Sibley coax them into pretending to be perfect, cream-white pearls.

Greene says he has no moral qualms about it because they ask the pearls to never, ever change back into shells.

★★★★★

ACKNOWLEDGMENTS

Thank you to everyone who read this book. I'm truly honored. And special thanks to those who read this book *many* times to help me get it right: my agent, Stephany Evans; my editor, Leah Mol; and my first readers through endless permutations, Jennifer and Zach. Thank you to the wonderful people at MIRA Books who performed the magic trick of turning my story into an actual, beautiful book with your work on the copy editing, the cover, and the marketing. Another thank-you to Zach for letting me sometimes borrow your amazing brain, and for your faith in me, and for your love. Finally, thank you to my children, Henry and Aesa.